THE QUEEN SPOKE—
AND A LAUGH RIPPLED THROUGH THE EARTH . . .

Ariadne raised her chin and reached into the purse at her girdle, taking hold of the Crystal. She withdrew it and in the blinking of an eye it began to glow, and then to flare. By the time the Watchman dared look directly at it, the thing was shining like a star in the confined space. As Ariadne closed her hand about the Crystal, her living flesh glowed red and translucent. When she spoke, her voice was strange, "Go." She opened her hand, and where the Crystal had lain, now there was nothing. . . .

GREENBRIAR QUEEN

Sheila Gilluly

A SIGNET BOOK

NEW AMERICAN LIBRARY

*For Mom who has seen this coming since an uncle missed a line in a picture book.
And for Dad who could get every kid in the room looking for the doggy.*

NAL BOOKS ARE AVAILABLE AT QUANTITY DISCOUNTS WHEN USED TO PROMOTE PRODUCTS OR SERVICES. FOR INFORMATION PLEASE WRITE TO PREMIUM MARKETING DIVISION, NEW AMERICAN LIBRARY, 1633 BROADWAY, NEW YORK, NEW YORK 10019.

SIGNET TRADEMARK REG. U.S. PAT. OFF. AND FOREIGN COUNTRIES
REGISTERED TRADEMARK—MARCA REGISTRADA
HECHO EN CHICAGO, U.S.A.

SIGNET, SIGNET CLASSIC, MENTOR, ONYX, PLUME, MERIDIAN and NAL BOOKS are published by NAL PENGUIN INC., 1633 Broadway, New York, New York 10019

First Printing, January, 1988

1 2 3 4 5 6 7 8 9

PRINTED IN THE UNITED STATES OF AMERICA

Prologue

All day the ravens had floated above the field, waiting. The defenders had been pushed back until they formed a tired knot under the very battlements of the castle. They had gone from despair to grim resolution: though the Greenbriar King of Ilyria, their lord, would fall, every manjack of them would lay down his life to make the victory more costly for the Bastard and his army of Barreners.

At the forefront of the First Watch, the young captain leaned on his sword and gazed out over the hillside that sloped to the river he could see twinkling through its ruff of willow trees. Across the water the land rose again to hills the color of dusty blackberry, and a warm cottage stood at the fold of the valley. With a pang as bitter as any venom, he knew that he would never live to see twilight, and he wondered whether Maeve watched now with her far-seeing eyes. She had dreamt of this. He had wiped her tears away and smiled.

He turned his eyes back to the battlefield and saw the next wave of enemy troops coming. Grasping his sword once more, he shouted, "Stand by, Peewit!"

Crouched in the shelter of the postern set into the fortress wall, his lieutenant, of the race of the Littlemen, had straightened to obey when he realized there was another presence in the narrow passageway. "The king comes!" He snapped to attention.

The captain turned with a disbelieving look and quickly ran back to cover the king with his shield, though it would have been a far shot for the enemy bowmen in the line of trees two hundred yards south.

1

"Sire, you must go back inside! We are going to set off the charges now!"

"You cannot," the king told him and lightly pushed the buckler away until he could see out over the field. Less than a mile away, the mounted horsemen of the enemy surged over the broken ground, leaping the earthworks that should have halted their charge. Before their host, a burly figure spurred a black stallion and by his side his standard bearer raced with the flag rocking in its saddle cup. The breeze snapped the pennant out straight and the silently watching troops of the king saw the device: red on black, a flaming blade sliced at the stem of the Royal Briar.

The king's gray eyes glinted and a bitter smile twisted his lips. "They're having a fine old hunt of it, aren't they? It's odd, you know, Tristan—when we were boys, my brother couldn't even sit a horse, much less ride like that." His eyes narrowed as he caught a flash of sapphire amidst the dense undergrowth near the riverbank. "Ah, the wizard who made him the sword is here too, I see. Both the buzzards have come to the feast." The captain raised his arm to signal a new defense, and the jingle of mail rings recalled the king immediately. He said in a low voice for the tense young commander's ears alone, "We can't set off the charges yet. There's a secret way out that leads back up there." He indicated the forested crags that lay behind the castle. "I've sent Melchior with the queen and the children. If we can gain a little more time, they may make it to the Guardian."

Turning his back to the watching men, Tristan whispered urgently, "Go with them, my lord. We will give you what time we can."

The king smiled thinly. "It's too late. The way is blocked behind them," he murmured. Drawing his sword, he raised his voice to be heard by the nearest troops. "So I too will fight here, and make an end among valiant companions. It is enough for any man." A rustle spread among the torn and weary remnant, and suddenly a ragged cheer went up as the ranks acclaimed him. "Poor fools," he breathed as he returned their salute, and met the look the captain shot him with one of his own: "Poor fools, all of us, to think we could stand against my misborn brother and his warlock."

He sighed and swung the royal sword in a whistling arc to limber his arm. The jewels of the hilt flashed in the waning sunlight. "Master Harper?" he called.

A lithe figure detached itself from the archer company to his right and the Yoriandir stood forth, his beech-green skin gleaming golden in the sunset. "Here, sire!"

"We would have a song, Imris," the king commanded in a hearty voice even as he watched the dark horseman jump the last bulwark.

The Yoriandir archer saw him coming too, but he laid aside his bow, understanding the king's purpose. "And what would you hear, sire?"

Tightening his fingers on the sword hilt, the king pursed his lips for a moment, thinking. Then he grinned. "Give us the lay of Marian the Fair."

The Yoriandir's fir eyes widened as he unslung his harp, and several men turned to the king in open-mouthed surprise. The song was a barracks favorite about a woman who kept a house in the nearby village—had kept a house—but they had not known that he had heard it.

Into the silence came a short bark of laughter and a gruff voice. "Sing, Imris! We'll give those mad dogs yonder cause to worry!" A dwarf jumped down from his vantage point on the low roof of the guardhouse thirty feet to their left and trotted up, followed by his dwarven axmen, whom he dispersed around the king in a rough semicircle.

The ground was already shaking from the thundering hooves as the Littleman left the gate and joined the group around the king. "Keep a way for me clear there," he directed the tall men behind him. Then as he took his place by the captain's side, the enemy was upon their first ranks while the harpsong rose clear above the screams, the curses, and the moans of the dying.

At the last, when they had endured beyond any telling of it and the black horseman reared above the dwarvish axes, the captain reached a long arm to clap the Littleman on the shoulder. The small figure flung his shield up into the face of an enemy pikeman, dodged the thrust that would have spitted him, and ran for the postern. Sprinting through the doorway, he glanced back and saw the dwarf grasping at the sword that hacked across his face, go down beneath the mashing hooves. The captain, his sword raised high, sprang to meet the horseman, and a blast of sapphire flame blew him backward like a pine knot exploding from a fire. And then the king stood alone, still as a statue, while the black figure slid from the saddle and walked deliberately forward.

The Littleman raced into the narrow corridor, seized the torch, and lit the fuse.

Book I   The Oath

The wizard drew in his sorrel mare in a copse above a small farm at Wolf's Glen. As his horse snatched a mouthful of sweet grass, the white-haired enchanter leaned on the pommel of his saddle to ease his tired back and thought that the tiny cottage below was an unlikely place to seek a princess. It was neat enough, and even from a distance he could see that care had been taken with the placement of the midden and byre, but the thatched roof needed patching and there were only a few fowl pecking about the yard.

He surveyed the tilled fields and hay pasture, and his gaze sharpened. The shrubs that he had first taken for berry thickets by the side of the house were in fact briar roses, thick and tended. Coincidence? Or did they suspect who their foundling daughter really was?

His vision had given him no clue. He had seen the swaddled baby, too exhausted to cry, picked from the ruin of bodies in a dell and borne here by a soldier wearing the red and black of the Bastard King. The wizard did not even know whether she still lived. In the past twenty years much could have happened to the child of a peasant family. But he trusted the vision had not been given to him for naught.

He pulled his horse's head up and was about to set his heel to her flank, when from the crest of the hill to his right came a sudden drumming of hooves and hoarse yells. Over the green brow of the hill swept a troop of at least twenty horsemen—there might have been more—galloping headlong down the slope as men do when they hunt. Their uniforms glowed bright crimson and sable, and for a moment he thought they were after *him*.

There was a confused spill of action in the open doorway of the cottage: a stout woman ran out, snatched up one of the hens, and returned with it just as quickly, while past her leaped a half-grown youth brandishing a kindling ax. A maid jumped after him, caught at his jerkin, and tried to lead him back inside. But the troopers never stopped. The one in the lead smashed the boy down with the butt end of a lance as easily as a man swats a fly, the next soldier caught the young woman, and a third flung a streaming torch into the thatch. They pounded through the yard and down the track that led to the neighboring farm.

As the thudding hooves receded, the wizard heard faint cries of astonishment and distress from the furthest field. Two men leaped over the rows of knee-high maize, and a maid and a child, tripping over their skirts, followed more slowly.

The enchanter gripped his carved staff and a bright flare of amethyst crackled from it, but just as quickly he extinguished his fire. He could not intervene; this was the most sacred vow of the Meld of Wizards. He had lived his long life by the Rule, and he could not now forswear it, though he ached to burn those red and black vermin from the face of earth. He clamped his jaw grimly and sent a fragment of his Warding after them; that much protection he could give the girl. When he opened his eyes again, the roof of the cottage was engulfed, and the matron was dragging the boy from the flames.

The wizard stared at the empty track where the marauders had ridden. Though he could not go after her himself, he knew who could. He had to get a message quickly to the Watchmen. Turning the sorrel's head up the hill, he guided the mare through the trees and broke into the open, urging the horse to a gallop.

The message had said it would be tonight.

The one-eyed dwarven landlord drew another pint while he kept a troubled watch on the door, where a leather curtain hung to keep out the rain. They should have been here by now.

Peat smoke hung blue beneath the roof trees, flicked through with firelight from the large open hearth at one end of the long public room. Pungent tobacco smoke from countless pipes and steam from cloaks spread to dry in the heat added to the haze. At the trestle tables, mutton pies and new bread were being devoured, washed down by frothing mugs of ale. The food at his Sword and Skull was known for its excellence, and the beer was legend.

The rumble of voices overspread the rattle of dice cups and the clink of coins from the benches placed round the walls. Kursh Korimson threaded his way through the room with a platterful of tankards, greeting friends, tossing bones to the mongrels panting by the fire, watching the door.

He circled the room and pushed through the swinging door into the kitchen. Roasting pork sizzled on the spit, pullets hung from the rafters, oatmeal cakes baked on the hearth, and his nephew and the cook maid stood frozen in a kiss across the breadboard. Their eyes rolled to look at him askance, and they sprang apart. Kursh had already taken two swift strides toward the younger dwarf, and now grasped him firmly by the collar and threw him headfirst through the wooden door. He turned quickly. The girl's eyes widened in a face pink with blushing and flour-spotted by work. She was terrified of his rages.

Abruptly, Kursh blew a short, sharp breath and growled, "Get back to your pots, girl." He stomped across to the cellar door, grabbed a candle lantern, and disappeared down the stairs. She couldn't see, but he was smiling.

Kegs of beer lay row on row down into the far end of the cellar. The aroma of hops and malt mingled with the thick hickory of the hams aging on their hooks, and the sharp tang of pie apples in bushel baskets by the foot of the stairs. Hanging the light, he picked up an apple and polished it on his leather apron as he gazed about with satisfaction. Suddenly he felt a cold touch of iron on the back of his neck, and a voice grated, "Yield, rebel, in the name of the king."

The dwarf dropped the apple and froze. Carefully

he raised both hands. Bile rose in the back of his throat and his palms prickled with fear sweat. The kiss of iron was withdrawn.

Immediately he whirled to attack, dropping a dagger from a concealed forearm sheath into his hand. His arm was already coming up, blade held low for the kill, but the small figure grinning back at him from the top of a barrel never even flinched. Kursh jerked his dagger back. *"Peewit!"* he exploded.

The Littleman hopped down off the barrel, laughing merrily, and offered a handclasp, but the dwarf slapped it aside. "You crazy little whoreson! I could've killed you!" the dwarf thundered.

Peewit Brickleburr snorted. "Not likely with a stance like that, Sergeant Major! You should have seen your face!" He burst into another peal of laughter.

" 'Tisn't funny, your pretending to be one of the Bastard's men!" Kursh snapped, replacing his dagger. He was scowling, but the Littleman continued to chuckle. "How did you get down here, anyway?"

"I haven't lost my knack completely," Peewit answered. He looked up at Kursh, who at four feet stood almost a head taller. "You haven't changed much—a little more girth, a little thicker in the head. In the olden days, you wouldn't have fallen for that one!"

"In the olden days, I would have killed you," the dwarf replied evenly, and it was no idle boast.

Peewit wrinkled his nose. "Thank the Powers you've learned some wisdom in twenty years." He perched on a small cask. "Yes, thank you, I believe I *will* have a pint of your best, landlord."

The dwarf shook his head and smoothed his mustache, but he went round the staircase to fetch a tap and mallet. He called back to the Littleman, "The others will be here soon, I expect, but there's no reason we have to wait for them."

"No, indeed." Peewit dug a short clay pipe and a pouch of tobacco from his pocket, and stood on the barrel to light a splinter from the lamp. Between puffs he questioned, "Do you have any idea what this is all about?"

"None." Kursh came into the light, rolling a small

barrel. "All my note said was 'We have a job. We'll meet usual place, second night of the quarter moon of the new month.' It was signed with the captain's mark, like always."

"Mine was exactly the same. I thought at first that it must be a joke, but then I had the feeling that I had better come anyway." Kursh muttered an assent and drove the tap in the barrel.

Through the pipe smoke, Peewit studied him. The dwarf had aged. There were gray streaks now in his beard and hair, and his beak of a nose stood out sharply against the eyepatch. His solid bulk still gave an impression of strength, but as the Littleman had already observed, he was slower in action than he used to be. Not much slower, though, by the Powers, Peewit thought.

"Peewit."

The dwarf had said it again before the Littleman heard him. As Kursh held out the dripping mug he was thinking, Ah, his hearing never did come back as good as it was. Giving no sign of what was in his mind, he nodded to the small figure and lifted his own cup. The candle flickered in the damp air; by its light Kursh watched the shadows slide over Peewit's rounded shoulders. Lines radiated from the corners of his brown eyes and his curly brown hair showed prominent salt-and-peppering. The Littleman had grown a beard to pass for a dwarf and he wore a scribe's robe of golden-rod with a dark chestnut cloak. He was pudgy, and his once-clever fingers were mottled now with what Kursh finally recognized as old inkstains. "What's this?" the dwarf asked, gesturing.

"Ink. I do genealogies now, keep accounts, copy manuscripts, that sort of thing."

"Did you ever finish that damned chronicle you were always working on? *The Greenbriar King,* wasn't that it?"

"That was it." Peewit smiled, then sobered. "No. No, I never did. With the Bastard on the throne, how could I?" There was no answer for that, so they each took a long pull at their beers. Kursh was wiping foam from his mustache when a squeal and a loud giggle came down to them from the kitchen. The dwarf glowered and the Littleman grinned and asked, "Your son?"

"Nephew. Dense as stone."

"Must run in the family."

The dwarf reached to cuff him just as a clear run of harpsong came down from the tavern. The Littleman raised his head. "Imris is here," he said, smiling.

"Aye," the dwarf growled, "and now I'll never get rid of that crowd up there." He brushed past the Littleman and led the way upstairs. Peewit was amused to see that despite his irritated tone, he took the steps two at a time.

As they went through the kitchen the girl was ladling broth into a bowl while the young dwarf knelt to stoke the fire for the bread oven. The lad did not look up, but the maid gave them a glance, then a second, longer look at Peewit. Kursh, whose attention was fixed on the music from the other room, did not notice, but Peewit did, and gave her a courtly bow as they passed through. She was frankly staring now and quickly nudged the lad. Then Kursh was pushing through the swinging door and the Littleman glanced back over his shoulder to see her stoop and whisper to the boy.

The tavern room was dim compared to the lamp-lit kitchen, and for a moment the Littleman had only a confused impression of dark silhouettes against the hearthglow. Here and there a cup was held motionless between table and lips, or a bright gleam of metal flashed as someone turned to the singer and the firelight caught his cloak pin or dagger hilt.

Imris Gravenleaf sat in one of the oak seats near the hearth. His green skin had a fresh cast in the light of the glowing peats, like sunlight on new beech leaves, and his head was tilted to one side as he listened to the chords. The azure fall of the Yoriandir's cloak was the color of a summer sky and his wheaten hair was unsilvered yet by age, for the Yoriandirkin were a long-lived people, and Imris was by their reckoning but a little beyond his prime.

As the dwarf and the Littleman stood by the kitchen

door—Kursh foursquare with arms folded, and Peewit leaning comfortably against the rough plaster wall—the Yoriandir raised his head and looked down the room to them. The forest green of his eyes showed dark above his harp. He nodded and smiled without interrupting the song, and Peewit, who had heard it long years before, surrendered to the spell and let it take him where the night sky burned with countless jewels and lovers sighed within a crystal tower.

When the song was done, the tavern erupted in a tumult of applause and cries for more, but Imris smilingly waved them off. Amid shouts for ale and the growing clatter of resuming dice games, the Yoriandir came to where they stood. "Well met, friends. Too long has it been since last I sang for you."

Kursh cleared his throat and pulled at his mustache. "It's good to see you under my roof, Imris. Peewit, here, will give you what news there is. I have to tend to this lot before they rip the rafters down. We're just waiting for the captain now."

The Littleman and the Yoriandir exchanged glances and it was Peewit who told him, "He's here, Kursh. Back in the corner there."

The dwarf looked through the crowd and a light came into his eye while Imris said, "But he says we are to wait for Master Llodin. It seems the old wizard is to be part of our council."

In the corner, the dark-haired man raised his head, caught Kursh's eye, and brought his fist to his chest in a brief sketch of the Greenbriar salute. So strong was the old training that the dwarf's fist was at his chest returning it before he caught himself. He covered by tugging impatiently at the leather apron. The captain smiled across the room and the dwarf said gruffly, "Well, let me know when he gets here. I've work to do. If you've left a pack outside, you'd better move it upstairs to my quarters."

Imris told him, "It is in the stable and will be well enough there; I will know if anyone tampers with it."

The dwarf's eyebrows went up, then drew down as he frowned. He leaned closer and looked up at the tall

Yoriandir. "You haven't brought that damned bird, have you?"

Smiling with a touch of sadness, Imris said, "No, indeed. Thrushes do not live so long. This is one of her daughters. But she is quite as intelligent as her dam, I promise you, and is watching my things for me."

"Bloody hell! The last time you brought a bird along, I was washing droppings out of my hair for weeks!"

"That was bat dung!" the Yoriandir laughingly protested.

"Just keep it away from me." Muttering, the dwarf left them and stomped into the kitchen.

The Yoriandir and the Littleman, still laughing, made their way to the corner table. Deep shadow covered it, but even so, Captain Tristan Faring sat back where he could watch the door yet not be seen. Now as Peewit slid onto the bench across from him, the captain reached a gauntleted hand to him. "Did you have any trouble getting here?"

One shoulder lifted in a shrug and Peewit said, "Who looks twice at a traveling scribe? You're the one likely to attract attention."

Though the tall man wore no expensive ornament, his cloak was thick and well woven, and he wore cross-gartered breeches and gusseted jacket in the style of the kingdom beyond Ilyria's southern border. He also wore a sword openly. None but the troops of the Bastard King were permitted to do so. Now his hazel eyes casually surveyed the room, and the Littleman could just see the gray that brushed the temples of his black hair, which he wore shorter than was customary these days but had been quite common a generation before among military men. "I have a pass from Ka-Nishon," he said, naming the neighboring king. "It should be enough to explain me to the patrols." His eyes came to rest on his old comrades and he lowered his voice even more. "Incidentally, I am Ra-Lippon, a trader. That is all you know about me, if anyone should ask."

"Trader," Peewit snorted.

A flickering smile played over the handsome features. "You needn't be so amused, First Watchman—I really *am* a trader for King Ka-Nishon."

"What do you trade in, then?"

The captain surveyed the tavern again. "Whatever is for sale," he answered lightly.

"I'll wager," the Littleman said dryly as Kursh's nephew came toward them with three tankards.

The boy was plainly curious, but he had the good sense not to ask any questions, merely handing around the brews and then dashing away to answer a call for another pie.

"Master Llodin is late," Imris commented. He slid his beer over to the captain, since he himself drank nothing but clear water. Kursh must have forgotten.

The man nodded and his quiet voice was troubled. "I know. And it was he who called this meeting."

The other two were surprised. "Then you don't know what is going on, either?" Peewit asked, frowning.

"No. Trouble, I would guess. When was it ever not?" He met their eyes directly. "I know, I know—you wonder what could be worth putting all our lives at risk. So do I. But Llodin does nothing lightly. When he sent me an urgent message, I listened. I do not trust many people, but the wizard is still one of them." He lifted his tankard.

Imris remembered the scars that the supple leather gloves hid, and he remembered too how the captain had gotten them: the snap of blue fire from the Bastard's enchanted sword was still vivid in his mind. "You are captain, Tristan," he said, and Peewit nodded.

But Tristan shook his head. "I command no one. I only thought we should all hear what Llodin has to say. Then, each goes his own way, as before." He could see an objection plainly written in Peewit's face and to forestall more talk of it, he lifted his cup in a toast. "Come now, we must drink deep or risk Kursh's wrath. To old friends, then."

"Living and dead," the Littleman added. He and the captain touched cups and drank. Looking about, he remarked, "It's a wild night for old Llodin to be on the Road alone."

Imris shuddered and passed a hand over his brow.

"What is it?" the captain demanded, setting down his cup.

The Yoriandir shook his head and twitched his cloak up further on his neck. "I know not. A draft, perhaps. Nothing."

The hazel eyes narrowed, but he did not pursue it. "We didn't get much chance to talk when I met you down at the ford. How are things among the Yoriandirkin these days?"

Imris, glancing around the crowd, spoke in a way of his people—a thought that communicated itself clearly to their minds. 'There is grave ill in the land, my friends, but even we of Yoriand cannot tell what is the matter. There is a wasting in the spirit of the earth. I have even seen grandfather trees in sore straits. It is as if they perceive some deep threat of ice coming. Sometimes, they do not even waken to our songs anymore.' The two listeners heard distress in his voice. Folk called the Yoriandirkin "tree-tenders," and rightly so, for the Yoriandirkin had retained the old kinship with living things that had long since passed out of other peoples. But the nature of their real work was little remembered, even in the oldest of Ilyrian songs or legends. With the name "Yoriand" was paired another: "Nilarion." A huge tree, the tales said, that gathered earth in its roots and caught clouds in its branches. This tree the Yoriandirkin tended. But why, not even the oldest Ilyrian grandmothers could tell.

Peewit sought to ease his friend's mind. "Maybe it's just a blight of some kind, and will pass soon."

"It is a blight," Imris replied, "but I fear it is not a natural one." Before they could ask what he meant, a drinker at the next table leaned to tug at the azure cloak.

"Pardon, Master Harper, but would ye mind singing us another tale? 'Twould be a rare pleasure for us."

Imris smiled and replied, "For such an audience, how could I not?" He glanced at the captain and sent to him alone, 'I am uneasy about Master Llodin. It is not his way to be late.' When the man nodded that he had heard, the singer picked his way through the crowd and approached his harp once more.

The song he chose, coming as it did upon the heels of their talk, was not the romance the crowd expected. Instead, he sang of the divers life of the woodlands, and—to one who knew—there was autumn and swelling ripeness in the lyrics. But to casual listeners there was only a long song about some trees and a bubbling spring. And in the middle of the refrain, trouble walked in the door.

The captain saw the five immediately and his hand was already resting on the hilt of his sword beneath the table when one of the uniformed men pounded on the bar and roared, "Landlord! Mulled wine, and be quick about it!"

The quiet strumming of the harp ended in a jangled protest as the Yoriandir slapped a hand along the strings to cut off the song. In an instant it was so quiet the peats could be heard hissing when rain strayed in through the chimney hole. Cautiously, all turned to the voice and hands dropped to daggers.

Kursh straightened from talking over a table and warned his nephew back with a glance when the boy started toward the soldiers. Slowly the one-eyed dwarf made his way amongst the tables. "As you will, sirs." His words were courteous enough, but even across the room Peewit could see the stiff resentment in his back and he could imagine what the proud dwarf must be feeling at being thus addressed in his own establishment. Kursh snapped his fingers at his nephew and pointed at the kitchen door. "Fetch the gentlemen's wine, Orin," he ordered quietly. The dwarven boy hastened to obey and the room lightened then darkened as he thrust through the swinging door.

The troopers shrugged out of their wet cloaks and one of them, a squat flat-faced fellow, collected them and approached the hearth to spread them there. The silent townsmen moved their legs out of his way. He was followed by the officer, who was thin, and florid with cold. The people in the tavern knew him well. For the past three years he had been overlord of the country roundabouts. He styled himself Robert of Dells, King's Reeve of the Southmark, but his fickle cruelty had earned him the whispered epithet, Snake Robert.

The reeve surveyed the tavern, one hand resting
easily on his sword hilt, and then his other hand dropped
to tap a tabletop. "We would sit here," he said quietly. The drinkers at the table hurriedly gathered
their trenchers and mugs and vacated the places. While
the others of his men swaggered up and slid onto the
benches, Snake Robert turned and looked down at
Imris, who sat still by the fire. "Play on," the thin man
ordered. " 'Twas a pretty tune."

The Yoriandir bent his head and swept his fingers
along the strings, picking up the melody again. Kursh
took the tray from his nephew at the kitchen door and
bore it through the room to the soldiers. Silently he
handed the hot wine round, gave a half bow, and
withdrew again to the bar. Peewit carefully turned to
look at him. Kursh caught his eye, and—unseen by the
troopers, who were already halfway through their cups
and riveted by the music—gave a nod at the wall
behind him. Hanging there like some trophy was a
broad battleax in a scarred leather sheath. The Littleman
nodded and returned his attention to the tableful of
the Bastard's men.

The crowd was beginning to relax and there was
some shuffling as ale mugs were lifted. But no one
dared start a game, or call for another round, and
Imris had probably never had a less attentive audience. He finished the song to scattered clapping and
set his harp down on the floor. Robert stated, "We do
not see many Yoriandir in the Southmark."

The fir eyes summed the officer. Imris did not know
the reeve, but he saw by the subtle deference paid him
by his men and even more clearly by the townsmen's
silence that here was a person to be wary of. "We
seldom journey outside our own land, sir."

"So I understand. And what purpose brings you
here, Master Harper?"

"I take the Road northward, going home. I was sent
to tend certain saplings we planted here in the Southmark."

"Ah, yes. The tree-tenders." Snake Robert said it
the way another might have said "swineherds."

Imris said nothing, only meeting his eye directly.

That in itself was enough of a challenge. The Yoriandir realized this immediately. He looked down and made a business of moving his harp further under the bench.

"Why do you put your harp by? We'd like to hear more. Wouldn't we?" The reeve did not even turn his head to his men. They all took up the cue and thumped on the table, grinning.

Calmly Imris set his harp on his knee once more and looked over it at them. "What would you hear, gentlemen?"

When Robert did not speak, only swirling the wine in his cup and taking a sip of it while staring the whole time at the Yoriandir, his men called for one tale or another until Imris opened with a chord and gave them a rollicking chantey. Soon they were clapping in time to the music. The reeve listened, but his eyes roved the room, noting every face. His gaze sharpened when he spotted the captain slouched at the corner table beyond the fire. Taking a final sip of wine, he rose and made his way past the nervous farmers. All eyes followed him, and though Imris kept playing, he sang more softly.

The reeve came to stand before the Littleman, at whom he glanced with some interest, but for now he addressed only Tristan. "I am Robert of Dells, reeve for King Dendron. Who are you, southerner, and why are you here?"

Tristan's left hand toyed with his beer mug, and his right was out of sight beneath the table. Expressionlessly he replied, "I am called Ra-Lippon. I came to trade."

"Trade what?" There was an edge.

"My lord King Ka-Nishon has business with your King Dendron. I am not charged to tell my commission to every minor official who demands an explanation." The captain said this levelly and he did not raise his voice, but everyone in the tavern heard him, and Robert knew it.

The heat stood bright in the reeve's face, but his lips twisted in a smile. "Then you will have a Pass."

"Of course." Casually, Tristan reached for the pouch at his belt, but even so he saw the troopers become suddenly wary. He extracted a folded parchment sealed with an official-looking imprint in wax and handed this to Snake Robert. While the reeve held it up to the light, the captain raised his cup to his lips and looked over it at Peewit. The Littleman brought up a finger to scratch his eyebrow. It was one of the old hand codes of the King's Watch: ready.

Robert had broken the seal and now scanned the paper. His thin brows drew down. "I cannot read this, trader."

Tristan gave him a slow, disarming smile. "That's all right," he said easily. "I can't read *your* language, either."

The reeve's eyes flew to him, but he could hear no sarcasm in the voice. Robert's gaze dropped to Peewit, who was trying his best to look insignificant. The parchment fluttered to the table at the Littleman's elbow. "What does it say, scribe?"

Peewit looked up with surprise, a humble traveling secretary. He took up the Pass, smoothed it, and cleared his throat. "Well, my lord, it begins thus: 'Greetings to whomever shall chance to read this commission. Know ye by our seal and sign that we here empower one Ra-Lippon, trader, to conduct our business at Ravenholt. Signed, Ka-Nishon, King of Shimarron, Lord of the Far Isles, etc.' It goes on with the rest of his titles, lord." He handed back the paper, with just the proper measure of deference. He had not the faintest idea what the thing really said.

Snake Robert stood slapping the thick parchment thoughtfully against his hand, regarding Tristan. After a moment, he threw it down on the table. "Keep to the main Road, trader. The wilds can be very dangerous."

The captain measured him. "I can deal with animals."

The reeve was restrained only by the official document. "Then you will need no escort from my men."

"None." The captain held his eyes. "But I will mention your offer when I come to court." He saw the promise of official recognition dawn in the man's face. He knew also that Robert's men would be watching his every step, parchment or no.

The reeve nodded curtly, looked sharply at Peewit, found him patently harmless, and turned on his heel. The Littleman let out his breath.

"Smith!" the thin man roared, and a burly man across the hearth jerked as though he had taken an arrow.

"Here, lord," he managed as he got to his feet. His thick hands, blackened from his work, twisted into a knot before him.

The reeve unhurriedly walked through the crowd. "I noticed that the planking in the bridge is still loose. I was nearly thrown from my horse coming across it tonight." As though he read the sharp disappointment that came to several minds, he smiled. "I mentioned that planking to you last week, did I not?"

"Aye, my lord, but—"

"Enough. You'll come with us. Perhaps your memory will improve under the lash." Two of the scarlet-and-sable-coated soldiers got up, anticipatory grins on their faces.

The smith went white behind his sandy-red beard and he thrust out two brawny arms. "But, my lord, I —"

"Silence! You will find"—the reeve's cold glance touched here and there in the crowd—"you will *all* find, that when I give an order, it is obeyed."

The captain nudged Peewit's foot, and when the Littleman looked across at him, Tristan passed Imris's bow and quiver under the table. The small figure swallowed, but got himself in position to run for the harper.

The smith was still pleading, and now as the soldiers caught hold of him roughly, his tablemate rose also. He was a miller, Tristan judged from the flecks of chaff still clinging to his clothes and beard. "But, my lord, he has been working on the new strapping for the bridge all week! I seen it myself! Why, it would ha' been put in today, but for the storm! Surely, ye can't expect—"

Now there's a loyal friend and a dead man, Tristan thought. He silently slid his sword part way out of its leather scabbard.

"I *can* expect!" Snake Robert roared. "And I'll have both of you flogged within an inch of your miserable lives!"

The miller's jaw worked with fury and he glared at the two of Robert's men who seized his arms. Tristan gestured to Peewit, sending the Littleman, bent double, dodging between the tables. Then he rose and kicked over his bench as a diversion. "Let them go, reeve."

Robert whirled and when he found who confronted him, hissed, "Stay out of this!" He swept his sword out of its sheath.

But as quickly the captain's was in his hand. "I think not." He had all the uniformed men's attention on him now and out of the corner of his eye he saw Kursh turn and lift his ax down from the wall, pitching the leather cover aside. The dwarven boy peered round-eyed from the kitchen door and the captain wished he would close it to cut down the light. Kursh's hand flickered and his nephew ducked back in.

The reeve was furious. "By Beldis, your commission will not protect you now! Take him," he ordered his men.

They dropped the two townsmen and headed for the Southerner in a rush.

Tristan leaped from the corner and easily parried their first clanging blows. Kursh rushed down the room and engaged one of the other men, and Imris nocked an arrow so quickly that his hands were a blur. He sent to the remaining soldier, 'You there.' When the man's eyes widened with surprise at the voice sounding in his mind, the Yoriandir sent, 'Over here.' The trooper looked about distractedly and saw the harper sighting in at him from across the hearth. Imris smiled. 'Hello.' The man stood amazed and the Yoriandir held him there. 'Yes,' he sent. 'If I can talk to you in your mind, just imagine what *else* I can do.'

By now the benches were empty, men stumbling out of the way, back against the walls. The ones who were close enough sprinted out into the town's main street. Kursh ducked a sword swipe and hewed solidly with his ax. The soldier was dead before he hit the floor, and the dwarf turned to the two who fought the captain.

As yet, Robert was merely watching with narrowed eyes from the far corner near the kitchen where he had retreated. Tristan was aware of him, but had to contend with the two before him. He drove in under a clumsy parry and caught one of them under the ribs, thrusting home. The other had his blade poised and began to swing. Kursh's ax clove his head from behind.

The captain straightened from a fighting stance, his back momentarily to the soldier Imris held under his bent bow. The man reacted instinctively, leaping forward with his sword raised. The arrow whizzed into his chest.

The captain took a quick inventory of his men, swept the confusion of faces along the walls, and found Snake Robert alone by the kitchen door. The reeve gripped his sword and started, not for the fight, but for the outside door. There was a blur of motion across the townsmen's legs and then Peewit leaped upon a table, launched himself furiously, and tackled the reeve from behind. Though his weight was not much, it was enough to knock Robert to the floor. As they rolled apart and the Snake scrabbled for the sword he had dropped, Kursh dropped his dagger into his hand and sent it spinning end over end. It caught the reeve through the throat.

For a moment there was frozen silence in the tavern. The local men stared from the uniformed corpses to Kursh and the strangers. The kitchen door crept ajar and Orin's face peered around it. Peewit got to his knees, shaking his head to clear it, for he had knocked into a bench and was a little stunned.

Then Kursh stooped to clean his ax on a scarlet and sable tunic, Imris slung his bow over his shoulder and strapped the quiver at his waist, and the captain stepped to the fire to inspect his sword for nicks.

The miller was the first of the tavern patrons to move. He went to bend over the reeve's body and then turned and nodded to the smith. The burly man approached Tristan. "Thank ye," he said hoarsely.

"No thanks needed. In fact, it was a pleasure." The captain polished the blade of his sword on a black cloak, and the metal gleamed in the firelight.

The smith stared as he saw the etching down the sword's length. He blurted, "That be the Old Briar!" The royal device had not been seen these twenty years in the country of Ilyria, for the Bastard had replaced it with his own.

Tristan looked up quickly and the smith stepped back. But the captain answered casually, "It seems so."

Now there was speculation in the smith's face, and when the captain looked up the room, he saw it reflected in others. "Aye, well, maybe it would be an antique that you've traded for somewheres," the smith said, but both he and the captain knew it was a lie.

Tristan smiled. "Maybe."

The miller cleared his throat. "Ye'll be needin' a place to hide away. I've a small place downriver that I use sometimes when we take the grain barge down."

"Thank you, no. Have no fear for us. As for yourselves," he said as he looked round at them, "you must protect Master Smith and Master Miller here. Let your story be that the reeve and his men tried to arrest us, and say nothing of what went before." There were nods.

The miller surveyed the mess. "I have my wagon outside. This lot can go into the river without anybody missin' them, I reckon."

Tristan clapped him on the shoulder. "Each of you lead one of their horses away and set it free near your home. They will find their way back to the reeve's stable, no doubt, but maybe not till morning. And now, good night. Go safely and have a care to have your stories ready. The murder of a reeve is a grave thing, and there will be those who will ask questions."

"They won't get no answers from us," the miller said vigorously, and several voices echoed his words.

"Get out of here, the lot of you," Kursh growled, and the miller slapped him on the back and, with the smith, bent to Robert's body. Soon the corpses were removed, and nothing remained but to sweep up the sawdust and put down fresh shavings. The one-eyed dwarf laid his ax on his shoulder and his fist on his hip and glared at the Littleman standing next to him.

"That was the bloody stupidest thing you've ever done. Unarmed, and you tackle him!"

Peewit fingered the bump on his head and winced. "It used to work."

"You used to carry a sword to back it up with!"

"I've *got* a sword, but it's out in your stable!"

"Fine place for it!"

Imris burst out laughing, and the captain cut in. "Leave it, you two. We've got to get this place straightened out."

But now the Yoriandir suddenly frowned and moved his shoulders as though something cold had touched him. "No, Tristan. First we must go looking for Master Llodin." When the captain looked at him sharply, he added, "I don't know why, but we must."

Kursh caught his cloak from a hook by the door and had a word with Orin. Peewit, the Yoriandir and the captain were already heading for the door. Together, the Watchmen slipped into the night and the rain.

But they were seen when they emerged from the stable a few moments later, mounted and fully armed. From across the street, a dark figure watched them ride past. He waited until the clop of their horses' hooves on the cobbles could no longer be heard and then he moved out into the street and stood staring after them. Finally he smiled and walked quickly toward the door of the Sword and Skull. He paused for an instant, looking left and right, and quickly shrugged out of his dark cloak. Beneath, he wore a black and red uniform with a chevron of bright blue across the chest. He wrapped the cloak about his forearm, drew his dagger, and stepped inside.

In the miasmal darkness the clashing tree limbs shrieked with wind and keeled before the driving storm. They had to duck their heads into the protection of a crooked elbow to look ahead or they would have been blinded with the stinging needles of spray. The banked road ran from the town gates out into the wilderlands that lay between the town of Swiftwater Shallows and the river. It had been cleared of saplings and underbrush earlier in the spring by companies of guildsmen and was considered a fairly decent highway, better maintained than most, and safer than some. But tonight it was fetlock deep in mud and treacherous underfoot.

The dwarf reined in his horse suddenly and wheeled it, rump to the force of the gale. In the dark the others couldn't see his face, but his voice held thunder: "He *must* have begged hospitality at one of the farms. He's not out here, and we're stumbling around like bloody idiots. If he's warm by a fire somewhere, I'll—"

"Hush!" advised the Yoriandir. "He may hear and take you up on the challenge!"

"Quiet, both of you!" the irritated Littleman snapped. "You're making enough noise for a den of wolves and I can't hear a thing out there!" He meant that he could hear nothing out of his bad ear because of the storm, and both of them knew this.

Kursh harrumphed and rode a few paces to the side of the road, looking into the woods on that side, and Imris smiled, though he too searched the night. His thrush nestled close to the back of his neck inside the blue hood and fussed at the storm. The wind had whipped their words away in an instant, and the captain bent his head and closed his eyes, turning his head to listen the better. "Not a thing," he finally murmured.

"What?" demanded the dwarf, turning to frown at him.

Tristan shook his head and raised his voice. "Nothing. I can hear nothing."

Kursh muttered something, fingering the pitted blade of the ax hanging in its sheath at his waist, and turned to scan the night again.

"Tristan, look." The Yoriandir's green hand, dimly seen in the swimming darkness, lifted to point off in the trees at the left of the road ahead. "Do you see, there?"

The captain narrowed his eyes. "Something," he agreed, unconsciously gripping the hilt of his sword.

The dwarf whirled to look where the Yoriandir had pointed. "Where?"

Imris did not answer, and the captain waved to indicate that they should dismount and approach the area from different directions. Kursh nodded, drew his ax, and followed as Peewit rode into the darkness to the right of the road. The Yoriandir slicked the moisture from his bowstring, fitted an arrow, and slipped gracefully to the muddy road. Tristan flung himself off his horse and led it under the trees. Circling, he and the tree-tender came quickly to the shadow at the edge of the grass underneath the forest's first branches and approached cautiously.

Imris was ahead, but he drew back sharply and an expression of disgust broke across his face. It was the carcass of a horse, belly-gutted. The ground was soaked with blood and he danced back quickly, glancing at the man beside him. They had both seen that it was a sorrel with a star blaze: the wizard's horse.

Sick with foreboding, the captain scanned the darkness and had pursed his lips to whistle a signal when the Littleman's choked cry was borne to him on the wind. Immediately he and the Yoriandir ran toward the sound, but carefully lest they be caught in a trap. But it was no trick; they saw that when they caught a glimpse of them through the trees.

The Littleman was crouched on the ground, and Kursh stood above him, shoulders bent and beard streaming. When Tristan and Imris were near enough to see the huddle of robes at their companions' feet, they slowed to a reluctant walk.

Neither Peewit nor Kursh looked up. The dwarf grated, "Some murdering scum shot him from ambush with a poisoned arrow." At Imris's questioning look, he explained shortly, "We found the place where the attacker waited over there." He jerked a thumb toward the forest. "There was a phial of liquid marked with a hex."

"Did you touch it?" the captain asked quickly.

"D'ye think I'm bloody simple?" the dwarf roared. He glared for a moment. "It was broken on the ground. He must have dropped it running. There is only one set of tracks."

"Show me."

They trudged across the road, where Peewit led the

way to a thicket of blackthorne and mutely pointed to the sparkle of crystal fragments by a jutting rock.

The captain took another moment to peer around through the trees. "Are there more of the Bastard's troops about?" he asked Imris. "What does your little friend there say?"

The thrush's bright eyes just showed next to the Yoriandir's ear. She peeped once and cocked her head to regard the tall man. "We are the only ones abroad," Imris reported.

The captain nodded and knelt. Drawing his dagger, he carefully probed at the shards until he could see the wax seal clearly. From over his shoulder there was a hissed word in Yoriand. Tristan looked up to see Imris shaking his head violently with the look of one who has seen the arch of the sky cracking.

"What is it?" Peewit asked quickly.

The Yoriandir licked his lips and backed away. "I have known this sign only once." His fir eyes came up to meet theirs. "It is the Fallen's mark."

"Are you sure?" Tristan demanded.

"I make no mistake," Imris assured him. He leaned against a tree trunk. "Would that I *could* forget such evil." He closed his eyes. Thought took him back there, back to the pit, to the place of torment for such of the Greenbriar King's loyal troops as were left after that last suicidal stand beneath the castle walls. The guards, half-savage brutes, had worn that sign openly, mockingly. And then they had taken hot irons and branded it into the flesh of the conquered.

Unconsciously the tree-tender raised trembling fingers to rub the place on his forehead, though it was long since healed by the power that ran through the Yoriandirkin. For a moment he could smell his own seared flesh again.

Kursh grasped him firmly by the arm and shook him, and the memory broke into the dripping leaves and soggy breeze of the present. The dwarf looked up at him out of his one good eye and said quietly, " 'Twas a bad time then, Imris, but it's more than twenty years gone now."

"Suddenly, twenty years is not long enough, my

friend," the Yoriandir sighed. The evil face of the
wizard Rasullis, called the Fallen because he had been
cast from the Meld, swam up before his inner eye. It
had been Rasullis who had supervised the tortures.

The captain was turning the shards of the phial this
way and that. "It was not the Fallen himself, I think,
who did this. He would not have needed poison." He
rose and jammed his dagger back in his belt. "I heard
rumors down on the border that the Fallen has insti-
tuted a new corps of assassins. Llodin's murder seems
to prove it true."

"Maybe that's the news Master Wizard wanted to
give us," Peewit suggested.

The captain's face was grave. "I don't think so. He
told me that it involved our Oath."

The Oath? the Littleman thought. Our Oath to protect the king's Blood with our own? Our Oath that
died with the King there on the Sweep twenty years
ago? What was old Llodin thinking of?

The captain carefully swept some leaf mold over the
broken poison container and ground it in with his
boot. Then they all went back to the wizard's body.
Tristan crouched and ran one gauntleted finger down
the fletching of the arrow, noting its markings, and
then gently drew a fold of the enchanter's stained
cloak to cover it. "And he told *me* to be careful on
the way here," he rasped with angry sorrow.

Kursh said, "I'll tell you one thing—if it was indeed
the Fallen, acting through an assassin, then he has
become much stronger. Llodin had the most powerful
magic I have ever heard of and yet, look—what good
did it do him? There is no sign at all of a fight. He was
dying before he knew that he'd been hit."

It seemed obvious. Everywhere they looked the
woods were undisturbed, except for the damage of the
thrashing storm. Tristan judged, "You're right, Kursh.
He was completely taken by surprise."

Imris was looking at something through the trees.
"Not quite." Picking his way through the gripping
briar underbrush, he reached into a thick patch and
drew out a carven pole of ash, broken off near the
middle. He peered, tried the branches this way and

that, and after a moment withdrew the other half.
Runes gleamed faintly in the rain. The Yoriandir said
quietly, "He made certain his power would not be
misused."

Somehow, it was this sign of the care he had taken
that finally broke through their numbed shock, and
sorrow overcame them. Each walked a little apart
from the others and nothing more was said for a time.
Finally Kursh swiped angrily at his nose and smote the
trunk of a young elm. "By the Three, I'll kill that
whoreson Rasullis for this!"

Peewit furtively dried his eyes and said nothing, but
he thought, How?

"We'd better be going," the captain murmured. The
dwarf went back to collect their horses, and he left the
others at the roadside, leading Tristan's bay stallion in
under the trees. Peewit meanwhile had picked up the
pieces of the staff. For some reason he did not understand, the touch of them made him feel comforted,
and he thought perhaps he would keep one of the
halves for a walking stick. He didn't think Llodin
would mind. The sharp break showed new-wood clean
against the darker grain where the wizard's hands had
worn oil into the staff, and on an impulse, the Littleman
fitted the pieces together, meshing the jagged ends
until they matched exactly. The runes ran coiled and
intricate around the ash pole.

The horse did not like the scent of blood, but Kursh
held it firmly while the Yoriandir and the man gently
lifted the body to lay it across the saddle bows. As
Tristan grasped the bony old shoulders, a low moan
broke from the wizard's bearded lips. For an instant it
was as if lightning had struck nearby and come up
through the wet ground, holding them rooted to the
spot and tingling. "By the Powers!" the captain gasped,
and then Kursh whooped mightily, so that the horse
threw up its head and tried to break away.

Peewit stared down at the staff in his hands. "*Captain!*"

At his tone, Tristan glanced back over his shoulder
even as he and Imris lowered the wizard carefully back
to the ground. He saw a web begin to grow, an ame-

thyst network that twined the surface of the staff, hovering over the Littleman's hands. But he saw too that the running of the runes was imperfect, the threads of purple fire winking out in sparks that tried to jump the break in the staff. When Peewit involuntarily trembled and the jagged ends separated for an instant, there was in the gap a bright gleam, like the furnace in the heart of a firelit gem. "Steady!" the captain hissed. "For the love you bear him, do not drop it!"

"What is it?" the Littleman demanded, his voice cracking.

"I know not, but he is alive because of it," Tristan reported as he tore open the wizard's robe and felt the heart staggering under his palm. "Kursh, is Fidelis still at the Retreat?"

"Aye, and grown to be a stronger healer than ever!" the dwarf answered with fierce joy. He vaulted to the back of Tristan's stallion. Imris and the captain lifted the old man into his arms, but when Kursh would have set his heels to the horse and raced away to find the dirt track that led up into the hills, Tristan checked him sharply and reminded him that the wizard must remain with his staff. So Kursh gathered the reins until Imris had brought the rest of their horses and Tristan had raised Peewit, staff clenched tightly in his fists, to his pony's back. Then they started off at a brisk pace, with Imris leading Peewit's mount. Kursh fretted and chewed his mustache, but he held the old man gently and finally they were climbing through the terraces where shadowy vines rustled in the wind, and the moon through the scudding clouds glistened on the clustered fruit.

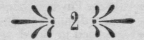

Once, the Retreat had been a small self-contained community, dedicated to the observances that honored the Powers. In the scouring aftermath of the war the place had been put to the torch. Belatedly, one of the local Barrener officers had discovered the quality of the wine stored in the cellars. The main buildings were shabbily patched, and to replace the religious community that had perished with the old scrolls and censers, the Barreners installed a steward and set the Ilyrian peasants to farm the place and keep the vines flourishing. For two decades the Retreat had been a village in thrall to the overlord of the Swiftwater area.

Now the roughly chinked stones of the encircling wall gleamed wetly and showed a blank face as they rode up, but Kursh directed his horse to a broad door set into the wall. Tristan knocked with his sword hilt, eliciting no response until Imris thought to look for the bell rope. He pulled it and they heard a clanging within. Shortly a wicket in the gate slid open and, dark against the lamplight behind him, the gatekeeper peered out.

"We have an injured man here. Get Master Fidelis the healer quickly!" Tristan ordered, forgetting the demands of courtesy in this great need. That voice had sent subalterns scuttling in former days. But the gatekeeper was fuddled by sleep, or else simple, and he only stared at the fretful horses with their dark trappings and at the company of strangers that wanted entrance in the middle of the night. "For pity's sake, man, admit us to the hospice!" the captain demanded again, striding up close to the wicket and trading stares with him. But the man now saw Peewit, and the staff with its fire flickering low clenched in his aching fists. He gasped, and the wicket slammed shut. The Littleman groaned.

"Fool!" Kursh yelled after him, while Tristan hung on the bell rope, intending to set up such a ringing as would wake the villagers in their beds a mile and a half away down in the valley. In the noisy confusion, the thrush peered from Imris's hood, trilled suddenly, and lifted into the air to flutter over the wall. The Yoriandir reached to stay the captain's angry pulls, and they waited in tense silence for what seemed hours.

Abruptly the wooden bars were thrust back into their sockets. The door swung in and slammed back against the arched passageway beyond. A wiry figure strode out, tying a hospital apron over his robe. "Kursh!" He stopped short as he saw the amethyst-robed figure in the dwarf's brawny arms. "Powers protect us! Oh, Master Llodin!" He beckoned urgently. "Inside!" He ran back through the passage himself and bore for the dimly lighted windows of the hospice that formed the left wall of the courtyard. Behind him, Kursh urged the horse through the echoing dark of the bricked tunnel and clattered across the old cloister. The young gatekeeper, not much more than a boy, stared after them for a moment, then hurriedly barred the gate again and followed.

Already they were pulling the wizard's crumpled figure from the saddle while Tristan explained, "It's a poisoned arrow."

"How long ago?" the healer asked, leading the way into the ward.

"We found him about an hour ago. How long before that he was shot, we don't know. I would guess another hour, at least—maybe more." They passed along a row of beds, and through a small door beyond into a chamber whose area was mostly taken up by a stout table upon which Fidelis gestured they should lay the wounded enchanter.

Peewit eased through the door, maneuvering carefully, and took a place in a corner, out of the way of a jostle. His fingers were numb and his arms ached all the way to his shoulders, but he set his face resolutely and held the staff together. The healer threw him an encouraging glance as he quickly cut away the blood-encrusted purple tunic. "How was the staff broken?" Fidelis asked.

"He broke it himself, we think," Imris answered with his eyes on the old man. "To protect it from the Fallen's assassin."

Fidelis stilled. "An assassin?"

"Aye," Kursh told him. "We found a phial where the attacker waited. It was marked with the Fallen's hex."

The doctor drew a hissing breath between his teeth, shook his head, and directed the boy now standing at the doorway, "Go to the kitchen and fetch us a kettle of hot water, Alphonse. And be careful crossing the courtyard. Don't spill it on yourself. I have all the patients I can take care of right now. Go on—off with you." They could hear the slap of his sandals as he pounded away.

Tristan had lit the lamps in the hanging tripod above the surgery table, and now they could all see the waxen pallor and black streaks of poison spreading out from the shaft of the arrow which still protruded from the right side of Llodin's chest. The wizard's struggle for breath was painfully evident, and when the doctor felt for the lifebeat a few inches to the left of the wound, he shook his head. The Serpent tattoo of the Meld of Wizards coiled about the old man's throat, and looking at it, Fidelis knew that whatever had been in the phial, it had not been poison alone. No poison could thus strip a wizard of his power.

Alphonse ran in with the kettle, set it on the hook in the fireplace, and fed the small blaze there. Over his shoulder Fidelis called orders to him. "Poppy liquor, in the blue bottle on the top shelf. That's it. Now moss, in the small chest there. No, the box next to it. Yes. Heat a stone for his feet, and fetch more linen and blankets. Hand me the kit there." The boy laid an open box of implements on the table and dashed out for blankets and a winter stone from the ward. Imris's thrush returned at that moment from the cornice of the cloister outside and trilled briefly. The Yoriandir reported, "Someone is coming. An angry man, she says, very fat."

Fidelis nodded. "The steward." Kursh stepped forward, volunteering to use his strength to pull the arrow. The healer shook his head. "I don't know what kind of tip it has; if it is flared or barbed and we pull it, we'll take half his lung with it." The dwarf smoothed his beard but said nothing.

The captain asked, "So what's to do?"

Over the body on the table, Fidelis met his look straightly. "Come now, Tristan—have you never caught your thumb on a fishhook?"

In the corner, Peewit murmured a nauseated "Oh,

no," and closed his eyes tightly, but he quickly opened them again when steps sounded in the doorway.

"What is the meaning of this? By whose authority were these people admitted?" It was apparent that the steward had dressed hastily; his outer robe was drawn on over his nightclothes and his sparse hair stood up in wild disarray. "Fidelis, what is the meaning of this?" he demanded again, while the dwarf, who had moved aside to make way for him, hovered protectively. Then the steward caught sight of the Serpent of the Meld tattoo. He went rigid and his breath seemed to stop. "Beldis! This is a *wizard*!" His eyes flew up to the healer's. "You'll get us all *killed*!"

Fidelis met his panicked look for a moment. "It is only a wounded old man, Ned." Calmly he folded a thick wad of linen and placed it between Llodin's jaws.

"The tattoo, fool!" The steward flung a pointing finger and then snatched it back.

A broad hand caught his shoulder and none too gently straightened him up. "Stay out of the light," Kursh told him.

The steward shook him off and his triple chins quivered. He glared about at all of the odd group now, his gaze going from the southerner to the green-skin, and then to the Littleman and the staff flickering with magic light. "By the Wolf!" he whispered hoarsely. "Get it out of here! Out!" Beside himself with fear, he made a grab for the staff.

Tristan's sword rang chiming from its sheath. "Hold!"

The steward's shoulders bunched as if he felt the tip of the blade, though Tristan merely held it leveled and ready. Slowly the fat man turned and beads of sweat popped out on his forehead.

Fidelis said quietly, "Leave us now. We will discuss this later. And Ned: it was dark when Alphonse let them in; he could not tell it was a wizard. He saw only a wounded man, and all these we have permission to treat. If we keep our heads, naught will come of this. You understand me?"

The steward's dubious gaze went again to the still form on the table, but he nodded abruptly and backed

out the door. They listened to him go. The captain
rammed the sword home in its housings and ordered,
"Imris, bar the hospice door and stand guard there."
He looked across the table at Fidelis. "Will he betray
us?"

"Can it matter right now?" The soldier made no
reply and the healer told them, "All right. Kursh,
stand by to push. Tristan, let's turn him on his side."
He looked over at the Littleman. "And by the Powers, Peewit, don't falter now!"

When it was done and the wound was packed, the
wizard slept a deep, drugged sleep while his fever
soared and the poison sought to break him with convulsions. There came a moment's respite and the
Yoriandir came through to the ward from the surgery
with two mugs of steaming herb tea. Handing one to
the doctor and the other to Tristan—who now watched
at the window lest the steward rouse the rest of the
villagers to action—he sat down on the edge of a cot
and whistled softly. The thrush flitted down from
the rafters and settled contentedly on his shoulder.
Alphonse had been dismissed (Fidelis sought to spare
him from the steward's anger), and they had taken a
long strip of linen, wrapped it about the break in the
staff, and sealed it with wax to form a brittle cast.
When they had prized the Littleman's numb fingers
away, the wrapping had held and the staff had retained its light. It lay now in the recess of the long
window casement, safe from accident. Peewit huddled
thankfully on another cot across from the Yoriandir,
his hands and forearms wrapped in steaming compresses
as Fidelis coaxed the overused muscles to relax and
cease their cramping. Kursh had held a mug of tea
laced with a liberal dollop of brandy to the Littleman's
lips and Peewit had regained his normal ruddy complexion. Now he winced as he flexed his hands and
asked, "What will the steward do?"

Fidelis shrugged as he sipped. "I think he is probably in his rooms right now trying to decide that, while
his wife curses him for a fool and urges him to send a
rider to fetch the constabulary." Seeing the concern

that flared in their eyes, he added quickly, "But he will do nothing till morning. Our Ned is not a hasty man."

Kursh folded his arms across his chest and regarded the healer out of his good eye. "And then?"

"Then I fear trouble. You will have to be gone as soon as possible."

Turning from the window, Tristan said, "We put you in a difficult position, I know, but I could think of nothing beyond getting the wizard here."

"It was fortune itself that you found him when you did. He wouldn't have lasted another hour." He set a hand to the old man's brow, and a reminiscent smile played across his features. "Somehow I have always known that the lot of you would come looking for my help some night. It's almost like old times."

They looked back with affectionate respect at the former chief physician to the king. Of them all, Fidelis had changed the least. He had still the same quick intelligence and sturdy common sense, the flashes of humor, and lean countenance that he had always possessed, and if the wiry hair was now gray, it was no matter—he was still Cedric, physician and counselor.

In the last battle, when the bastard brother of the king and his ally, the Fallen, had suddenly struck by surprise, Cedric had been in the village a mile from the castle, tending the merrymakers of a riotous marriage party of the night before. So swift had been the attack that he had not been able to get to the king's army, and thus escaped the final disaster. Later, when they had heard in the village that the king was dead with all of his army, Cedric had cursed the restraining arms of the villagers and wept with rage and shame. Two shepherds spirited him away when they took the flocks to the high pasture a few days later and he was free. The bastard king had never heard rumor that the doctor was not among the corpses that had been unceremoniously burned on the battlefield.

Cedric had parted from the shepherds in the mountain passes and wandered alone, paying his way by his skill. By autumn he had come down into a river valley near the southern border and found himself in a free-

hold village that guarded its liberty jealously and re-
sisted any suggestion that the new king might want to
strengthen his claim on them. But within a few months
it became obvious that the Bastard was out to destroy
everything of the old order—the Ilyrian kingdom and
especially the old Ilyrian religion. Worship of the Three
Powers of Earth, Wind, and Fire was forbidden under
strictest penalty, supplanted by the cold religion of the
one the Barreners called Beldis, Lord of the Wild
Fire, whose incarnation was the Wolf. This god the
Barreners had brought with them from their mountain
heights, whereto they had been driven an age of the
world ago by Beod, first of the Greenbriar Kings.

When the Bastard's troops smashed the chapels of
the old religion and tortured its priests to death, worship of the Three Powers went underground. Gradually there grew rumors among the common folk of
secret fastnesses, cunningly hidden, where the old
ways were preserved. Hearing of one such Retreat in
the hills above Swiftwater Shallows, Cedric set himself
to find it.

Whether he found it, or whether the brethren found
him and led him to it, he was never sure, but as winter
came on he stumbled into the hidden dell and found
them waiting for him. He begged sanctuary and was
accepted. In time, he took the vows and became a
Retreat Master, one of those whose very lives were
sworn to keep alive knowledge of the Three.

Because of his skills as a doctor, it was deemed that
he should live outside the Retreat so that the people
roundabout might have access to his healing. He took
the traveling name "Fidelis" and his brothers and sisters sent him to the village at the burned-out former
chapel.

One day when he was attending at a birth at one of
the outlying farms, Fidelis had heard of a one-eyed
dwarf who had returned to Swiftwater Shallows to
take charge of his uncle's tavern. At first he had
thought nothing of it, but when the stout midwife
whispered that the dwarf had been one of the old king's
men, his interest was piqued. He had borrowed the
farmer's plowhorse and made his way down to the town.

He would have known Kursh anywhere, despite the eyepatch.

He was made welcome and they had spent the afternoon making inroads in a keg of ale and sharing such news as there was: Tristan and Peewit had also escaped, though the captain had been grievously burned and the Littleman partly deafened. When each of them had recovered from his injuries, they had together rescued Imris from slavery—how, Cedric had never asked. The survivors of the King's First Watch would be meeting from time to time here at the tavern, Kursh told him.

Over the next couple of years, they *had* met, but as time went on and the Bastard's hold over Ilyria strengthened until it became dangerous to travel, the meetings became less frequent and each of them went his own way. An oath to a dead king is no oath at all.

Now it seemed, Fidelis thought as he glanced around the ward at them, the web of the past had brought them all together again. But the key to their purpose lay locked in the wizard's fevered brain. He looked down again at his patient and frowned.

Llodin's spasms were growing stronger and the fever burned in two bright spots on his cheeks, the only color he had. Fidelis had propped him half sitting against the pillows to ease his breathing, but in his flailing he had slipped. The doctor had just grasped his shoulders to settle him again when the next seizure hit, arching the old man until it seemed his backbone must surely break. Fidelis came to a desperate decision. "Hold him," he directed the Yoriandir, and when Imris had taken his place, he ran for the inner chamber. He mixed brown liquid from several jars and boxes, working quickly.

"What is it?" Kursh asked from the doorway.

"I've never tried it before, but I heard of a case something like this many years ago. I have no idea of the *proportions*, though," he said to himself in frustration. He bit his lip and stared uncertainly at the flask, stilled by indecision.

The dwarf came into the room slowly. "Whatever chance there is, you must take it, Cedric. Llodin is an old man. I don't know how it is with wizards, but I am sure that his own power has done everything it can do. Have you noticed the staff?" When the Retreat Master looked up quickly, he added, "It grows dim again. I think he's going."

They stared at each other until Kursh finally said, "We *must* know his message. Otherwise, he will have died for nothing."

Fidelis drew a breath, clenched his teeth, and nodded shortly. Taking the flask and a knife, and pausing to cut a hollow straw from a broom standing near the fireplace, he strode out into the other room with Kursh following.

The spasm had passed and Imris and the captain had eased the old wizard back to the pillows. Tristan made way for Fidelis and cast a quizzical look at the flask and other articles. "I'm going to make an incision here." Fidelis pointed to the swollen vein that knotted up the inside of Llodin's right arm as he lifted it clear of the blankets. "And then I'm going to try to force some of this potion into the cut." He looked around at them. "If it works, his fever will break and there will be no more convulsions. If it doesn't . . ." He paused and looked down at the man in the bed. "If it doesn't, his heart will stop."

The captain said at his shoulder, "At least it will be quicker for him than this." Imris nodded agreement. Peewit walked to the casement and reached to touch the staff; then he too turned to watch.

Swiftly, precisely, Fidelis made the cut. He slipped one end of the straw into the vein, capped the tiny geyser of blood with his finger, and took a sip from the flask as Kursh tipped it to him. Bending, he carefully blew the potion into the free end of the straw.

For a long moment nothing happened. Fidelis turned his head to accept more from the flask, thinking that it needed a greater dose. Simultaneously, there was a loud snap near Peewit, the Littleman yelled something indistinguishable, and the wizard sat up suddenly, breaking Tristan's grip. The startled doctor found himself face-to-face with his patient, and the old man gasped hoarsely, "The staff, fool! Give me the staff!"

Galvanized, Peewit slipped his hands through the blazing amethyst fires that now webbed the stave and brought it for him. He fairly hurled it into Llodin's hands in his excitement. The wizard grasped it weakly at first, closed his eyes, and slowly, painfully, raised it above his head. There was an explosion that drove them all back, shielding their eyes, but when they opened them seconds later, there was only a little smoke and some bright purple sparks drifting down to snuff out before they hit the coverlet. The old man laughed delightedly and struck the healer on the arm with the pole. "By the Three," he panted, "I'll make an adept out of you yet, Fidelis!" Sweat sheened his brow and he slumped back into the pillows. The doctor checked his pulse and assured them that this time it was a healing sleep. He took the staff gently, unsurprised to find the wax melted, the linen burned free, and the wood fused across the break. He stooped to place it on the floor by the cot, and then they withdrew the length of the room to the fireplace and dragged stools close to talk without disturbing the wizard.

In the still of the night, long after the others had stretched themselves on cots to sleep while Tristan kept a sharp-eyed watch at the window into the cloister and even Fidelis drowsed on the stool he had set near the bedside, Llodin rode the surface of a dream. He was there in the candle-lit infirmary and he was not; he was sleeping and he was not; it was his dream, but it was not.

A clangor rose through his dream-drifting and resolved itself into the clash of arms. He was on a battlefield. Sharp and clear he saw the weapons flashing in the late afternoon sunlight, heard horses screaming, was stunned with the frenzied movement of color around him—the bright emerald surcoats and pennants of his own troops, the spill of heart-red blood that ran in trickles through the trampled summer grass, and the red-on-black banner that snapped in the breeze.

He felt again the horror as he watched them all fall, the dwarf with blood welling between the fingers of one hand as he tried to hamstring the black stallion with the ax, the young captain smitten by a sudden roar of blue flame, while the harper played and the Littleman scrambled back through their tottering line in the direction of the castle. But the dream lent him a certain detachment; he knew how the moment had ended.

He let himself float away from his body up into the golden sky as the black horseman reined in and swung his leg to dismount. Thus it was that when the outer battlements crumbled, he was already too far away to hear the explosion. He went where his heart willed.

The dream became confused; things he had not seen with his bodily eyes were dimmer, blurred, like a reflection in a shady pond. He had an impression of pine forest, a drowsy hum of insects, small rocks rolling on a scree. "Careful, Your Majesty—the ground is broken here." Melchior's voice, gasping with exertion.

"Mama, I want to ride my pony."

"Yes, my sweeting, and so you shall. But not today," she answered. Even in his floating dream, he was proud of the way her voice sounded; but because it was a dream, he could also hear a whispered fragment of what she did not say aloud: 'Maybe never again, my Gerrit.'

The sturdy little legs pumped up and down, climbing the slope through the trees. "Why is my uncle come with his army, Mama? Is it a festival time? Will I have a new tunic like my father's?" The thin treble shook a little. Even at five, he knew it was no festival.

In the dream he saw the glance that passed between Melchior and the queen over the boy's head. How do you tell a child?

It was the chamberlain who answered, "Your uncle Dendron is not a good man, Lordling. He has not come in peace."

"Hugh said there will be war." It was a question.

Melchior turned to lift the boy up over the trunk of a fallen tree. "Hugh would do better to stick to his duties," he muttered, and gave the queen his hand to steady her.

"Wait, Melchior, this is pointless," she said calmly.

He bowed his head but said nothing. "We must leave the trail. Here, they can follow on horses. We must take away that advantage."

The chamberlain gave her a quick, surprised look. "That is so, madam, but if we leave the path, we may lose the way. I have only been there once," he said in quiet apology.

"And I have never been there. My husband the king does not—" She caught her breath and forced herself to say, "Did not feel the need to show me." Her eyes reddened, and she looked quickly away. Then her chin came up and she put on courage like a mantle. Sitting down on the log, she drew the child to her. "Gerrit, we are trying to reach a safe place where your father will come to find us." She drew a steadying breath and continued, "Now, Melchior and I may not be able to go all the way with you, so I want you to know how to find the place, all right?" At his serious nod, her face softened, and she cuddled him close, laying her cheek against the fine hair. Inwardly she wept, Ah, my little girl, where are you?

"Madam."

Melchior's sympathetic voice recalled her and she straightened, putting Gerrit from her a little so that she could look into his face. "Now, my son, do you see that spire of rock up there?" He looked in the direction she pointed, up the ridge. A finger of rock thrust from the tall pines at its base. Time out of mind, tales had called it the Guardian. It was said to be a magical sanctuary, a place outside time, created by Ritnym for the Greenbriar Kings. But darker rumors called it Ritnym's Gate—the entrance to the land of the dead. The queen would not let herself think of that now. "If you go to that rock and look carefully, you will come to another rock which leans against the base of it, hidden in the trees. In fact, it is a wondrous big boulder, as smooth as the rocks you play with down by the river. And through the middle of this rock, there grows a tree."

"A tree?" he asked uncertainly.

"Yes, but not like these." She waved a hand at the pines surrounding them. "It has red leaves all the year 'round, and white berries. When you see the tree, climb the boulder, and in the cleft, the place where it is split, you will find the opening to a tunnel. It will be dark, Gerrit, but you must be brave and go into it. There may be an old torch with a flint and tinder so that you can have a light. The tunnel leads to a room made ready for you."

"For me?" he asked with childish innocence.

"There is not time to explain," she told him.

Clear through the forest air they heard the baying of hounds. She started and the blood drained from her face, but then she said, "The waterfall, Melchior—it is near here?"

"Yes, my lady."

"I remember a tree that the lightning had blasted. It was hollow."

He understood immediately. "This way. Come, Lordling, I will carry you for a bit."

They fought through the whipping branches, and even in the dream the pitch clung to his hands and the needles pricked. The dogs were closer now, and there were many of them. They could hear a horn, and in the distance, hunting calls. Finally they crashed through the brush to the steeper sides of a ravine and the land pitched sharply down. The roar of the water forced Melchior to raise his voice. "The falls are just over that cliff, my lady."

The Powers are merciful, she thought. At least Gerrit will not see.

She stooped to the boy. "I will need your cloak." As her hands fumbled with the clasp, she could see fear in his eyes. "We are going to play a trick on your uncle. It is sort of a hide-and-seek. You see this hollow tree here? Well, I think that this will make the perfect hiding place for you!" She tried to make her voice light and merry as if this were, indeed, no more than a child's game. "Melchior, give him a boost up to that branch." As the chamberlain raised the boy, she caught at his arms and kissed the trembling mouth. "There. Now you will stay hidden till everyone is gone, won't you? You mustn't spoil the game. Your father would be angry."

"Where are *you* going?" he whimpered.

She faltered. "Oh, Melchior and I are just going to lead them on for a bit. Now remember, go to the rock with the red tree and wait there." She nodded to the chamberlain.

Melchior tousled the boy's hair affectionately. "Stay well, little master," he said gruffly and swung the child up. Gerrit caught at the branch and straddled it. The trunk ended just above his head as he perched there.

"Stand up and you'll be able to climb down inside the tree," she urged. Her heart caught in her throat as he did her bidding and his dark curls disappeared. "There. Are you all right?"

"Yes." And then in a sharp tone of discovery: "Mama! There's a bird's nest in here!"

Tears came and she called back in a choked voice, "That's nice. Stay there now."

She turned away blindly and Melchior gave her his arm. She tried to speak but could not, and he led her some distance up the path toward the roaring falls. He bent to shout into her ear, "We must wait until they see us, my lady."

She forced herself to nod and began to say, "Melchior, you have been a good and faithful steward, and I—"

"I'm sorry, my lady, I cannot hear you," he shouted.

And suddenly, there was no time left. In his dream he saw the mounted hunters spur their horses over the lip of the ravine, and heard the horn blare to signify that the quarry had been sighted. They turned and fled toward the cliff and when they were near the place she looked back once, clutched the small cloak to her for an instant, and then let it fall.

Like the mist that rose above the roaring water, the vision wavered and broke as the connection between the king and the dreaming wizard weakened. When the other turned, there was in the shadowed eyes beneath the war helm an agony of despair. "Find him. You must find my son." As Llodin swam up out of the dream, he heard a woman's voice implore, "And my baby, my little girl," and the wave of her sorrow spun him like a piece of wood on a whirlpool toward the daylight world.

Llodin woke to a bright spatter of sunlight filtering through the shutters. At the window, Tristan—who had been enjoying the swooping play of the swallows in the crumbling cloister—suddenly stiffened and peered between the slats. The wizard moistened his lips and spoke softly, not to wake the others. "Let him come. It is"—he searched in his mind for the name, and it came to him out of the darkness of the night before— "Alphonse."

The captain cast a quick look over his shoulder. "I didn't know you were awake."

"I wasn't."

Fidelis, who had been propped against the wall by the side of the cot, woke and moved stiffly to the bedside. "Blessings!" he whispered, a grin showing white in the dim room. "By the Powers, I am glad to see you behind those eyes!"

"No gladder than I am to be able to see out of them. I know your labors last night. It was not easily done. I thank you."

The doctor was embarrassed and covered it by assuming a sterner countenance. "You shouldn't be talking."

It is all I have left, the old man thought, but aloud he agreed, "It will be good to rest, later. But first, there is much to be told, and a decision to be made. Alphonse is on the way to tell us that the steward intends some petty evil. So tea is in order, I think, and be sure to add a dram of brandy, if you please."

Fidelis opened his mouth to argue, caught the wizard's raised eyebrow, and laughed instead. "Your staff is there, by the bed."

"I know."

The Retreat Master shook his head and went through the arch into the inner room. Llodin could hear him dipping water into the kettle.

By now, Imris had risen lightly, and was stringing his bow. He darted a look bright with relief in Llodin's direction as Kursh sat up, tugging at the eyepatch to settle it. "What's the matter? What's going on?" the dwarf rasped in a gravelly morning voice.

"Not to worry," Tristan told him. "We are just about to have our 'meeting,' that's all." He raised his voice to call to Fidelis, "I've lost the boy."

The healer reappeared. "He'll be coming 'round back through the garden, I should think."

The Yoriandir put an eye to the shutter on that side and nodded in confirmation. Llodin painfully pushed himself up until he was sitting propped against the pillow. He was so tired, and the task just begun!

There came a tapping at the garden shutter. "Master Fidelis?"

The doctor walked over, undid the latch, and threw the shutter wide. "Come in, Alphonse. It's quite safe."

A warm scent of herbs blew past the boy on the light morning breeze riffling his red hair. "The steward is coming here," he blurted, peering into the infirmary as if he expected to see salamanders as big as sheep or dragonets perching on the bedstead.

Llodin did not move, but his eyes widened. "Alphonse," he said softly, "you must give us leave awhile. We have matters to discuss which are not for the steward's ears. Keep him away, would you?"

The youth reddened. Squinting, he regarded the old man in the bed, and suddenly a wide grin stretched his freckles. "Right enough, sir. I am glad to see thee well," he offered as he lifted one hand in a wave and slipped back into the garden, stumbling over the rain barrel.

Kursh snorted and rammed his ax back into its sheath. "You should have told him he was a toad."

Llodin darted him a look. "There's more to that young man than meets the eye, Master Longbeard. You will do well to go gently with him." He reached for the steaming mug Fidelis had fetched, winced, and asked the captain, "What is the situation out there?"

"The boy ran out and said something to the steward, waving his arms about and pointing back here. He must have been convincing—they've all pulled back into the shelter of the chapel door."

The enchanter knew a moment of satisfaction: even

with the Fallen's poison still working in him, he could summon enough command to cast a Warding upon the villagers outside. And time altering was no mere adept's spell, either, but rather one of the major Wardings. With this small glimmer of pride came the sobering realization that the spell was weakening him moment by moment. No matter, he thought with hard resolve. *I must have time to instruct them and, left to their own devices, the people outside would never give us these few precious instants.* (For so it would seem to the steward and his group.) Llodin sipped his tea and savored the sweet brandy-fire that underlay the herbs. "Excellent," he pronounced. "Come now, all of you, and hear."

The tall man took one more look through the slats and seemed satisfied with what he saw. Turning away from the window, he said, "I have been wondering what could possibly bring you away from your scrolls, Llodin—and at the time of the Meld-Meet too. Ill news, obviously. It *was* the Fallen's hex, then, that we saw on the poison phial?"

"It was, indeed." *Oh, it was indeed, and none of you begins to suspect its power.* . . . "And I left *after* the meet, not before it."

"Ah," the captain said as if his suspicions had been confirmed.

Kursh stood at the foot of the bed, his thumbs hooked in his broad belt. "Your message to the captain, here, mentioned the Oath," he stated. He cleared his throat and looked away for a moment, but then, being Kursh, he met the old man's eyes straightly. "I want to say that counsel taken by the Meld of Wizards about *our* Oath is offensive to me." Into the strained, surprised silence, he added, "I speak only for myself, and mean no disrespect for you, Master Llodin. But it was ill done," he reiterated stubbornly. "The Meld has no right to command us under the Oath of the First Watch."

There was a glimmer in the old eyes. "And who do you think wrote the Oath in the first place, Master Korimson?" he asked in a deceptively quiet voice.

"It is in the Roll of Kings," the stout dwarf answered.

"And did it come out of the evening air one fine night when Ilyria was a collection of huts by the river, think you? Or perhaps a dragon perched on the Sweep and whispered it to Beod of the Singing Sword when first he dreamt of building his castle there? Or maybe" —his voice rose—"your forefathers brought it with them from Jarlshof when they came to trade and then to fight on Beod's part against the Unnamed!" From beside the bed came a warning crackle as the warmth rose in the wizard's haggard face. "Dolt! We wizards *wrote* the Oath!"

Kursh chewed his mustache, while Tristan made a small movement of surprise and the Yoriandir nodded, smiling.

Llodin went on impatiently, "Now, I did not return from the porches of Ritnym's Realm to bandy words with you, so if I may be forgiven, I do indeed have news which may be of interest to all of you. Whether it is binding upon you under the Oath you once swore is for you to decide."

Fidelis was worried that he would fever himself anew and he sought to get the business over with as quickly as possible. "Say on, Master Llodin. And forgive our seeming reluctance. It is long since we thought of ourselves as members of the First Watch, that is all."

The old man regarded them for a moment and then he suddenly sighed. "Well. It is as the First Watch that you must act now, else I fear greater ill than any we have seen so far." Something had been knocking at the gates of his awareness and now he sent his mind questing outward, touched the group in the chapel, passed on over the walls, and found them: red and black uniforms showed in the forest, and among them was one with a blue chevron. He heard Tristan say something about Ilyria never seeing a worse ill than the Bastard on the throne, and the wizard's eyes focused again. He looked up at the lean figure of the captain. "I have put all of you in jeopardy. The Fallen had an assassin watching when I left Covencroft, and now he is here in the valley of the Swiftwater. In following me, he has found you. Foolishly I have given you away. I am sorry."

The captain was waving the words away before Llodin was done speaking. "It is no great matter. The Bastard and the Fallen have been seeking us for a long time. Now at least we shall be together when they come for us. We will not be taken easily."

His voice held grim resignation, and Llodin knew this was perhaps their greatest danger, so he snapped, "For shame! Think you of death as comfort when *the Blood still lives*!"

Their shocked silence lasted a full half minute and then Fidelis stooped to take the pulse in the thin wrist. Tristan's eyes met the doctor's over the cot and the captain of the First Watch said quietly, "You've been very sick, Llodin, and—"

"Damn you, Tristan! Leave me alone, Fidelis!" His eyes flashed dangerously. "I am not made senile by the fever! Hear me!" He looked slowly round at all of them and continued, "It is as I have said: the Blood still lives." In the stillness they could hear Imris's thrush fluttering in the roof coping outside, foraging for wood beetles.

The captain's hand closed about the hilt of his sword. "We were there," he said thickly. "The king fell. The Greenbriar bloodline ended."

"So we thought."

For a moment, hope danced in the air, as tangible as the steam from the tea or the dust motes that rose in a cloud as Peewit felt behind him for the edge of the nearest cot and sat down suddenly. But then they read in the other faces the doubt in their own minds, and the flicker died as quickly as if it had never been. Llodin saw this, and he waited until each had thought past the specter of the dark horseman, the exploding castle wall, and the battlefield corpse. He was not talking about the king.

Peewit's head jerked up and at the same time Imris leaned forward to say, "You cannot mean the children! We searched for them!"

"Months later," the wizard reminded him. "It was a long time before Tristan, Peewit, and Kursh were healed enough to leave Covencroft. Then they had to get you out of the rathole that the Bastard and the

Fallen between them had made of the castle at Greenbriar. By the time all that was accomplished, the trail was long gone cold. I doubt that anyone else could have found it.

"Then, when your tracking had led you to the point where the trail forked, you quite properly followed what you felt to be the prince's trail, where the queen and Melchior the chamberlain had taken the young heir to the kingdom. That trail ended above the first falls on the mighty Willowsrill."

"My lady queen, Melchior, and the Lordling must have jumped from the cliff into the falls," Imris said. "At least, that was the rumor among the Bastard's troops at the time, and we found nothing to tell us otherwise."

Stricken to the soul, Peewit burst out, "Were we wrong?"

The wizard did not mean to be cruel, but he did not answer directly. Instead he addressed the captain. "And what of the princess?"

Tristan stared back hard-eyed. "Long ago the Meld knew what we found. You agreed with us then that neither of the children survived. You know that the trail forked; the queen, Melchior, and the Lordling went by one way; the princess, who was naught but a babe in arms, was sent with Hugh the groom and the nursemaid, Keridwen. When we followed their trail, we came in time to a small dell. There were tatters of the garments they had worn and—"

When he paused, Kursh filled in firmly, "Bones. The wolves had savaged the bodies."

"Yes," the old wizard agreed. "And having come upon that dismal scene, you returned to Covencroft. So we thought the royal family massacred. All of them gone."

Tristan controlled his husky voice with difficulty. "And now?"

Llodin studied the swirl of leaves in the bottom of his cup. "Now, I have reason to believe that one, or both, of the children lived." He held up one hand to still their incredulous exclamations and amended, "Rather, I *know* that the princess survived, and therefore I suspect that the heir to the Greenbriar throne may have, as well."

They were all speaking at once, but Imris's bard's voice carried through the others: "How?" he demanded. "How do you know that Princess Ariadne is alive?"

"Because Rasullis the Fallen has her, and was rash enough to send a message to the Meld demanding that we ransom her with—something that he wants."

"But this is unbelievable," Peewit objected. "Do you mean that he found her all those years ago, and only now has flaunted her before your council?"

"Of course not. No, until recently Rasullis did not know of her existence, either. And that has been the luckiest piece of fate in this whole sorry business." He sighed and rested his head against the pillow. "Apparently not all of the soldiers in the Bastard's army are brutes. The trooper who first found that dell must have discovered much the same sort of evidence you did, with one exception: he also found the baby, still alive. The animals had not harmed her in any way.

"Well, this man had children of his own, and at the thought of killing the helpless infant, his conscience smote him. He hid the child in the brush, called the others of his company, and let them think that the princess's small bones must be among the others. Later, on the way back to the castle, he contrived to fall from his horse, appeared shaken, and said that he would ride back alone slowly, as he didn't want to keep the rest from reporting straight back to the Bastard.

"When they had gone, he went back and took the child to a peasant's hut they had passed in the foothills. He left the baby there, and never knew—nor dared to find out—what had become of her." You would have thought he had put a spell of silence on them, Llodin thought, looking around at the Watchmen. Not one of them moved. "Until about a month ago, that is where she remained, brought up as the daughter of the family. Then, a raiding party swept through those hills, and the youngest and strongest of the women were taken. You know why."

Kursh nodded savagely and the Littleman gripped the hilt of his short sword.

Imris asked, "Has Rasullis told her who she is?"

"I have no idea. But the Fallen was immediately struck by her likeness to the late king, and then he perceived my Warding upon her, so he made inquiries and found the soldier. He had him tortured and found out what he wanted to know. The poor fellow did not survive, I will not need to tell you." He could see the realization of what they would have to do growing on them, and he knew by small signs that they were afraid.

The captain's shoulders straightened. "And what of the heir?"

Llodin shook his head. "I do not even know for certain that he is alive." A fragment of his vision of the night before echoed in his mind. '. . . the red tree with the white berries . . .' "But I can suggest one place to begin the search."

Peewit had been reckoning. "The princess must be what? one-and-twenty now, almost."

The wizard's blue eyes regarded him steadily. "Yes. Breedable age."

The crassness had its intented effect. "Even the Bastard would not . . . !" Imris gasped.

"Of course he would," Kursh said flatly.

"It is not that, exactly." Llodin smoothed the coverlet. "Or rather, it is not *only* that. There is more danger to her than lust." He looked up at Tristan. "You recall the myth about the Crystal of Healing?"

The captain of the First Watch shrugged. "Every mother's child in the land has heard of it. Supposedly, it was given to the Greenbriar Kings at the beginning of the world by the Lady of Earth. But like all tales of the type, it loses something once one comes of age to hold a sword. I saw the Crystal once: my lord the king showed it to me. But I saw nothing so special about it; a pretty thing, an heirloom." Too late he remembered he was talking to a Wizard of the Meld, for whom study of ancient lore and artifacts was the substance of his life.

"Your lessons have not been well learned, Captain." There was ice in his voice. "Some 'tales of the type' have meaning beyond a fanciful story to lull a tot to sleep."

Tristan's face grew hot and he absently kneaded his fingers inside the heavy gloves, as though they pained him. But mindful of the old man's weakness, he only answered quietly, "I'm sorry. It has been long since I stayed at Covencroft and I have fallen out of the habit of talking with wizards."

"Yes. Well, then." Llodin sounded mollified, but in fact he knew he was growing weaker and thought only to hasten the tale. "It is no mere bit of poetic fancy that Ritnym of the Earth gave the Crystal to the royal house of Ilyria; it is true fact. You will forgive me, I hope, if I dwell upon this a bit. No doubt Fidelis, Retreat Master that he is, could recount the story in fairer form, but my point is only to refresh it in your memories, for there are currents moving on the face of earth that have not been seen since those early days, and unless I miss my guess, your part in the doings will be greater than you know." Despite their quick glances at one another, he went on. "So then: this you know . . .

"In the Dawntime, there were Four Powers who nurtured earth and its kindreds. These four were: Ritnym, Lady of the Earth itself; her brother Aashis, Lord of the Wind; and the twins, Tychanor and Tydranth, Lords of Fire.

"At that time, earth—or at least the part of it that we know—was peopled by the same folk as now: Men, Littlemen, Yoriandirkin, and Dwarves. Each of these peoples recognized the Four and paid reverence after their own fashions. They lived in peace, the first three in the forests of Yoriand (which in those days stretched from the sea up beyond the furthest reaches of Willowsrill), and the Dwarves apart on the three home islands of Jarlshof. There were no wizards yet, and Covencroft was a fire mountain.

"Now, Tydranth fancied himself slighted because he was not present when each of the Powers chose a portion of earth to care for in an especial way. He grumbled to his twin about Aashis's and Ritnym's 'conniving' until Tychanor lost patience and told him to be still. From that day, Tydranth began to plot. He would subvert all the good his brothers and sister tried to do for the puny creations.

"The more he brooded, the worse became his anger. He began provoking discord and then one day, one man struck another with a stone. The wounded one fell to earth and a terrible change came over him. Had Ritnym not granted him a portion of her own Power, he would have died.

"This was a stunning moment. Until that time, not even the Powers themselves had realized that life could cease. Somehow, perhaps without even intending it, Tydranth had created a new and horrifying condition. And as soon as he did it, he knew what power he had. He began to incite fighting, for he realized that not only were the kindreds mortal, but so was everything else on earth.

"Now, Aashis, Ritnym, and Tychanor had not watched idly while all of this happened. They took counsel among themselves and invited the wisest of all the kindreds to deliberate with them, realizing that those to whom the danger was gravest should have a say in their fate. Beod was for Men; Ochram for Dwarves; Comfrey Lichen for the Littlemen; and Dlietrian Silverstar for the Yoriandirkin. By this time, Tydranth had seduced followers of his own—the forefathers of the Barreners fought on his behalf and it is from this that the ancient enmity between them and the house of Greenbriar springs.

"The Three and the council decided to try to drive Tydranth off the earth into the Zones Outside. They did not want to harm him because of their kinship, but they determined to keep him away from the fragile earth." When Llodin stopped, he saw them slowly rouse themselves as though they had been listening to a bard and now found the infirmary around them again. "You know how the tale ended: Tydranth was indeed driven into the Zones and so the Three and their allies won, but at what cost! The forests of Yoriand were destroyed until only a bit remained, sheltered by the sea on one side and by a rampart of mountains on the other; Ritnym herself set the great tree Nilarion there to be the Earthgate, and made the Yoriandirkin

its caretakers. This prevented Tydranth from returning, but sealed the doom of the kindreds. For by
Tydranth's conniving, Death had entered the world
and the kindreds had become mortal. Beod of the
Singing Sword was the first to fall, fighting Tydranth
himself in the final battle. For a sorrow payment to his
heirs, Ritnym gave the Crystal of Healing."

Fidelis's eyes were glowing with a reverent light.
"You tell it well, master," he said softly.

"Not as well as could be, and too quickly."

The captain looked uncomfortable. "I am sorry I
spoke so, before. I had heard of the Crystal, of course,
and I knew somewhat of the Great War, but it is plain
that I did not know much."

Old Llodin smiled. "You may be forgiven for it. It
has been a long, long time since the Crystal has been
used."

Imris asked quickly, "It is not just a fable, then?
The Crystal really does heal?"

"It did once. As every mother's child knows," he
said, his eyes twinkling, "the Crystal of Healing, when
in the hands of the rightful heir to the kingdom, is
capable of mending the most grievous hurts. This is
the bare essence of the myth. As is usual with such
lore, it has become embroidered with all sorts of other
details. To hear some tell it, the Crystal works on
anything from bunions to a flux of the bowels. Accord-
ing to other versions, only deathly injuries are serious
enough to use such magic on. There is even one arcane branch of knowledge that claims that the power
of the Crystal far exceeds this, and that it was intended to be used to heal even the *land* of Ilyria,
should that ever prove necessary." Now they were
coming to the crux of it, and he made sure that he
held the ones outside still in the time spell before he
went on. He tapped Peewit on the arm suddenly and
asked, "Do you know why Rasullis is called the Fallen?
What tales have been told about why we of the Meld
cast him out?"

The Littleman glanced at Tristan, plainly wondering
whether the fever was coming back upon the wizard,
but he answered, "I think it was because he broke

your Rule. The one about not meddling in human affairs. When he sided with the Bastard against us."

"No," the Yoriandir objected. "Rasullis had already been shut out of the Meld before he met Dendron. In Yoriand, we heard that the Fallen had betrayed the Meld itself, and *then* allied himself with the Bastard."

The shaggy eyebrows drew down. "You are both correct, up to a point. It *did* have to do with the Rule, Peewit, and yes—as Imris says, he betrayed us.

"Rasullis had always pushed at the edges of the learning permitted to us. He studied all manner of spells, he pored through the ancient scrolls, he learned more and more of the—" Here he stumbled to a halt. There were some things one just could not make sensible to the uninitiated. "Well. Enough to say that I began to perceive in him an unwholesomeness—a wrongness that lay so deep that it was nearly hidden. I spoke of it to some of my brethren, but they believed me jealous of him." Remembered shame ignited in his pale cheeks. "So I deluded myself into believing that they were right, that I was wrong, and I tried very hard to accept Rasullis as one odd in his ways, but sound to the core." A bitter smile pulled down his bearded lips. "My mistake. And a costly one.

"For as I watched Rasullis and pondered his actions, it gradually came to me that this man believed in *nothing*. Not in the Powers of Earth, Wind, and Fire which we of the Meld serve, not in the ancient wisdom of the scrolls of our community, not in the unity of the Meld itself. He took all and gave nothing of himself back, like a leech, like a tick. And like a tick, he brought disease—a discord rose in our ranks and almost we lost the Song."

Tristan looked across the bed at Imris, but the Yoriandir could not explain just then what he knew of the Song and the Meld, so he merely nodded slightly.

The enchanter had not noticed. His low voice, rasping with weariness, went on. "A special Meld-Meet was called, and those who were journeying were summoned to discuss the source of the strange disharmony, for many still did not believe that any wizard would so corrupt the Meld. They thought there must be something from outside disrupting the Song.

"The night before the Meld-Meet was to begin, while the rest of the community slept, I was drawn by a restless spirit to leave my rooms and go to the Keeping—a hall in which ancient scrolls and artifacts are kept for careful study. There I found Rasullis. Can you guess what scroll he was poring over? No, how could you? The most ancient, the most prized manuscript in our care was written during the First Age, and it is the one that tells how the Crystal of Healing was made."

The Littleman sucked in his breath. "But the Crystal was given by the Lady of Earth, I thought! How can you say that it was 'made'?"

"The Lady directed its making, and gave her gift to be the heart of it," Llodin corrected, "but the fashioning of it was done by an Ilyrian smith. The scroll set forth the manner of the making, together with instructions for how the Crystal was to be used. Fortunately, as it turns out, much of the language in that old manuscript is so archaic that even we of the Meld cannot decipher it. Attempts have been made, but all we have managed to read is what seems to be a recipe of sorts, though for what, we cannot tell. Rose hips are mentioned, and the thing is named the 'Grene Bryar Elixir.' "

"Elixir?" Fidelis questioned. "It's a medicine, then?"

"It would seem a reasonable guess, but no one in this age of the world knows hows to work the Crystal. Now, we come to the evil part of the story. As I say, I went to the Keeping that night, and Rasullis was there before me, the scroll unrolled on the table in front of him. I asked if he had made progress in the reading of it, since I knew that he had long been working on the problem. 'Some,' he said, 'some.' And then he added that when he did finally discover how the Crystal was made, he would attempt the feat himself. I reminded him that the Power of Earth herself gave the Crystal to the Greenbriar Kings and he laughed. 'Still believe the cottagers' tales, Llodin? I would have thought by now that you would have outgrown the old lore and made some new for yourself.'

"I was stricken by such blasphemy and I am afraid I said a few rash things, and this angered him. We struggled over the manuscript and it tore. Both of us stood there with the tatters in our hands, and I think for a moment he was as stunned as I. Then"—the old man winced—"he threw his Fire at me." Llodin read the sudden knotting of Tristan's hands. "Yes. I have scars too, Captain, but mine are not in my flesh as yours are." He looked around at the Watchmen. "By the time I came to, it was near dawn and he was long gone. With half the manuscript. The part I held in my hand when I fell was protected by my Warding and he could not retrieve it. Likewise, the Crystal itself was still hidden, though he had turned the place upside down searching for it." His voice hardened. "We cast him from the Meld that day, and ever since, I fear that he has worked on the ancient scroll. I think he is near to reading it, and I fear his is the portion that tells how the Crystal was made."

The captain frowned. "Even if he someday makes another, what harm would it do? It is a Crystal of Healing, after all."

The wizard shook his head on its pillow impatiently. "No. We have read that the Earth-Power in the real Crystal is protected by the Lady herself: a curse will be loosed if ever mortals attempt to tamper with it. I fear Rasullis disregards this, deeming it only another musty bit of lore. And greater than this, the thought that chills me to the bone, is that Rasullis himself will fall prey to his own folly. For you must know that Tydranth has long sought a way to return past the Earthgate. Out of his pride, the Fallen may give it to him."

Though the new summer sun laid gold stripes across the long room and they could hear twittering from the garden, each of them shuddered as if suddenly it were midwinter and they stood naked in a gale.

The old man was silent a moment and then shook himself free of his musings. "Now Rasullis presents us with a foul choice: we may abandon Princess Ariadne to him, or we may save her and give him that which he demands in ransom." He reached painfully over the side of the low bed and brought the staff across his lap. "Which is this."

The runes surged at once into flame so that the whole length of the wand was limned with a brilliant glow. In the dim room, they watched as a second, spell-image staff materialized out of the thin air, seemingly, and hovered there above the real wooden stave in Llodin's hands. Each of the watchers felt his breath come a little quicker, but the spell held them, and they would not have looked away even if they could have. Two ghostly hands appeared, a mirror of the wizard's own, and seized the light wand. With an abruptness that startled them all, the magic hands moved quickly in the manner of someone breaking a twig, and the spell staff snapped in two. Peewit cried aloud, remembering the night before, but the real staff remained firmly in the wizard's grasp. As they watched, the two halves of the broken staff drew apart in the air. In the gap between the two pieces, a piercingly bright gem shone like a star, caught and held there, distant and unattainable. "Not quite a tale for children, I think."

"Is this really the Crystal, Llodin, or only an image that you show us?" Peewit breathed.

The vision disappeared. There was no puff of smoke, no explosion. It was simply gone.

From beneath his deep brows, the wizard regarded him. "What you have seen is real enough. But the Crystal is hidden within the spell to prevent its falling into the wrong hands." A kindly note entered his voice. "So you see, Master Littleman, you did me a greater service last night than you knew when you picked up my broken staff to keep for a walking stick."

Thunderstruck, Peewit exclaimed, "You knew!"

The old man merely smiled a little and closed his eyes, weariness coming on him in waves now. At any time, casting two spells at once was taxing, but he had had to show them the Crystal. The Watchmen were the pivot of matters even he did not fully understand, but only felt, like the brush of fur in the night.

But now his hold on the steward and the villagers outside was broken, and he knew even as he sighed and spoke that the Fallen would win this day. He tried to put bitterness from him, but it was hard. "You must escape now, my friends. Over the garden wall is the quickest and easiest way, but beware the other side!"

The captain jumped to the cloister window, drawing his sword. He put an eye to the shutter and swore, "Damnation! Here they come! And they've got a caldron of pitch—they're going to burn us out!"

Kursh was checking the garden side. "All's quiet here, so far," he reported, fumbling to draw his ax.

"Go now," the wizard repeated. "There is no time."

"We're not leaving you here!" the Littleman declared, dashing to the bedside to try to help the enchanter to his feet. Imris, his bow slung over his shoulder, leaped to join him, but the old man waved them off.

"I have seen this, I tell you," he snapped. "Leave me, and *go*!"

Fidelis went for the door. "Maybe I can stop them." Before anyone could prevent it, he had flung back the bar and stepped outside. "Neighbors! Think what you are doing!" those inside heard him say.

Kursh threw open the window into the garden and, with surprising agility, jumped through it. In a moment, he stuck his head back in to whisper, "The way is clear. Make haste. Fidelis cannot hold them for long."

From the cloister came the steward's voice, with an edge of wary fear. "Get out of the way, Fidelis. We'll settle with you later."

"This is bravery—to come with fire against those who only seek healing for a friend!"

Tristan gestured to the others and they lifted Llodin despite his furious protest as the steward answered, "Fire's the only way to be rid of a wizard. Everybody knows that. The others will have to suffer the same—we can't risk letting one of them get away, maybe with the enchanter's spirit in him." A chorus of assenting voices rose. "Move, Fidelis—or you'll get the same. We've no time to waste."

They had the wizard to the window now, though he staggered and his lips tightened with pain as Tristan on one side and Imris on the other tried to hurry him as gently as possible. Peewit was behind them carrying the staff. Through the courtyard window there came the sudden sound of a torch crackling in the wind, and the steward said, "Very well."

"Let them go!" the Retreat Master shouted desperately. "Ned, friends, you have no idea of the evil you do! Fear not the wizard; fear the darkness inside you!"

"Hurry," Kursh urged needlessly, reaching through the window to grasp the old man's arms. Irritably Llodin shook him off and awkwardly managed the window himself. The dwarf steadied him as the other three scrambled outside.

A voice in the crowd shouted, "The Meld of Wizards is an enemy to our king, and the troopers'll massacre us one and all if it's known we let one of 'em escape!" An angry roar greeted the words.

They crashed through beds of pungent herbs, making for the outer wall. Tristan ran ahead to boost them to the top.

"No!" Fidelis cried. "May the Powers forgive you!"

On his last word, a gout of flame leaped skyward over the roof of the hospice. Peewit dropped the staff and ran back toward the building, but Fidelis was already tumbling through the window into the garden. "Go!" he gasped, slapping at his smoking robe as he ran.

Kursh was sitting astride the wall, leaning down to grasp Imris's hand and pull him up by brute strength. There was a clatter from the small archway in the corner between the hospice and the ell that housed the communal kitchen. "They're coming!" Peewit yelled. The Yoriandir scrambled to the top of the wall, and both he and the dwarf bent to take the wizard's hands. Tristan lifted him as far as he was able with Fidelis's help and somehow they got him up. "Your turn," the captain told the Littleman and hoisted him easily.

"The staff!" Peewit groaned, even as the first of the villagers burst through into the garden.

"I'll get it!" Fidelis raced to where it lay amidst spires of foxglove, snatched it on the run, and doubled back to the wall with the men gaining on him by the second. "Catch!" He tossed it like a spear up to Peewit. Sprinting, he flung himself up the rough stonework, scrabbling for a toehold as Tristan gave him a push upward. As the captain lunged to catch Kursh's outstretched hand, Fidelis and the Yoriandir lowered the old man to safety. One of the villagers came close enough to hurl a pruning knife at the captain's unprotected back. Luckily the dwarf had seen the movement and jerked Tristan aside as he gained the top of the wall. They both cast down their weapons on the other side and made the leap, rolling to their feet. Together they led the way down through the vineyard.

The Yoriandir and the doctor between them supported Llodin, who was white and gasping for breath. "Tristan!" Fidelis called urgently. "He can't run like this the whole way!"

"What would you have me do, then?" the captain snapped, but he sheathed his sword and made ready to carry the old man.

Suddenly, hoofbeats pounded on the cart road behind them. Their hearts sank. Imris nocked an arrow with one fluid motion as Kursh ran to the back of their small column and raised his ax high. The horseman appeared as a blur above the grape stakes.

"It's me, it's me! Don't shoot!" Hauled up short by the inexperienced rider, Tristan's horse reared, and the tall man darted forward to grab the bit and pull the animal's head down just as the rider slid off in a heap.

"Alphonse!" Fidelis exclaimed, and on his arm, the wizard closed his eyes and smiled slightly.

"Bless you, boy." Imris laughed.

But the young bondsman shook his head. "No, you don't understand! I looked down from the belltower and—oh, by the Powers!" He broke off, staring past them.

When they turned to follow the direction of his terrified gaze, they saw the small party of horsemen ride out of the trees at the foot of the terraces. Black-and-Reds, and among them was one with a blue chevron slashing down the front of his tunic. The troopers rode at ease; apparently the group of fugitives had not yet been spotted. But then one of the soldiers must have caught sight of the thick billows of oily smoke, for he flung up an arm, pointing. They set spurs and galloped up the road for the gate.

The captain came to a swift decision. "We'll send Llodin and the boy on the horse. They cannot defend themselves, and the horse is trained to war. The rest of us will have to fight our way out if we cannot escape their notice." He helped the frightened boy remount.

"But I don't know how to ride, sir," Alphonse said desperately.

"That's no matter now. Just give him his head—so—he'll take care of you." They lifted Llodin to the saddle in front of the youth and Peewit passed him his staff. "I am sorry about this, Llodin, but there's no help for it," Tristan apologized.

The wizard gazed at the sun-livid blue chevron. In a curious way, it seemed to be all he could see. Then he looked down at the captain. "As you say, it does not matter now," he said softly. "I'll be fine. Farewell."

The captain grasped his hand and then pulled away. "Let's go," he commanded, and the others followed him down the vineyard path. Over his shoulder, he called, "Wait for us down at the tavern!"

Llodin raised one hand slightly. He bent his head, closed his eyes, and poured out his Warding on the Watchmen, and on the boy.

Saddle leather squeaked as Alphonse leaned to peer beyond the wizard's shoulder. "What do we do now, sir?"

Llodin fingered the runes. "We wait. When they have split up the troopers, we ride. And then life begins where it ends."

After a little moment, the boy said hesitantly, "I don't think I understand."

The wizard's shoulders shook with a silent laugh. "I shouldn't think you would. But it will all be clear soon enough, my boy." After another moment in which the Watchmen came within bowshot of the enemy troopers, he said, "Tell Tristan that he must seek the Guardian."

"I beg your pardon?"

But even then the Black-and-Reds saw the Watchmen and set their horses into the rows between the vines, leaving the cart road free. Llodin sat straighter, taking up the slack reins. "Just hold on to this for me, would you?" he said, and pressed the staff into the youth's hands. Before Alphonse could reply, they were pounding down the path and charging through the tangled knot of figures. The boy saw Kursh's bearded face fly past and the curly top of the Littleman's head, and suddenly the horse reared, pawing at the black uniform that had leaped into the path. The iron-shod hoof struck, and the man went down, but his flung dagger had found its mark: Alphonse heard the wizard gasp, and then the stallion jumped again to a gallop, mashing the blue chevron beneath his flying hooves.

When Alphonse was finally able to pull the horse to a halt in a meadow some way from the old Retreat, the shaking boy found he held the wizard dead in his arms, and a gray staff bleached of magic like a weathered stick. As tears slid down his cheeks, a thrush swooped into a currant bush nearby and began to sing.

Kursh stumbled on a loose cobblestone. "Damn guild! What do we pay taxes for, then?" Peewit heard him say. Around them the housewives chattered, baskets on their hips and a child or two clinging to their skirts, as they returned to their homes from the market in the village square. The Littleman envied them. He suspected that nothing in *his* life would ever be that simple again.

They had buried the wizard in the peaceful meadow. With all of them helping to cut turf to cover the small barrow, it had not taken long—not as long as they had wanted to give it. But Llodin would have been the first to understand their haste; with the Retreat village roused, they could afford no long speeches or honoring ceremony.

On nearing the outskirts of Swiftwater Shallows it-self, they had met up with one of the men who had been in the tavern the night before. The corpses had been disposed of in the river, he had told them with a wink, and added that, No, no more of Snake Robert's troops had ridden in.

Kursh had thanked the fellow for the information and mentioned something about going on along to the baker's house to get his nephew (for he assumed the boy had gone home with the girl to her parents' house, as he had told him to). "Was he supposed to?" the man asked with surprise. "Well, he didn't. Stayed right there in the tavern, Kursh. Said he had to mind the place, with you gone."

If the dwarf was impressed by this attention to duty, he gave no sign, merely grunting something as the man waved a hand, slung his bow, and strode off.

Now Tristan led his horse, while Fidelis walked alongside with his hood cast about his face. The boy brought up the rear, trying to keep the staff from scraping on the ground. A cat skittered into the dark blur of a narrow lane that opened off the main street and a moment later they heard the high, thin screech of a rat. The thrush nestled closer to Imris's neck, and he absently raised a finger to caress the spotted feath-ers of her throat.

When they reached the Sword and Skull, it was as they had expected—the curtain had been taken inside last night and the door swung to and barred. The establishment had not yet opened, and would not until noon. The dwarf knocked on the stout oaken planks. There was no sound inside. Again he banged on the door. When there still was no response, he gave the latch a sudden vicious pull. "Bloody hell, ye dimwit, open the door!" When this failed to work, he pulled at his beard with anger that was not all for his nephew.

Peewit gestured to the second-floor window. "Give me a boost." For once, not even the dwarf teased him about his skills. As he gripped the casement and wig-gled his knife blade between the shutters to lift the latch, the thrush flew up and perched on the sill, cocking her head and regarding him with bright eyes.

"You wouldn't be able to do anything about this, would you?" She fluffed her feathers and preened, unconcerned. "I thought not." Finally he got it and swung the shutters open. Holding the knife in his teeth, he pulled himself through. From the street he heard Kursh's snarl: "Don't wake him up, Peewit. I want the pleasure myself."

Grinning, the Littleman sheathed his knife and made his way to the door of the room, which was a guest chamber by the looks of it. The daylight did not penetrate well to the hall outside, and he felt his way along until he found the banister of the stairway. Moving carefully in the dimness, he went down to the kitchen.

Regardless of what Kursh had said, Peewit didn't want to startle the boy awake and find himself walking into a blade in the darkness, so as he came to the foot of the stairs he gave a soft hallo. There was no sound in the room. A cat's-paw of fear touched the nape of his neck and his hand found his dagger without conscious thought. Underlying the rich smell of new-baked bread, there was something—some odor he had breathed before—that stopped him on the last stair, eyes widening to pierce the gloom. After a moment he crept forward, moving as silently as only a Littleman can move, making for the window. He had to have light, and that was the quickest, though by no means the safest, way.

Carefully he reached up and eased the latch open. Just as he swung a shutter wide and dove away to the place where he had seen the table the night before, there arose a crashing clatter. His heart leaped into his throat until he realized that it was only Kursh pounding on the front door with his ax haft. Simultaneously he jerked his hands back out of the puddle into which he had skidded, and now he knew, even without the daylight streaming in.

Near the banked hearth Kursh's nephew lay in a heap. His throat had been cut.

From a very great distance, Peewit heard his name being shouted and he focused on this and gradually the sickness passed. Shaking, he lurched for the wash bucket and plunged his hands into the clean water, scrubbing them vigorously as the water slopped over the brim and made wet stains on the floor. Turning his back on the body, he grabbed for a towel hanging on a hook by the fire and ran from the kitchen out through the swinging door into the tavern. "All right—I'm coming!" he tried to shout in answer to the ruckus outside.

He wrested the stout bar out of its holders and flung it aside. Kursh came charging in but Peewit used all his strength and shoved him back. "Wait, Kursh. Don't go in." Something in his voice stopped them on the threshold. "Captain, in the kitchen . . ."

Tristan narrowed his eyes, glanced quickly at Kursh, and clapped the Littleman on the shoulder as he ran past, fumbling at the hilt of his sword.

"What—" the dwarf started to roar, but Imris, seeing that the Littleman was white as milk, grasped his arm to quiet him.

Then Peewit saw it happen in Kursh's one good eye; the dwarf understood that some horror had come to his house in the night. He pushed the Yoriandir away and walked slowly toward the kitchen. The Littleman leaned against the front door. "Don't, Kursh," he repeated quietly, but he heard the creak of the swinging door behind him. Resting his head against the planking, he sighed.

"Stay here," the Yoriandir directed the boy quietly, and Peewit heard Alphonse sit down at one of the trestle tables, puzzled and frightened, but mercifully silent.

Neither of them had moved when Imris came out sometime later and mutely handed the Littleman a small horn of mead. Peewit sipped it slowly, wincing as the sweet fire bit its way down his throat. The tree-tender sent, 'The Captain thinks whoever did it must have hidden upstairs sometime last night. There was a crowd, you recall, and it is possible the killer came in then.'

"I was hoping to find him asleep with the girl by the fire," Peewit said, and drained the horn in one swallow. Some color was returning to his face as he asked, "How is Kursh?"

"He said very little, and I could not reach him with my thought," Imris answered. "But I think he was much fonder of the boy than he wanted anyone to believe. You know Kursh."

Peewit nodded. He shouldered himself off the door and looked up. "What's to do now?"

"Kursh is downstairs, taking inventory in case it was a robbery, unlikely though that seems. The captain sent him down there to get him out of the way till . . . the kitchen can be made decent again."

The Littleman pushed the drinking horn back into the Yoriandir's hands, saying, "I'll help with that." He went into the other room.

Imris slowly swung the front door shut. He stood with his head bowed for a moment, and then walked over to the boy, who sat with his fists knuckle-white on the staff. The Yoriandir's dark green eyes took on the hue of a forest pool. "Pray that you see no worse days in your life, lad."

Alphonse swallowed and licked his lips. "Someone else has died?" His glance flicked to the kitchen door and back to the blue-cloaked figure across from him.

"Kursh's nephew has been murdered."

The boy's head went down on his hands, and in a strangled voice he said, "I don't think I am cut out for faring in the world after all."

"Master Llodin knew the hearts of people to a hairsbreadth, Alphonse, and he chose you to bear his staff. Let that count for something when you weigh yourself."

The ginger hair came up and beneath it the blue eyes. "What do you mean, 'bear his staff'? He only gave it to me so that he could manage the horse."

The Yoriandir regarded him. "I do not know much of the Meld of Wizards, but I believe that the master passes his staff or ring to the one whom he chooses as his adept—his apprentice, you would say."

The youth's eyes went round and he flushed. "I—I am to become a *wizard*?"

Imris held up a hand. "I do not know. We will find the answer when we get to Covencroft."

"The Isle of Wizards? We go there?" It was a name out of legend.

"Eventually," the Yoriandir answered evasively. He did not know yet what the captain would decide. He fell to thinking about the task facing them and a bitter knife of pain drove itself through him. He did not know how they would ever accomplish the job without Llodin. Grief rose up in the back of his throat.

When Imris remained silent, the boy hesitantly asked, "Is there anything I could be doing to help?"

"I think not. Such work does not require many hands, only time. But there is something *I* must do," he said, rising from the bench and going to the hearth where his harp still stood from the night before. "Do you know music, Alphonse?"

The boy shook his head. "I have no ear for it. But I like to listen," he added hastily.

"And so you shall. It is a custom among my people to make a song for the passing of one whom we loved well." The Yoriandir bent his head, seeming to listen for the trueness of tone as he turned the silver keys to tune the instrument. Then the chords lengthened into song, the words of which Alphonse could not understand, but the music made him think of the cries of white birds wheeling over a salt strand, and he did not know how he knew this, because he had never seen the sea.

In the kitchen Peewit straightened from dumping sawdust onto the stained floor. "Ah, leave be, Imris— let him go," he said softly as the song came from the other room.

"It's the Yoriand death dirge." Tristan listened, leaning on the broom. He followed the song a bit and murmured, "It sounds like him," and the Littleman knew that he was not referring to Imris.

"Best sing one for the boy too, and have them both over and done," Peewit muttered bitterly. They had rolled the body in a blanket and carried it upstairs. "Why would an assassin kill an innocent like that? He must have known it wasn't Kursh!"

"You know their way is to terrorize. It was done as a warning to the townsfolk, I would think. And as an added measure of pain for Kursh himself. The killer must have planned on pursuing us all back here, where he would pick us off after disposing of Llodin. That is, of course, assuming that there was only one assassin, and that the fellow with the blue stripe up there at the Retreat was he."

"He had a quiver full of the same kind of arrows as wounded Master Llodin," Peewit pointed out.

The dark-haired man nodded thoughtfully. "At a guess, I would say that he was sent alone. But the Fallen may still have had a report from him before last night. I doubt that we are safe here. We cannot delay long." He went back to sweeping up the red sawdust.

"What will we do with Alphonse?"

"We have no choice: we'll take him with us. It seems Llodin wanted it that way."

"Do you really think he knew what was going to happen?"

"I think there was little he didn't know." He frowned. "But I must admit, I am surprised that his choice fell on such an ill-seeming young fellow." He looked down at the Littleman. "I would have thought you might have been the elected one."

"Thank the Powers I'm not!" the other said fervently. "I'd not care to try to master their lore at my age. Some of it is dangerous!"

"I know. I hope he can measure up." The tall man mused, "Llodin knew so much that *we* need to know. I still do not understand why he thought the heir might be alive. Though the boy has told us that the wizard instructed me to seek the Guardian, I can only guess at his meaning. The only Guardian I know is that landmark near the First Falls on Willowsrill."

"It would make sense that there might be a clue there, if anywhere, but how we could possibly find it after almost twenty years I have no idea. And then, if he lives indeed, the heir could be anywhere in all the earth!" the Littleman said with frustration while he knelt with a pail of water and a scrub brush to try to wash the stains out of the floor planks.

The captain gestured absently for him to hand him the other brush which sat still drying near the dead fire. "Then there is the problem of the Crystal itself, of course. Hidden in the spell as it is, it is out of our reach, and unless young Alphonse is much cleverer than he seems, we may *never* retrieve it."

"Perhaps the Meld will know what to do."

"I hope so."

"Well, then." The small figure sat back on his heels. "For a starter on our other problem, how do you propose to get the princess out from under the Fallen's very nose?"

Tristan's face grew strained. "I have an idea," he admitted, "but it has small hope of success, and will require risks so great that I do not know whether it is worth it for one who, at best, can be only the bearer of the Blood, and not the heir."

"Do we have a choice? The Oath is clear:

'Heart, mind, and spirit his.
Hand, eye, and body his.
My blood for the Blood,
Now and forever.'

We were sworn, Captain."

"I remember the words of the Oath well enough!" He threw down the brush angrily and rose. "Think you to tutor me in my duty? Better to tutor the king who would not try to save himself! Dying, he made us all forsworn!" He struck both hands flat on the tabletop.

Peewit stood up. "That was fated," he said with a calm he did not feel inside, for he too carried the guilt. "Our vow was not broken because we outlived him; short of running on our own swords, we fought till the end."

"So you say."

"Yes! So I say!" the Littleman flared, and now his eyes flashed, and despite the extra pounds and the years that weighted his countenance, he looked suddenly very much the lieutenant of old. "And I say too that we had better put grief behind us and get on with our job! Because, whether we are out of practice or no, twenty years too late or no, still we are all that stands between the princess and that pig, Rasullis, and sorry lot that we are, we've got to find a way into that bloody castle!"

"That will be *enough*, First Watchman!" Tristan barked.

Eyes locked, they stood across the table from each other, the breath whistling angrily in the man's nostrils as he glared down, and a flush of choler raging in the Littleman's face. The moment stretched and then suddenly Peewit dropped his eyes and swallowed.

Tristan shook his head ruefully.

The ill feeling evaporated like a morning fog burning off, and half ashamed of their fear, they laughed and began to weigh Tristan's plan.

Downstairs Fidelis lifted his head to listen to the harping. Laughter came down the stairs to them from the kitchen, and he winced and glanced at Kursh. He would have thought Tristan and Peewit could have had more respect for the dwarf's feelings, but Kursh made no sign that he had heard. He had said not a word since the Retreat Master had followed him down to the storeroom.

He had gone first to some barrels down at the far end of the cellar and bent to check the seals, or so it seemed at least from where Fidelis stood near the foot of the stairs. It had crossed the doctor's mind to wonder what the dwarf had thought could be wrong with the kegs, but grief affected people in different ways, and it could have been that Kursh was aimlessly wandering, just trying to find something for his hands to do. Fidelis did not want to intrude, so he sat down on a crate stamped with a potter's mark (new crockery, he guessed).

"You don't have to hang about like a mother hen, Fidelis," the dwarf suddenly rasped. "I can count barrels, and I have an eye in my head to see that nothing's been touched anyway."

The healer wanted to keep him talking. "If there is someone else who should be told, Kursh, I will do it," he offered.

"Someone else?" the dwarf repeated, and for a moment there was puzzlement in his voice. "Oh, his parents you mean." He shook his head. "My brother's been dead these many years and his wife was taken last winter. There is no one," he said flatly.

"You were a good uncle to him."

A quick shrug. "I needed help in the tavern."

"Still, it was something to have given him a home."

"Leave off, doctor. I want none of your professional sympathy." Kursh flung away, took a key from its hidden place between two crates, and made for a small door set in under the stairway itself.

"You have it anyway," Fidelis told him quietly. He stayed where he was as the dwarf disappeared through the doorway. He heard a flint strike, followed by candleglow from what was evidently a small chamber. From the sound, the dwarf was prizing the top off a keg. In a moment he came out carrying two dripping mugs. He pressed one into the healer's hands and Fidelis looked down into liquor as black as a mine shaft. "What is it?"

"Good dwarfish flotjin, that's what it is. We drink it at weddings, births, and"—he took a mighty swallow—"wakes."

Guest to host, Fidelis raised the cup to him, and when the dwarf nodded gravely in acceptance of the salute, he took a sip. It was as if he had swallowed molten rock from the depths of the earth! He could not even cough, and he thought the burn must surely have swollen his windpipe shut.

Kursh nodded again, this time with satisfaction. "You will find it will clear your mind."

"And everything else," Fidelis managed to gasp, wiping his tearing eyes on his sleeve. But it had the most extraordinarily pleasant aftertaste, he thought, rather like . . . well, like licorice? Or maybe juniper berries? No matter. I like this, he thought, and swallowed some more.

"I am glad you do," the dwarf said, pulling a keg near and seating himself, though the doctor had not realized he had spoken aloud. "I rather favor it myself."

"It's really very good once you get through the fiery part," Fidelis insisted.

"Yes."

They both raised their cups again.

Kursh set his drink down on the floor, and a quick movement of his wrist dropped the dagger into his hand.

"Oh, wait, now, Kursh. Don't do any—anything foolish."

"Drink up, Cedric."

Fidelis half rose and grabbed for the knife, but his hand closed on air, and the dwarf merely regarded him expressionlessly. "I have to shave," he said. "In token of honor to the dead."

The healer regarded him stupidly and then sank down again. "Sorry."

The dwarf methodically began to hack off his long beard.

"Your drink's too strong f-for me, Master Dwarf."

"Most Outlanders find it that way." He was making a neat pile of hair on the flat top of a cask.

Desperate to reach past that stony mien, Fidelis tried to focus. "I really am sorry about the boy, Kursh."

The hand holding the dagger did not waver. "Yes. 'Twas a bad way to die."

Small in the stillness of the house, they could hear the harp's plaintive melody.

When he was done, the dwarf set the candle flame to the clippings, drained his mug, and went steadily up the stairs.

Fidelis hunched on a crate, disgusted with himself.

Later in the day the captain made arrangements for horses with the local hostelry, and Imris went to a small house down the lane where the cook girl lived to break the news and to leave Kursh's heavy ring of keys with her father. Peewit, Alphonse, and Fidelis busied themselves with buying provisions for their journey and packing.

Kursh had gone off near noon with his nephew's body wrapped in a shroud in the bottom of a cart that he normally used to haul goods from the river barges. The dwarf would allow no one to accompany him, and when Tristan warned him to be careful, he only flung him a glittering, hard-edged look, slapped the reins against the horse's rump, and rumbled down the cobblestone street. But Peewit saw that his ax lay beside him on the seat, unsheathed.

*   *   *

Trees arched over the path by the rushing stream and Kursh squinted up through the green canopy to check the sun's position. It was getting on for late afternoon, and he urged the horse to a faster trot. He had unharnessed the gelding and left the cart on the hillside where he had buried the boy next to his parents. Now he rode the cart horse bareback with only a halter for reins.

Even in the fog of the past few hours, he had realized that it was a beautiful day, with a savory smell of damp earth on the wind. For a Yoriandir, the breeze itself would have been a tonic, but Kursh was a dwarf, and like his fathers before him, when he was hurt he sought the comforting dark of a cave. There was one above a pool on this brook. He had found it long years before on the night his wife had died giving birth to their son, and the boy had lived only long enough to be buried by dawn light.

Ever since, whenever the mood threatened to overmaster his stern control, he had come up here to sit in the dark and rebuild himself.

He needed to do it now. He saw again the two youngsters kissing over the bread board, and how he had thrown the boy from the kitchen. A line furrowed his forehead beneath the strap of the eyepatch.

The stream began angling upward, much swifter here than when it crossed under a small bridge on the Road a mile or so back down toward Swiftwater. The path was mossy underfoot and close in to the water, and the horse picked its way carefully, splashing through the shallow running water at times. Kursh was watching the ground to see that the gelding did not put a foot wrong when he noticed a hollow depression in the moist verge. He reined in and swung down from the horse's back, bending to peer closely, and then he grabbed the ax out of his belt: it was the print of a boot, a nailed boot, and he had never seen a civilian who had a pair.

Squinting he looked back along the way he had come and followed the course of the stream in his mind till it met the highway. It was less than a quarter mile from where they had found Llodin. He made a quick inspection, but found only the one print, and concluded that no troop had passed that way. Only one. But had it been the same one Tristan's stallion had trampled? Would the Fallen have sent *two* assassins, confusing even Llodin? If so . . . When Kursh looked up the stream, his eye glinted. He was just under a half mile from the cave.

Leaving the horse securely tethered, he crept forward. Near the place, he crossed the brook and climbed the embankment to approach the cave from above. His eye roved ceaselessly and he listened intently for some telltale noise, but if the murderer was at the cave, he was keeping himself very quiet.

Finally the dwarf reached the slope above the waist-high opening. He stopped to scan for traps, but he saw none and picked his way through the undergrowth closer and closer. When he was positioned directly above the entrance, he opened his mouth to draw a silent breath, made sure of his footing, and raised the ax over his right shoulder. He knew a moment of absolute calm. Then he pitched a bird's whistle to sound as though it came from across the pool.

Nothing happened.

Some moments later, he slid down the slope and jumped into the cave. Inside it was warm, and the dappled sunlight slanting in gave him enough light to see. The assassin's pack and provisions were strewn about: a bow leaned against the rocky wall with a quiver of black and red arrows propped beneath it; a leather bottle and the remains of a half-eaten meal stood on a flat rock by the cold ashes of a fire; a bedroll was slung carelessly to the rear; a leather case of the kind some scribes used to carry their inks was set higher up on a ledge. This he unlaced and opened. Five phials were securely nested in the straw with a depression for a sixth, and he knew even without taking the case to the light that each would be marked with the Fallen's hex.

"One left for each of us," he said aloud. "Five for the Watchmen."

A scrap of bundled cloth lay next to the case and he reached to unroll it. In the dim light he could see the ruby in the center of the intricately worked pin, a brooch of ancient dwarfish design. It was an heirloom of his house, and had been a gift to the boy, since he had no one else to pass it on to. He had seen that it was missing from Orin's corpse, but had assumed that the lad had presented it to the girl.

He took back the keepsake and clenched it in his fist until the golden pin drew blood.

The peats glowed on the hearth. Imris strummed softly on the harp and the others sat at the table nearest the fire, listening to him, but even more, listening beyond him for footsteps outside. It had been dark for over an hour, and Kursh had not yet returned. Peewit got up and went to the packs heaped on the floor. Idly he retightened a thong, though there was no need. "We should go after him," he said much too loudly.

No one answered, but they were all inclined to agree. The dwarf was quick-tempered and they did not wish to risk losing his friendship by interfering, but it was after dark.

"We'll give him another half hour," Tristan decided quietly.

The Littleman flushed. "If we had given Master Llodin another half hour by himself on the Road, he'd have been dead!" Like an echo of that thought came another: And now he's dead anyway. Peewit knew that the same idea had darkened their minds too.

After that, no one spoke again.

Suddenly, on the rafters above, the thrush untucked her head from her wing and cocked her head, listening. She whistled sleepily and a smile broke across the Yoriandir's face as there came a pounding at the door. Fidelis flung it open, and Kursh brushed past him, already running for the steps to the second floor. "I'll just get my things," he said over his shoulder.

Tristan caught at his arm. "Where the hell *were* you, Sergeant Major?" That wasn't exactly what he'd meant to say, and he regretted the words as soon as they passed his lips.

The dwarf jerked to a stop and swung to face him.

The razor burns stood out redly on his clean-shaven jaw, and he looked directly up into the captain's eyes. "That's none of your business."

As the tall man colored, Fidelis said quickly, "We were worried about you."

"No need." He was still looking at Tristan. "There's a troop of soldiers on their way here—I saw the torches at the head of the valley. We have about a quarter hour to make it to the ford, otherwise they'll cut us off."

They moved quickly then, and by the time the dwarf came down again, they had doused the fire, loaded the packhorse, and were mounted and waiting for him, the horses stamping nervously in the street. As the dwarf stepped through the door and pulled it closed behind him, Imris and the captain exchanged a glance: he was wearing his old campaign clothes—a slate-gray cloak covering a leather tunic cured so that the hair still remained on it, breeches of some toughly woven fabric dyed muddy gentian, and otter-fur boots. The leather tunic was unbuttoned to allow for his extra weight, and cinched with a wide belt on which hung the sheath for his ax, and the otter-fur boots looked a little moth-eaten, but suddenly the picture was the same as it had always been. Except for the beard.

"I'm sorry I kept you waiting," Kursh said gruffly as he swung to the saddle.

Tristan returned his salute, clapped his heels to the bay's sides, and led them toward the ford.

Kursh had noticed the extra horse as soon as he'd seen them all waiting in the street, and now he urged his own mount up beside Imris as the lane widened. He indicated Tristan with a thumb. "He has a plan for getting the princess out?"

The Yoriandir's azure cloak flowed out behind him as they trotted, and the thrush cocked her head and regarded the dwarf from his shoulder. Imris nodded. "I'll tell you when we are clear of the ford." He did not want to let the dwarf know just then how much depended on a song, a flint, and some chalk.

Tristan fed another stick to the small fire. As it

snapped and caught, Imris winced. The Yoriandirkin did not make fire. Wood to them was living, whether in tree form or lying stretched at full length on the forest floor, toppled by a storm. He would have felt the same revulsion warming himself at a funeral pyre.

His green eyes avoided the blaze. By his elbow, Alphonse misunderstood his shudder. "Would you like my blanket, sir?"

"I am not cold. Thank you."

The captain turned at his tone. "I'm sorry, Imris. I *did* take only dead stuff."

The Yoriandir clasped his harp more tightly. "But the wood did not know that it was dead."

The tall man thought, Oh, by the Powers! First Kursh, and now Imris too! He got up impatiently and went to check the horses' pickets, though he could hear them cropping grass and knew that they were safely tied. He passed Kursh standing on guard several yards outside the circle of firelight. The dwarf's ax lay easily on his shoulder, ready for instant use, though they were not expecting attack.

They were following the course of the Swiftwater down its steep valley. For the first few days they had expected the soldiers to catch up with them at any time, but after a while it seemed apparent that these had been returning to their barracks on the road that bisected the river about fifteen miles east of Swiftwater Shallows. If the officer in charge had sent a courier toward Ravenholt, some fifty-five miles northeast, the Watchmen had never heard him, or seen him on the river paths. Probably there had been no such message. The matter of a few outlaws disturbing the retreat village was, after all, insignificant and it would not have been pleasant for the king's troops to have to report from this outlying post that they could not even punish six civilians. The reeve's murder and the loss of the assassin, however, should have been noteworthy. Tristan guessed that the second-in-command had taken the not-unusual step of declaring himself heir to the reeve's powers—and tax collections. Ravenholt would be notified when this one had consolidated his power.

"Quiet night," the captain remarked as he passed

the dwarf. Kursh grunted something incomprehensible, and Tristan did not venture more conversation. They had all noticed Kursh's taciturn brittleness and left him pretty much alone, but once when he had been especially sharp with Alphonse, the captain had intervened with a quiet word and the dwarf had not spoken to him since. Whether this was out of anger or merely part of his mood, Tristan could not tell. Peewit had said the obvious: that Kursh was mourning the dwarven boy.

Imris had disagreed. "It is not that. That kind of grief would not leave Kursh so angry," the Yoriandir argued as he, the Littleman, and the captain had ridden at the rear of the party with Kursh up ahead, out of sight, scouting, and Fidelis and the boy riding side by side ahead of them.

Peewit leaned across the pommel of his saddle, peering across Tristan to watch the Yoriandir's lips; they were both on his bad side. "But now he's alone," the Littleman observed quietly. "At least as far as I know," he amended. "He's never spoken of any other family." The other two nodded confirmation.

Imris shook his head thoughtfully. "I don't know. This mood has rather more of anger than sorrow. It is as if he resents Alphonse in particular."

Tristan said, "Because this boy lives and his did not?"

The green face was troubled. "Yes. I think that is it exactly."

The three of them watched the youth ahead as he tried to obey Fidelis's advice to "hold the reins looser" and "keep your heels tucked in."

Thinking back to their talk, Tristan brushed aside a hanging limb and patted his stallion's neck. The horse nuzzled his chest. He pushed him away and stood looking up at the stars, hoping that Kursh could be counted on to play his part when they got to Ravenholt. Much of their defense would depend upon him.

They would reach the castle in two days if there was no unexpected trouble. For the success of their plan, they *had* to arrive on Dendron the Bastard's birthday. If they were late, or if they could not gain access to the stronghold, Imris would have sacrificed his life, and this was not Tristan's intention. Not now, when they were being given a second chance to fulfill their Oath. Even if the princess was not, strictly speaking, the Blood (for only males of the royal house were counted in the Bloodline) and therefore could not be the heir, she was the bearer of the Blood. Through her lay Ilyria's hope: her son, if she lived to bear one, would be king. As long as a member of the royal family lived, the captain's duty was clear.

But it had been ages since he had thought this way.

For the first few months after the disaster on the Sweep, he had first lain and then sat about the wizards' seaside retreat at Covencroft, silent, shocked, and inwardly raging. The fire from his burns kept his skin open and suppurating all the length of his right hand, arm, and shoulder. The left was much less damaged and healed soon enough. Finally Llodin, seeing the worm that gnawed at the proud man's spirit, goaded him into speech, saying, "So the Greenbriar King was mortal. You did not know this? Come, Tristan, you behave like an unseasoned boy!"

"Don't presume to lecture me! You do not have the right. I am not one of your pupils, who still believes in your wizard's tricks and deceits!" the young soldier flung at him.

The wizard, who even then had white hair and a deeply lined face, regarded him with compassion, but did not relent. "In what way have you been deceived?"

Tristan pushed himself to his feet, the effort making him scowl with pain. "The Bastard had his wizard," he said in a tightly controlled voice. "Yet my lord the king, who had revered the Meld's knowledge and valued its counsel, was left naked before that enchanter's spells." Suddenly he exploded, shouting, "All of you *knew* we could not stand against them without help! And you did *nothing*!"

Llodin saw fresh blood break through the captain's bandages as Tristan clenched his fists and struck the fireplace mantel in the small guest chamber. He knew whatever he said next was likely to cost him the young man's friendship. He lifted a finely wrought cup of silver and sipped the spiced wine, giving Tristan time to regain control. When Llodin saw his head drop, he said softly, "That is our Rule, Tristan—we cannot enter into human affairs to change them."

"Then you should have killed Rasullis before he broke your Rule, Wizard."

There was no point in telling him that a wizard could not be killed. Not in the way the soldier meant, at least. "Yes. We should have. But none foresaw how warped he would become. When we cast him out of the Meld, we knew only that he could not master his desire for power. We thought that by cutting him off from the flow between us, he would become only a mortal man—dangerous still, but within human limits."

Tristan slumped into the other chair, gingerly lifting his injured hand into his lap and reaching with his other for his own cup. "What went awry? He still has plenty of power"—his mouth pulled up in a humorless grimace—"as you can plainly see. And this was not even the full of it, only a bit that he had put into the sword he had made for the Bastard."

Llodin gazed into the ashes in the fireplace. "We underestimated him." He hesitated, glanced at Tristan, and added, "You must remember, we had never had to deal with the problem of corruption before. In all the long ages of the world, no Wizard of the Meld had ever failed his charge. It diminishes all of us."

The young captain regarded him steadily. "And now what will you do about him? Casting him forth from this place had little effect; he still has power, and he has used it to break your Rule. Ilyria is destroyed, the Bastard sits on the Greenbriar throne, and now his army of Barreners burn and pillage at will. The charge to get rid of them both is the Meld's, it seems to me."

"I know," the wizard answered, "but there are many of the Meld who do not see the matter this way. They argue that if we stoop to Rasullis's tactics, we are as guilty as he, no matter that we did what we thought was good at the time." The violet embroidery at the square neck of his robe shimmered in the sunlight from the open window into one of the gardens, and the Serpent tattoo writhed as he turned his head to

listen to the fountain splashing in the courtyard of the
guest wing. After a moment he said, "I will do what I
can to convince them." Tristan made an impatient
movement and Llodin laid a hand on his uninjured
arm. "I tell you, I will do what I can. But if you need
hope, then I will say that though this doom seems
dark, yet it is not the worst that could have befallen."
He spoke across the soldier's incensed exclamation:
"And while life is, you may yet have your heart's
wish. Mayhap Ilyria will return."

"The Bloodline is dead."

The wizard frowned at him. "Yes. I know." He
seemed ready to say more, but rose suddenly and left
the captain to his bitter thoughts.

Remembering back through the years, Tristan knew
now that Llodin had been speaking of the Crystal's not
falling into Rasullis's hands, and he wondered whether
the wizard had suspected then that the heir might have
lived. Surely not. He would have given some sign.

Tristan raised one gauntleted hand and flexed it,
feeling the scars still pull tightly. His burns had finally
closed, but there had been nothing even the wizard
healers at Covencroft could do about the puckered
brands where the sapphire flames of the Bastard's
enchanted weapon had laced his sword arm. They had
saved his limb, but he was left with shiny tissue stretching from his fingertips to his right shoulder. None had
seen those scars but the healers, Peewit, Kursh, and
Maeve. She had tried to pretend that it made no
difference, but he read the look in her eyes and left
the next morning for Ka-Nishon's court. When next he
had returned, the small cottage had been burned to
the post holes.

A twig snapped behind him and Tristan clapped a
hand to his sword hilt, already turning, but Kursh's
broad hand came down on his forearm and the dwarf
looked up at him. "It's about this boy," he said without preamble. "I don't think we should take him with
us into Ravenholt. We'd do better to leave him to
watch over the baggage down by the river."

The tall man leaned against his horse's shoulder.
"Why?"

"Because he'll only slow us up, and he won't be able to fight if there's need of it."

"But if something goes wrong and we can't return to the rendezvous, we won't have to worry about trying to get back to him—we can just go on toward Covencroft." They planned to head for the wizards' sanctuary, the only place that they might be safe from the pursuit the Bastard would surely send after them. If they got the princess out, she would need a secure place to wait while they returned to the Guardian and tried to find out what Llodin had meant. Also, they would leave Alphonse with the wizards and be done with the responsibility of watching after the youngster.

But Kursh was shaking his head, the stubble on his chin showing silver in the moonlight. "I don't like it. We'll have to move fast, and we'll have to move sure, and I don't think he can do either."

"Shall we not give him the chance to see?" He reached to take a leaf from the tree that arched over them, and let a smile show on his face. "I seem to recall a cadet once, the son of a glassblower, I believe, who was so clumsy at swordplay that the sergeant-at-arms was moved to pity and gave him an ax instead, advising him to become a charcoal cutter." His eyebrows lifted.

"That was different."

"Was it?"

"Of course! I wasn't going into battle the next day!"

"If we're all very sharp about this scheme of mine, neither is Alphonse." The dwarf snorted and turned angrily away, and Tristan asked, "Come now, Kursh: why do you really want to leave the boy behind?"

The black eyepatch tilted to meet his gaze. "Because he'd be safe." His lips tightened as though he had said something he hadn't meant to.

The captain belatedly understood. "There is no place safe, Kursh. Not while the Bastard and the Fallen rule Ilyria." He hesitated. "You, better than any of us, know that."

The dwarf tugged at the eyepatch angrily. "I am thinking of the Crystal of Healing," he snapped. "The boy has Llodin's staff, and that's the way Master Wizard wanted it, I guess. But if he loses the bloody thing, who knows what wickedness Rasullis would do with it—"

"He can't do anything with it," Tristan interrupted. "The Crystal only works for the rightful heir, you remember."

"But the Fallen has Princess Ariadne, and if we fail and Rasullis has both her *and* the Crystal, he'll—well, you know damn well what he'll do. And if she bears a son, he'll have both the Crystal *and* the heir. Won't he?"

In answer, Tristan told him, "Then we can't fail."

"By the Powers, look at us, man!" the dwarf exploded, though he kept his voice down lest the others hear. "You can't raise that bloody great sword of yours without pain, I can't see a damn thing coming at me from the right, Peewit can't hear, Fidelis and the boy don't bear arms, and we're going to send Imris in there to do a task that already has him in a funk, and small wonder!"

"You are not bound by the Oath, Kursh: the king is dead. Go back to Swiftwater Shallows if you wish."

"Say that again and I'll take your toes off, just for the practice."

The captain laughed. "Save it for the Bastard's guards."

Kursh looked at him incredulously. "You really think this is going to work, don't you? We're just going to slip in there, find the princess, and take her to safety?"

The captain raised his eyes to the stars, took a deep sniff of the night air, and said to the moon, "Ask me two nights from now."

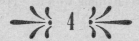

4

In a room hollowed out of the guts of the Sweep over which the castle of Ravenholt brooded, the twisted figure of a long-bearded dwarf stilled as he heard the approaching footsteps on the other side of the thick door. He suddenly scuttled across the room to hide and drew a long, thin blade from a thigh sheath. He waited.

The latch lifted and a tall man in a dark shimmering robe swung through. Soundlessly the dwarf sprang from behind the door, the blade whipping up to take the man under the breastbone, but the knife never struck. Instead, blue fire erupted in a gushing fountain that arched over his head like a wave breaking and bore him down to the floor. Enveloped, he writhed in helpless agony, his mouth stretched wide, screaming—but no sound escaped. His tongue had been cut out long ago.

Through the sapphire heat, the enchanter watched impassively, noting for future reference the dwarf's contortions, the veins bulging in the mute throat, the mouth and gullet red and gaping, indecently exposed. He felt an urge to raise the magic flame to a higher power, to test the dwarf's physical limit, but he clamped an iron control on his curiosity and withdrew the spell.

The blue fire snapped out and the dwarf lay gasping on the floor, his muscles still locked in mortal fear. "I told you never to try that," the wizard told him quietly.

The twisted dwarf tested his limbs and found that he could move. Slowly he got to his feet and then bowed low, his crooked body hunching in on itself. He remained in the posture.

"Yes, you do well to apologize. I do not suffer stupidity lightly. It irritates me to find you suddenly stupid, Nolin." When the dwarf raised his head fearfully, the wizard added, "I thought we understood each other better than that." There was an answering gleam in the dwarf's deep eyes.

The enchanter turned his back and went to the work table. He drew the oil lamp nearer and stared down at some sheets of vellum. "You have everything prepared?" He swung around to catch the dwarf's nod, and in the brightly lit chamber the unnatural paleness of his skin against the dark robe was accented. Rasullis the Fallen was tall and ascetic, his sharp features planed like a whittler's carving. He had black hair and black eyes set deep beneath eyebrows that flared outward and met in a solid bridge across his nose. His hands were sepulchral, and the sapphire ring he wore on the index finger of his right hand seemed too weighty. The shimmering material of the dark robe was cut with a square collar to show off the tattooed Serpent that coiled about his throat.

The dwarf raised an inquiring eyebrow and jerked a thumb at an iron door set into the opposite wall of the room.

"In a moment. First I have to deal with you." The twisted figure shrank away. "Oh, no, I shan't do away with you." Hope leaped in the eyes raised to meet his. "Not yet, anyway. Despite your imperfections, you are a useful tool." He leaned back on the stool, arms folded. "So what will we do with you, hmm? Shall it be the fire again?" A wild shake of the head. "Or perhaps you'll test a potion for me: what do you say to that? No? Well, then perhaps you will like this: I shall not punish you in any way." At the other's widened eyes, the wizard smiled, his bloodless lips stretching mirthlessly over perfect white teeth. "But I shall not reward you, either. You will not get that which you want."

The dwarf swallowed but did not dare scowl.

The wizard rose from his seat. "No, my dear Nolin, no princess for you. Too bad. She is no great beauty— but then, neither are you." He laughed and cuffed the smaller figure as he strode to the iron door. Behind him the dwarf looked down at the floor and his jaw worked. After a moment he bent, picked up the curved knife, and slipped it back in its sheath. Taking the lamp, he followed his master through the open door into a smaller room, which was lit only by firelight.

Rasullis looked about, checking the arrangements. The room was warm, but not stifling; the fire blazed brightly and Nolin was lighting the hanging tripod; there was fresh sawdust on the floor; the golden bowl had been scoured. His tilted writing table stood nearby, fresh paper and quill prepared. As the dwarf went out to the other room and returned bearing a silver tray on which were placed two goblets, the wizard told him, "We'll have to rush this one a bit, I'm afraid. The king's birthday feast will begin early and last late, and I'll have to be there for the whole thing. But I wanted to get to this test first; tomorrow Dendron will be in no condition for it." He went to the shelves lining one wall and took down an ornately carved box. When he flipped back the lid, the polished silver knife shone against the plush velvet lining. This knife he put on the table, next to an amber sphere which contained what looked like two or three wizened seeds. "All right, Nolin. They'll be expecting you." The dwarf bowed and went out.

While he waited, the wizard sipped his wine. Maybe this time, he thought. Maybe the original Crystal holds luminos seeds, bright herb-flower of the ancients. He smiled. If Ka-Nishon—the oaf—ever knew what a treasure we've raided from his palace garden . . .

"Again?"

Lost in his thoughts, Rasullis had not heard them come in. Now he swung to face the king. Dendron was wearing hunting clothes and it was apparent that he had just ridden in when Nolin had delivered the enchanter's summons. His hunched shoulder, crooked since he had been caught beneath the exploding castle wall twenty years ago, gave him a truculent attitude, as though he were always leaning forward for a fight. He had been a big man, and he was bigger now, but it was mostly about the belt line, and his cheeks and nose were red with a heavy drinker's false health. From his tone, the wizard knew that he was in one of his surly moods. But then, coming down here always scared the Bastard.

"Maybe this will be the last time, my king," Rasullis suggested easily. He saw, behind the king, how the commander of the Home Guard, the king's constant attendant, stiffened, reading a threat into his words. The Fallen felt a small smile tug at the corners of his mouth. He lifted the other silver goblet and offered it to the man to test. The commander frowned, but he took it, as usual. Someday, Rasullis thought.

"By the Wolf, why don't you give it up?" Dendron demanded. "You'll soon have the real one, anyway, if this scheme of yours with the girl works." Grumpily he sat himself down in the high chair drawn close to the fire.

"Because we are very close to discovering the secret of the Crystal, my king. If we go on, soon—today even—we could have both a Crystal *and* your niece. And then there would be no gainsaying us, would there?" This was familiar ground; they had been over the plan many times. Dendron was stalling. He hated the bleedings, but that much of the scroll fragment Rasullis had deciphered. Somehow, it was the conjunction of the Crystal and the Greenbriar Blood that triggered the ancient magic.

Briskly the wizard stepped to the table and took up the knife and golden bowl. He looked down into the Bastard's glowering blue eyes. "Ready?" When Dendron nodded abruptly and extended his wrist, Rasullis cut him.

It was only a nick to open the vein; the king's arm was crosshatched with tiny white scars. Not much blood was needed. Very soon the Fallen stemmed the flow with a silk bandage. While Dendron washed his bloody fingers in the laver Nolin held before him, the wizard quickly took the bowl to the table and shook into the collected blood two of the luminos seeds. His face was intent.

Dendron sat sipping his wine and looking into the fire, and did not even bother to turn his head. After a long silence, the Bastard pushed the empty cup into the dwarf's hands and rose. He told the wizard coldly,

"You should try making the sacrifice to the Wolf first. Perhaps he would aid us."

The Fallen lifted his head, but did not look at the king. "Superstition, my king. There is no Wolf; there are no Powers. We must aid ourselves." He heard the commander gasp. Such blasphemy from anyone else would have brought swift death.

"Keep your unfaith to yourself," the king snarled. "You'll be at the feast, at least? That much of our petty custom you'll stoop to?"

Rasullis turned a bland face to him. "Of course, my king." He smiled. "I even have a gift prepared for you."

Dendron grunted. "Is it still alive?" He laughed then as though he'd made a joke, clapped the commander on the shoulder, and strode from the room. Rasullis and the dwarf could hear them laughing all the way up the long corridor.

The Fallen suddenly hurled the golden bowl at the opposite wall. The blood splashed and slowly trickled down in thin lines.

The flames spit and flared as the grease from a joint of meat basted the logs. The men sitting closest to it cursed and jumped from their benches, while the others laughed and commented crudely on what had been burned. One who had been insulted flushed deeply, drained his horn of drink, and went for his dagger. A laugher sprang backward over his bench and grabbed for his own knife. Swiftly their squad leader caught them by the throats of their tunics, hauled them upright, and bade them be seated again before they caught the king's eye. In the crowded hall the roar covered his words, and both glanced uneasily up the length of the cavernous room to the raised dais. Sullenly they moved to do as they had been told.

As he sat, the laugher was jostled by a maid servant carrying a great jug of mead. "Watch what you're bloody doing!" he erupted and backhanded her.

Half blinded by the stinging blow, the girl fell against the table across the aisle and dropped the vessel. It shattered in a puddle of drink and heads turned toward the sound. When her punisher saw her face in the guttering light of the smoky torches, he sucked in his breath and quickly looked down. "Damn! It would have to be her," he muttered to the man next to him.

The scattered catcalls were abruptly silenced as the girl dragged herself to her feet and gave him one swift, piercing glance before she bent to gather the broken pieces into her apron. Studiously they ignored her and resumed their talk.

But at the head table, eyes had seen.

Rasullis touched the rim of the goblet to his lips and followed her with his gaze until he lost her in the shadows at the back of the hall. He set the wine down with a click, smoothed the impeccable folds of his white court robe, and leaned over the carved armrest of his chair toward the king. "Your leave, sire?"

"What?" Bleary-eyed, Dendron swung his ox-maned head. Cloth-of-gold shimmered in the torchlight, rippling from his thick neck down over the hunched shoulder nearest the chief counselor.

"Your leave, sire?" the enchanter repeated, carefully schooling his face. Dendron was rank with drink and spackled with gravy from the shank bone he waved.

"But there's a singer to amuse us after dinner," the king slurred and winked. "One of the patrols caught him out on the Road without a traveling pass. If he sings well enough, we may be inclined to be merciful, eh?" He guffawed and stifled a belch with the back of his hand.

Rasullis smiled thinly. "He'd have to be *very* good, sire. I'll be back in time to hear."

"Where are you going?" Dendron asked, idly picking at the roast.

"Business, my king. Nothing to trouble you."

The king suddenly looked him full in the face and said softly but clearly, "When I ask a question, wizard, I expect a straight answer."

Rasullis stiffened fractionally, and his nostrils flared. After a moment he reached for his wine and drank.

Dendron chuckled and said behind a chunk of fine white bread, "Yes. Take a drink. Cool your ire. And let us not forget who has the Blood."

Deliberately Rasullis set down his cup as he murmured for the Bastard's ears alone, "And let us not forget how he came by it."

The Bastard king grasped the dagger which was sunk up to its hilt in the roast before him and wrenched it free. Unmoving, Rasullis focused his gaze on the blade as it swerved toward him. In the torchlight the pupils of his eyes dilated, and suddenly the king hissed a curse and dropped the knife. A snapping arc of sapphire glowed between his fingers briefly and then was extinguished as Rasullis closed his eyes and quietly told him, "Save the theatrics for the peasants, Dendron. You and I need each other too much to engage in these childish displays of temper." Calmly he opened his eyes and surveyed the noisy hall over the heads of the crowd. He noted the stewards hovering just out of earshot behind their chairs, the servants bustling to and fro, the silent figures of the Home Guards standing well back in the shadows against the walls. But he did not see the girl, and a frown creased his forehead as he returned his attention to the king.

Dendron too was scanning the smoky room, and now the corners of his mouth drew up in a grin. He leaned back in his chair and picked his teeth. "Ariadne, is it?" he asked lightly in a voice from which almost all anger was gone.

"Yes. One of the soldiers struck her awhile ago. She went to the kitchens and has not returned."

"Ah." He scratched his beard. "You should have told me right away. Of course you can have our leave to go." As Rasullis pushed back his chair, Dendron put a hand on his arm. "And tell the trooper who did it that if he's marred my niece in any way, I will personally gut him out with a rusty meat hook." The magician nodded, bowed for show, and made his way down the steps onto the floor of the hall.

A Home Guard stepped out from his post beside one of the pillars to attend him. In an undertone, Rasullis questioned, "That soldier by the lower hearth— you saw it?" When the man nodded briefly, the wizard ordered, "See to it. And keep watch on the king. He's in a strange mood tonight."

"Yes, my lord."

"You have the singer ready?"

"Yes, my lord."

"Very good, but let him not be brought until I return."

"So it shall be done." The guard, his eyes hooded in the shadow, hesitated. "Will my lord require further service?"

"No, thank you. There is no danger in the bakehouse, I think."

"I could fetch the girl and bring her to thee, my lord. Perhaps it would be more seemly."

"Doubtlessly. But I prefer to do this myself. Stay here." The guard touched his forehead and withdrew.

As he paced the length of the hall, Rasullis was aware of the ripple of silence that spread out before him and closed in after. The men were afraid. They had witnessed his power, and it was recognized that his temper was unpredictable. He exited the room through the massive wood portals and behind him heard the volume of voices increase dramatically. He smiled.

His footsteps echoed off the tiles of the wide corridor, almost a hall in its own right. The weaving torchlight, caught by the drafts that ran up the walls, made of his shadow a towering ghost that marched along beside him. As he came near the huge mosaic-bordered fresco that covered the entire length of the left-hand wall, he slowed, remembering the original picture as he had first seen it. For generations the fresco had been periodically re-touched with shades of green, brown, blue—life colors—appropriate to the subject: the royal crest of Ilyria. Against a sky of washed blue, the Royal Greenbriar had twined up the wall, graceful but unyielding, with large thorns to prick enemies and crowned with roses of a curious blue green, though no one could remember why the artist had represented the flowers in such a hue. The Greenbriar had been rather more fanciful here on the wall than in the standard depictions on the shields and banners of the Ilyrian army, Rasullis remembered. He had been amused to see a startled hare crouched in the lower right corner and a bird, perhaps a thrush, winging high overhead, up near the gilded beams of the corridor ceiling.

That was all gone now.

Soon after they had taken the castle, even while Dendron still kept to his bed and his broken shoulder had mended crooked, he had given orders that the picture that infuriated him should be obliterated. In its place he had commissioned a new crest, the sign of his victory. Like the standard under which his troops had fought, this new mural showed a much less impressive briar caught in the moment it was severed by a flaming sword. Dendron had ordered that the whole be done only in red and black; he wanted to make it clear, he said, that the old order had passed forever. His Barrener army had cheered, and taken his order as tacit approval for the havoc they wreaked on the castle interior and even on the land of Ilyria itself.

Ravenholt, as the new king styled his castle, had become a gray, miserable place, the tatters of glory standing everywhere like wakeful dead retainers. In place of the fine furnishings, the artful tapestries, the polished metalwork, Dendron's craftsmen—if such they could be called, Rasullis thought—had made coarse hangings and fittings, and gaudy baubles such as would please the king's taste.

If the Greenbriar Kings had not been such fools, Rasullis could have missed them.

So now, from long habit, the wizard looked up as he was passing by the fresco. He jerked to a stop. The echo of his last footstep went on alone toward the end of the corridor. The light from torches spaced at regular intervals along the opposite wall foundered and flared in the contrary whispers of wind that crept along the floor. The wavering light made the gargoyles that crowned the lintel behind him seem to move and stretch their jaws. That was a familiar effect and ordinarily he would not even have noticed. But tonight there was something about the picture that made him regard it anew. In the dim light, the black of the background seemed to fall away, as though he were looking into the bottom of a well, or up at the sky on a

night of no moon. The brilliant scarlet of the Briar and
Sword leaped into bright relief, like isolated autumn
leaves floating on black water. But suddenly it seemed
to him that the whole fresco was suffused with the
barest cast of green, a shade so subtle he couldn't be
sure he saw it at all.

"Odd trick of the light," he said aloud. The echo
ran away and was soaked up by the empty corridor.

His wizard-trained senses sharpened and he knew
that he was not alone. He turned quickly, but there
was no one there. Still the feeling persisted. The Fallen
was breathing hard, and he was annoyed to find that
his hands trembled. "Idiot," he muttered. "Miss a few
nights' sleep and scare yourself with your own imagin-
ings. It's a mighty enchanter that can put himself under a spell! You might as well go back to being an
adept afraid of his master's staff and start all over
again!" Irritably he rearranged the folds of his robe
and ran a thin hand through his hair.

For three nights dreams had disturbed his sleep;
three nights he had wakened in a cold sweat and spent
the rest of the dark hours in a chair before the fire,
afraid to sleep again. It was the same dream too. He
thought that he stood in some place where the earth
would not be still, but bucked like a horse, and he had
a feeling of horror or perhaps of fear. Nothing else of
the dream could he remember, except that the only
color he could afterward recall seeing was amethyst.
He supposed, in those long hours before the fireplace,
that old Llodin—meddling fool!—had been too much
on his mind of late. This business of the girl and the
Crystal brought up all the long-standing anger he har-
bored against the Meld, and it had been a rare pleasure to dispatch the assassin to deal with the doddard.

He shook himself and took a deep breath. Maybe a
sleeping potion would do him good tonight. A thought
flickered through his mind, and he smiled. Maybe a
potion of another sort. He swung down the mural hall
and went left into the utility corridor leading to the
kitchens.

The air was much cooler here because of the open
window arches that in the daytime looked out into

one of the servants' courts. The second-quality torches burned sulkily and blackened the stonework of the damp walls, but he paused by a window and lifted his face to the night air. He was facing west, toward the crags that protected Ravenholt's rearward flank. King's Hall from which he had just come was the highest point in the cluster of buildings that formed the stronghold. Sitting high on the Sweep, it had an unbroken vantage out over the castle itself, down over the battlement walls on three sides, and southwestward across Willowsrill to the mountains from which Dendron had drawn his army of Barreners.

Up in those hills there was little arable land and the mountain folk had coveted the rich pastures and black soil of the Willowsrill valley, out of which they had been driven by Beod of the Singing Sword. They never forgot that the broad valley was their ancestral land, and they had hovered on the edge of the kingdom of Ilyria, a distant threat even down to King Theobold's day a generation ago. But they had never been a power to be taken seriously until Dendron, Theobold's bastard by a captured Barrener slave girl, was thrown into the wilderness by his younger, legitimate brother, Dhonald after their father's death.

Dhonald had been young at the time, and his counselors loud in their demands, and so on his coronation day he had looked Dendron in the eye, placed a hand sadly on his shoulder, and sent him from King's Hall in the sight of all the people. The onlookers had cheered, glad to be rid of the Barrener and his brooding presence.

Dendron, then a man in his prime at twenty-three, had cursed his fate and the younger brother—only eighteen—whom he considered hardly fit to be king. But with a troop of Greenbriar soldiers at his back, he had no choice: he left.

The soldiers escorted Dendron far into the mountains and then took his horse, his provisions, and his weapons, and left him. If he tried to return, he would be executed, the officer informed him coldly before they wheeled their horses and cantered down the rocky path. He had spat after them and made the mountain ring with his hoarse curses.

When night fell, he climbed a tree to be safe from the wolves he could hear howling over the next ridge. He woke from dozing when he heard the snuffling around the base of the tree. He looked down through the stunted branches, winter-twisted, to see the gleaming eyes watching him. Even though he knew that the beasts could not reach him, ice spilled through his bowels and he clasped the trunk with a grip so tight that he broke a blood vessel in the heel of his hand. In the slave stables of Greenbriar, and later in the rough-and-tumble violence of the squires' mess when he served his half-brother as a menial, he had never been as alone as he was now. He had been hated, but never alone.

Before morning light the wolves left, drawn perhaps by the lure of some easier game, and when the sun came up over the peaks, Dendron climbed stiffly down, knowing that he must find shelter and food if he meant to survive. In later years he often thought it strange that he had never considered simply following the path back to Ilyria and his doom, but instead resolved to live as long as he could.

Live he did. By that autumn, as the trees beneath the high cave he had been lucky enough to find flamed gold and russet, he had fashioned stone and wooden implements, woven snares out of vines, and managed to dry some hare meat and the remains of a deer the wolves had brought down. He had worked with sticks to make fire and tended it faithfully, for in it lay his only chance for survival.

Living like a wild thing, he had developed a wild thing's instincts, and one day as he culled over some acorns by the mouth of the cave, he knew that he was not alone. He went about his work, but managed to get closer and closer to the rude spear he had left standing against the cave mouth. Just as his hand closed on it, something struck him from the side. His head exploded with pain, and he fell into an echoing blackness.

When he woke, he was lying by a campfire. As his

vision cleared he was staring into the face of an elderly Barrener, gap-toothed and shaking with palsy. But the eyes were piercing beneath the scraggly brows. In halting Ilyrian, the old man asked, "You were left here to die by the Iron Men. Why?"

Dendron licked his lips and gingerly sat up. Two stone spears flashed down in front of him and he froze. The old man barked something in his own language, and the polished flint points withdrew. The Bastard answered, "Because my mother was a Barr— was a woman of the mountains, and my father was the king of the . . . Iron Men, and now my little brother is king and fears me."

The flat black eyes regarded him expressionlessly. "You are not much," the old man said. "Why should he fear you?"

Below his shag of hair, the color rose in Dendron's face, but he held back his anger and said, "Because he believes I would kill him."

"It is a serious thing to kill a brother. Would you do it?"

Flatly, with utter hatred, he answered, "Yes."

The old man's face strained into a smile, then a grin split his face and revealed many missing teeth. He was chortling, wheezing, so that for a moment Dendron grew afraid that he would not be able to catch his breath. But in a moment the old man lifted a merry glance to someone standing behind Dendron, and said something in his own language.

And from behind him came an amused, cultured voice saying in perfect Ilyrian, "We must see that you have the chance, Dendron the Bastard." The speaker stepped around him into the firelight and Dendron had an impression of a tall man with black hair and eyes, gaunt and clad in a smooth robe that shimmered in the light. When he leaned with a smile to pull Dendron to his feet, the neck of the garment fell away and the Bastard saw the serpent tattoo.

"You're a wizard," Dendron blurted.

"Yes. I am Rasullis, called the Fallen," the dark man said. His red lips smiled again. "And I too would kill the Greenbriar King."

As they shook hands the firelight caught the sapphire ring on the wizard's index finger.

Rasullis came out of his reverie with a start. He was staring up at the pine forest and upthrust rock formations, the one called the Guardian dominating the rest. The dark spears of the conifers jutted against the stars, and the wizard felt unease drifting over the battlements on the evening breeze. The castle had never been attacked from up there, he knew; the way was too steep for an army and the crags inaccessible to bowmen. Still, he thought, if anyone had been up there, they could have been looking right back at him. His skin prickled and for an instant he saw—imagined that he saw—a gleam. A spark, no more, as a sunlit dewdrop in the night. He blinked and squinted and it was gone. As he stood staring, a patrol sauntered across the top of the battlement wall and the moon caught the buckle on the soldier's sword harness.

The wizard made a mental note to have the careless sentry relieved at once and flogged. He had stressed to Dendron that the Meld would not suffer extortion without retaliating. He himself had spies watching the ways from the sea isle retreat of the wizards, but he had heard nothing from any of them for almost a month.

An eddy of wind whistled in the stone passage, and he pulled the robe up at the back of his neck. His gaze fell to the courtyard below, attracted by a brief scurry of movement in the shadows. He leaned out over the sill, but presently he saw a small figure—a page, probably—cross the patch of moonlight to enter a door directly below his vantage point. He relaxed and moved down the hallway.

Firelight and heat boiled out of the main kitchen and he sniffed appreciatively as he stepped through the double doors now lying back against the rough plastered walls. Within the flurry of activity at the center, serving maids lined a table and carefully dotted the tops of cakes with rosettes of honeyed fruit rind to honor the king's birthday. Near the door a bored

Home Guard watched, surety that Dendron's food and drink would not be tampered with.

As the soldier caught sight of the chief counselor, he levered himself off the wall and came to rigid attention. Rasullis acknowledged him with a nod while the room quieted except for one lad basting a roast, who was cheerfully humming under his breath. The boy turning the spit thumped him in the ribs and the cook's apprentice turned with his fist cocked, saw the white-robed enchanter, and froze.

Rasullis ignored him. "Ariadne."

She had known he was there; she was the only one in the room who had not turned or looked up. Now she took a moment to place another bit of fruit before she dusted her hands lightly and stepped around the end of the table. "Come," the enchanter ordered quietly, and she followed him out into the corridor.

When he had led her some distance from the open kitchen door, he stopped and waited, and she halted a few paces away, her rough red hands clasped before her over the shabby peasant's dress. He went to her and gently turned her head to the light of the torch, raising a finger to touch the bruise already darkening on her softly rounded cheekbone. In the tanned face, her smoky gray eyes watched him warily. The torch caught gold highlights in her light brown hair. He said, "Some valerian ointment should take care of this. I'll order it for you."

She moved away from his lingering touch and looked at the floor. "Thank ye, m'lord."

"I have told you, Ariadne, my name is Rasullis."

"Mum and Dad raised me to speak well to elders, m'lord." There—chew on that, ye randy old goat, ye, she thought angrily.

A smile slashed across his face and his teeth showed white in the gloom, but she knew by the sudden knotting of his hands that she had stung him. "I am no graybeard, though certainly I am older than you, Princess, and as for you parents, you know well enough by now that they were the king and queen."

Her eyes came blazing up to meet his. "I know nothin' of the kind! 'Tis only people *here*, in this wicked place, who say so! Though to what end, I cannot guess. And you can all leave off callin' me Ariadne too. My name is Robin!" The tinder of her anger burned out in the sudden gust of fear that shot through her veins. Powers protect me! she gasped inwardly, horrified that she had dared use that tone of voice to the dangerous wizard.

He was inclined to be amused, a cat who has had his fill of mice. "As you wish, my lady." He took her arm. "Will you walk with me?"

Having no choice, she did.

"I wanted you to know that the drunken lout who struck you will be properly disciplined," he told her. She absorbed this without answer. "I spoke against putting you in the kitchen," he continued, "but your uncle is a rather unforgiving man, and he still holds the grudge against your father. I think it gives him certain pleasure to see you so humbled." They were in the fresco hall now, and he stopped in front of it. "So you remember nothing of this place? That is not surprising, certainly. You were less than a year old when you left." She flushed and he could read denial plainly in the sudden tilt of her chin. "It is true, my poor little Robin: you are not who you think you are. That must be a terrible feeling."

"I know who I be, m'lord."

He smiled. "I envy you."

They were standing side by side before the painting, and now he gazed up at the picture and was silent. She glanced sidelong at his face, and her eyes widened as she saw a dwarf slip through the outer archway and duck into the kitchen corridor. The furtiveness of his movement proclaimed that whoever the dwarf was, he wasn't supposed to be here. Good for you, she thought. Run for it! She realized that the wizard was looking down at her. "What is it, my dear? Are you cold? How thoughtless of me." He unpinned the light summer cloak that fell from his shoulders, and slung it around hers. "There. Better?"

Lips dry, she nodded. Oh, come back, Master Dwarf, and take me with ye!

Rasullis saw the way she clutched at the edges of the

cloak. "I think perhaps you are more hurt than you know, Robin. I think you should rest. If you came to my rooms later, I would fix you something for the ache in your head."

It needs no great brain to guess at what would happen *then*, she said behind her eyes. "Ye must have women enough to your needs, m'lord. One more can mean nothin' to ye."

"You could mean very much to me," he told her truthfully.

"I think I will not, m'lord."

He bent his head and studied the ring on his right hand, twisting it so that the sapphire shone and darkened, shone and darkened. "I could force you, you know."

"I know," she agreed calmly, but inwardly she tensed.

At the flatness of her tone, he looked up. "But you need have no fear of me. I would not hurt you."

Before she could guard her tongue, it slipped out. "I would not let ye."

His dark eyebrow lifted, and then the glimmer of a condescending smile played over his features. "And how would you prevent it? You are only a woman, after all—even without the power, I could still take you."

She made no reply and he moved suddenly, catching her hands and crowding her back against the painted wall while his lips fastened on hers like a fish striking to the hook. She struggled and finally, laughing, he broke off the kiss and held her helpless, watching from a few inches away the wildness in her eyes.

"My father and brothers will kill ye for this!" she hissed.

"Yes, little farm girl? Do you think you'll ever see them again to tell them?" She was stilled. "Think about that. Your life is likely to be right here for a long, long time. And I could make your lot sweeter than it will be in the servants' kennels. So consider well before you spurn such comforts as I offer." He released her and stepped away. She made no movement. "We will go into the hall now. There is some business to which I must attend, and then perhaps you will be glad to accompany me to my chambers, Lady Robin," he said with heavy mockery.

Benumbed, she let him lead her into the hall and when he spoke briefly to one of the thick-shouldered guards and motioned her to a stool, she hardly noticed. He had been working up to this for the past two weeks and now the trap had sprung. She felt its teeth in her very soul.

Beside her, the guard watched the wizard's back until he was well up the length of the hall, and then glanced with pity at the girl.

Through her staring fog she heard the sudden blare of trumpets cut through the hubbub, leaving silence after the blast. Then *his* voice. "Men of the Sword! In honor of our lord the king's birthday, we have a special entertainment tonight."

He paused, and she could just hear a nearby trooper saying, "Good sport, this. Watch."

"Out on the Road this afternoon was a singer, begging to be allowed to sing for His Majesty tonight, and His Highness has graciously consented to hear him. Was this not handsomely done?" Drunkenly they cheered. Rasullis held up his hands to quiet them. "Indeed it was." He made a slight bow to Dendron, who waved regally. "So now you will hear and judge. If this Yoriandir bard sings well, His Majesty has decreed that he shall go free. But if he grates on your ears, my lords, well—I think I have heard a few of you complaining that the recent rain has rusted your swords?" Coarse laughter rose from the benches. Rasullis looked toward the rear. "Let the fellow be brought."

All attention was focused on the great doors and in a moment the girl could hear the measured tread of boots on the floor outside. As they were passing by her stool, she looked up.

Between his two guards, Imris caught his breath. The eyes of the girl sitting by the doorway were his king's! He forbore to kneel only by the greatest effort and thought, *if only we had known she would be here in the hall, this could have been so much easier.* But now they were committed, and the plan could not be changed. He would have to play his part and hope. Quickly he sent, 'Courage, lady. You have friends near.'

Her head jerked at the voice that sounded clearly inside her mind, and her eyes darted about, seeking lips on which to hang those words. Her wild glance crossed his and he winked. For an instant her gray eyes started, wide and staring, and then she deliberately dropped her gaze. Ah, no fool, this one, the Yoriandir thought; she will not give us away.

Imris looked neither left nor right as the guards marched him up the aisle toward the wide circle that had been cleared below the dais. A chair had been set ready in the middle. He kept his head down. It had been twenty years, but still, some of these troops must have been in the Bastard's army then, and even more importantly, Dendron himself, the black horseman of Imris's worst nightmares, sat on the platform, now leaning over to say something to the wizard and laugh. The singer sent, 'Peewit, the princess is sitting on a stool just inside King's Hall. There is a soldier there— guarding her, I think. Watch for him when you come in.'

On the stairway that led up to the mural corridor, the Littleman heard the Yoriandir's words and double-checked the action of the forearm-dagger Kursh had lent him. He was clean-shaven and dressed in the red and black of a page, and they had remembered at the last minute down in the servants' courtyard that a page would not be wearing a sword, of course. Peewit leaned from a step and took a torch from its holder, carrying it down a flight to extinguish it in the urn of sand that stood there for the purpose. He crept back up the stairs, replaced the torch, and shrank close to the wall in the deep pool of shadow to wait. The brim of his boy's hat flopped down over his forehead, and he pushed it back impatiently.

Because it was cool after the warmth of the summer day, the leaded panes of the great windows stood open to let in the breeze, and over the heads of the seated crowd the Yoriandir could look out over the Sweep. Imris Gravenleaf, child of the starlight, your old friend is there to comfort you, he thought as the moon hung full and silver over Willowsrill. He found that his forehead stung where the brand had been, and he withdrew into his own mind. From that safe distance, he watched himself bow to the Bastard and the Fallen, remembering to make it ungainly, as if he had never before sung in a king's hall. He straightened and stood cradling his harp, waiting.

"You may begin when you are ready, fellow," Dendron said, puzzled by the singer's composure. But then he saw the hands shaking as the bard sat and tuned the strings, and he was satisfied. "Would you like a drink to wet your throat?"

Imris shook his head, a tree-tender too afraid to speak. He sent, 'Tristan, I see no staff. He wears a ring, though.'

The captain drew on the helmet of a Home Guard, grimacing as the Yoriandir's thought came to him. He had seen enough of the Fallen's fire to last a lifetime. He bent to rip the insignia brooch from the baldric of the unconscious soldier lying bound and gagged at his feet. Getting the uniform had been ludicrously easy. He took a close look at the brass insignia; it betokened the rank of commander of twenty. Quite a step down, he thought to himself as he clipped the thing to his own sword belt, and he grinned in the moonlight. He was standing on the veranda just through a short passage from the king's high table. One part of his mind was amazed at how much he was enjoying this. He heard the first chords from the hall, and hastily finished dressing. He loosened his sword in its sheath and went back inside.

Even as he began to sing, Imris noticed Tristan appear suddenly against the draperies behind the high table. At least he presumed that the tall red-and-black-uniformed figure standing there with his hand grasping the hilt of his sword was the captain. The man's free hand came up to his chest, and the Yoriandir was heartened at the salute. During the run of chords between the first two verses, he cast his thought toward Kursh. 'Well, all is in place, Master Dwarf. I hope you have not forgotten to bring my bow and quiver with you. I feel like a hart circled about with spears.'

"I've got your bloody equipment," the dwarf growled under his breath. He stood with several others at the servants' entrance where a cool breeze steadied heads. The soldier next to him looked down and then, finding that Kursh hadn't spoken to him after all, jerked a thumb toward the Yoriandir. "Pretty good ain't 'e?" he remarked conversationally.

"Not bad."

Listening to the music, the other swept a glance over the dwarf's weapons. "Been out on patrol?"

Kursh thought quickly. He nodded at the green-skinned singer. "Brought *him* in."

"Do say? Lucky catch. Imagine the reward must o' been a tidy bit of change? Don't get many lawbreakers nowadays."

The dwarf looked up quickly. The man seemed harmless enough, standing with his arms folded on his chest, tapping his toe in time to the rollicking chantey Imris was singing, but the one-eyed tavern keeper was acutely aware that they were surrounded by enemies. He made no reply and the man seemed to forget him, but he heard a fragment of conversation pass between two who were standing further up front: "Looks familiar, don't he? Feel like I seen him someplace before, but can't quite call it to mind, you know?"

As he swept a long chord, Imris sent, 'Now, Peewit.'

The Littleman marched confidently into the hall and right up to the guard standing over the girl. Covered by the clapping that had sprung up in rhythm with the refrain, he told the man, "My lord Rasullis sent me for this girl." He let the guard think what he would.

Captivated by the music, the man merely glanced down at the chubby boy and waved.

"Come, miss," the Littleman said. He took her by the hand, almost pulling her to her feet, and led her from the hall. Once outside, he hugged the mural wall and walked briskly toward the stairway. "Quickly, my lady. If they look up from the singer, they can see us from the head table."

"You be not one of Lord Rasullis's men, then?"

"By the Powers, no!" Peewit swore. "I can't wait to get these damned colors off!" They made it to the balustrade and clattered down the first flight. He paused an instant to listen, but heard no pursuing footsteps. He squeezed her hand. "All right. Now we run!"

They rounded the landing, flying hand in hand. She tripped and he steadied her, but she put his hand away, hiked up her skirt to her knees, tucked the excess into her girdle, and pulled off the cheap servants' slippers she had been given. "There. *Now* we run," she told him mischievously, and barefoot shot down the next flight of stairs so quickly that Peewit could barely keep up. The last torch caught her hair streaming honey brown out behind her and the flush of excitement in her cheeks, and she sprang through the wide doors that gave onto the broad lawn outside the hall with a giggle of pure joy. The Littleman had to stop her or she would have run straight for the road leading to the main gate.

Imris sent, 'Now, Fidelis.'

Grasping the last two horses by the bridles, the Retreat Master felt the Yoriandir's words. "Is that all of them?" he asked the boy.

"Yes. I've got the others ready in the paddock." Alphonse was white with excitement and fear, but he had a quick way with the animals, and Fidelis was glad after all that they had brought him along.

"Good job. And just in time too." He urged the animals into the corral with a slap to their flanks and turned back to the barn.

Alphonse was intensely curious about how Fidelis knew this, but said nothing. "Are you sure the others have found the princess?" he asked doubtfully, peering up at the tall gables of the hall that he could just make out over the other buildings further up the hillside.

Fidelis stooped to the groom who was sitting propped against a sack of oats. The man was dead drunk on the holiday rations that had been handed out in honor of the king's birthday, spiked by a little of Kursh's flotjin when the fellow wasn't looking. He would sleep for several hours yet, the doctor guessed. "I'm going to assume so," he replied to the boy's question. "Now, drag this one around the corner of the shed there, where the stone will protect him from the blaze, and then stand by to open up that paddock gate." He took a flint and a short length of iron from the deep pocket of his robe and went into the stable.

With all the dry straw, it took but a spark to get a small tongue of flame going. A wisp of smoke meandered up into the loft, and suddenly the blaze threw out fingers and grasped the pile of bracken for the horses' bedding. There was a whoosh and the first two boxes were engulfed. Fidelis ran past the empty stalls and called over the crackling, "Let go the gate!"

He heard the squeak of hinges and, as he passed into the cool moonlight, felt the ground shake to the hoofbeats of the frightened steeds of the mounted regiment. Riderless and panicked, the horses fled through the streets of Ravenholt. As he became aware of an anxious meowing behind him, Alphonse dove past into the flaming stable. Grasping at the boy's sleeve, he followed.

Alphonse had followed the sound, and knelt at the back of one of the stalls, gathering mewling kittens into a fold of his robe as the mother stood up on his knee. "Give here," the doctor gasped harshly in the smoke, and the boy thrust a couple of scratching bundles into his hands. They ran together for the door and tumbled into the open air. The mother cat emerged from the smoke a moment later and circled them, craning her head to see her kittens. Alphonse led the way around the stone tack shed and up the alley. Already the smell of burning was on the air, and they feared discovery at any instant.

Their own horses stood heads up and ears pricked while their nostrils tested the air, and as they came around the next corner into a small court outside what might have been a granary, one of them gave a long pealing whinny. Fidelis set down the two kittens he carried and went at once to hold the horses' heads and muffle their nostrils against his robe. Alphonse knelt and gently set three other young cats onto the ground, where the female at once began to wash them. They were about weaning age, the boy judged, and the one still clinging to the homespun of his robe was a tabby with dainty white feet and bib. "Come on, little one, let go," he told it, trying to disentangle the claws.

"Alphonse, get these other horses," Fidelis called over his shoulder, impatiently trying to hold the restless animals.

But the more the lad tried to get the cat to let go, the harder it clung, and it looked up into his face for a moment and mewed.

"*Alphonse!*" The doctor turned his head and opened his mouth to say more, but seeing the boy still kneeling there with the patch of fur high up on his shoulder, a sudden insight came to him, and he saw the youngster as only a boy, far from the only home he had ever known. He smiled. "So you miss your Patience, do you?"

Alphonse blushed and pulled at the kitten to separate it from him, and then scrambled to his feet and ran for the nearest horses.

In King's Hall Imris bent his head as the applause and cheering swept over him. He was seated with his back to the windows through which the firelight from the burning stables must surely be visible now, and he knew that he would not have to hold them much longer. Memory slanted across the broken and dirty tiles of the floor, and he remembered the last time he had sung here in the hall, with the heavy spring rains beating against the stained-glass windowpanes, counterpointing his melody. The war had not yet begun, though they had heard from the outer marches that a vast army was being raised by the Bastard. It was obvious there would be heavy fighting before the newly planted crops ripened. But they had not known how bad it would be. They had not known that when the crops came to ripen, there would be so few to harvest them.

He looked at the cracked floor. When there was a king in Ilyria, he thought, his hall was a thing of beauty, of fine workmanship, of careful stewarding. There would not have been a broken floor with roaches scuttling under the rushes. And suddenly anger woke in him and with a kind of fey disregard of the danger, he lifted his head, looked straight at Dendron, and began to sing for the king.

Kursh started violently as the first strains of "Marian the Fair" rolled out over the rapt crowd, but none of the other soldiers nearby seemed to take note of him, and he tugged at the bristling hairs of his short beard as a tide of emotion brought a swelling to his throat. Pride stiffened his back even as he cursed the Yoriandir for being such a fool.

Tristan closed his eyes behind the iron helm as the hot fire constantly smoldering in his breast woke to sudden flame. He wanted nothing more than to draw his sword and smite the two who sat at the table barely a half-dozen paces away. But knowing that he could not, not until Princess Ariadne was safe, he clenched his jaw until his teeth ached.

There was some stirring in the crowded hall now as men leaned to murmur to their neighbor, "Don't I know that song from somewhere? Haven't we heard this before?"

At the head table, Dendron suddenly inhaled sharply and leaned forward to study the singer's face, but even then someone sitting near the southwestern windows cried out and rose from his place, pointing. *"Fire!"*

"The stables!" came several voices at once, and they scrambled from the benches and crowded to look.

The king yelled over the confusion, "Don't stand here looking—*go!*" As the hall emptied, he looked down at the Yoriandir. The whole sky was lit behind Imris as he stood now with the harp resting at his feet. "I know you, don't I?" Dendron asked with full knowledge in his voice. He had expected no reply and got none, and as Rasullis got to his feet, beginning to comprehend, the king held out a hand to the soldier next to Tristan. "My sword."

The guard shot Tristan a confused look, but began to unsling the ceremonial sheath in which he bore the enchanted blade. The captain's sword swept out and he knocked the weapon spinning from the man's grasp. Diving for it, Tristan caught it and jumped from the platform. Dendron found his voice and shouted, "Treachery! Guards, to me!" They came running out of the shadows along the sides of the hall. Rasullis automatically brought up his ringed hand, but something held him back, as though he had suddenly encountered some other will. Belatedly he realized the strangers were Warded.

Imris was sprinting for the doorway where Kursh waited with his ax upraised for the first of the pursuers, and Tristan covered the Yoriandir's back, parrying one thrust and sweeping aside another as they raced past the dwarf into the narrow passageway. Imris snatched up his bow, swept an arrow out of the quiver, and shot the leading soldier through the throat. Kursh cast him a quick, disgusted look, saying, "I had him, I had him," and then the fight flooded over them. They were pressed back into the corridor, which ran along the hall the back way to the kitchens and down a spiraling stair to ground level.

The captain wrenched his sword free from the body of the man he had just killed and saw behind the nearest uniforms of red and black, a white robe that seemed to gather all the light in the dim passage. "Imris, the Fallen!" he shouted, and the Yoriandir swung his bow in that direction just as the wizard threw up his ringed hand and every motion in the crowded confines was frozen. Imris struggled to make his muscles obey and let go the arrow, but he could not. Through a blue glare, as though in the side of a glass, he watched helplessly as the enchanter picked his way over the bodies and through the frozen figures of the Bastard's soldiers.

As the Fallen drew closer, it seemed to the Yoriandir that there was a change in the color of the mist; it deepened, and Rasullis suddenly halted and looked down at his ring. The aura took on a violet cast around the edges of Imris's vision, and then, for an instant, he saw a bright gleam of amethyst wink in place of the sapphire, and the enchanter hissed a curse, flinging his hand from side to side as though it burned him. The Yoriandir's heart gave a great bound and he was able to let the arrow fly.

It struck true, taking the wizard through the fleshy part of the arm. He screamed, releasing the spell. Tristan's sword swept down, and Kursh's ax flashed from side to side, and then the way was clear and they ran down the echoing corridor with the sound of hobnailed boots and the enraged curses of the wizard following them.

Peewit and the girl raced around the corner of a warehouse, almost crashing into one of the horses, and Fidelis grabbed for its bit as it shied. The Littleman bent double, gasping for breath. "This is Fidelis—my lady, and—this is Alphonse," he managed between gulps of the smoky air.

The doctor moved forward. "Can you ride, my lady?"

She looked at him with a frown. "Of course," she said and then laughed, "though my father thinks it be not seemly for a girl to race her brothers and win! Aye, I can ride, master!" She gave him her foot to help her into the saddle, gathered the reins competently in one hand, and sat easily controlling the sidling horse.

Fidelis turned to Peewit, bumping against Alphonse to wake him out of the staring trance into which he seemed to have fallen when he saw the princess. But the youngster did not move, and Fidelis looked at him sharply, only then seeing the dilation of his pupils and the way his hands gripped the staff. There was no web of power, however, and the doctor was confused. Peewit started to straighten and say something about the horses to the boy, but the Retreat Master gripped the Littleman's arm and he broke off in midsentence. "I think he's casting a spell," Fidelis said doubtfully.

"Or in one," Peewit whispered.

Ariadne leaned over the pommel curiously. "Is he a wizard?"

"It's a long story," the Littleman replied shortly, forgetting for the moment that he was talking to a member of the royal family. Just then the boy dropped the staff, grasped his temples with both hands, and came awake, groaning.

"Alphonse, what's happened? Are you all right?" the doctor questioned urgently, taking hold of him.

The redhead nodded painfully. "The others are coming," he told them. Peewit and Fidelis exchanged glances.

"We must be quick, then," the healer said, and dug in his saddlebag for a small box. From this he began to smear a white salve of chalk onto the boy's face. When it was done, they wrapped him in a blanket and bound it with leather thongs. "Up you go now," Fidelis told him, and with Peewit helping as best he could, he slung the boy belly-down over his horse's saddle and tied him there. "All right?" he asked.

"I suppose I'll ride this way as well as I do the other," Alphonse said, carefully straight-faced not to flake off the makeup. "How do I look?"

"Horrible," Peewit told him. "Worse than usual, even."

Then the doctor and the Littleman mounted, and they all waited in silence while around them ash drifted down, people's hoarse cries could be heard, and the mighty bell atop the watchtower tolled the alarm.

Imris raced fleetly down the alley and stopped short at the corner, cautiously peering around the warehouse as the other two came pounding up in the moonlight. He waved them back warningly and they withdrew a few feet. "Troops. Four or five—I couldn't tell. They are down at the bottom of this alley, staying out of sight under an archway."

"The Bastard must have posted reinforcements," the captain said, turning his head to listen for pursuers.

"One squad only—at least to this approach," the dwarf contributed. "If they suspected where we were headed, there'd have been half the army here by now."

"Cut through the cellar under the row of smiths?" the Yoriandir suggested.

The captain shook his head. "No time. They're sure to discover us soon, and the others are too exposed, just waiting for us."

"Right," Kursh rasped. "Let's go, then."

"Sergeant Major, draw them out," the tall man

ordered. "Imris, wait until he gets at least a couple of them in the clear."

"Stay to the right, if you can," the Yoriandir told Kursh. "I'll need a clear shot."

The dwarf stepped out into full view of the soldiers. He strode along stolidly, his ax lying on his shoulder. "All right now, you blackguards in yonder doorway," he called pleasantly. "Let's have a little to-do, shall we? What's the matter? Can't attack unless it's from behind? Yes, you, in there. Of course I'm talking to *you*. See anybody else? But I'm forgetting—you're the magician's men, of course. Can't even squat unless—"

He had come too close now, and they leaped from their hiding place and ran at him. Imris dropped the first, but the dwarf had to circle to avoid the flashing blades and his body came into the line of fire. Tristan was already running forward, darting into the fray, and drawing off two of them. The dwarf put his back to the captain's and another arrow came whirring in to fell a second victim, making it an even match, two against two. But the Bastard's men were fresh and Tristan and Kursh had already fought their way out of King's Hall. As the dwarf hewed at his man, the captain was a fraction of a second too late in parrying a thrust—the trooper's sword slashed in under his defense, and though Tristan managed to turn away the full force of it, the other's blade sliced through the uniform surcoat and tunic and just caught the flesh beneath. As the captain fell back a step, the dwarf heard his grunt of pain, caught the blade of his own opponent with his ax haft, and stepped in to grapple the man back by force of strength. The man went off-balance and the dwarf had his opening. He swung once, and the trooper went down. The sergeant major whirled and found Tristan clumsily weaving and bobbing, holding his side, while his enemy sought to get in past his guard. "Duck!" Kursh yelled, and even as he swung his ax, another arrow whistled out of the darkness and the enemy soldier crumpled. The dwarf leaped backward, shaking his hand where the fletching of the arrow had stung him.

The Yoriandir ran up. "I'm sorry, but you moved so quickly I had not time to slacken the string."

"Fat lot of good that would have done *me* if I'd been any closer to him!" the dwarf roared.

"Hush. You are not hurt much," Imris said, laughing, as he put out an arm to Tristan. "And you, Captain?"

"It's not bad—just a graze. Let's get away from here before Kursh brings the lot of them down on our heads!"

They covered the next street, dove through a luckily empty wainwright's shop, and emerged less then twenty feet from where the small party of mounted figures waited. Ariadne's eyes widened as she saw the Yoriandir harper and she exclaimed with surprised pleasure when she recognized Kursh, "I saw ye in the hall with the picture!"

"Aye, m'lady."

Beside her, the captain vaulted to the back of his bay stallion. She knew a momentary fright at his uniform, but reason told her this stranger too must be one of them. "You're hurt!" she said.

"Nothing to matter, my lady," the captain answered as he swept an appraising look over her, noting the way she sat on the horse: Good, no problems there, he thought thankfully. He glanced past her to where Alphonse lay across his horse. "Courage, boy!" he called, and kicked his horse to a trot toward the north gate.

Where the way opened into the main cart road to the gate, the green-skinned harper dismounted and ran forward to peer around the corner. He came back to the party and announced grimly, "It is manned, of course, and barred. There is a complement of archers on the platform above the gate itself. I see no other troops, though."

"Small wonder," the dwarf muttered, leaning forward in his saddle to ease his aching back. The strain of overused muscles was beginning to make itself known.

"Well, this is my part," Fidelis said. "Whew! I had not thought how much I would be shaking when I said back there in Swiftwater Shallows that I would do this!"

"You may decline now with no dishonor," the captain told him.

"You forget, my friend—I swore the Oath too, though it was to heal, and not to fight for the Blood. Still, it is all one now, it seems." He was looking at the girl, who was listening intently for some clue about who these strangers were.

Tristan saw the direction of his gaze. "It is all one," he echoed quietly.

Without another word, the doctor cast his hood about his face and nudged his horse to a walk befitting a merchant's steed.

As he rode out of the protection of the buildings, Fidelis was aware that every archer above the gate saw him immediately and that every one of them had an arrow aimed straight for his heart. He wondered how many of them he might be able to feel when they hit. Though he tried to open himself to feel the Powers flowing through him—as he sometimes could—the cramps in his belly kept him rooted in his corporeal body and he was mortally afraid.

Keeping close in the shadows, the princess's rescuers watched the two figures ride out, knowing that if the archers fired, there would be not one thing they could do for Fidelis and the boy. And if they failed, the rest of them stood very little chance of escape.

"Good even, good men!" the Retreat Master called clearly as he neared the gate, though the people he wished this for were not in front of him, but behind.

"Halt and stand!" The command rang loudly from beneath the platform. There must be an officer there, Fidelis thought. "State your name and business."

"Robert of Dells, Guild Master of Herbalists," Fidelis answered. "I brought our tribute for our lord the king's birthday, and I am returning home now."

"At night?" the officer barked suspiciously.

"Well, truth to say, I had intended to start earlier, but there seems to be quite a fire over yonder"—he jerked a thumb at the nearby glow—"and I had a hard time getting through. There are many horses running

wild in the streets," he added with just the right touch
of befuddled amazement in his voice.

"What is that bundle on the other horse?"

"Ah, that is my apprentice, Giles. Or rather, that
was Giles."

"He's dead?" the voice questioned sharply.

"Alas, yes. I knew he had been sick for many days
on the journey here, but the way was so long and we
did not wish to miss the ceremonies today, well, I am
sure you can understand, sir, that I would not have
made him go on if—"

"Enough!" There was a subdued order, and then,
"Stay there."

In the alley, the captain drew his sword.

Two soldiers marched briskly out from the tower,
and the archers still kept their arrows targeted. Fidelis
sat waiting for them and prayed that his voice would
not betray him. Hanging head down across the packhorse, Alphonse thought his eyeballs would burst from
their sockets with the pressure of the blood that had
run to his head, and he hoped desperately that he
could play his assigned part. Within the cocoon of
blankets he felt suffocated. When he heard the first
pair of boots stop near his head, he quickly shut his
eyes and tried to calm his breathing. Oh, Master Llodin,
he thought, I wish you were here.

The soldier standing by the packhorse took out his
knife and quickly cut the thongs that bound the blankets. "Oh, sir, I wish you hadn't done that," Fidelis
fussed, turning in his saddle to watch.

The soldier standing by Fidelis's horse's head reached
for the bit and held him there, while the first trooper
grasped the bundled Alphonse and dragged him off
the horse's back to the ground. Even in the alley they
could hear the bone-jarring thud. Peewit winced, and
Imris sent a quick reassurance, hoping that the boy
was still alive to hear it.

As the soldier knelt to the blankets, Fidelis found
his voice and said, "Really, sir, I don't think you
should do that." The man ignored him, flipping the
wrappings aside. "I wouldn't want to see you die too."

The soldier paused, looking up at him. "How's that?"

"Well, the fever, so they say, can be caught from a corpse. Though, to be sure, I myself have never seen that. But then, of course, I have never seen this fever, either, so maybe—"

"Fever? This boy died of fever?"

"Oh, yes. It was terrible. Poor Giles screamed so much, you see. He did until his throat swelled shut, that is, and then, of course, he couldn't scream very much anymore—"

Shielding his face with his sleeve, the trooper gave a yank at the blanket and it fell away to reveal a twisted, chalk-white visage with purple showing in veins through the pallor. In the moonlight, the effect of Fidelis's makeup job and Alphonse's own very real pain was ghastly. The soldier sprang up hastily, backing away, and then he ran toward the guard tower to make his report. The man holding Fidelis's horse looked scared and backed off to arm's length, peering around the horse's neck to see the corpse.

A moment later, the huge gate began to swing open.

"Get out, you."

The trooper let go the horse and snatched his hand away, wiping it on his tunic. Fidelis looked bewildered. "But won't one of you put poor Giles back on his horse?" When there was no answer, the doctor dismounted and stooped over Alphonse. While wrapping the blanket over his face again, the healer passed his hand around the boy's neck, making sure that it was not broken. He found instead a lump already raising on the back of the lad's head. Fidelis lifted him carefully and slung him over the saddle with some difficulty, retying the ropes and making sure he was securely fastened.

"Hurry up, there!"

The Retreat Master made haste to remount and rode toward the gate. He glanced surreptitiously at the archer company. They were leaning over the platform wall, frankly curious, their bows slack, but he felt the skin on the back of his neck tighten as he rode under them.

In the alley, Tristan commanded, "Now!" and they broke for the gate in a wild gallop, riding down the

trooper who still stood staring after the corpse, and
bearing straight for the barrier. Imris's bow sang, and
the officer dropped where he stood. Then they were in
the dark tunnel and out the other side, and a hail of
arrows slanted into the ground all around them. Ahead,
Fidelis led the packhorse, the bundle on its back bumping sickeningly. Ariadne bent low, urging her horse
with heels and knees. Tristan kept close with her,
admiring her skill, even as he checked the others.
Knowing that he could do nothing against the archers,
Kursh simply rode, while beside him Peewit clung like
a burr to his pony and the Yoriandir tried to give them
some cover by answering the fire from behind.

And then they were plunging down the Sweep, out
of bowshot, the grass soft beneath their racing hooves,
and the moon bright on their faces. Tristan looked
back once and saw the keep wall limned against a
firelit sky, and he laughed with an ease he had not felt
since he was a much younger man. Catching the sound,
Ariadne looked across at him and smiled at the uniformed man.

Book II   The Heir

5

Tristan reined under cover of a gnarled oak and gave a hand signal to the others. In the silent forest the crackling of twigs and underbrush as their horses bunched close behind him sounded alarmingly loud. The captain frowned and looked over his shoulder. In former days he would have had the hide of any man who had not taken care to have his horse's hooves well wrapped when he went out on patrol, but of course that was not to be expected now, and anyway, the old posting station was falling in on itself and—even in the moonlight—obviously deserted. Brambles grew through the windows, gaping cracks showed where the winter ice had heaved the stone walls, and a sapling reached right up through the roof.

Someone still used the weed-grown track, though; there was a discernible path leading up to the sagging door.

A flash of brown and white went hurtling past his head. The tall man ducked instinctively, but it was only Imris's thrush returning. The Yoriandir reported, "Safe. She says no one is near."

"All right. We'll rest here for a half hour," Tristan ordered. "It will take them that long to make the climb up from the valley, and then we shall still have an hour's lead on them." He swung down from the stallion, and his hand went to his side, where the blood had crusted, and tugged now at the cloth of the black and scarlet uniform. "Kursh, if you will fetch some water from the spring—you remember where it is? Then Fidelis can tend to Alphonse's head. Imris, we'll need to know from your little friend there if Dendron has sent scouts ahead of the main party down there; he'd be a fool if he didn't, and he's never been a fool where tactics are concerned. Peewit, check the station." He turned to help the girl from her mare, but she jumped nimbly from the saddle. "My lady, if you'd like to sit down here beneath this tree, we'll break out food and drink for you."

Standing crowded against her horse's shoulder, Ariadne looked up at him. In the moonlight she could tell that his eyes were dark, but whether brown or dark blue, she couldn't be sure. She smoothed the skirt of her dress. "I be no fine lady, sir, but I do thank ye for fetchin' me out of that horrible place." She felt awkward. This odd group hadn't said much, but she was certain that despite their rough clothing and only middling horses, they were all highborn folk. "Now, if ye'll just lend me this horse and point me on my way, I'll be goin' home." Her heart pounded. She had them figured for escapees from the castle's slave quarters, and she had no wish to be wife (or worse) to a fugitive. She had acted without thought back in the great hall when the Littleman had duped the guard, but she'd had plenty of time to think since then.

"Home?" Tristan repeated, as though he had not heard her clearly. The others were staring.

She swallowed and lifted her chin. "Well, to the South Riding, anyways. I warrant I can find me own way once I'm there."

Peewit began, "But, lady, the whole of the Bastard's army lies between—" The captain's hand made a downward chop and the Littleman broke off.

Tristan told her, "We take you to a place of safety, lady. It is too dangerous for us to be abroad in the land, and so we must hide for a while."

"I'd rather be on me own," she said, quickly adding, "Not that I ain't beholdin' to all of ye, but still."

Imris began to smile. "You are wondering who this group of strangers is, and whether after all you might not have been better off back in the castle." He looked to the captain and sent, 'To you goes the honor, my friend!'

The tall man cleared his throat. "Please be seated, my lady." He gestured again to the embankment the tree's roots had made and, when she still hesitated, added, "I do assure you, we would not for all the world wish you ill, but the explanation is somewhat . . . hard to believe, perhaps."

After a moment more in which she studied each of them, Ariadne sat.

Tristan did not know how to begin. Had the Fallen told her who she was? "Did the wizard Rasullis have anything to say to you, lady?"

"Much, and none of it such as would turn a sow's head."

Kursh fingered his ax and glowered. "Did he hurt you?"

She was taken aback at his tone and merely shook her head.

The captain grasped the dwarf's shoulder and Kursh fell silent. "Did Rasullis, perhaps, tell you . . . anything about yourself that you had not known?"

She shrugged. "He spun a story about me bein' a princess. Can ye believe it?" She looked around at them and laughed merrily.

They all looked at Tristan. He said quietly, "It is true. You *are* the Princess Ariadne."

She shook her head firmly and got to her feet. "Sorry, sirs—ye've got the wrong girl. Everybody knows the old Greenbriar King and all his family is dead these many years."

"No," the captain said. "Not all."

"Oh, by the Powers, not you too!" she swore. "The Lord Rasullis kept after me about it till I thought I'd go mad. 'You're the princess,' he said. 'The king's yer uncle.' (And I'd just as lief be kin to a great warted toad!) Well, I can tell ye, I am *not* the princess—I'm Robin of Wolf's Glen!"

"You are the image of the late king," Fidelis told her gently.

"And how would ye know that? I suppose ye'll tell me that ye was personal friends of his!"

The captain's hand found his sword hilt, while Kursh bent his head and rubbed at the eyepatch. "I would not presume to say friends," the tall man said, "but certainly we knew him. All of us here except the boy were members of the First Watch."

She drew herself up and said scornfully, "Look you, I may be nothin' but a country-born girl, but I been brought up proper. Me mother and father have told me all the old stories. The King's Watch never left the Sweep alive."

"It is convenient for us to let the Bastard and the Fallen think so." Tristan smiled grimly. "But as you see, we are very much alive. We go now to the wizards at Covencroft, lady. There perhaps will be further proof for you if you require it. Surely you would believe *them*?"

Ariadne grew suddenly still. "Covencroft?" she repeated and her eyes were wide. "There really is a Wizards' Isle, then?" Her eyes flew to Alphonse. "Meanin' no disrespect."

The boy put up one hand hastily and said, "Oh, no! I am not a wizard!" Then, as if realizing only after he said it that Llodin's staff was in his other hand, he added lamely, "I'm only . . . minding this for . . . someone."

"Are ye now?" she said softly, plainly thinking more than she said aloud. She gave them all a swift, summing glance, and Tristan felt as scrutinized as he ever had during a snap inspection. "I'd give a deal to see Covencroft, sirs, but I'm needed at home." Her face, which had by turns been wary and then curious, turned troubled and tired. "The soldiers hit me brother a terrible clop and burned our house." Her chin came up and she swore, "By the Powers, I'd like to see them eat barn-muck for breakfast!"

Maybe it was only the fire in her voice, but the captain was sure he saw her eyes flash. He looked down at her, and despite himself a smile crept over his face. She came barely to his shoulder, but he'd not like to cross her! Close on this thought came guilt: she was the princess, and here he was thinking about arguing with her. No matter, he thought, she's got to go with us to Covencroft, and by the Three, it's got to be now!

Luckily Imris was already saying, "On the way to Covencroft, we must first pass through my homeland, lady. Some of my kin are abroad in the land, and a message can be sent through them to your . . . family. That way, you may stay in safety with us, and still reassure your folk that you are well and among friends. In the same way, you may receive word of them."

Still she hesitated, and Fidelis saw that she doubted them. "My lady, I am a Retreat Master," he told her. "You know what that means?" At her cautious nod, he went on. "Then you know that I would not lie. And you must see that by doing as we have at Ravenholt, and by telling you what we have about ourselves, we have placed ourselves in your hands." Shrewdly he pointed out, "If you tried to make it alone through the Bastard's army, you would endanger us."

She nodded a little. "I get yer meanin', sir. And I can see the sense of it. Well, bein' as Master Harper says I can get word home, and seein' that I probably would get caught straight off by the king's men, I guess I'll be goin' with ye. But all this talk of the First Watch, and the old king and his daughter, well, that'll have to wait betimes. With them hounds on our trail, this be no time for long tales. So, shouldn't we be goin'?" She dusted moss off her hands and stood expectantly regarding the captain.

He hid a smile and answered, "I think we may tarry yet awhile." He glanced around at his troop. "To work, gentlemen." As Kursh fetched the bucket and went past, and Fidelis eased the protesting Alphonse to the ground, Tristan rummaged in the saddlebag on his horse for his own clothes. "Are you warm enough, lady? I have a cloak here."

"Thank ye, no. I'm fine." She saw him wince as he reached to retie a thong and his hand went again to his side. "Ye should have that hurt tended," she advised. "Else the night air'll get to it."

"When Fidelis is done with Alphonse," he assured her. He was silent for a moment and then she heard him chuckle. He slapped the stallion lightly on the flank so that it sidled away from him.

"Why do ye laugh?" She put up a hand to stroke the horse's neck.

He looked across the saddle and shrugged, embarrassed at having revealed a private thought. "I still can't quite believe that we pulled it off. It's been a long time since the Watch has seen any kind of action and—" She was looking at him with her head tilted to one side, and the things he had been going to say about his men being unprepared and about how worried he had been at the risk to them evaporated. "And now here you are, and with luck, we'll be beyond the Fallen's reach by midmorning."

She had marked his change in tone. "Did ye really come to Ravenholt just to get me out?"

The horse stood quietly between them. "Yes."

She frowned. "Ye're more brave than smart, ye know."

"Probably." He gave a low laugh, and it drew an answering smile from her.

A twig snapped behind them and she turned with a start, but it was only the Littleman returning from the broken-down shack. He had changed into his own goldenrod robe and brown cloak, and he looked suddenly older and stouter to her than he had in the page's uniform, which he carried under his arm.

The captain was gingerly settling the Bastard's enchanted sword under the stirrup leather. "Keep it," he directed as Peewit was about to cast the hated uniform into the underbrush. "It may come in handy again."

"Oh, well, all right—if I must. But a page, for pity's sake!" He sounded so aggrieved that Tristan smiled.

"The Barreners have none as short of stature as your people. Besides, it got you into the hall and that's all that matters." He came around the horse's rump. "Did you find anything in the station to show who's been using it?"

The Littleman shrugged as he buckled a short sword in a plain leather scabbard around his waist. "There are remains of a campfire and some bedding piled in a corner. I'd guess hunters."

The captain's eyes narrowed, but he nodded. "Why don't you go back up to the lip of the dell, and see if you can spot anything."

"Thought that's what the bird was doing," the

Littleman muttered. "I was looking forward to a pipe."
But he went back across the glade and up the path the
way they had come.

Tristan looked over to Fidelis as Alphonse stood up,
carefully leaning on the staff. A new bandage, soaked
in the cold water Kursh had fetched, was bound about
his brow. "How now, young Master Wizard? How do
you?"

"Oh, I am not much hurt—I landed on my head,
after all, and that's the best thing I could have done,"
the boy answered, walking toward him with the healer
hovering at his side and Kursh following.

"You gave us a start," Imris told him. "My own
head ached!"

"There has not been time to say so, Alphonse, but
you showed real courage back there. Master Llodin's
staff was well bestowed." The captain extended a hand
for the boy to shake, and the others followed suit.

This time, the youth did not cast his eyes down to
the ground. Instead he met Tristan's gaze levelly.
"Thank you, sir."

Tristan nodded gravely, man to man.

The Yoriandir repeated thoughtfully, "Well bestowed,
indeed. Captain, a word with you?"

Tristan nodded and gestured him to the derelict
station. "Kursh, you will attend the lady."

Imris took his arm and turned him toward the shack.
The boy and the doctor went to the packs, Fidelis
saying he had a draft he wanted Alphonse to take.

A few minutes later, after the Yoriandir had told
Tristan he had it from Peewit that Alphonse had apparently cast a spell back at Ravenholt, they came
back down the clearing, striding toward the boy. When
they were near, the captain glanced down to avoid
tripping over the wizard's staff, which Alphonse had
left propped against the baggage. He recoiled sharply
and his hand went out to grip the Yoriandir's shoulder
even as the amethyst network flared and spilled along
the length of the wand like a spark struck into a thin
line of oil. At the same moment, Alphonse rose swiftly
to his feet as though some invisible hand pulled him
straight up by his ginger hair. He dove across the

bundles to snatch up the flaming staff. His mouth stretched wide and the voice that came out of him was a familiar one, and sharp with vexation: "The *tree*, fools!"

The boy leveled the wand at the oak over Ariadne, but froze when a rough voice yelled, "Move an inch and the girl dies!"

Imris, the bowstring already drawn back to his ear, held his fire, though he targeted the rustling leaves above and to the right of Ariadne, who turned carefully and peered up.

Tristan glanced sidelong at the still-flaming staff, furious that Alphonse did not release whatever spell was gathering there and shaken because the voice that had come out of the boy had been Llodin's, and the captain did not know what that meant. Kursh was nowhere to be seen, and the tall man could not hear Peewit returning through the brush. Tightly, the captain called, "Who are you, and what do you want?"

"Tell yer green friend to throw down that bow, and call off yer wizard."

Where was the thrush? Why had they been given no warning? Tristan made a slight downward motion of his hand, and Imris brought the bow down and laid it on the ground. "Alphonse, if you can hear me, please stop."

The amethyst web winked out at once. "All right," Llodin's voice replied.

"Good," the raw voice in the tree said. "Now, if nobody does anything stupid, missy here don't get hurt."

"Who are you?" Tristan demanded again.

"I gets to ask the questions, gent. Who are *you*, and why is the Bastard King's army hell-bent-for-leather coming after you?"

"Are they?"

"Hah! You're a cool one, and no mistake." The voice hardened. "But so am I, mister. One more answer like that, and missy ain't half as pretty as she be now. Understand?" The captain nodded, his jaw corded. The voice grunted, "What you done?"

Tristan had no way of knowing what reply might set

the man off, but if he were an outlaw, as seemed likely, he would be no friend to the Briar and Sword. "We left Ravenholt without the king's permission," he answered cautiously.

"Did you, now? That weren't too bright, were it?" A hoarse chuckle shook the leaves. "The Bastard ain't forgivin' to deserters."

The captain realized that he was still wearing Ravenholt's scarlet and black. "He isn't forgiving to anybody," Tristan suggested, thinking to draw the man out.

"Right enough." The tree limb bounced a little. "I tell ye, I been up here listnin' a long time, and even though I couldn't hear much o' what ye said, I got enough to tell me that you folks stole missy from the castle." Abruptly he asked, "She your woman?"

The night had lightened to the gray of early dawn, and Tristan could just see Ariadne's movement of protest. Knowing he had to cut off whatever she was about to say, he quickly answered, "I'm her man," which was true enough.

"King take a shine to her?"

"Rasullis the Fallen did."

"Ah." There was a taut silence. "Then you're not likely to go back. Good enough. All right, lads—take them!"

From every side there was a rush of figures. Before Tristan could draw his sword, before even Imris could catch up his bow, they were both grasped roughly from behind and wrested to the ground. Alphonse was flung down next to them, the staff falling to the leaves. Fidelis was held standing, with a stout stick laid alongside his ear. Twisting in his captors' arms, the captain broke the outlaws' grip and was trying to get his feet under him to spring up when his angry eyes met the boy's, and the wizard-adept winked. "It's all right," Llodin's voice told him.

By that point there was nothing he could have done anyway, because one of the outlaws had pulled Ariadne close to him and was holding a wickedly long blade at her throat. "Settle down, or she gets it!" the voice ordered sharply from the oak.

Seething, the captain let them take hold of him again as, from a clump of saplings behind and left of the monarch tree, another three of the band pushed a gagged and hand-bound Kursh forward into the clearing. The dwarf's good eye flashed and his back was stiff with resentment, but he too had apparently been taken by surprise. The ax was missing from his belt.

"That's better," the voice said, and a patter of twigs showered the girl and the man who held her as the outlaw chief jumped to the ground. As he landed and the outlaw behind her released his hold to put his knife back in its sheath, Ariadne bunched her fists at her sides and, as she had seen her brothers do, whirled and delivered a roundhouse swing straight to the man's nose.

The outlaw staggered back a pace, both hands going to his face and eyes wide with shock. The girl followed him, fists cocked for another round. She whipped a look over her shoulder at the Watchmen. "Well, come on!"

There was a stunned tableau. Some thirty-odd dirty and unkempt men with rude weapons ringed the clearing and stared at the girl. Tristan was held half lying back on his elbows by three of them, while next to him the Yoriandir crouched with four more holding him down. Alphonse sat hugging his knees with one arm while his other hand crept out and found his staff. Quietly he drew it close. Across from them, Kursh had gone bright red under the gag and was choking with laughter. The outlaw chieftain's eyebrows were drawn up and a smile seemed ready to break across his face. The man Ariadne had punched sputtered curses and gingerly fingered his swelling nose. The girl herself stood now with her hands on her hips, for all the world like any village harridan, glaring from the outlaws to the Watchmen.

A hearty laugh shattered the tension. Tristan thought it came from Alphonse, but he couldn't be sure because suddenly everyone was whooping and guffawing, men slapping each other on the back and dabbing at their eyes. The leader of the outlaw band hooked his thumbs in his belt and threw back his head, thoroughly enjoying the joke, but Tristan's own smile faded as he saw the man clearly. The sky above reflected a warming pale yellow down through the trees and revealed the owner of the voice from the oak to be a huge man, easily a foot taller than Tristan, and thicker through the chest than Kursh. His skin was burned brown by the summer sun, and his hair was dark and nearly as shaggy as a spring bear's. Like his men, he was dressed in roughly cured hides—foot coverings, leggings, and knee-length tunic. A tatter of sheepskin cloak hung over his shoulders, and a long knife was thrust through his belt. One of the men handed him a wooden spear tipped with iron as he came forward into the dewy grass of the clearing, square teeth showing in a wide grin. He nodded over his shoulder to Ariadne, who followed him with her eyes. "Feisty, ain't she?"

Tristan eased himself to a sitting position.

"Now mebbe our Taran will keep his hands to home, eh?" He looked back at Ariadne's guard and called in a bantering tone, "You watch her now, Taran—from a distance!" A fresh outbreak of hoots went around the group. The big man regarded the captain, and his eyes went cold. "Now, what did you really do back there at the castle? And don't give me none o' yer talk about leavin' without the king's by-your-leave. They don't send an army after one deserter and his leman." The spear point came down level with the hazel eyes. "See, if we don't get movin', they're goin' to be here in a little while. And until I figgers out what to do with ye, we ain't movin'. Right now, it's goin' through my mind to take ye back down the trail, and see how much the king's willin' to pay for yer hide. Must be a reward, hey?"

The captain held his eye. "Probably. But I am on urgent business, and I may not reveal what it is. Except to say that if we succeed, this land may be rid of the Bastard and the Fallen once and for all."

"Fine words. And who hasn't wished 'em more than oncet over a horn of drink?" He looked around at his now-silent men. "There ain't a man here who wouldn't like to see things back the way they used to be, when a man could spit free and say what come to mind without a fear that they'd come and burn him out in the night." There were nods among the outlaws. "But them days are many a year gone, and talk don't put bread in the bairns' mouths, do it?" Growls answered him. He looked down again at the Watchmen. "Nowdays, a man's got to take what him and his family needs from them that's got it." The spear point winked in the rising sun. "And you looks like folks that have more than we do."

"You are welcome to anything in our provisions," Tristan told him quietly.

"Ain't that handsome, though!" The man grinned. " 'Specially seein' as how you can't do nothin' about it anyways."

The captain deliberately cut across his words. "Only leave us our horses and weapons: we'll need them to outrun Dendron's troops and fight them if we must."

"Whoo-ee, crowin' mighty loud, ain't ye! All six of ye—plus missy, o' course—goin' to take on the King's whole army!"

The captain answered, "We already have. That's why they're chasing us. We burned a good part of Ravenholt last night and wounded the enchanter."

The outlaw cocked an eyebrow. "Oh, aye, and I'm the Greenbriar King," he said sarcastically.

Llodin's voice came out of the boy, incongruously deep in that slight frame. "It is true, Master Quint."

The huge man swung his head suspiciously. "How'd you know my name, wizard?"

Alphonse slowly unfolded himself and stood with the staff looking like nothing more than a hiking stave in his left hand. Below his red hair, his deep blue eyes widened. "I know many things about you, William. How is your little one? It is hard to keep the smaller children warm in a cave, isn't it?"

William Quint's hand came up in the sign against enchantment and he backed away. "Stay away from me, you!"

Several of the outlaws were sidling toward the cover of the surrounding trees as Alphonse, still with the deep tones of Llodin's voice overriding his own, told him crisply, "I have no intention of harming any of you unless I must. But you have been dunderheaded fools and my patience is wearing thin. The outriders of the king's army are already through the ravine and have climbed the trail from the Willowsrill valley. They will be here within moments. However, there are only a dozen of them and they are expecting to have the upper hand, so you can take them easily if you wish. We have no interest in betraying you to Dendron's soldiers, but we will not allow you to do it to us. Is that clear?"

Even to the captain, the boy's control was impressive. The huge man was nodding, but Tristan could see anger beginning to furrow his forehead. If Quint let them go like this, he would be smaller in the eyes of his followers. The same thought had obviously occurred to the wizard-adept. "Now, Master William, you are just the man we have been looking for. You spoke awhile ago of wanting to see things set to rights here in Ilyria. Was that just talk, or are you prepared to do something about it?"

Quint spat through the gap in his front teeth. "I was a true man to the Briar in my time."

"In fact, you fought for King Dhonald at the Battle of the Southmark, didn't you?"

William's eyes narrowed and he folded his arms on his chest. "Aye."

"In First Watchman Peewit Brickleburr's troop—correct?"

A reminiscent smile flickered over the weathered face. "Aye. He were a scrappy little whoreson."

The wizard-adept stepped toward him and pointed with his staff down to the end of the clearing opposite the old posting station. "Look. Have you eyes?" he said quietly.

Two of the outlaw's men were manhandling the Littleman between them and Peewit was fighting them every step of the way. His goldenrod robe was rent from the brambles and a livid weal showed on his neck where a whipping sapling had caught him in the fight. Quint's face seemed to light up from within as the sun broke over the treetops. "By the Powers!" he shouted.

He broke into a shambling run and caught up the Littleman at arm's length as a man of normal growth might catch up a child. *"Shorty!"* he roared in Peewit's face.

Peewit flailed wildly and caught the giant a glancing blow, but William ducked it off. Then as what the man had said got through to him, the Littleman took a closer look. "Quint? It can't be!"

"Well, it is!" The outlaw chief shook off his men. "Leave him be, ye jackasses! Can't you see this is an officer o' the Watch?"

The Littleman's nose wrinkled. "It would probably help if you set me down."

He was deposited with a jolt that stung his heels. "Them bastards down in the valley is after you, First Watchman?" Quint demanded.

Peewit rubbed his wrists where they had forced his hands behind his back. "Yes. After all of us," he amended. "William, you were assigned to the Southmark regiment and so you probably don't recognize these other gentlemen. These are the other living members of the First Watch."

Beneath the dark tan, a flood of red suffused the huge man's face. "Ye don't mean it! We heard ye was all dead there on the Sweep!" His eyes went down. "Fact is, we give up then, and made our way home best we could."

Tristan got to his feet. "That was the wisest thing you could have done, Master Quint. Otherwise, you wouldn't be around to aid us today."

A scruffy man with a bow piped up from the crowd of outlaws, "Who said anythin' about aidin' ye?"

"Shut up, Ian Rigby!" the big man bellowed. "Of course we'll help 'em!"

"Not so fast, William," another of the band said quietly. *"You* know these men, but we don't, and even if they were our own kin, should we stick our necks into the hangman's noose? They're rebels, by their own account, and I say we don't need the trouble. We stay quick and quiet in the woods, like we always have, and send these on their way. Maybe the king's army will follow their trail, and miss ours."

There were murmurs of agreement. Quint glared. "These is the *Watchmen*, by the Three!"

"And the Greenbriar King is a story you tell your young ones," the same man retorted. "If you've got any left."

William walked over to him and put a hand on his shoulder. "Ye had a fine farm oncet, Harry. Wouldn't ye like to have it back? Wouldn't ye like to see them that took it served good and proper for what they done?"

"My land's gone to thistle, and my wife and children are under it. What's the use of the First Watch to me now?" He shook off Quint's hand and walked away into the forest.

"Time is running out," Alphonse reminded them all. "The seekers are almost upon us."

Peewit was desperate. "William, we have to get away. We must keep this woman from falling back into the Fallen's hands."

He glanced to Tristan, who made a hand code to Imris, and the Yoriandir sent, 'Yes, tell them.'

The Littleman went to the chieftain's side. "Take a good look at her. Who does she remind you of?"

Ariadne, who until now had stood quietly, walked out into the sun when Peewit waved her forward. A blush of pink came into her cheeks as the big man peered at her.

Quint scratched his beard. "I don't know," he said doubtfully.

"Look at her eyes."

Ariadne kept her chin up, though his breath was bad and she was a little frightened of him. She saw his eyes go wide. "By the Powers! It's the king! But who. . . ? No. It can't be!"

"Yes. It is," the captain confirmed.

"But she weren't nothin' but a baby!" Quint protested.

"Baby has grown up," Peewit said.

Quint whirled to face his men. "This here lady's the Princess Ariadne! Never mind how I know; I do. Now we got to get these villains that're after her out o' the way, else we're never goin' to get a chance to talk to her 'bout gettin' our lands back. Come on, boys—let's

get 'em!" He covered the clearing at a run and led the
way toward the place where they would set the ambush for the attackers.

The outlaw band looked from him to the Watchmen, who were snatching up their weapons. "Might as
well," Ian Rigby said. "They're too close now to let
them go. We'll reason with Quint afterward." They
scattered through the woods to catch the scouts
unawares.

Tristan stopped for a brief word with his own men.
"Be alert for any sign of treachery," he told them. "I
trust Quint, but the others aren't sure yet that they're
in this to the finish. Fidelis, Alphonse, Imris—stay
here with my lady. Your best cover will be the shack,
but you'd do well not to wait for us. Imris, the land of
your people is near. I leave it in your hands." The
Yoriandir nodded gravely, took Ariadne's arm, and
urged her toward the broken building.

The dwarf, Littleman, and captain raced toward the
path. Alphonse called after them, "Hurry, gentlemen.
We have much yet to do." Again his voice was the
familiar wizard's. "And besides, I want my breakfast
tea."

His quiet laugh followed them down into the dell.

Ariadne sat with her back against the crumbling
wall of the posting station as Imris had requested her
to do, while he stood above her with his bow swung up
and ready at the window hole. "I hate waiting like
this," she whispered.

Fidelis, who crouched beside her on a pile of debris
that had once been part of the roof, searched through
the bag of healing herbs and ointments he had scrounged
from Kursh's small stock back in Swiftwater. He was
frowning, and paid her no attention. His thoughts
were fixed on the boy, who was standing woodenly
against the opposite wall. Alphonse was staring, and
his pupils had widened until they nearly swallowed his
blue irises. Try as they might, they could not shake
him out of the trance under which he seemed to have
fallen. He had followed them all into the shack and
then not moved again, and it had been nearly half an

hour ago. Fidelis did not know whether Llodin's spirit still held him, but he was afraid that, with the knock on the head he had received the night before, the strain of possession might prove too much for the slender youth.

The Yoriandir stood very still at the window, only his eyes moving constantly, swinging from the edges of the clearing to the sky and back. "I don't understand why she hasn't come back," he murmured to himself.

"Who?" the girl asked.

"Tabindrinath," he answered, and then, catching the lack of understanding in her expression, he explained, "My thrush." His face was troubled.

"I'm sure she's all right," Ariadne tried to reassure him, not yet realizing that the bird was something more than a pet. "Maybe she just got hungry and stopped for a grasshopper or two."

He did not smile, and she feared she had offended him. Instead he told her in a low voice. "Tabindrinath would never have let danger get so close without returning to tell me. I fear . . ."

Ariadne looked to Fidelis for help, and now the Retreat Master said, "Why would they hurt her, Imris, even if they saw her? They could not know that she was *your* thrush, and they had no reason to suspect what she can do."

The Yoriandir's green eyes caught the reflected morning sunlight as he nodded. "True. Still—my heart is heavy, and I know of no other reason why it should be so." A grimace passed across his face. "I must go look for her!"

He was halfway to the sagging door when the healer caught his arm. "Imris! You can't go out there! We don't even know whether any of the king's troops got through to the dell here. We have to stay with the princess, and you're the only one of us who is armed." Imris's hand clenched on his bow.

From somewhere outside came an ear-piercing shriek, the cry of a hunting hawk that has sighted its prey, and the Yoriandir flung off the doctor's restraining hand and leaped to the doorway. "Tabindrinath, ya nekumin!" he shouted with fear, and high in the blue

sky, the thrush heard and tried to obey his order to
come home. But the bird of prey was much faster, and
even as the speckled thrush dove down the air currents, slanting for the dark oblong of the shack door,
the peregrine struck.

Tabindrinath crashed dead to the moss in an explosion of feathers, the cruel talons driven into her back.
The falcon bent his hooked beak to feed.

With a hoarse cry, the Yoriandir let fly an arrow.
But it burned in a searing blue flash. The peregrine
gorged, unconcerned, as from the side of the clearing
over which the huge oak arched, a man in a black and
red uniform banded across the chest with blue stepped
out onto the grass and began to twirl a whistling lure
to coax the falcon back to his fist.

Imris, his face contorted with angry horror, swung
the bow to cover the man and fired. This arrow too
was burned to ash faster than the winking of an eye.
In a kind of blind fury the Yoriandir fired again and
again, while the uniformed man walked closer, stoop-
ing to take the peregrine off the thrush's body and slip
a hood over the red-stained beak. He spent a moment
grooming the bird and, when he was satisfied that it
had broken no small feathers in its hurtling strike,
held it carefully and looked toward the station. "All
right, Master Harper. You may put down your useless
bow, and leave off wasting arrows. As you see, they
do no good."

Fidelis put a hand on Imris's arm, and met the green
figure's wounded look.

Outside, the falconer stood at ease. "I am come to
you from Lord Rasullis. My rank is Master Assassin,
and my name is not important: you may call me the
Hawk."

Across his words, the Retreat Master hissed, "He is
protected by the Fallen's power!"

The assassin told them, "The princess will come
back with me." He smiled without mirth. "Lord Rasullis
does not choose to be without her company."

In the gloom of the posting station, Imris slowly laid
aside his bow. His eyes had taken on the hue of
green—a breathing glow—that country folk some-

times see rise over a swampland in the dark. Fidelis let
go his arm. "What are you going to do?"

The Yoriandir looked past him. "He has angered
my fathers." His voice, though kept carefully low, was
charged with an overtone that the human sensed more
than heard.

Ariadne heard it too, and whether it was the
Greenbriar blood in her or whether she simply was
more intuitive, she saw the violence in the gentle
harper and guessed something of the form it might
take. She rose quickly to tug Fidelis back. "Let him
go," she whispered. "Listen!"

As the Yoriandir stepped through the doorway into
the sunlit clearing, a murmur rose, a swelling of uncanny voices like the sighing of pine trees in the wind.
But there was not the slightest breeze stirring the
leaves. The assassin's gaze traveled quickly around the
clearing and then fixed on the Yoriandir, who had
halted a few paces out from the shack. "Don't try any
of your tree-tender tricks. The Lord Rasullis will not
tolerate minor nuisances."

Imris made him no answer, but from the woods on
every side there was a snapping of twigs and rustling
of leaves. Yet nothing moved. The last of the morning
mist smoked through the treetops.

The assassin called, "Princess Ariadne, unless you
would have me hurt this green-skin, come out of there
now!"

Fidelis glanced down at her. Her hair was filmed
with spiderwebs, but when she peered past him through
a chink in the stone wall, her eyes sparkled. "Sounds
scared to me," she whispered.

The healer opened his mouth to answer, but the
assassin suddenly stripped the hood from the peregrine and launched the bird at Imris. Before it had
given two swift wing beats, a loud crack rent the air
from the side of the clearing. As slowly as though it
were happening in a dream, the monarch oak crashed
down, killing both the Fallen's assassin and the bird of
prey beneath its summer-green boughs.

Branches tossed lightly in an unseen breeze all around
the posting station and borne on the wind was a dis-

tant murmur, like sad humming. "Askarion, ampiere,"
Imris said softly. I thank thee, grandsire. He picked
his way carefully to the packs heaped still on the
leaves. Unstrapping his harp, he took it up and softly
began to play.

Nearby, the remains of the speckled bird stiffened
under the coverlet of green oak leaves.

The ambush had gone well; the trackers were disposed of quickly and quietly, and the only casualty
among the outlaws was a turned ankle suffered in a
dash to capture the army scout's horse before it bolted
all the way back to the main party of the king's troops.
Kursh and Tristan were so stiff and sore from their
exertions breaking out of King's Hall the night before
that glances of suspicion were cast their way by some
of Quint's band, who thought they were slacking. However, when the dwarf dropped his ax to send a slender
dagger through the throat of the last scout as the
Ravenholter raised his sword above Ian Rigby's head,
there was an approving whistle from another of the
men.

After some careful scouting of their own—which
Tristan noted was carried on in absolute silence in an
old Greenbriar battle mode—the outlaws headed back
to the clearing. They heard harping before the trees
thinned enough for them to see, and at the sound the
captain's lips tightened and he made a hand code to
Peewit and Kursh to split up and approach from different directions.

From the cover of the undergrowth just outside the
bright sunlight in the clearing, the tall man saw the
Yoriandir and the fallen tree. There was a dark pile of
cloth in the tree's branches, and the princess and Fidelis
sat listening amidst the broken twigs, while the boy
sprawled, apparently asleep. Puzzled, the captain whistled a greeting code, and Imris laid a hand across the
strings and turned his head to the sound. "It's all
right, Captain. The danger is over."

Walking out into the clearing, Tristan picked his
way over branches to the small group, with Peewit and
Kursh converging and Quint's people following, ex-

changing looks, for they had heard no ax, yet the massive tree was down. "What happened?"

Fidelis gestured to the black-clad body. "Another of the Fallen's assassins. He knew exactly where we were, Tristan, and he came straight for the princess." The healer continued, "He killed Imris's thrush, and would have killed us too, but the tree fell on him."

The captain nodded almost imperceptibly at the Yoriandir, who had not looked up, and asked, "Just—fell?"

Fidelis nodded back.

"I see. What's wrong with Alphonse?"

"Nothing. He's only asleep. He came out of his trance, shook it off like a spaniel, and said—in his own voice—to wake him for breakfast."

While the captain absorbed this, William Quint wanted to know, "What's to do now, First Watchman?"

Peewit looked up at the captain, and the tall man said, "We're already in your debt, Master Quint—and that of your good men. But from here on, we can't ask you to share our road. It is too dangerous, and besides, we seven may pass where a larger group could not."

The huge man frowned. "Ye'll not say we can't help the princess, surely, now we know who she is?"

"You have already helped, more than you know."

"That? Pshaw, that weren't but a bit of stalkin'. We want to help ye fight 'em! Don't we?" he roared to his men.

There was silence. Quint flushed.

Ariadne thought that if they didn't move soon they'd draw Black-and-Reds thicker than midges in springtime. She stood up, dusting twigs from her dress. Be royal, she told herself—that's what they'll believe. She dropped into an imitation of her mother, Nelia, telling stories of highborn folk while the distaff spun by the open hearth. "Sir William, I thank thee right well for all the troubles ye've been put to on my account. Thee and thy men art brave, bold, and true. If my father the old king was alive, he would reward ye with golden treasure, I am sure. But thou knows my sad tale: mine uncle sits upon a throne he wast not born to. Because

of this, I cannot offer ye even thy own land back."
The men's eyes were on her, and she realized with
sudden shock that, for them, this was not just a handy
bit of cheeky nonsense. High color came into her
cheeks. "But I believe that if these Watchmen can get
me out of that castle, they canst do other wonders.
And if by chance I come again to my family's castle,
mayhap you too shall come to your homes." She swept
her gaze over the rough-looking men and read the
hope in some of the faces. Now ashamed of her lie,
she dropped the pose and said simply, "I don't like to
make promises I can't keep, but I do promise I will
remember ye."

Quint stared at her, and then shook his head. "Ain't
she just like him, though?"

There was a small smile on the captain's face. "Very
like," he agreed. "And now, we must go. If you would
do something more, get safely away and spread the
word to others like yourselves that the royal Blood
still lives in Ilyria. But keep it very quiet: if it is openly
spoken of, the Bastard and his wizard will redouble
their efforts to capture her—or worse. Let it be a mere
whisper. It will be enough."

The outlaw chief settled his sheepskin to his shoulders. " 'Twill be done. Even this lily-livered crew is
good enough for that," he said with disgust.

"Don't be hard on them, Quint," the captain told
him quietly. "They were not officers of the Briar, as
you were."

The brawny man grinned. "I weren't no officer, sir,
just an ordinary slogger."

Tristan made a snap decision. Raising his voice, he
said clearly, "You're an officer now." It felt good to
use that power for the first time in twenty years. He
told the openmouthed Quint, "When we need you,
you'll know where to report. Until then, keep yourself
well."

"Aye, sir, I will do that." If possible, William grew
taller. "Will we be goin' to war, then?"

The captain of the Watch tried to be honest. "I
don't know. There's nothing I'd like more than to lead
an army against theirs, but that day may have to wait

for others younger than you and me, since there is no
heir for whom to take the throne. It may be a long
time, Quint, but yes, I think the day will come."

"I've waited nigh onto twenty years. I guess I can
wait a few more," the man replied sturdily. "Now, we
got to get out o' here and see if we can confuse a trail
for them rats. G'bye, Your Highness." His fist came
to his chest in the old Greenbriar salute. When the
captain whipped him an answering one, the big man
grinned and turned on his heel. "Come on, lads. Let's
play a little fox-and-hounds." They made way for him
and before they followed him out of the clearing, one
or two looked Ariadne's way and tried a clumsy imitation of his homage. The Watchmen answered them.
Within moments, the outlaws were gone.

Peewit twinkled. "Superior recruits these days."

"Imagine the amount of provender it would take to
keep *him* in the field," Kursh mused. He looked up at
the tall captain. "Well, that tears it—now we'll *have* to
take back this bloody kingdom."

"One day at a time," Tristan reminded him. "Let's
just get out of here." Fidelis stooped to waken
Alphonse, and Peewit and Kursh went to pack the
horses once more.

Imris lifted his harp from the ground, looked toward
where Tabindrinath lay, and swallowed. Ariadne put a
hand on his sleeve. Then she quickly stooped and tore
a strip from her hem. She said, "We can bury her
under the tree. That way, none o' them will find her."

His fir eyes considered the cloth gratefully. "Yes,
that would be well. I must take a twig of grandfather
too, that he may be remembered in Yoriand."

She did not understand, but told him, "Why don't
ye do that, then, and I'll take care of Tabindrinath?
Go on, now." She gave him a gentle push away from
the mess on the ground and he went.

Her eyes met Tristan's, and his were warm. "Thank
you, my lady," he said quietly, and raised her hand to
his lips. Then he too went to make ready for their
flight.

As she dug the small hole under the fallen trunk,
Ariadne was scarcely aware of what she was doing.

She could feel her cheeks flaming, and her hand actually seemed to tingle a little. Her hand closed around the stiff little bundle and she was suddenly ashamed of herself for dreaming over the poor Yoriandir's shattered pet. She placed the cloth-shrouded thing in the shallow depression she had scooped out, and a speckled feather sifted out of the wrappings. She regarded this a moment, and then picked it up and carefully tucked it into her girdle. She did not know whether, after a time, Imris would want this remembrance, but if he did, she could give it to him.

She covered over the hole, fluffed some leaves on top of it, and walked toward the horses. They were all waiting for her. "I'm ready," she said, and the captain helped her to the saddle.

P eewit's pony ticked a hoof sharply against an outcropping of marbled stone, and he hauled its head up. They were climbing steeply, the mixed woodland of birch and oak below having given way to spruce and cedar. Beyond this ridge lay Yoriand.

Behind them was the king's army. The Littleman turned in the saddle to look back, and he could see the sun winking off spear points down the shoulder of the mountain. The metallic sparkling was strung out across a broad meadow and into the trees. "Go back, you poxy bastard," he muttered.

Rising in front of Peewit, Fidelis heard the Littleman's pony stumble and glanced back to see that he was all right. His eye was drawn over Peewit's head to the line of soldiers pursuing them. "They have not slackened," the healer remarked.

"No, and they've nearly made up the distance we had on them when they stopped back at the posting station."

Brickleburr looked forward where Imris led their group up a rocky defile. "I hope the Yoriandirkin don't mind us bringing a little company."

At the head of the column Imris's keen ears picked up their talk, and he called back to them, "My people already know we are coming and who rides behind us. I think you need not fear that the Bastard will be able to find us. The tales of the forests of Yoriand are not all mere tavern talk."

He referred to the old stories among the Ilyrians, and even among the Barreners, that the land between these mountains and the sea was protected by an enchanted forest. Not many travelers ventured to Yoriand, although the legends of a lush valley and wondrous fountain of silver excited more than passing interest. From time to time, adventurers would take it into their heads to climb the high hill passes to the land of the green-skinned tree-tenders. Whether they were bent upon treasure or simply upon being one of the few ever to see the fertile water-valley sloping to the ocean, they all found the same thing: once into the forest that lay below the ridge, they were met by courteous Yoriandirkin who entertained them with music and singing, gave them food if such was needed, and returned them firmly back to the crest. If the travelers attempted to return to the valley after their guides had left, they became lost in the woven woods, and were shunted upward by the impenetrable trees to finally emerge where they'd begun.

It was not, however, an entirely pleasant legend. Some of the would-be plunderers had never returned to the taverns where they had sworn to seek out the hidden land and come back with silver. So the enchanted forests of Yoriand were regarded with as much fear as eager curiosity.

Had the Yoriandirkin wanted, they could have told the story aright—that there was no harm done to those who did no harm. But let a benighted wanderer who had disdained the gentle order to go home break boughs from the forest for bed or fire, and the trees themselves took vengeance. Not even the tree-tenders could stop them. A spell older than the Yoriandirkin them-

selves wakened at such times, and the traveler was
doomed to wander the forests for a period proportion-
ate to the damage he had done. If he had but broken a
few sticks for a small fire against the night's chill, he
would be lost in the forest for a few days while murmuring voices told him repeatedly that he must not
abuse his brethren. Then he would be cast up, dazed
but unhurt, on the borders of his own world with no
memory of what had passed, but with a lifelong aver-
sion to cutting wood.

For more serious offenders, the wandering was longer,
the voices more insistent. It was said among the
Yoriandirkin that the trees had held some captives for
years, and during this time the outlanders were only
voices that not even the tree-tenders could find, but
only heard sometimes on the murmuring breeze. When
these unfortunates were returned to their own land,
they had been gone for so long and talked so strangely
that they were taken for mad and shunned.

In all the years the rest of the Watchmen had known
Imris, none of them had ever journeyed with him to
the land of his people. Now Peewit glanced back over
his shoulder again at the Bastard's army, and wondered what welcome his party could expect.

Alphonse—who had shown no signs of reverting to
Llodin's personality since leaving the clearing—had
heard only the vaguest of stories about Yoriand, and
these chiefly from the tenant farmers who worked the
retreat lands and who had delighted in filling the gull-
ible young bondsman's ears with tales of bewitchments.
As he rode, the freckled lad was a little frightened of
what lay immediately ahead after they had crested the
ridge, but he thought that it probably couldn't be
much worse than the dangerous time at Ravenholt,
and he had survived that well enough, though he still
had a beastly headache and would be glad to get off
the jolting horse.

Ariadne handled the tricky ascent with smooth
horsemanship, but she was weary and wondered
whether William Quint and his band had escaped the
king's army. Too, she was thinking. I'm Robin, she
told herself. My father is Sten and Mother's name is

Nelia. She was a Burrows before she married. Gran didn't like Papa when first he came from over the hill to woo Mum—she thought he looked too much and said too little. She heard her mother's husky voice retelling the story for the hundredth time, while the red stood as brightly in her cheeks as in a girl's, and she glanced merrily over at the wiry man who smoked his pipe and planed barrel staves by the light of a sheep's tallow candle, his oldest son Gil helping.

"Knew what I wanted when I saw it," her father always rejoined to this teasing and, clenching his pipe between his teeth, would add, "Din't see no need to palaver about it." And Gran, until she had passed away three years ago, would pipe up from her chair drawn close to the fire, "I din't want my daughter marryin' no dumb man, Sten Cooper, so you could ha' saved yeself a peck a trouble by bein' more forth standin'!" Robin and her brothers and sisters would shriek with laughter, and Sten would play at being miffed, but he never could hold the pose long. More often than not, he would put a stop to the teasing by starting to whistle, at first low and as though he weren't paying much attention to the others, but then so loud and clear you could tap your toes to it or clap.

There was suddenly water in her eyes and she thought fiercely, They *are* my folks—they've *got* to be.

The Yoriandir's clear voice interrupted her. "My lady, if you can pass by the others, would you come up here? I'd like you to be the first to look down on my home with me."

She dashed a sleeve across her eyes and hoped none of them would mark that she had been weeping. Urging her horse past Alphonse and the captain, who crowded close to the edge of the path to make way for her, she saw that the trees opened against a bright blue sky further ahead. The earth must drop off steeply there, she thought.

Imris was smiling and had turned on the light blanket that served him for a saddle. "I thought the sight might cheer you. It is not given to many to see it."

She made an effort to respond to his obvious enthusiasm. "I'm sure 'twill be very nice."

He waited until she was behind him and then nudged his horse forward. They rode past the outthrust branches of the bristlecone pines that crowned the ridge and emerged on a wide promontory. Below them spread a panorama of sparkling streams tumbling downhill through the most brilliant autumn landscape Ariadne had ever seen. Yet a warm summer breeze lifted her hair and tickled her nose. She caught her breath and let it out in a slow whistle of surprise.

The Yoriandir laughed. "I thought you might like it."

"Oh, Master Harper, 'tis beautiful! But how can it be fall down there and summer up here?"

The others were scrambling their horses through into the open space as he replied, "It is always autumn in Yoriand. Or at least, the trees always wear their brightest foliage, even though by the moons we can tell that it is spring or summer."

"Or winter."

His flaxen hair caught the sunlight as he shook his head, looking down into the land. "There is no winter there."

Tristan was leaning on his saddle horn, sweeping the valley with admiration. "Llodin told me about this once," he said, "but I must say he didn't do it justice. It's marvelous. I wonder that you weren't applying for leave at every chance, Imris. I don't think I could have stayed away as long."

The Yoriandir looked back at him. "I was sent by the elders to fulfill our pledge to the Greenbriar King." He stared down into the russet glory. "But my heart has always been here."

Kursh shifted uneasily in his saddle. "It's a bonny sight," he agreed, "but I don't much care for the one back the other way, if you take my meaning. I'll feel better when we get down off this ridge."

Imris drew a deep breath, as if he were savoring some odor of home the others could not smell. "Yes, it is well. They will be waiting with refreshment for us. Master Dwarf, do me the favor of keeping your ax in its sheath. My people are distrustful of those who bear such tools: in our experience, only grief has come of them. Oh, you need not look at me that way! You are already well known to my kindred, and are regarded with the honor befitting one who was high in the favor of the Greenbriar King! I reminded you about the ax just as a precaution."

"I'll not take a swing at your precious trees, never fear," the dwarf rasped. Beneath his breath he added, " 'Twould ruin the blade, anyway."

"Come then, and be at peace in Yoriand," Imris invited formally. His horse shook her mane and neighed, and Ariadne heard an answering whinny from somewhere in the trees below. The Yoriandir's horse suddenly leaped forward, frisky as a colt despite the long night behind them and the distance they had come from the tavern before that. Imris's laugh floated back to her, and Ariadne found herself smiling, and clapping her heels to her own horse's sides to follow him.

The grass under their hooves was lush and still wet with dew, though by now the sun was high, just past midday. There was a most delicious scent on the air, and she found herself thinking of bursting April mornings when Sten and Gil went out to do the plowing, and she and her sisters spread the bedding over the briar bushes to air in the spring sun.

But the landscape was pure autumn.

The maples, birches, and chestnuts spreading over her head as she rode down into the forest glowed with color. The turf beneath the boughs was as freshly green as if it had poked through the rich earth just that morning. Many of the trees were the largest of their kinds that she had ever seen. On the hill above her home there were huge hickories, for which the place had been named, but she knew that they would have looked tiny compared to these. Each tree stood in its own place, and there was none of the undergrowth around them one would have expected. She thought that the Yoriandirkin must be extraordinary foresters to manage with such care even the rise of saplings along a trail. But if they didn't clear the wood by cutting it, how *did* they do it?

Imris led the way to an open pocket of meadow in the midst of the woods, and as Ariadne came up behind him, she had her first glimpse of the Yoriandirkin.

There were ten of them and her first impression was that they all looked rather a lot like Imris: flaxen hair, with maybe a shade or two difference—a little redder— to some of them, the green skin and eyes, of course. Most wore tunics like his, of some woolly stuff left its natural color, and over this a cloak. These were of different hues: saffron, rust, scarlet, violet, and a beautiful forget-me-not blue that would look well on her youngest sister, Iris.

While Imris was greeted with joyful welcome, she studied them more closely and decided that they were not as like as had first seemed. One was considerably shorter than the others, another much stouter—not Kursh's size, but still—a third wore a neck torque and cloak clasp of finely chased silver. Imris alighted to bow before this one, and she guessed that it must be their king. His hair was silvery too, she noticed.

The older Yoriandir smiled down. "Welcome home, Imris. You have been gone but a short time, and still we have missed you. The music is never quite the same without you here."

"I shall play for you this evening, Eldest." Imris straightened. "May I present my guests?"

"I can guess who most of them are, but you must name them formally for me."

And so Imris introduced each of the company. Only twice did the Eldest's gaze linger: once when Alphonse was named and bowed, clutching his staff, and the other time when Imris presented "the Princess Ariadne, daughter of the Greenbriar King."

When the boy recovered from his bow—trying to keep from wincing at the sudden burst of pain in his head—the Eldest said to him, "Be welcome here in Master Llodin's name, Alphonse. He was our dear friend, and such shall you be also; the forest of Yoriand shall never be closed to you."

The youth stood straight. "I should like very much to sojourn here whenever I am able, lord. Thank you."

The dark green eyes swung to Ariadne. "We knew your father well, lady Ariadne. He lived peacefully with the earth. We were sorrowed at his passing, and thus your presence here is an unexpected joy."

She was aware that behind her, the captain and all the others had dismounted and were bowing before the Yoriandir king. Ariadne slid from her mare's back. "Thank ye, m'lord. I'm afraid I've brought trouble to ye and to your people, though."

The Eldest smiled serenely. "King Dendron has come to our border more than once, child. Do not fear him while you abide with us."

Imris said, "Rasullis is with him."

At that, the king looked surprised and, Ariadne thought, even a little fearful. "Is he indeed?" he murmured. To Imris he sent, 'We heard Tabindrinath's cry and feared you lost until we saw your party coming up the mountains from Ilyria.'

The harper responded in the same way. 'The Fallen has a corps of assassins now, Eldest. They have sought us since we left Swiftwater Shallows. One of them set his hawk on Tabindrinath so that she could not return to warn us that they were close." His eyes flicked to the girl and back to the older tree-tender. 'Even more than the princess or the rest of our company, Rasullis wants Llodin's staff for that which it holds within its spell.'

'The Crystal of Healing, you mean.' The Eldest nodded, 'Yes, when he came through here last, Master Llodin spoke of it to me. He had had a dream, he said, that told him the time was at hand for it to be restored from the Meld's protection to its rightful owner.' His eyes too regarded the girl as she accepted a fine silver goblet of some clear liquid from the smiling Yoriandirkin of the king's party. 'He would not say exactly what he meant. . . . Has this woman a son, perhaps, who could be king?'

'Llodin told us the Greenbriar Lordling may also be alive, though how this had come to pass, or where the grown man might now be, Master Wizard did not have a chance to say.' Imris's brow wrinkled. 'Much has happened since I left home, Eldest.'

'I see the heaviness of your spirit, sister's-son. We will hear the details of your journey later. For now, be at peace. You are home. And even Rasullis the Fallen dare not work his black will against us. He must remember the lore he learned on the Wizards' Isle: "When Yoriand falls, comes the world unhinged."' The Eldest smiled down at his nephew. 'Now let me speak to our guests, who surely must be wondering by now what you and I are sending to each other.'

Imris bowed and moved back.

The Eldest made a quick, graceful move, and suddenly he was off his horse and standing before Ariadne. "You must forgive me, lady. We have been remiss in hospitality. You are all weary and hungry, and I have kept you waiting."

Ariadne had drained her cup—it had contained sparkling, curiously bubbly water from some sweet brook, she thought—and now the stout Yoriandir appeared at her side to receive the goblet. She told the Eldest, "We are much beholden for your kind welcome, m'lord. 'Tis a great relief to be safe at last."

She saw a glance pass between the king and Imris, but the Eldest looked back to her with a smile. "If you can bear to mount and ride again but a short distance, we will offer you a proper welcome at Aspenglade. Our hall is there, and places are prepared for you." At his sign, the taller Yoriandir came forward and helped her into the saddle once more. She followed the Eldest as he led them further into the woods along the broad path. Turning her head to study the other treetenders as they escorted the Watchmen and chanted a welcome, she was astonished to notice that the trail they followed closed behind them. It was not exactly that the path vanished or that the trees moved, but when she looked back, she suddenly could not discern a way through the stately forest. It all seemed equally dense, as though no one had ever passed that way before.

Ariadne blinked and looked again. She was beginning to suspect that the Yoriandir drink might be stronger than water, but she wasn't dizzy, and she didn't think she was seeing things. Her mystified expression caught Imris's attention, and he guided his horse beside hers. "Now you see why outsiders do not venture into our land," he told her with an amused glance back at the trees.

"I wasn't sure for a moment there. It made me wonder what was in that goblet."

He laughed. "You have tasted the water from a wondrous spring we call Nose-Tickler. The drink we name Sileaught. Among my people the saying is that it smells like the forest, tastes like dew, and makes you merry, like a summer morning. One may drink as much as wanted, and suffer no ill effects such as your wine and beer produce. You will have the chance to hear the legend of Nose-Tickler if we have time."

"What do you mean?"

His fir eyes regarded her. "Our path lies still across the water to the Wizards' Isle, my lady. After we rest tonight, a boat will bear us thither in the morning."

Ariadne looked up at the trees. "I could almost forget that, here." The Sileaught had sharpened her sight in some way. Colors were brighter, and each leaf stood out in relief. Hearing too had grown more powerful, and she became aware of a vast twittering near and far. "Imris, be that the sound of birds?"

"Yes, my lady."

She caught a shadow on his face. "What's wrong?"

His head was tilted, listening. "They tell of the king's army behind us. The little sisters are upset."

"The little sisters?"

"The birds."

The princess bowed her head. "Oh." Like Tabindrinath.

At her tone, Imris shook off his own mood. "Wait till sundown," he told her. "You shall hear all of them singing then. What a great fest that is!"

The influence of the Sileaught made it impossible for her to stay sad. She felt the cloud lift from her mind, and she drew a deep breath of the tangy air. The breeze was threaded with a rich smell that made her think of honey-dipped nutmeats, piping hot, and tall mugs of mulled cider. She tossed back her hair and lifted her face to the sun.

They wound down the mountainside, the turf thick and springy under the horses' hooves. The sharp incense of pine blew strongly down from the ridge behind them. Apples hung juicy red and green in the boughs, and there were nut trees ripening in the warm sun: she saw acorn and chestnut, beech and hickory. Wild pear and cherry trees heavy with fruit stood apart in the meadows.

They passed into a clearing where birds she had never seen before took sudden flight and circled into the trees. Their white plumage showed bright against the tangerine foliage, and the brilliant emerald of their sweeping tails was glossy in the sunshine. Ariadne caught her breath. Imris told her, "These we name Binoyr, lady. We believe that something of our land's magic lies in them, for they exist nowhere else in the world. It was said by our sages an age of the world ago that the Binoyr are the Yoriandir spirit—if ever something should happen to them, doom would come to us, though none can tell what that doom would be." As he spoke, the party walked their horses through the meadow, and the Binoyr hidden in the trees began to sing in a curiously bell-like warble, a lovely fluting tone. One of the birds flew across to perch on the girl's shoulder, and another swooped to her hand when she instinctively raised it. The Yoriandirkin of the Eldest's escort turned on their mounts to stare, and next to her, Imris's eyes were wide. "They have never accepted a guest so!" he gasped. "How did you call them?"

"I didn't call them. At least, I don't think I did," she replied in confusion. Apparently she had done something to infringe on the hospitality of the green-skinned folk. She looked to the Eldest. "I'm sorry, m'lord."

He alone of the Yoriandirkin was smiling, and now he guided his horse back to her. "There is naught to be sorry for, lady. The Binoyr have chosen you." His green eyes were clear and solemn as he looked down at her. "And now you have the right to claim anything of us that you wish. In whatsoever way we can aid you, we are bound to do so, as long as earth shall last."

Troubled, she frowned at the birds. "I wouldn't think of asking for anything more than ye've already given, sir: welcome and safety."

The Eldest bowed his head and closed his eyes. When he opened them to look down at her again, his gaze was gentle. "So it shall be," he said quietly, and there was such sadness in his voice that Ariadne was brushed by a grief she could not name. Seeing her distress, the king reached to grasp her hand. "It is well, Lady of the Greenbriar. Come now to our hall. You are looked for and it will be a merry meeting. You shall behold Yoriand's glory. We shall drink deep of Nose-Tickler and make such a feast as ne'er will be forgot." He raised his voice and called, "To the glade!"

Flanked by the Eldest and by Imris, Ariadne found her horse trotting eagerly down the path with one of the Binoyr on her shoulder and the other balancing lightly on her fist. The escort had fallen in behind them and she could hear Peewit jesting back and forth with them.

They were passing fields planted with regularly spaced saplings, sturdy and well branched. Their leaves were bright green with a reverse of silver. Imris was craning from his horse's back, and the Eldest laughed. "Does the work seem good to you?"

"They look well enough—perhaps a trifle dry," Imris responded.

The king informed her, "Though he would be too modest to say so, lady, most of the garden you see here is Imris's responsibility. When he is here at home, he holds the title Master of the Leafkins. There is no more important work among us than caring for the young ones, for in them is the future of Yoriand." Ariadne glanced doubtfully at the rows of trees. When she looked back at him, she had the uncomfortable feeling that he had read her mind. "Have they lost so much lore in the outside world?" the Eldest asked softly. "Can it be that folk no longer remember that hallowed Nilarion, the Earthgate, holds the earth together with her roots, and keeps the heavens from crashing down?"

"Oh, I have heard that"—she was about to blurt "story," but collected her wits in time—"that lore."

He swept a gesture over the fields. "These are Nilarion's children."

While she was still pondering this, the path before them led over a slight rise and before them spread an open meadow bordered with aspens, shining gold in the sun. But she had no eyes for the aspens or even for the host of Yoriandirkin—flaxen-haired women and children too—who waited in the glade and sent up a glad shout at their approach. Irresistibly, her eye was drawn to the overspreading branches of a mammoth tree that dominated the whole scene. It reached from one side of Aspenglade to the other, and its crown of red leaves and clusters of white berries were a striking contrast to the gnarled trunk, which was bare of bark in some places and showed long cracks running up its length.

The Eldest said at her shoulder, "And that is Nilarion."

"Ye can't mean it!" she whispered. "I mean, if I heard the stories aright, Nilarion was there when the world was new!"

"Yes. Just so. Whenever Nilarion fails, a new seedling is set in her place. But not all the seedlings live to mature. That is why it is so important to foster the leafkins carefully: we must find the one among them that will be Nilarion when it is time."

The Eldest held up a hand to the crowd, which had settled to a murmur at the sight of Ariadne with the white and emerald birds gracefully preening on her hand and shoulder. "We return with the guests. The Chosen of the Binoyr is daughter to the Greenbriar King, whom all of you will remember." Before Ariadne had time to wonder how the children could possibly remember the old king, the Eldest went on, "These are her companions, the First Watch of old. The boy with the staff comes in Llodin's name. They have come out of great danger and go in the morning to the Wizards' Isle." Then he added a sent thought: 'Bastard Greenbriar and renegade wizard pursue them, and even now are on Rimwall.' He saw the fearful glances. 'Rasullis the Fallen may try to force his way into our land. Go you, Yedo, and take some others with you. Keep watch on the Outlanders and aid the grandfathers, if it is necessary.' One of the taller Yoriandirkin bowed, gathered his gray cloak over his arm, and nodded to several others.

The Eldest himself handed the princess down from her saddle, while the Binoyr swooped into Nilarion's lower branches. As their tired horses were led away, the Yoriandirkin showed the Watchmen to woven cushions strewn on the soft grass. Ewers of steaming water were brought, and basins, and the guests refreshed themselves, washing the grime of travel from their hands and faces. (Except that Tristan only waved away his smiling server and hoped the Eldest would not think offense was intended.)

Then at a signal from the king, the feasting began. Baskets of fruit and nuts, fine loaves, honey cakes there were, and steaming broths of savory vegetables and roots seasoned with sea salt and herbs. Again and again the guests' silver cups were filled with clear Sileaught, and when the singing and harping began, even Kursh bellowed the refrains.

As the dusk approached, the birds of Yoriand began their evening chorus, as Imris had promised. The Yoriandirkin and their guests fell silent, entranced, and from every side each species contributed its own call or trill, all making a harmony at once entirely natural, and yet as intricately patterned as the march of the seasons, or the bursting to bloom of a single buttercup.

The first stars were piercingly bright in the violet evening sky when the chorus finally ended with the clear sliding note of a nightingale. The tree-tenders and the princess's company stretched themselves as though waking from a pleasant sleep. "Now you are truly of Yoriand," the Eldest told them, looking around at each as they reclined or sat at ease upon Aspenglade's broad lawn. "Once one has heard evensong, he—or she!—cannot choose but return someday."

The captain answered formally for all of them. "It is a rare privilege, indeed, lord, and we hold it as a precious gift. If there is ever aught we can do to aid the Yoriandirkin, the Watch stands ready."

The starlight caught the silver torque about the Eldest's throat as he tilted his head back, regarding Nilarion pensively. Seated at his right hand, Ariadne had the feeling he was "sending" to the great tree arching over the meadow. After a moment, he brought his eyes down to them. "Thank you, Captain. The ancient ties between the men of Greenbriar and we Yoriandirkin shall be renewed." A slim youth refilled their cups, and they drank the pledge while others of the tree-tenders went about with what seemed to be covered pans. Ariadne thought there was more food to be served and didn't know how she could manage one more bite, but she soon realized that the pans were some sort of devices.

A maiden of about her own age knelt to set one of the lidded pans on a circular stone slab at the king's feet. She carried it as though it were heavy, and when she placed it carefully, Ariadne could feel heat radiating from the black metallic container. The girl took a hook from her girdle and deftly slipped it into a ring in the lid, pulling it open. At once bright light, like the glow of a lantern, lit up the area. Ariadne squeezed her eyes shut for a moment and then opened them to stare at the brazier. As nearly as she could tell through the bright heat, the pan seemed to be filled with a quantity of rocks that glowed red-hot. A small wind had come up and it sent a chilly draft across her neck. She stretched her hands to the fire-pan. "I have never seen rocks that burn," she remarked.

"We call it friava," Imris told her. "As you see, it serves us well for both light and heat."

Despite her interest, she found her eyelids suddenly very heavy. The fatigue she had been holding off by force of will through last night and all this long day threatened to overwhelm her, no doubt helped along by the Sileaught. The Eldest noticed her sudden silence. "Sleeping places have been prepared for you all. I know you are weary. Let us say good night now." He motioned to two women to accompany the princess.

They led her to the ranks of aspens which surrounded the glade, and there she found a pavilion of brightly dyed cloth billowing in the breeze. Inside, the rugs were of thick fleece and the blankets sweet-smelling and soft.

*   *   *

Upon the Rimwall, Rasullis the Fallen sat immobile on his horse, which had its ears pricked at some noise down in Yoriand. To the wizard's right King Dendron curbed his horse roughly as the stallion reached to crop some grass. "Do you plan to sit here all night? Or can we mere mortals make camp and have a piss and some sleep?" He spoke in a low tone, and whether the Home Guard who were strung out left and right of them along the ridge heard he did not really care. He was still seething from the ignominy of losing his hostage and the foolish, flat-footed way his troops had reacted. They had left the commander of the guards dead on the cobbles of Ravenholt; he had killed the man with his own hands.

The enchanter turned his head slowly. He had the hood of his white court robe cast about his face, and the king could see nothing of his features. "You can make water any time you wish, my king, and anywhere you want to—as you have often demonstrated in the past." He paused, and could feel anger boiling out of the crooked figure beside him. "As for sleep," he continued, "I think there will not be time."

"Why not? They've obviously gone to rest down there." Dendron gestured with his chin toward the valley. For some time they had watched the glow of campfires, all grouped in the same place far down near the sea, and reckoned that the Yoriandirkin were feasting.

The white hood nodded, and the king could hear satisfaction in Rasullis's voice when he answered, "Yes. They are asleep."

"That's no advantage to us. We can't attack *this* place by night—no more than we can attack it by day. If we go into the enchanted forest, we'll never come out. Don't tell me it's a fairy tale, either. I've sent men to watch the borders before." He stared challengingly at Rasullis. "They've never come back. Not one of them."

"Of course not. Everyone knows the forests protect the Yoriandirkin. Only fools venture to go down there."

One of the Home Guards behind them must have checked his horse suddenly; Dendron was aware of

the animal's surprised trampling. He could guess why.
The last patrol sent here had been handpicked members of the elite unit. "Sometimes brave men may dare
it." He knew that reply would be reported back at the
barracks. The guards were loyal to him and hated
Rasullis, for they correctly perceived him as the single
greatest threat to the king.

The Fallen looked full at him then, and his shoulders shook silently. Dendron saw that he was laughing, but when the wizard spoke, nothing of it could be
heard in his voice. "Send your captains down the line,
my king. Order them to have their men ready. It is
possible that some of the Yoriandirkin will try to escape this way, though I doubt it." The breeze blowing
up the valley from the sea brought the tang of salt to
them, even here on the uplands, and Rasullis pushed
back his hood. "The sea would be safest for the tree-
tenders, but they will not take that way out." He had
been thinking aloud, and Dendron could follow nothing of what was in his mind.

"What are you planning?"

The Fallen twisted the sapphire ring on his finger,
looking out across the dark stretch of black water
beyond the Yoriand shore. In the night, with no moon,
they could not see the Wizards' Isle. "You want the
tree-tenders and those they harbor punished, do you
not?"

Dendron felt a clammy touch on the back of his
neck. "I want my sword back. I want the bard and his
fellows. By the Wolf, I'll not be made mock of in my
own castle by such low-life scum!" He was aware that
his gauntleted hand had bunched into a fist and his
voice had risen. Hang it, he thought. Let the men hear
my orders. "But the girl, my niece, you will not harm."

The wizard raised one dark eyebrow. "Of course
not, my king. She continues to be under your royal
protection. We do but try to claim her back." I won't
play the villain for your purposes, my dear Dendron. I
too have my reasons for wanting Ariadne unhurt.

The king shifted in his saddle. "How do you propose to get into Yoriand?"

"I don't. At least, not while it is still Yoriand. But

what do you think would happen if the forest somehow lost its power?"

Dendron shrugged. "I can't see how that would ever happen. The valley's been here since the beginning—at least if you believe the bards' tales."

"The tales are true lore. In fact, Yoriand *was* the beginning, if one wants to be precise." He did not explain, and Dendron assumed this was some wizards' learning, for which he cared not a whit. It all sounded like claptrap to him. But the power Rasullis wielded was real enough, and the king wished he'd get on with whatever he was going to do.

"You grow impatient, my king. But it is no small thing to destroy such a myth as that of the tree-tenders and old Nilarion."

"Spare me the book learning. Get the rebels out of there!"

There was a stretched silence. The evening breeze snapped the pennon over the king's head and the Flaming Sword glowed with some trick of the starlight. The Fallen said in a distant, cold voice, "Very well."

In Aspenglade the pavilions were quiet, the sleepers within dreaming of sunlight on crimson leaves. The Watchmen were all quartered in a large tent near the Eldest's own, and from this one Kursh's snores rose, but disturbed no one.

Suddenly a wild wind tossed Nilarion's boughs and the tent ropes creaked in the darkness. A few frighted sleepers rose on an elbow to listen. Over the rustle of the forest, a harsh scream rent the night and Alphonse, clutching Llodin's staff, stumbled out of the pavilion. "Fire!" he shrieked in a hollow voice overlaiden with Power. "Fire on Rimwall! Wake, Nilarion's children!"

In the same instant, every one of the Yoriandirkin was wakened by a sent shout from Yedo, who watched with his men while Rimwall exploded with gouts of blue fire: "Wizard's fire is kindled! Rise and help the grandsires!"

7

Ariadne pulled her ragged dress over her shift. Outside the tent she could hear shouting in the Yoriandir tongue, and she was sure that it had been Alphonse's voice that had screeched through her sleep. The two Yoriandir women were gone from their bed places.

Her fingers were clumsy, and she had to force herself to move deliberately. Her heart was pounding and her feet seemed to have turned to ice. She didn't like storms, even when she was safe at home while the wind roared through the thatch. This one seemed ready to blow the entire glade down the hill into the sea, but it sounded as though they needed help out there.

When she finally fought her way past the curtain at the doorway, she stopped short, sheltering her head with her arms. Above her, Nilarion writhed like a living thing in a trap. A blood of red leaves already spread over the grass of the glade and twigs of pearled berries littered pavilions, banquet cushions, and even the friava braziers. While she stared, a branch as thick as a man's calf crashed through the roof of the tent behind her. She jumped and could not master the overwhelming impulse to run.

Strong arms caught her from behind. The captain's voice shouted in her ear, "Not that way, Ariadne! If Nilarion comes down, you'd be under it! Over here!" He tugged her back toward the aspens and she let herself be guided.

In the panic one of the Yoriandir children crashed into her and buried his face in her skirts, shrieking. She scooped him up, and the captain put his arm around both of them as they ducked into the partial protection of the gray tree trunks. While she hugged the child close, Tristan put his fingers to his lips. He gave a loud, two-tone whistle that did not carry far in the wailing wind. Still, from somewhere to the right came an answering signal, and then Peewit came fighting his way through the flying debris with Kursh behind him.

"Where's Alphonse?" the tall man yelled.

The Littleman gestured toward the glade. "He was out there, last time I saw him."

"With the Eldest," Kursh roared. "They're over by the big tree. The boy was shouting something about a fire."

A golden aspen cracked and snapped off behind them, and its crown hung tangled in the tossing branches of the other trees.

"And Fidelis?" Tristan yelled.

"There by the well." The captain peered in the direction Kursh pointed and could just make out the doctor's brown robe bending over someone on the ground.

"Get him," Tristan ordered, and the dwarf ran into the glade. "Have you seen Imris?" he asked the Littleman.

The nearest pavilion sheared and catapulted twigs and Nilarion's berries at them. Peewit threw up an arm to shield his eyes and shook his head.

In the clearing Kursh thrust roughly through a knot of Yoriandir women who were all staring northwestward to Rimwall. He glanced once in that direction and stopped in his tracks, his mouth falling open. He turned and beckoned urgently to Peewit and Tristan. When they did not move quickly enough, again—angrily.

The two ran out, leaving Ariadne and the child rocking together on the grass. When Tristan looked where the dwarf was pointing, he felt sick and he was aware of Peewit choking curses beside him.

Yoriand was burning.

From right to left the horizon was flame. Already the leading edge of the fire was more than halfway down the Rimwall. Even as they watched, immobilized by shock, an orange finger of it, shot with blue, thrust forward pointing at Aspenglade. At them.

The captain came to himself first, and gave Peewit a push toward Fidelis. He raced for the mighty tree at the center of the glade with Kursh following. As they drew closer, they could see Alphonse and the Eldest standing together at Nilarion's very roots. The Yoriandir king had his head pressed against the rough trunk and the wizard-adept grasped his arm. Tristan did not hear until he was almost upon them that Alphonse was speaking. "Come with us, sir, I beg you!"

The Eldest straightened but kept his hand on the wood. "Would you, if you were I?" He looked across at the young wizard. "Of course not." He smiled, and the emptiness in his face sent a shudder down the captain's back. Tristan realized that he was hearing the end of an argument, and it seemed, strangely enough, to have been a debate between equals.

The captain had drawn breath to yell a question when the boy suddenly flung away from the tree, his face contorted and tears streaming down his cheeks as he faced the Rimwall. *"Damn you, Rasullis!"* he shouted, and the Power in his tone rent through the storm's howling. He threw up both arms, clenching the staff in his fists, wild with rage and grief. The runes leaped to life and then, with a charge that knocked the two Watchmen to the ground, a bolt of purest garnet light arched from between his hands over the burning valley to the top of the Rimwall.

For a moment it hung against the smoky black sky, while a roar like the fires of a thousand foundries filled the glade. Then it was answered. From Rimwall a lance of sapphire caught the garnet and beat it back in a snarl of sparks. Alphonse closed his eyes and his arms shook as he grasped the staff. Moment by moment the sapphire gained. When it was halfway to Aspenglade, the boy extinguished his fire and spun around, sweeping the wand in a circle around the glade as if trying to cover the heart of Yoriand with a shield. When he again faced the Rimwall, his shoulders slumped and he brought the staff down to lean upon it like an old man. "Damn you, Rasullis," he whispered. Ash blown by the storm stung his skin.

The Eldest had not moved. "You have done what you could, my friend. Go now."

Tristan and Kursh scrambled to their feet as Peewit came up with Fidelis. Alphonse looked to the Yoriandir king. "I will come back," he vowed, but his voice broke on the words.

The Eldest watched the approaching fire. "Do not," he counseled quietly. "I beg of you."

As the youth turned blindly away, the king stepped from Nilarion's trunk and touched his arm. "Alphonse." When the wizard-adept looked up, the ancient Yoriandir took the silver torque from his own neck. Handing it to the boy, he said, "This is for Imris."

Alphonse nodded shortly, grasped the Eldest's arm for a moment, and then faced Tristan. "Come, Captain. There is a boat." As he broke into a run across the glade, the first sparks singed the aspens, and thick smoke caught in their throats.

The lean man's strides carried him beside the boy. "Where's Imris?"

"The Master of the Leafkins is in the nursery. Where else would he be?"

The situation was too desperate for the soldier to take offense at his tone. "We must get him!"

Alphonse's face was set. "We can try."

They crashed through the aspens, and nearly ran into Ariadne where she stood with a group of the Yoriandir women and children about her. The captain reached to take her arm. "Come, my lady!"

But Ariadne pulled away from him. "We've got to get these people out o' here!"

"There's no time! The fire is almost upon us! A boat awaits!"

"Just one?" Then, as she understood, horror and disgust came into her eyes. "Ye can't be serious!"

"Please, my lady," Peewit pleaded, batting at a glowing ember that had settled on his chestnut cloak.

Alphonse whirled back and grasped her shoulders. They were of the same height and he shook her. "Don't you understand?" he shouted. "They *can't* leave! *They're bound to the trees!*" As she stared at him, his voice lashed out at her. "Why did you *think* they are green!"

Her eyes widened and her breath stopped. Then suddenly she shoved him away, but there was angry acceptance in her face. The wizard-adept put his hand on the head of a little girl and told the Yoriandirkin, "Go into Aspenglade. There is protection, if anywhere." Without waiting to see that they stumbled through the trees, he turned and led the way at a run for the nursery.

Racing behind him, the Watchmen and the princess held their sleeves over their mouths and noses, but still the smoke choked them. They could see fire through the trees now, and Tristan's heart sank within him, for the nursery of the leafkins stood higher up the valley, closer to the Rimwall.

They broke through into the meadow of the Binoyr, where the turf was ablaze in patches and several of the trees were already burning like torches. Ariadne looked for the white and emerald birds, but could see no sign of them.

Once through the meadow they were in the lower part of the nursery and halted, peering through the smoke and shouting for Imris. Three figures materialized out of the night and Tristan recognized two of them as cup-bearers at the feast. "Where is Imris?" he shouted.

The Yoriandir had their arms full of bare-rooted saplings, but they turned and gestured up the field. "The master is there, with the smallest!"

The Watchmen ran past them. But within a hundred feet they stopped, for the wall of the fire rose up above their heads just through the open space ahead. The young saplings around their feet were already curled and brittle from the heat. Kursh cupped his hands around his mouth. "Imris!" he bellowed.

Each of them listened intently, willing a voice to answer. "Imris!" the dwarf roared again.

"Over here!" a hoarse voice called, and they looked to the right and found him emerging from the smoke with a bundled cloak on his back from which tiny green and silver leaves protruded. He was limping and moved so slowly that exhaustion seemed about to overcome him. They ran to him, and the dwarf swung the bundle onto his own back. Fidelis reached him next and the Yoriandir clasped the healer's arms. "Help me save the leafkins," he panted desperately. "So many of them have already died! Who knows whether the next Nilarion was among them?"

"We must get out of here!" the captain shouted above the roaring fire. "The Eldest promised a boat to get us to Covencroft. Come on!"

The Yoriandir shook his head. I cannot leave until the leafkins are safe—it is my duty. Help me!"

"There's no time!" the captain yelled. "We can't dig up all these trees!"

"Pull—just pull them, they come easily," the frantic tree-tender panted.

Tristan grasped his shoulder roughly. "Imris, we must get the princess to safety. *Come.*"

The Yoriandir was silent. Then he shook his head. "I cannot, Tristan." He pushed the gauntleted hand from his shoulder. "You have your duty, though. Go. Quickly." He pointed behind him. "The sea is that way."

Suddenly and with surprising strength he broke away from them and ran up the field toward the fire. He shouted back, "Guard those leafkins well, Kursh!"

"Ye bloody fool!" the dwarf thundered. "Come back here!" He dropped the bundle of trees to the ground and ran after the dim figure of the Yoriandir.

"*Kursh!*" the captain shouted, furious at both of them. As he hung indecisively, torn between his instinct to go after them and his duty to get Ariadne out of danger, there came a great whooshing blast and the tops of all the trees about the nursery burst into flame. The tall man struck Alphonse on the back. "Take her out of here!" Then he raced for the place where the dwarf and the Yoriandir had disappeared into the smoke.

Before the wizard-adept or Fidelis could move to obey, Ariadne glared at them. "Wait! There be time yet!" Neither of the men was willing to abandon the others, so they all turned and faced the fire. Within moments they heard a great shout above the roaring. Ariadne leaped forward toward the sound with them close on her heels.

When she was near enough, the princess saw three

silhouettes against the red maw of the fire. They were spread out and she realized that they were retreating toward her. She stopped and held up a hand to Fidelis and Alphonse. As the three of them looked fearfully around at the encircling flames, the figure of the Yoriandir stopped suddenly and bent to pull a leafkin, while the other two raced on, unheeding. Ariadne had opened her mouth to shout to them that they were leaving Imris behind when the tree directly in back of the tree-tender fell.

She saw Imris look up and then the flaming branches smote him to the earth and covered him from view.

Even as a scream ripped from her throat, Ariadne ran forward. The captain and the dwarf, smoldering themselves, were already stamping their way through the flaming limbs, beating at the fire with their cloaks. She did not think they could reach him, but they did. She saw the dwarf stoop and then he was dragging Imris out. She reached them just as Tristan rolled the tree-tender over, smothering his burning tunic on the dirt of the nursery floor. Kursh reached to feel the pulse in Imris's throat, unmindful of his own burned hands. "He lives."

The captain wrapped his cloak around Imris, and Kursh lifted the Yoriandir easily. Fidelis grabbed Ariadne's hand and they led the way in the direction of the sea. Alphonse veered to where Kursh had left the bundle of leafkins, and bore it toward the one gap at the end of the field where they might be able to get through.

Tristan watched them all go safely and then he moved to save himself. At his feet lay a bare-rooted leafkin, flung out of Imris's hands by his fall. The captain bent swiftly, seized it, and ran after his company.

Imris lay in the bottom of the boat, dying. Fidelis had not had to say so; they could all plainly see for themselves. Despite this, Kursh bent his broad back to the oars, and the Yoriandir craft skimmed through the choppy waves as though racing on a placid lake. From where she sat across from him, Ariadne could see blood dripping down the oars, and she knew that the palms of his burned hands must be stuck to the wood.

His head was sunk on his chest and sweat matted his graying hair, beads running down into his good eye. Impulsively she reached forward and wiped them away. He grunted his thanks, but had not breath for more.

She did not want to look past him, but her eye was drawn irresistibly over the hunched figures of the other Watchmen where they tried to keep Imris from thrashing, past Alphonse, who sat with his head bowed so that she could not see his face, across the churning strait to the burning shore. Yoriand was one vast funeral pyre.

She knew that there should be tears but her eyes, though swollen from the smoke, were dry. The horror she felt was too deep for weeping. If she had sobbed, it would have been more from anger than from grief.

She kept seeing the Eldest, the Yoriandir women spooning steaming broth into their bowls, the little boy at the glade who had been petrified and screaming for his mother. Imris pulling one final leafkin. The Binoyr. Nilarion.

All gone, she thought, or soon will be. All that lovely land. Something is passed from the earth and from me, and I be hollow. A burnt-out tree. "They can't leave," Alphonse had said back there. Neither can I, she thought.

I didn't know what I was askin' of them when I claimed "welcome and safety" as the chosen of the Binoyr. The Eldest knew what was comin', though, I'm sure of it. I knew I saw something in his eyes. And Imris knew—I saw the look that passed between the two of them, but he didn't say anything, either. Damn these people! Why do they throw themselves at death on my account? I can't bear any more deaths, don't they know that? These men here could all ha' been killed at the castle tryin' to get me out. We got out o' that by luck and by darin' and now—

Now I've done this.

Oh, please the Powers, take me home. Just let me go home. I be no royal lady for people to die for. I keep a goat and I can weave a little, that's all. I am Robin. Ariadne, this princess, is *their* dream, not mine, and I can't live with the pain o' their dream any longer. *They* can't live with it. 'Twill kill all o' them if I don't put an end to it.

But this I swear to any Powers that hear me: I will kill Rasullis for this. I will.

By the time they reached the stone pier thrusting from Covencroft's shore, an ironically beautiful day was dawning over the high volcanic shoulder of the island. They were met by grave-faced wizard-healers, who spoke soft words of welcome even as they helped Tristan and Fidelis lift the injured Yoriandir from the boat onto a waiting litter. Four adepts, boys of Alphonse's age or younger, bent to the handles and set off at a trot along the pier and up the road that led to the buildings set within the extinct cone itself, which was open to the sea on this side. The healers hurried with them and Fidelis ran alongside.

When the physicians had gone, two wizards remained on the wharf to greet the Watchmen and the princess. One was bent with age and leaned on his staff, regarding the strangers out of coal-black eyes. His skin was stretched tight over the bones of his face and across his bald head, giving him a curiously youthful appearance. The other was perhaps Tristan's age, and he leaned to steady Ariadne when she stepped up onto the boulders. Both wizards were dressed in elegantly embroidered robes, with surcoats of some shimmering material. The old man's was emerald; the younger's copper. The Serpent twined about the throat of each.

Ariadne heard the younger wizard introduce himself as Hrontin and present the old one as Chiswic. She looked up to find the bent figure staring at her—or so she thought until she realized he was looking at Alphonse.

Hrontin was saying, "You are welcome all. We have looked for you these two weeks past, and feared you lost in Ravenholt."

Weary beyond thought for courtesy, Tristan settled his sword in its harness. "Llodin is dead."

The copper-surcoated wizard said, "We know." He did not explain how, and no one questioned him.

As Kursh painfully grasped the mooring line and

came ashore, the captain added, "This is Princess Ariadne of Ilyria."

Before the words were out of his mouth, she cut across them: "My name is Robin. Where have they taken Imris? I want to be with him."

Hrontin's eyes widened, but he inclined his head courteously and pointed to a large whitewashed building near the road which wound from terrace to terrace. "They have taken him to the house of healing, lady." He beckoned and an adept wearing the gray robe of his class trimmed with copper came forward onto the pier from where he had waited with Chiswic's servant on the shore. When the boy reached them and bowed, Hrontin told him quietly, "The lady will be shown to the healing rooms where they have taken the Yoriandir. You will wait upon her, Nels, and send one of the other second levels to me." The adept bowed again, and gestured the girl to precede him. Her face set in a smudged mask, Ariadne walked off.

Those left on the pier followed her with their eyes until she began to climb the road. Hrontin observed compassionately, "She suffers much. She believes that heinous deed over there"—he did not need to name Yoriand, for the smell of burning reached them even here—"is her fault."

Alphonse was still sitting in the stern of the boat, Llodin's staff held across his knees. "It is not her fault. It is yours." When Hrontin looked down at him with surprise, the youth added, "You must have watched Yoriand burning all night. You certainly saw our Flames—Rasullis's and mine—yet you did nothing." His eyes sparked and his face was flushed beneath his red hair. "In the name of the dead, I demand a reason!"

The copper wizard regarded him sternly. "Until your understanding is schooled to the ways of Earth, Wind, and Fire, I suggest you pass no judgments, Llodin's adept!"

Alphonse leaped to his feet, setting the boat rocking dangerously, but old Chiswic put a hand on Hrontin's arm and stepped to the edge of the pier. His bright eyes, starred like black gems, regarded the youth. Alphonse stared back at him. The old man said in a soft musical voice, "This is not Llodin's adept, Hrontin. This is the Wizard Alphonse. Let us welcome him home to the Meld, for this is his proper place." He leaned on his staff and now his voice took on a gently chiding tone: "Step ashore, young Master Freckles, and think no worse of us than you would of men who kill the thing they love with too much cherishing."

Whether Alphonse understood or not was unclear, but after a moment he stepped over the thwarts of the boat to the land. "The Eldest is gone," he said to Chiswic alone, and his voice sounded all at once very young.

The old wizard nodded slowly. "Yes."

"I tried to save him."

"I know, little one."

"I could not stop Rasullis alone, and none of you would come."

"It was not time." The boy's eyes—watery blue in the morning light—met the old wizard's black ones. "But a time there will be, Freckles, and then the Fallen will be damned in truth."

After a long moment in which they measured each other, Chiswic placed his hand on Alphonse's arm and the pair slowly walked up the dock and onto the road.

If Hrontin smarted at all under the old wizard's rebuke, nothing of it showed. "Will you come to your rest, sirs?" he asked. "Guest chambers have been prepared for you, and a healer stands ready to tend your hands, Master Dwarf. Such poor welcome as Covencroft can give this cursed day I give to each of you."

Kursh said gruffly, "I believe I'd rather go sit by Imris too, if ye don't mind."

"Certainly." The group began to move toward the shore just as there came a deep rumbling in the earth and the stones under their feet shook. Bracing their feet wide apart, they were able to stay standing, though their hearts pounded with fear. When the rumbling had passed and the earth grew stable again, Hrontin looked across the strait to the charred ruin. "So," he murmured. "Already it begins."

"What was it?" Peewit asked, his knees trembling.

The wizard looked down at him. "Nilarion's roots

no longer hold the earth together. The world is beginning to crack apart."

Without another word, he turned and walked away to the road. The Watchmen, looking from smoldering Yoriand to each other, silently followed.

Rasullis poked at a smoking ember with his boot and it broke apart, still glowing. He watched it flare and then meditatively ground it out beneath his heel. His doeskin boots were black with soot and the thought crossed his mind that he would need a new pair made immediately.

A pall of gray smoke hung over the valley, but already it was shirred by the prevailing wind from the sea, which had returned to its normal direction and strength just before sunrise. He had let the spell that had called up the maelstrom lapse then because the destruction was sufficiently complete.

Alone on Rimwall, he had watched the sky lighten the sea to dull pewter while behind and below him on the ridge the king's army slept—or tried. The moans of the soldiers who had been seared the night before by the sudden shaft of garnet made it impossible to drift off for long.

Alone on Rimwall, he had watched the small boat put out from shore and scull for Covencroft. Though he had expected this, he was surprised to find himself angry, and even more shocked by the flicker of fear that shot along his veins.

Cinders crunched behind him, jarring him out of his reverie. He glanced over his shoulder and Nolin made a hand sign. "He does, does he?" the enchanter murmured. "Well, we mustn't keep him waiting, then. Where is he?" The dwarf turned and pointed further down the sea slope to where the Briar-and-Sword fluttered over the gray stallion. With a final scuff of his foot across the ashes, the wizard walked to meet the king.

Only a company of guards had accompanied Dendron and Rasullis into the mess that had been the tree-tenders' valley. There was no point in moving up the whole army; not one survivor had been glimpsed among the blackened stumps. At Dendron's signal, the men had gone harrying down into the valley, eager to find the silver treasure they believed would be, in spite of the fire, strewn about and free for the taking. But the eerie silence of the forbidding ruin had reduced them to the occasional sharp command or nervous obscenity.

Now, as the wizard picked his way across the charred turf that had been the meadow of the Binoyr, the scarlet-surcoated troops of the king avoided his glance and busied themselves hunting for any small objects they might have missed in their first hasty search. The Fallen knew they stopped to stare after him when he had passed. He had left his white robe up on the ridge, not wanting to ruin it with ash, and his square-necked blue tunic contrasted sharply with the colorless landscape.

The new commander of the guards, sitting watchfully on his horse to the king's right hand, saw the enchanter approaching and inclined his head to Dendron, saying something brief. The king pulled his own mount around and stared coldly and without speaking until Rasullis stopped a few feet away to pick up something which he examined then cast away. "Well, wizard."

"Well, my king?"

Red suffused Dendron's face. "Damn you, don't mock me! Where are they?"

"On the island."

The king's eyes, bloodshot with anger, narrowed. "You let them escape."

"I did not 'let them escape'; I simply could do nothing to prevent it when they did. There is a difference. Once in the strait, they were protected by all the Warding of the Meld." He shrugged. "I warned you that this might happen, you will recall."

"You said you could get them out of this damned forest!"

"And so I did." The wizard smiled slightly.

"Sending them pelting to the one place we can't possibly get at them!" the king roared, and his horse half reared, curvetting nervously. He pulled the animal around roughly and spat, "If that's your idea of action, spare me! For all the good your bloody magic did, we could all have stayed in Ravenholt, biting our nails and nursing our ass-boils!"

"So that's what's bothering you."

Dendron went purple and clapped a hand to his second-best sword. The commander spurred his horse forward, but Nolin was already beside the exchanter, the long burnished throwing knife ready. Blue fire glowed at the tips of Rasullis's fingers, though he kept his hands at his sides. He said flatly, "Stop."

The Bastard King mastered himself first, and grasped at the commander's sword arm. "Put up," he said harshly.

The man held Rasullis's gaze. "I am sorry, sire, I will not. Not until the dwarf throws down the knife and the enchanter puts out his fire." He sat implacably, his naked sword catching the morning sun.

For a long moment, no one moved. The Fallen let the time stretch, taking the man's measure, and when the commander did not show any sign of wavering, he nodded. "This one has better stuff in him than the last, my king. I believe you've blundered onto a worthy man. All right, Nolin, that will do. Return to the clearing back there and fetch my horse." The dwarf thrust his knife into its thigh sheath, bowed, and strode away. Rasullis folded his arms on his chest and looked at the soldier. "You must forgive Nolin, Commander— he does his duty as he sees it, but he is somewhat lacking in wits. As for *my* intentions toward the king, I do assure you that if I had wanted to cause him harm, I could have done so countless times these many years past. I am sure His Majesty realizes this." He left the thought unspoken: And if I wanted to kill him, there is nothing you and your sword could do to prevent me.

The man's eyelids flickered, and Rasullis knew that the threat had found a mark. When the commander spoke, there was pride in his voice, but also wariness. "I have my duty, lord, and I will do it, come what may."

"Of course you will. We expect nothing less. I would suggest that you look to your duty now, and order your men to be ready for hard travel. We will be returning to Ravenholt with all haste, leaving the wounded behind.''

Dendron shot the wizard a quick glance as the soldier frowned and asked, "Is this true, sire? Are these my orders?''

"They are not. At least not until the chief counselor and I have had words.''

Rasullis lifted one shoulder in a shrug. "As you say, my king. Come over here, then; there is something I would have you see.''

Dendron bristled at his tone, but the wizard had already turned his back and was walking toward a belt of tree skeletons. "Wait for me, Commander." Their eyes met. "He is useful, but dangerous, as you have seen. I would like to catch him without that ring someday. I would give a great deal to see that happen. You understand me?" The man nodded once. Dendron clapped his heels to the stallion's sides and trotted after the Fallen.

Amid the splintered black skeletons of the aspens, Rasullis waited for Dendron to catch up with him, and could guess the gist of the king's private speech with the commander. But the paltry threat represented by the Bastard's surly mien caused him no more than a moment's pause. It was the faint trembling under his feet that brought him to a halt. In that moment, he began to suspect that something had gone seriously wrong.

There was nothing of this in the countenance he turned to the king.

Continuing their argument, Dendron stated without preamble, "We'll stay camped up on the ridge, and patrol the shoreline. The rebels have got to leave Covencroft sometime.''

Rasullis was frowning, squinting as he studied the clearing that lay beyond the grove of stumps. "Why?'' he asked absently. "They have reached the only sanctuary there is. Would you ever leave it, if you were they?''

The Bastard snorted and flipped his long cloak over his arm to keep it from catching on the jagged log fells. "What, will they live out the rest of their miserable lives amidst all that mumbling magic?''

"There are worse fates." The Fallen shrugged his shoulders as if suddenly cold, and this seemed to break whatever dark mood held him. He glanced up at the king. "Come, Dendron, there is something you should see."

"Unless it's silver, never mind. The men want to get out of here, and so do I."

Rasullis opened his mouth to reply, but a dull rumbling under the earth quickly built and the ground shook, flaking brittle pieces of char off the tree skeletons. The gray stallion jumped and bucked and tried to get the bit between its teeth, but Dendron had it mastered by the time the swelling ground settled and the noise died away. Ashen-faced, the Bastard flung himself off the horse and stared about wildly. "Beldis's balls!" he swore. "What wakes under the earth?"

The enchanter said quietly, "It is not what wakes, but what dies. The roots cannot live without the crown."

Dendron flung him an openmouthed look of fear, but when the wizard seemed calm, he came to himself and was shamed. He waved back the commander, who was already coming toward them. Wrapping the reins about his fist, he held the stallion while it jibbed and then rapped it sharply. When it rolled its eyes and subsided, trembling, he turned to Rasullis. "Speak plain."

"I told you I had something to show you. This way." Without waiting to let Dendron precede him, the Fallen trod across the warm cinders into the clearing. He stopped and gazed over the scorch to the mighty shaft of astonishing girth that climbed like a broken-nailed black finger toward the pale blue sky. Still smoking, the tree gave off such an aura of doom that Rasullis could not go further.

Beside him, Dendron's ale-heavy breath blew. "Another tree? What of it?"

The enchanter's gaze was fixed. "*The* tree, my king. That is what is left of Nilarion Earth-Pillar."

The Bastard looked unimpressed. "A pretty name. And like the Yoriandirkin to give their worship to a tree. They hadn't juice enough to serve more powerful gods." He turned his head and spat the reek of smoke out of his throat. "Where's their treasure?"

Rasullis's mouth twisted with disgust. "You pox-ridden bung hole, you."

The Barrener king grinned at the venom in his tone. "Gone dainty on me, have you? First you roast the poor green buggers, and then you pretend their old myth is worth some kind of respect. You have a funny way of showing piety, wizard. If I was old ghost tree, there, I'd take offense for it."

"*Shut up,* you fool!"

"Oh, come. You're not afraid? I didn't think there was anything that could give you pause, what with all your fancy tricks to protect you!"

Rasullis pressed his lips together and fought for control of his temper. After a moment he was able to say, "Your ignorance is appalling, do you know that? You stand here on the brink of doom and think to belittle me because I have glimpsed a future that your blackest nightmares could not encompass." His voice held Dendron still, wondering what was coming next. The wizard's eyes went to the tree. "It is well that you serve a god with 'juice.' You will need him, unless I miss my guess."

The Bastard regarded him with bravado. "Why? What do you see in the future, king's enchanter?"

Despite his sternest self-control, the vision came again, shattering the bright summer day into bits of charcoal glowing sapphire and amethyst and garnet. " 'When Yoriand falls, comes the world unhinged,' " he said hoarsely. "The ceiling of earth-cave falls with an echoing crash, smothering with void. Land-floor tilts; men cannot stand, oxen and sheep begin to slide. There is no sun, there is no moon; the earth-candle is blown out by a great wind and the stars burn in the ether for none to see. Then shall be silence forever, and waste beyond reckoning, and never a leaf shall unfurl again." He drew a breath and his eyes began to clear. His voice was nearly normal when he added, "This I have seen, King, and this I tell you: get you back to Ravenholt and make your sacrifices to your cold god, if you think it will do any good. There is a path clear through this doom, but I cannot see its beginning; perhaps other Powers may hold back the end for their own purposes. But right at this moment, we have wreaked the unspeakable, you and I, and the warp threads are singed from the loom." He passed a hand over his face, wiping away beads of perspiration.

Dendron was staring and his hand clasped the amulet at his throat. He had heard the enchanter speak in that voice before, and he recognized Power when he heard it. "I did nothing." His voice stuck in his dry throat. "You. You made the fire."

The wizard exploded. "To try to gain back the princess and whatever chance I had to breed Greenbriar Blood with you, you rotten carcass!"

The Barrener king's hand was on his sword hilt. "What do you mean, 'breed' it? Did you think I would—" He looked at something loathsome. "I may be a knave, but by the Wolf, I don't diddle with my own kin." Suddenly the sword swept out and he dropped the trailing rein to spring at the wizard.

The Fallen flung up his ring hand and the Bastard was knocked backward by a cold blue flash. Rasullis swiftly kicked the sword away and stood over the king, who was shaking his head and now struggled up on one elbow. The enchanter did not have to look to know that the commander of the guards was spurring his horse across the other field. Without even thinking, he pointed at the hoofbeats and heard the horse go down in a crash of snapping aspen skeletons and armor. The animal screamed once and he could hear it thrashing. Of the man, there was no sound, and the wizard knew he was dead beneath the horseflesh.

Dendron was staring up at him, dazzled by sun in his eyes and by the aftermath of the spell. Shimmering in his blue tunic, Rasullis bent over the king and the Serpent tattoo rippled around his throat as he said, "What you think you are, little king, does not concern me. You are a lecher and she is a maid, and there would have been a spell for the two of you to ensure a child. And that child would have been mine." His eyes bored into the Bastard's. "I would have taken him away and raised him as my son. And when I had found the Crystal of Healing, or made one—it cannot be so hard if a Yoriandir smith could do it!—then my

boy would not have grudged me his Blood, and I
would have opened the gates. I, Rasullis the Fallen,
would have been the gatekeeper, to say who should
pass and which way they would go!"

The king shrank back. "You're mad!"

The word seemed to turn the Fallen's fire to ice. He
straightened and wiped a bit of spittle from his lip.
Then he smiled. "That's what my peers in the Meld
said. You, and they, are deceived. I shall prove that to
you all someday." His breathing slowed. "For now,
Dendron Brother-Slayer, I must take pains to protect
you from your own folly: I would not see my only
channel to the Crystal spill his Blood senselessly under
the shadow of an old tree stump." The blue fire lit at
his fingertips and he danced them in front of Dendron's fearful eyes. "So don't force me to defend
myself that way again, all right?" When the king nodded shakily, the enchanter extinguished the flames and
left him to crawl to his feet. He himself cast an appraising glance at Nilarion's black spire and walked
toward it.

Behind him he heard Dendron scramble into his
saddle and jump his horse through the smoking belt of
trees back toward his guards and the safety of the
camp on the ridge. The wizard walked on, letting him
go.

His arm hurt where the bandage had pulled tight
against the arrow wound as he had raised his ring
hand, and he fingered it gently and put it from his
mind. He came to stand at the foot of the cracked and
wizened husk, tilting his head to look upward along
the stubbly column. Some of Nilarion's boughs, twisted
in the tree's last agony, jutted from the trunk to hang
at odd angles, sending thin wraiths of smoke to join in
the pall about the glade. He circled the stump, looking
upward still, and stumbled over a lip of rock. He
reacted quickly, saving himself a fall. Glancing down,
he realized that he had tripped over the rim of a well,
the surface pool of which had boiled almost dry in the
fire. As he stood staring down at the stonework, he
recalled that this must be the famous spring of the
Yoriandir. Well, it was gone now, except for a puddle.

He stepped around it and continued his inspection of the world tree, but he found no sign of life.

He pursed his lips. The breeze must have shifted then, because the smoke from the stump made him wave a hand in front of his eyes. His fingertips brushed the trunk and exposed a glowing patch. Snatching his hand back from the burning place, he cursed and examined the blister that was already rising on his index finger. The enchanter stooped to the puddle and plunged his hand into the tepid water. When the burn had eased somewhat, he angrily flung a handful of spring water at the charred hulk and strode away, shaking his fingers to cool them. Behind him he thought he heard a murmur and he swung around with a chill bunching his shoulders.

For a moment he thought he saw the pale shades of green-skinned men, women, and children standing under the twisted branches. They all pointed at him through the gauzy curtain that separated him from them, and he could hear them chanting. When he pulled his eyes away and then looked back quickly, they were gone.

Rasullis clenched his fist about the comforting weight of his ring, and strode past the aspen spikes. Nolin waited with his horse, and he leaped into the saddle and galloped away over the dangerously broken terrain. The dwarf looked back at the clearing with a frown, but shrugged and made his slow way back up to the camp.

In Aspenglade, a handful of Sileaught trickled down Nilarion's steaming trunk and was consumed by the parched wood.

Thinking of the Binoyr, Ariadne felt the lump rising in her throat again and knew that this time she would not be able to hold back the sob. All that morning and into the afternoon while the Yoriandir sank into a coma, she had watched by his bed with Peewit, Kursh, and the captain. The wizard-healers and Fidelis continually wrung cloths of herb infusions over the open tissues of his back, shoulders, and legs. The hysteria hung just in back of her teeth and she did not dare

speak for fear of going to pieces in front of all of them
and shrieking. When Imris moaned, she jumped to her
feet and ran outside. Peewit called a question, but she
scarcely heard him through the ringing in her ears and
then she was through the colonnaded portico and on
the lawn.

Nels had been waiting on the bench outside the
archway of the sickroom and now he fell in behind her
as she stumbled along half blinded by tears. She did
not know where she was going, and she did not care.
Hearing the adept's footsteps behind her, she whirled
on him furiously. "Leave me alone, can't ye!"

The boy's handsome face betrayed surprise. "Of
course, lady. I meant no intrusion—I thought only to
follow my master's orders."

"Well, you and your master can both go hang! I'll
not be clogged about with a lot of fussin' foolishness!"
Tears spilled over and ran down her face and she
swung away from him to hide them. She was vaguely
aware that she was looking across a flower garden.

"I am truly sorry. My presence obviously offends
you. I will go. If you wish a private place, an Aparting
has been prepared for you yonder." He pointed past
her to one of the small wooden cottages that dotted
the terrace. Each in its own grove of small trees and
flowers, the houses were angled to give the others
privacy. Nels was saying, "It is the one with the blue
delphiniums beneath the window—the one with the
green door." He hesitated and when she made no
response, added, "I took the liberty of laying out
some raiment for you. We had things in the storeroom
and master said they would be suitable. There is also
hot water, lady; you have only to turn the handle." He
assumed that she would know what he was talking
about. "If you need anything, ring the bell and I shall
come." Bowing, he backed away. "Excuse me." He
hastily walked back toward the hospital porch.

Ariadne could see the green door only as a blur, but
her feet carried her along the gravel path and she
began to run unheeding through the perfumed herbs.
As she burst through the rounded opening of the
house they had given her, she caught her foot on the

threshold. She lay where she had fallen on the clay-tiled floor and a black tide of grief swept over her.

When she finally came to, she felt calmer, but empty and cold. She gathered enough will to push herself to a sitting position and dragged a portion of her skirt across her eyes. Smoothing her tangled hair out of her face, she let her gaze travel about the sunwashed interior of the Aparting.

The walls were of some honey-colored wood and the boards had been laid on the diagonal, a style she had never seen, but it seemed to go well with the rounded arch of the door behind her and the round window in the middle of the wall facing her. On her left a tapestry covered the wall, its brilliant hues seeming to glow with some inner light. It was a cunning picture: a thorny vine crowned with blue-green flowers showed bright against a blue sky, and there were strange forked lines woven into the bottom of the scene. She was too tired to guess what these might represent, and let her eyes slide to the two high-backed chairs that stood facing each other on either side of the round window. The seats were carved with graceful, flowing lines and rubbed with oil to a deep chestnut finish. An ornate bronze candlestick stood by the arm of one chair and there was a honeycomb candle ready for lighting. A low table of the same wood was set between the chairs on a thick sea-green rug. On the table were a lidded silver flagon, two goblets, and a hand bell. A fireplace was built into the right-hand wall, and this too was of a style she had never seen, being a conical-shaped affair of mortared stone with a chimney. There was no vent in the roof for the smoke and she could not see how it could be very pleasant to burn a fire in it, but there were logs set ready, so someone must use it. There was a stool drawn close to the fireplace.

Immediately to her right beside the open door, a narrow table was tucked under the front window, and this was covered by a cloth runner in deep crimson. A glazed earthenware pot was centered against the casement and a beautiful bouquet of red sage and delphin-

ium spires fanned outward. She surmised this was
Nels's doing, and she felt tired and ashamed of the
way she had treated him.

There was a door in the fireplace wall at the back,
slightly ajar. Ariadne got to her feet, swung the entrance shut and latched it, and then walked across to
the inner door. Again there was a rounded arch and
she pushed the door open and stepped under it.

This was a bedchamber. Ariadne had never been in
one—at home, she slept in the loft above the one-
room cottage with the rest of the family, and at
Ravenholt she had shared the straw pallets of the
female servants' quarters—but she knew from songs
that great houses had separate rooms for lords and
ladies. The chamber was nearly as big as the room
outside and paneled like it with the same wood. The
floor here was covered with rich workings in blue and
green wools, and a latticed round window was opposite her. Under it stood the bed, with its carved head-
and footboards and coverlet of wool that repeated in
embroidery the motif of the tapestry. A carved and
painted clothes chest stood open beside the bed, and
the same kind of fireplace was to her right, where she
saw that it would join back to back with the one in the
other room. She stepped through the doorway and
froze. On the right-hand wall, something had moved.
She looked that way. Against the wood was hung a
polished silver mirror. These too she had heard of, but
never before seen. Hesitantly she stepped toward it.

She beheld an image whose black-streaked face stared
out of a wild muss of brown hair. Her eyes traveled
down the reflection, and then her gaze dropped to her
dress and she tried to brush away some of the ash and
grime. There were holes where embers had burned
through unnoticed in last night's panic, and as she
brushed at her girdle a red leaf and a speckled feather
that had been caught in the folds drifted to the rug.
She froze, and then stooped to pick them up. The
burning started in her eyes again and she squeezed
them shut as she raised the tokens to her cheek.

After a moment she turned away from the mirror.
There had been a door set to the left of the one she

had come through and now she walked to this and pulled it open. This room was small and the walls were of whitewashed stone, not wood. There was a chair holding some folded cloths in one corner and beside this several pegs had been set into the mortar. She glanced once at the length of drape hanging from one of them, and then the central feature of the room claimed her attention. She had not a clue what it might be, but it looked for all the world like one half of a huge wooden cask set into the floor. There was a swan's head of silver arching over the side, looking back at her. A dye vat? she thought. Why would they have a dye vat here inside? The work was too messy to be done indoors and besides, there was no stain of color in the wood. And what did the swan's head signify? Something Nels had said joggled her memory. "There is hot water . . . you have only to . . . *turn the handle.*" She went to the silver ornament and gently twisted it. A stream of water gushed down through the swan's head into the tub. It *was* hot; she could feel the silver growing warm beneath her startled touch.

"By the Powers!" she said aloud. She shut off the water hastily.

Now that she was close enough to look into the cask, she saw that there was a square cake of what looked like the soap she herself had often made, together with a patch of linen floating in the little puddle that had already collected. "Why, this is big enough to get into! I do believe 'tis a sort of indoor washing pool," she murmured. "Well, they may laugh at me when they find out, but that's what I'm goin' to use it for, anyway. I can wash this thing too, and dry it in front o' one of the fireplaces," she said, glancing down at her dress. "And if Imris . . . if they come to tell me . . . no doubt they'll find me something to wear. Wait. Didn't Nels . . . ?" She swung around to look again at the length of material hanging from the peg near the chair.

Snatching it off the hook, she shook out the material and caught her breath. She was holding a woman's gown the green blue of the summer sea, woven of some stuff so soft it was like the down of an unfledged nestling. The neckline was trimmed with a double thickness, and she saw that it would stand up in a teardrop-shaped collar. The sleeves were long, lightly puffed and tapering to fit at the wrist. The robe was unornamented with stitchery, and she thought that odd until she plucked the shift that had been hanging under it off the peg and found the girdle.

Gleaming in the light of the one high window, the gold tracery was spun as intricately as a spider's web. The wide belt depicted leaves wrought with such like-ness to real briar roses that Ariadne half expected thorns. At intervals a golden rose, its petals etched and folded to look dew-fresh, studded the girdle.

She let out her breath, and only then became aware that she had been holding it. Reaching a tentative finger, she touched the golden thing. After a moment she shut her mouth firmly and hung the turquoise dress back up beside the belt. "Those are clothes for a princess, indeed. If I wear them, I'll be turnin' into the person they want, and I can't let meself do that. I'll never get home that way."

She would bar the outer door and bathe. She would dry her own dress before the fire. She would be Robin.

"I will be Alphonse," the boy called through the open door.

Chiswic pulled a rug over his knees and pointed at the ready logs in the fireplace of his Aparting. "You there," he murmured. "Fire. Light." The split kin-dling flared and the fire sent a welcome billow of warm air out into the room. To the youth who was dressing in the bedchamber, the old wizard said, "You have the right to choose another name, if you wish. Alphonse is not, after all, your real one—it was given to you by the steward when you were orphaned."

"I know. But it's the only one I've ever known. I suppose my other is in the record scrolls somewhere, but I was only young and can't remember it. I'd feel strange now choosing something else."

Chiswic smiled. "As you wish."

Through the open window he could look out on the sea. Before last night, he could have seen the autumn colors of Nilarion's garden across the channel. As the wizard gazed now on the smudge that had been the valley, he was remembering another boy, a lad with blue eyes and raven hair and salt blisters on his lips. That boy had made himself a boat and set out for the Wizards' Isle from his home fishing village days below Yoriand, and he had been blown by a storm out beyond the ledges that rose just above the surface of the sea thirty miles off-shore. By the time the Meld-Mariners had found him and drawn his boat into the cove on the other side of Covencroft, the boy had been half dead of thirst and broiled by the sun. But he had shrugged off the arms that reached to help him ashore. "My name's Llodin," he had said. "I want to be a wizard. And don't give me any fuss about it, because I've been through a lot of rot to get here."

Down the years Chiswic could still hear the shout of laughter that had risen from those who had gone down to the strand to meet him.

"What are you smiling at?"

The old wizard started and looked up to find the new boy standing before him. "I was only remembering another lad very like you."

"Really? Who was it?"

Chiswic smiled. "Llodin."

Alphonse had been tugging at his surcoat to straighten it, but now he grew still. "But . . . you remember him as a boy?"

"Oh, yes." The old enchanter watched the awe grow in the redhead's eyes. "In fact, Llodin was my first adept." He added gently, "Acquaintance with the Three lengthens life, Alphonse. You will understand how when you have time to study the ways of Earth, Wind, and Fire."

The youth swallowed and made his way to the other chair. He fell silent, thinking, and Chiswic studied the way tension tightened his shoulders under the new robe of gray, embroidered with wine red about the square-cut neck. The light purple surcoat shimmered in the waning sunlight slanting in through the window. "I am sorry your own coat is not ready for you. The garnet has not been given for many years, and we did not know that you would appear among us so suddenly. The coat you have on was an old one of Llodin's. I thought it might serve well enough until tomorrow. Yours will be done then."

Alphonse lifted his face. "I don't understand very much of what you're telling me, you know."

The old man waved one bony hand. "Do not worry overmuch. It will come. You haven't even had time to find your own Warding yet. Poor Freckles—your power found you before you were ready for it. Ordinarily it does not happen this way."

The boy sat forward with his elbows on the armrests of the chair. "How *does* it usually happen? And what is my Warding?"

The ancient enchanter picked at the rug on his lap. "A wizard is made over the course of long years of discipline and study, Alphonse. What those studies are is not important now—you have somehow overpassed them. It is arcane lore and dangerous and requires subtle testing of character. If the adept is unworthy, the training can kill him." Chiswic did not say his next thought aloud: And one who should have failed the tests, passed them. But perhaps he was not unworthy then.

He shook his head, and resumed, "After the apprenticeship is served and the candidate has been tested by the Meld-Meet, he is sent into a place of isolation and there he listens for his Warding."

Alphonse made an impatient gesture. "I am trying to understand, but still I don't. Is this Warding some sort of spell, or charm, or what?"

The corners of the old man's mouth turned up. "Oh, no. By the time the adept goes to his Imprinting he knows all the spells he will need. No, the Warding is more a fragment of music, a muted, mysterious song as clear and as piercing as the music of the spheres." The black of his irises had spread and he seemed to hear something far beyond the crackling fire or even the boy's beating heart. "In fact, some say it *is* the very Great Song itself, the symphony of elemental Earth, Wind, and Fire." He closed eyes and when he reopened them, he was back in the small room. "I do not know the truth of that," he said softly, "but I soon will. At any rate, each of us hears some of the Song. Others hear different pieces. Together, we have listened to much, and from this comes the Meld's power: when we unite our minds, each of us can call on the Great Music itself to create, to unlock or bind, to know things as they are, and not as they but seem. Thus we pass our knowledge in an unbroken circle. For this reason is each of us imprinted with the symbol of our Meld." He pointed to the Serpent tattoo about his throat.

He went on, "Our particular shades of power come from one of the Three. You and I and Llodin, and yes, even Rasullis, find our power from Fire. Hrontin is one of those who finds his from Earth, and the Wind wizards ply their great barques upon the face of the sea, staying in touch with us here through the Song." His aged eyes rested on the boy. "You have not yet heard your Warding, have you?"

Dry-mouthed, Alphonse shook his head.

Chiswic looked away, out through the window and across the strait. "Last night when you fought the Fallen, how did you summon your fire?"

Confused, the youth shook his head again. "I—I don't know. I didn't think about it, to tell the truth. I just did it. Well, rather, I didn't even know it was going to happen. I was just so angry at Rasullis that I exploded."

At the word, the old man looked at him sharply. "And you were not burned?"

"By the fire from the staff? No."

Chiswic's face showed nothing. "How did you extinguish it finally?"

"Rasullis sent his fire to meet mine," Alphonse remembered. "I knew my strength was no match for his. When it seemed he might overcome my flame, I . . . just . . . withdrew." He shrugged helplessly.

The old man was looking out the window again. "Was that all? Did you, perhaps, try to protect Aspenglade from the fire?" He did not want to let the boy know how important the question was. If Alphonse could remember nothing of ending the spell, then some outside force was controlling him. Chiswic did not want to think that this appealing youth might be an Abomination, but beneath the rug on his lap his fingers were spread and ready to hurl a bolt that would kill the boy in the blinking of an eye.

The brick-red brows drew down in a frown. "Yes, I did. How did you know? It did no good, as you can tell." He nodded at the view that lay beyond the window.

"Tell me about it," Chiswic suggested casually.

Memory assailed Alphonse. "Already the fires were racing toward us. It came clearly to me that the Yoriandirkin could not leave. That they would . . . suffer the same fate as the trees. And Rasullis *knew* that. He didn't care, he took no thought for them at all." The youth went quiet, listening to the screams.

Watching him, the ancient wizard heard them too, and thought, Oh, yes, boy. The Fallen thought long and hard. That is what makes his evil worse than plain ignorance. He prodded, "And then?"

"I begged the Eldest to flee with us, but of course he would not leave Nilarion. And when I saw, when I knew . . . that they would all burn to death, I tried to kill Rasullis. I couldn't. So I flung what remained of my . . . power . . . about Aspenglade and I thought, or willed, to protect them." His voice was strained and Chiswic saw the telltale pounding of the pulse in his temple which meant that the boy was feeling the aftermath of Power; he had not yet learned how to make it come without rending his flesh. If an outside force had been controlling him, he would not have experienced any aftereffect. The old wizard sighed and relaxed his hand beneath the rug.

Alphonse was saying, "Now Nilarion is burned and Rasullis has won."

"No. He has not won, despite the loss of Yoriand. For because of you, the Fallen did not get the two things he wanted, either one of which would have been disastrous for us."

"What do you mean? I'm sorry I'm so slow—I've got a beastly headache and I can't seem to think at all."

"I know. Here." Chiswic leaned from his chair to pour a goblet of liquor from the glass bottle on the table between them. "Drink this. It will ease the pounding." When Alphonse looked into the cup doubtfully, the old man laughed. "Come, it is no vile potion, just some willowbark steeped in tansy tea and honey. I'd wager Master Fidelis has fed it to you before."

Wrinkling his nose, the boy sipped and winced. "Yes, sir. I know the taste."

"Tomorrow I will teach you a way to avoid the headache."

"Good. Now, you were saying something about the two things Rasullis wants?"

Chiswic leaned back in his chair and pointed at the copper lamp hanging in the corner. The wick flared and the oil caught; a yellow glow filled the room. Outside, evening was darkening the shadows across the broad lawns. The old enchanter sent his thought toward Ariadne and knew that she was in the Aparting assigned to her. He lit the honeycomb candle behind her as she knelt at the fireplace and she jumped. He let an amused chuckle float her way. She may have heard it, for she stopped suddenly and cocked her head to one side. Her hair was braided about her head and glowed redly in the firelight and her body was outlined through the flimsy material of her shift. The wizard admired her form as he might have a beautiful statue's—with not a shred of desire, but with a keen appreciation. He withdrew his gaze, and said to Alphonse, "Rasullis wants Ariadne. And he has an obsession for the Crystal hidden in your staff's spell."

"For the what?"

"You didn't know?"

"Know what?"

It was patently obvious that Llodin had not had a chance to instruct his adept. "The reason Master Llodin gave you his staff, Alphonse, is that he sealed into it by means of a powerful spell an object of surpassing importance. You had no inkling of this?"

"No. He just gave it to me, and then—he was killed. I knew it must be important because the others—

the captain, Peewit, Kursh, Imris, even Master Fidelis—
seemed to think that Rasullis was after it."

"He is," the old man confirmed. He gestured to
Llodin's carved wand, which stood with his own by the
door. Alphonse got up and brought it for him. "Watch
now." The wand lit with emerald fire. Eventually the
amethyst web grew under this green, twining the runes.
Suddenly, with a sharp crack, the staff broke in a
shower of emerald and amethyst sparks. A glistening
object was hurled into the air and floated above the
stunned youth's head. Chiswic beckoned it, and the
Crystal settled into his palm. The fires went out and
the enchanter lay the two halves of the staff on the rug
at his feet. He held up the Crystal. "This is what
Rasullis desperately desires."

He held it toward Alphonse, and the boy licked his
lips and reached to take it. Carefully cupping it, he
examined the treasure. The crystal sphere was capped
with gold filigree and glowed with its own light. Within
it, he could see tiny round wizened pellets. "What is
that inside?"

"I do not know. No one does. How they came
there, I *do* know. My master helped a Yoriandir smith
to make the crystal when the world was young. It is
my guess that they may be berries of First Nilarion."

"Why does Rasullis want this?"

Chiswic told him the myth of Ritnym of the Earth's
sorrow-payment to the house of Beod. He finished,
"It has something to do with the Greenbriar Blood;
apparently the Crystal itself knows who its master is at
any given time, and waits for him to act with it."

Alphonse studied the bright thing in his hands. "Does
Rasullis know how to use it?"

"I don't think so. I hope not."

The youth handed the precious Crystal back to
Chiswic. "Why did Master Llodin have it?"

The old enchanter looked down at the object in his
hands. "He had had a dream. He thought the heir
might still be alive." Chiswic seemed remote, walking
in memories, and Alphonse could see that he was
weary. He himself was growling with hunger. The old
wizard suddenly sighed. "It was Llodin's fate, I think,"

he said in a low voice as if to himself. "Still, it goes hard for us to be robbed of his wisdom, especially now." He looked into the boy's eyes. "You will have to take his place. *You* will have to be Rasullis's Unmaker."

Before Alphonse could ask what this meant, a bell rang somewhere with a sweet tinkling and the old man struggled to his feet. "Time for the evening meal. Come and meet your peers, Freckles. Eat hearty. You will need to be prepared for tomorrow's ceremony."

Alphonse fetched him his staff and they went out the door together. Chiswic paused just outside and surveyed the last layered colors of the sunset over Rimwall. He looked up at the boy. "Tomorrow you get your own staff, young wizard—and the Serpent tattoo."

The redhead followed at his elbow as they wended across the broad lawn to the lighted hall further up the hillside and wondered whether he could get the wizards just to mend Master Llodin's staff for him.

8

Beyond the shuttered window and the barred door there was a crunch of gravel and Ariadne heard the captain's voice call, "My lady?"

Crouched before the fire in nothing but her shift, she caught up her damp dress from the tiles where she had laid it to dry. "Yes?" She began to back toward the bedchamber. Ice shot through her veins. "D'ye bring news of Imris?"

"No. There is no change." He hesitated. "My lady, may I come in?"

Now what's to do? she thought. I can't put on this

damned thing while it's still wet. She told him, "Just a moment. I . . . I am not decent."

"I am sorry to have disturbed you." He sounded embarrassed. "It was just that they told me you had been here alone all afternoon, and I thought to see if you were well. I'll go now."

The weary grief in his voice cut through her hard resolve not to play the princess for their dreams. "Wait!" she called. "Don't go! I'll be out in a bit."

She heard him walk a little way down the path and stop.

Running back to the bathing room, she plucked the beautiful turquoise gown off its peg and thought that at least it was dry. And then, with a rueful smile, she was honest with herself and admitted that for just this one time in her life, she wanted to know how it felt to wear a dress like this. Me own clothes will be dry by morning, she thought; this is just for tonight.

When she had drawn on the robe and clasped the golden girdle about her waist, she stepped into the matching slippers she had discovered by the side of the bed. She crossed quickly to the mirror and scarcely recognized herself, but she was not displeased withal.

Tristan regarded the first stars of evening as they shone in the cooling blue sky. Bees droned past him, bound for their hives, and the spicy sachet of the herbs surrounding him blended with the salt tang of the sea air which was blowing in a moist touch up the hillside. He watched gulls wheeling against the western sunset, their cries sounding like people in torment. He closed his eyes and tried not to see flames.

The door opened behind him and a round shaft of light streamed out. "Captain?"

He turned and was brought to stillness. With warm candlelight behind her and the last rays of the sun lighting her face, Ariadne stood framed by the rounded archway. The glowing aqua of her gown draped gracefully to the ground and when she moved slightly the golden twining roses at her waist caught the apricot of the setting sun. "Will ye come in?" she asked.

He came to himself and moved toward her. "Allow me to compliment you, my lady. The dress does you justice." He looked down as she stepped back to let him enter and their eyes met. She blushed, and he went quickly past her.

She wanted to tell him that she was only wearing it because her own was wet, but . . . she did not. "There be wine in the vessel there. Can I pour ye some?"

As she shut the door, he stood near one of the chairs. "No. Thank you." He was aware that his clothing was dirty and torn and he knew he should have taken the baths before coming here.

"Ale, then? I could ring for Nels—I'm sure they must have beer about this place somewhere." She faced him from beyond the other chair.

"No. Not that either." He held up a gauntleted hand. "It's all right; I don't need anything right now, thank you." That wasn't true; his lips were as dry as they'd ever been on a hard march.

Her eyes were on his face. "How is Imris?"

"He lives still, though for how much longer, the wizards will not say." He looked away into the honeycomb candle. "I do not think it can be through the night."

"Is he still . . . does he seem to suffer?"

He shook his head, tall and somber. "They have fed him a potion. It seemed to give him some ease. I think he does not know much now." His voice was strained.

She sank into the chair.

"May I?"

She looked up to find him gesturing at the other chair, and it took her a moment to realize that he was asking her permission to be seated. "Oh, of course," she said, flustered. The thin edge of her resolution pushed its way to the front of her mind. "Don't be treatin' me that way, Captain," she told him quietly. "Please."

"What way, lady?" His brows were drawn down.

"I cannot be your princess. I do not want this."

He sat stiffly. "Surely one cannot choose one's birth," he ventured, uncertain of her mood.

She thought to reason with him. "Captain, look at me. D'ye see a royal lady?"

She knew immediately it was the wrong question.

His hazel eyes intense, he nodded slowly, and then seemed to start in surprise at his own effrontery. "Well, but I only meant to remark on your likeness to your father the king."

A thrill ran through her, for she knew well that wasn't what he'd meant at all. Upon the heels of that thought, though, the flames of Yoriand flickered between them, and she retorted, "So people keep tellin' me. But do ye know, I have no way of knowin' whether or not it be truth? Other than the fact that people are dyin' on my behalf, o' course." She bit her lip and looked quickly down.

When after a long moment he spoke his voice held an unlikely amusement. "If you need more proof, lady, I will tell you that you have a birthmark. For delicacy's sake, I will not say where."

Horrified, she gasped, "Ye were spyin' on me when I was in the bathing vat!" She was on her feet, ready to slap him.

Jumping up, he caught her hands easily and laughed a good, deep laugh. "No, but I was there the night you were born!" And then, as he heard himself say the words, he remembered the twenty years between them and the gulf between their stations, and he was ashamed of the glow he felt as he held her hands entrapped in his own. Guiltily he moved away. "I was one of the official witnesses to attest to your birth," he said apologetically.

Faced with this stunning proof, Ariadne went to the fireplace and stood looking into the crackling blaze. "It is true, then."

"That was indelicate of me, my lady. Your pardon, please."

She found the stool and sat. "How could I be angry with ye for tellin' me the truth?" she asked absently. He came around the chairs and bowed low, holding it. "Don't do that. It makes me nervous," she said softly. "I may learn to be royal, but right now I don't know anything about courtly ways. Give me time to find meself."

After a moment, he dragged one of the chairs beside her and sat down. "My lady—Ariadne—serving

your father was my life. I mean to serve you, if you
will permit it."

She lifted her eyes from the flames. "I'm afraid I'll
kill ye—and the others—the way I have killed Imris
and his people."

"You did not!"

Firmly she owned, "I did. If I had not been in
Yoriand last night, Rasullis would not have been there,
either. I brought the trouble with me, like something
rotten brings the crows."

"My lady, you must not think of it that way. Think
rather that your presence all of a sudden out of nearly
twenty years of darkness brings hope to people who
desperately need it." When she made an impatient
gesture of despair, he rushed on, "Can you know how
bitter it was for us to think that the Bastard and the
Fallen had won utterly, that our pain had been for
naught? That the fairest kingdom in all the earth would
topple to nothing with the mark of their brand upon
it? That all we had ever known of honor, and justice,
and good lay ruined beneath the Sweep?" The passion
in his voice and the shining of his eyes in the flickering
light told her more than his words did. Again the stern
control came down over his emotion and he looked at
her directly. "Now you are found, and with you comes
the hope that the Ilyria we cherished may someday be
redeemed. The Greenbriar Blood is in you, lady, and
if you were to bear a son, he would be the rightful
heir. Unless . . . well, leave that for now. I tell you
that to restore the kingdom to a son of the Blood, I
would lay down my very life before the Great Gate of
the castle and count it a boon to die so."

She had absolutely no doubt he meant what he said.
As they sat with the words hanging between them, a
bell tinkled somewhere, but neither of them paid attention. After some time, she stirred. "Is that why
Rasullis wants me? To bear a son to him?"

Something in her tone made him wonder whether
the wizard had made advances. "I fear so." He did not
mention the Crystal.

"I see."

"You need not fear him now."

In the hearth, a knot of wood popped and spilled an
ember onto the terra-cotta floor. He pushed it back
with the toe of his high boot. Watching, she murmured, "That's true enough. There be no hurt he can
do to me now greater than what he has already done."

Hard-eyed, he too stared into the flames. "There
will be a reckoning, I promise you."

"Small good 'twill do the dead." She sighed. "Ah,
well, we may all join them soon anyway, if what the
Eldest said was true. Now that Nilarion is burned,
how can the earth stand?"

He got out of the chair and went to the wine flagon,
judging that a drink would steady her. "The Yoriandirkin
were a strange and ancient people, and I never understood much of what Imris used to tell me of their
beliefs. But I cannot think that the Powers would set
things thus: that men cannot choose to battle the evil
that befalls them, but instead must wait for the stroke
of doom." He came back and presented the cup to
her, and though she had only rarely tasted wine in the
past, she took it and sipped. He did not drink, but
went instead to the front window and peered through
the crack in the round shutters to reassure himself that
the lamp still burned in the hospital room across the
way.

Despite what he had just said, he was thinking about
what Llodin had said: "for you must know that Tydranth
has long sought a way past the Earthgate and . . .
Rasullis may give it to him." Dread whispered past
him and he steeled himself against it. "Still, I have no
doubt that there was a mighty truth in the story of
Nilarion, though clothed perhaps in fancy. There was
some connection between the tree-tenders and their
trees. The wizards know all of it, perhaps; I do not."
He raised one gloved finger to touch the starred bells
of the blue delphiniums in the pot.

She saw the gesture. It was as if a curtain had been
drawn aside and she saw him clearly in that moment: a
man made stern by the hard loyalty that drove him
and by the dream that, in spite of years of hopeless-
ness, was still alight in his eyes; and yet a man who

could be moved by the beauty of a flower against a
darkened nighttime window.

The knot of her resolution loosened. "I am Robin
. . . but maybe I am his Ariadne too," the small voice
within her whispered. "If the Eldest, and the little
boy—and perhaps even Imris—are not to have died in
vain, then we the living must make Rasullis pay dearly
for his wickedness. And if we are to do that, I must
play my part, for the others will not go on if I do not
give them reason to. My son . . . a king. 'Tis too long
to wait for vengeance."

"Captain?"

When he turned, dark in the candle-lit shadows, she
said, "Tell me now about me father, please."

From his place in an alcove of the dining hall, Chiswic
looked in his mind to Ariadne's Aparting and saw the
tall captain of the Watch talking with her. He saw the
way her eyes never left his face and he heard Tristan's
heart beating. The old man smiled gently and turned
his attention back to the thick stew before him.

Later, as he walked back by the garden path to his
own cottage, he surprised in the furthest part of the
tilled ground a small figure with a lantern. Peewit
turned with a dipperful of water in his hand. "Oh,
good evening, sir," he bade the bent old man.

Chiswic looked from the Littleman to the dipper.
"Do you water our gardens for us, Master Littleman?
'Twill take many trips to the well, I fear," he teased,
for he knew Peewit well. When the Littleman, together with Kursh and Tristan, had come to Covencroft
for respite and healing after the Bastard's army took
the castle, the old man and the First Watchman had
often played at draughts together.

Tonight the Littleman did not smile. "No, sir—only
this one. The rest we planted further up the hill, but
this one was forgot, since it was separate. Tristan
brought it out of the fire, and it was not bundled with
the others." He bent and carefully trickled water about
the sapling's base.

Chiswic peered. "A leafkin, is it?"

"Yes."

"Ah. My mind must have been filled with other matters; I should have thought of this myself. You planted the others, you say?"

"Yes. Near the fountain on the highest terrace. Master Hrontin said it would be a good place. He seemed to think the splashing water would remind them of Nose-Tickler and home." He picked up the bucket and stood regarding the curled leaves. "Most of them look like that. I don't think any will root."

It is our strongest hope, Chiswic thought. And the Yoriandir's only one. His gaze went to the Littleman. "Was it Hrontin who remembered the little trees?"

"Well, no, actually it was my idea. Kursh's too. It just seemed that we had to be doing something to try to help." He switched the pail to the other hand and picked up the lantern. In his muddy, soot-begrimed goldenrod robe he looked forlorn.

"That is twice now that you have saved some part of a very dark day, Peewit. You have a good head on your shoulders."

The Littleman looked up at him, surprised. "What do you mean?"

"You were the one who fitted together the halves of Llodin's staff, were you not?" He laughed as Peewit's mouth dropped open. "Never mind how I know. It was well thought of, and so was this. Go now to your rest. You have done what may be done." He clapped the astonished Littleman on the shoulder and left him staring.

As he walked on, the ancient wizard was fingering the Crystal of Healing in the pocket of his robe. Where the path forked, he did not head for his Aparting after all, but took the loop back to the House of Healing. A sudden thought had come to him about the Yoriandir who lay within the tiny trees. There were lamps in hanging holders in the portico outside the sickroom, and by their light he saw the dwarf sitting on the steps of the garden.

Kursh was holding a small knee harp, and as the wizard came noiselessly across the lawn, he heard the faintest sweep of fingers across the strings. Kursh's head jerked up as he heard the first tap of the enchanter's staff on the stone flags. "Good evening, Master Dwarf. Pray continue. I am just going inside for a bit," the old man told him in a soft voice.

Kursh now held the instrument stiffly. "I have not craft to play this. I wish I did. I had a notion . . . well, that it might ease him to hear music." In the deep shadow Chiswic could not see his face.

After a moment, the old wizard came up the steps and as he passed by, placed a hand on the dwarf's shoulder. "Play it anyway. You may know more than you think."

The one-eyed dwarf did not move for moments after the wizard had gone inside. Then he balanced the harp on his knee, reached for the strings, and the music seemed to come out of the air itself, a melody as light and as sweet as a summer day.

Inside, even as he looked down at the Yoriandir in the bed, Chiswic let a whisper of his own Warding go out to Kursh, and the dwarf played on, enraptured.

Fidelis rose from the stool in the corner and came to stand by him. "There is no change," Chiswic observed.

"None. But that in itself may be a hopeful sign. If there were to be any change, it would probably be for the worse."

The wizard took the Crystal from his pocket and regarded it meditatively. "It doesn't seem so much, does it? A glass, some gold, some round pebbles, or whatever they are. And yet"—he glanced at the healer beside him—"we read in the ancient scrolls that this could once heal an entire army if there was need, or bring health to a whole village afflicted by fever. Though no such use of it was ever recorded, it was made to heal the earth itself."

"Llodin told us as much, the day he was killed."

"I know. And I wonder whether Llodin's vision of the boy was a true one."

"What boy?"

Chiswic's black eyes were fixed on Imris. "The Greenbriar Lordling. The heir, if still he lives, to the power of the Crystal."

Fidelis turned away tiredly and sat down again. "What

would it avail? No one knows how to use the Crystal, anyway."

Chiswic held the sphere up to the oil lamp and rattled the pebbles. Then he shook his head, and left the shining thing on the bedside table. He went to his Aparting to see whether he might be able to hear the Great Song tonight and build from it a net to catch the Yoriandir's spirit as it passed from Earth into the Zones.

But the Music of the Spheres was silent, and in the coldest part of that cold night, Imris died.

It was Kursh who came to tell her.

She had not long been asleep and woke to the light tapping on the green door. She knew before she opened it. There was no other reason someone would have come to rouse her at this hour. One look at the dwarf confirmed her thought. She held around her the embroidered coverlet from her bed. "I'll be right there, Master Dwarf." And then she could not stop her tears, and threw her arms around him.

Against her cheek, his stubbly beard was rough. After a surprised moment, he awkwardly patted her back. "There, now, m'lady, there now. It's best for him this way—he'd only have suffered terrible pain like Tristan has, and Imris worse, for his burns covered more of him."

She stiffened in his arms and for a moment Kursh feared he had sounded careless of the Yoriandir's death. Ariadne pulled away. "What's this ye say about the captain?"

Too late, the dwarf knew that Tristan had not yet told her. He swallowed, but remained silent. When she still stared at him, he said gruffly, "We had better get over there, m'lady. The others wait for you to join in singing him on his way."

The gloves, she thought. He always wears those gloves. She composed her features. "Yes. Yes, of course." She retired to the inner room, and when she came out again a few moments later in the turquoise gown, she took his arm to let him lead her across the dark garden with a gesture as natural as if she had been brought up to royal ways.

The hospital portico was lit and gray-attired adepts lined the steps and the broad porch. They silently made a path for her and bowed her through to the sickroom. Just inside the door, Peewit was standing almost hidden in the crowd of tall wizards. Ariadne did not even pause. With Kursh on one side, she extended a hand to the Littleman, and so with the dwarf, he led her forward. On the far side of the cot, Fidelis and Tristan stood looking down at the body, and Alphonse, with Chiswic behind him, stood at the foot. The captain's haunted eyes came up and she met them for a moment before moving to the bedside. There was a wizard-harper in one corner of the room, and he began to play softly.

Already someone had dressed Imris in a silver robe trimmed with emeralds. His flaxen hair had been combed carefully to hide the singed places, and a silver torque that she recognized as the Eldest's own was about his neck. They had put a harp in his hand, and on his breast rested a single small silver and green leaf. A shimmering white funeral pall covered him from the waist to his toes and draped over the sides of the bed.

His face, faded to the hue of a dried leaf, looked peaceful and gave no hint of the agony he had suffered. "Oh, my friend," she breathed, and a sob caught in her throat. "I never even had the chance to know ye." Her hands came up to cover her face and she was thankful that the singing drowned out the sound of her weeping.

It seemed to her to go on forever, but at last the respects had been paid and the wizards spoke words of condolence. The burial, Hrontin said, would properly take place at dawn: there would be boats to take all of them across the strait with the body, and Imris would lie with the rest of his people. When the members of the Meld retired from the room, only the Watchmen, Alphonse, Chiswic, and she herself remained.

The captain was the first to lean over the bed and grasp the cold hand. His lips moved, but none save the ancient enchanter standing behind the boy heard what he said. When the tall man straightened, he suddenly snapped one arm to his chest in the salute of the First Watch. Peewit, Kursh, and Fidelis did the same. Rigidly, Tristan intoned, "Heart, mind, and spirit his." The others joined in as he completed the Oath, "Hand, eye, and body his. My blood for the Blood, now and forever."

After a respectful silence, the others of the Yoriandir's old companions filed forward to bid him this private farewell before the ceremony in the morning. When it came Ariadne's turn, she kissed the icy forehead and placed a red leaf and a thrush's feather over his heart. She dashed the tears out of her eyes, determined not to make this any harder on the others.

Chiswic caught the captain's arm as the tall man turned to the door. "You will leave after we lay him to rest tomorrow?"

Tristan realized that the old enchanter had read his mind. "Yes. The task is not yet done—we must find out whether the heir lives. Llodin told me to seek a sign at the Guardian above Ravenholt."

"I know. I have seen part of Llodin's vision—and I will give it to Alphonse before you all go—but I doubt that you will find sign of a murder done twenty long years ago."

"The dream showed the Lordling's death?" Peewit asked before the rest of them could.

"No. Forgive me, I did not mean to dash your hopes. I only meant that the boy was left in desperate circumstance, as you can guess, after Melchior and the queen leaped to their deaths to confuse the trail. I do not think he could have survived alone, but if he did, it will be because he made his way to the Guardian. The queen had told him that he would be safe there. That is why Llodin told you to seek the tall rock."

To each of them came a glimpse of a small boy in a gold-trimmed tunic, lost and alone amidst tall pines. Ariadne said quietly, "This is my brother of whom ye speak, yes? The prince who is some five years older than me? Forgive me, but don't ye think he would have been discovered by someone before this if he was alive?"

Chiswic told her gently, "*You* weren't, my dear. It is possible that, like you, he has been hidden somewhere, raised in ignorance of who he is."

" 'Twill be a great shock to him I can tell ye," she said with what could have been, under other circumstances, humor.

The black eyes crinkled. "If he give proof of the Blood he bears, as you do, the kingship will shine from him." She wasn't sure, but she thought it was a compliment, and she glanced guiltily at the body in its silver funeral raiment. Chiswic saw. "Imris would not have gainsaid me, Lady Ariadne. You have the Greenbriar light about you for eyes to see that can. In fact," he murmured, "I could almost think—except that it has never happened that way, not once since the beginning."

"Think what?" There might as well have been only the two of them in the room, though Alphonse seemed to be getting an echo of the old wizard's thought, because his startled glance darted to Ariadne's face as if he had never seen her before.

Chiswic started out of his meditation, and then waved a hand depreciatingly. "An old man's mumbling, my dear. Forgive me. It is late, and I need my sleep." At the door he paused and then turned, leaning on his staff. "On the table there you will find an heirloom of your house, Princess. It belongs to you now to hold in trust for your firstborn son, or for your brother if by chance he lives. I intended to give it to you earlier, but other thoughts crowded it out. Take it from my care and keep it safe. Good night."

When he had gone, summoning an adept to light him across the garden, Ariadne picked up the glassy sphere. "This be the Crystal you told me about, isn't it? The one that is supposed to cure any hurt, no matter how bad?"

The captain replied, "Yes." Standing over the body of their dead friend, he did not need to say, Would that the king had been here when Imris was dying.

Her eyes slid to the corpse, and she saw a faint stain

spreading from under the shoulder nearest her. Body fluid was still leaking from the open tissues.

It broke her. Bringing her arm back, she hurled the Crystal to the slate floor, shrieking, "What *good* is magic when it cannot save the ones we love!" The small sphere shattered and the gold casing skittered across the stone flags. The wrinkled pebbles lay scattered about her feet.

Immobilized by shock, the others could only stare in horror at the fragments sparkling in the lamplight. Ariadne went red with shame and then drained pale. "I'm sorry. That was stupid." She crouched quickly to clean up the shards.

A wave of dizziness swept over her and she threw out a hand to steady herself. She felt a sharp pain and through the blackness narrowing her vision, she could see blood spurting from a deep cut in the palm of her hand. Tristan shouted something and then his arms were about her, while Fidelis grasped her hand and tried to stem the bleeding. Her eyes sought the hazel ones near her own. "I'm cold," she told him, but her ears were ringing so that she could not hear what he said.

Chiswic hurried through the doorway, stumbling in his haste. The old wizard had heard the captain's shout and now beheld the princess half lying in Tristan's arms while the healer crouched at her side applying pressure on a cut that bled copiously. The enchanter saw the gold chasing of the Crystal on the floor and all at once he knew what had happened.

But before he could say a word, Kursh—who was bending over the people on the floor—backed off suddenly. "What the hell is this?"

Chiswic sent a blast of his Warding to summon Hrontin and the others and then caught Peewit's hand as the Littleman stooped. "Don't touch it!"

There on the slate floor amidst the crystal shards, one of the pebbles lay in a tiny puddle of Ariadne's blood. Before their amazed eyes, the husk of it split and a creamy taproot pushed into the liquid. So quickly that they questioned their own sight, the seed swelled and burst, and a brilliant green shoot sprang for the ceiling, twining about the tall poster of the deathbed. Branchlets with five leaves waved from the main stem and thorns armored it.

" 'Tis a rose!" the Littleman breathed.

"Yes." Chiswic smiled. "The Greenbriar. Watch!"

The rambler sported a bud from every branch by the time the doorway was filled with the masters of the Meld and their adepts, all staring in wonder. But suddenly the plant began to fail, the lower leaves beginning to wilt, and the buds shriveling. The ancient enchanter, his eyes on the vine, commanded, "Fidelis, loose your grip on her hand! She must bleed!" When the healer looked at him with shocked disgust, Chiswic struck his staff on the floor and thundered, "The Greenbriar Blood feeds the Rose! Loose her!" A couple of the adepts started into the room, but the old man glared at them and they froze. Meanwhile, Tristan had realized what Chiswic was saying and pushed Fidelis away. Hrontin immediately threw a spell of command at the doctor, locking him crouched off-balance and falling away from the captain.

Freed of the pressure of his hand, the gash in Ariadne's palm bled. Alphonse went quickly to her and bent to help the captain. "Closer to the Rose," he told him.

Sprinkled with her Blood, the Greenbriar revived immediately. Now the buds unfurled, and the watchers gasped, for the velvety petals showed clear robin's-egg blue with a reverse of deepest teal. "The old scrolls were right!" Hrontin exclaimed. "I didn't think they could be!"

"It's just like the mural at the castle!" Peewit cried.

And just an hour too late, the old man thought. And then . . . he thought again. It seemed worth a try. "And if the description was accurate, then the formula for the Greenbriar Elixir will be too. Quick, some of you, get the manuscript and have the other materials ready! Nels, make the next room ready for the princess. A fire, blankets, linen. Off with you!"

Alphonse stooped to Ariadne, who was pale and leaned her head heavily against the captain's chest. He wasn't sure she could hear him, for the emanations of

a trance struck him, but he called, "Courage, lady.
This will soon be over." The fingers of her uninjured
hand moved slightly and he took it for a response.

The blue-green Rose was showing brown-edged and
blown now, a late summer rose. A first petal drifted to
the slate floor and then there was a shower of them. In
their place, rose hips swelled red orange. Chiswic moved
to the base of the rambler expectantly, his black eyes
shining in the lamplight. When the fruits were full, he
reached to snap off the one nearest him, and Alphonse
leaped to his side to do the same further up the vine.
Together they gathered the hips, seven in all, putting
them into the pouch the boy had made of his surcoat.

"What now?" the captain asked from the floor.

"Now," the wizard said with deep satisfaction, "we
distill the Lady of Earth's gift to Beod's line. Carry
her to the room next door, Captain. The healers wait."
He saw the look in the man's eyes. "Fear not! The
trance is broken, and from here on she is no more
than a maid with a cut hand. We of Covencroft can
take care of that!"

Kursh rasped from beyond the funeral bed, "This is
the healing of the Crystal? This rose? How can it be?
The Crystal only works for the heir—everyone knows
that."

"Quite so, Master Dwarf!" Chiswic told him with
deep joy, and then something in Kursh's face caused
him to frown, and he looked around at the rest of
them. He could see awareness dawning in each. Peewit
swung his gaze from Ariadne to the silver-robed
Yoriandir's body and deep thought wrinkled his brow.
The dwarf chewed his short mustache as he stared at
the top of her head over Tristan's shoulder. Fidelis,
released now from Hrontin's spell, straightened slowly
and stood staring down at her. And the captain pressed
her dizzy head under his chin and looked speculatively
at the old wizard. "Quite so," Chiswic repeated, speaking directly to him. "And that is a wonder unlooked
for: this woman, this unknown peasant girl, is the
rightful heir to the Greenbriar throne." Their eyes
were on him. "Gentlemen," he told them, "behold
your queen."

The dwarf sputtered, "but there hasn't ever—" and then he bit off what he had been going to say.

Chiswic nodded. "I know, Master Dwarf. My memory is somewhat longer than yours, I think. But you are quite right: there has never been a woman who wielded the power of the Crystal. To me, the matter already seems clear, but if you require further proof, you shall have it as soon as the Elixir may be concocted." He smiled at all of them and said softly, "You may just want to pop over to the storeroom and fetch some more suitable clothes for Imris. We wouldn't want him to wake up dressed in his funeral robe, would we?"

Book III   The Queen

9

She woke to the swimming lamplight with a throbbing pain in her right hand. When she could focus, she became aware of a dark shape in front of the lamp and she squinted, trying to make the edges of shapes come clear.

"Ah." The soft syllable held satisfaction and relief. He moved then, releasing her uninjured hand, and withdrew to a respectful distance.

"Tris . . ." Her tongue came out to moisten her parched lips, and from the other side of the bed, someone offered a goblet.

"Sip this, my lady," Fidelis urged.

When she had swallowed some of the bitter-tasting medicine, her vision steadied. "What happened?"

The two men's eyes met. The healer set down the cup. "You do not remember?"

"Well, yes, a little." The dark memories were sorting themselves out. "I broke the Crystal, and then I cut my hand. And then . . ."

"Yes?" Fidelis prompted.

She looked thoughtful. "I must have fallen into a faint, I guess." She remembered a ramble rose and Chiswic's eyes.

"You remember nothing else?" the captain prodded.

Her heart was pounding. Something had happened to her—*because* of her—but she did not want to touch the magic because she knew instinctively that it could swallow her whole. With asperity she snapped, "Why, what should I remember?"

Chiswic left the doorway where he had been listening. "Gently, child. Your friends do but try to lead you to knowledge you already have. Is it fair to them to pretend that you do not know what they are talking about?"

She swallowed. "I thought 'twas only a dream."

Kindly he corrected, "No. You *hoped* it was only a dream. But you saw the Greenbriar, Ariadne, and even through the trance that came upon you at the shattering of the Crystal, you could hear what we were saying. Couldn't you?"

Tristan was looking from the woman in the bed to the wizard as though he would have liked to throttle the old man for talking to the queen in such a tone, but he kept silence. Fidelis, who recognized a therapeutic if bitter medicine when he heard it, moved to bring up a stool for the ancient enchanter. Chiswic thanked him with a nod, but his eyes never left Ariadne's face.

Finally she blew a frustrated sigh. "Yes. I heard." Her chin firmed. "Ye called me queen."

Now the wizard smiled. "So I did. You see? Not all dreams are sour when we drag them into the light of day." On the word, he waved at the lamp, and it went out. Without its radiance the small room took on the ordinary dimness of a shuttered room where the sun has not yet come.

The barely surpressed joy in the old man's expression lit some answering emotion in her. "Well," she said. "Now that I am who I am, mayn't I have breakfast? Or do nobles not eat it?"

The captain had been taut with tension and suddenly it went out of him like a released bowstring. He laughed. "Just this once. What would you have?"

"Oh, oaten bread, I think, and goat's milk, and maybe some blackberries if ye have them here on the island," she told the old man.

On a golden plate, child, on a golden plate and a fine glass goblet for you to drink from, Chiswic thought. If she lived to see her kingdom restored, her waiting maids would disdain such simple fare. To the healer, he said, "There's a boy outside. Would you tell him?"

A moment later, as Fidelis's low voice came from the portico, she suddenly sat bolt upright, pushing herself up with both hands but snatching the hurt one back even as she reached for the wizard's sleeve. "By the Powers! I forgot! The potion—Imris—did it . . . ?"

His starred black eyes twinkled. "Why, I thought you could remember very little of all this!"

"Chiswic!" He only grinned, so she implored, "Tristan, *tell me!*"

He was smiling broadly. "If you could manage to walk a bit, my lady . . . ?"

"*It did!* Oh, it did!" She brought the bandaged hand to her mouth, staring over it at the captain and the wizard, who nodded and grinned like foolish puppets at a fair. She flung back the coverlet and leaped off the bed, and would have gone down were it not for Tristan's swift reaction. "Whew! I'm still a little shaky," she apologized as he lifted her back to the bed.

He tucked the quilt around her. "I shall carry you, then." He lifted her easily and lightly bore her past Fidelis and the adepts crowded outside, with Chiswic's stick tapping behind him.

She caught a breath of sweet morning air and then he stepped sideways to navigate the door to the Yoriandir's room. "Imris!" she shouted, and the tall man laughed again and set her carefully into the armchair drawn close to the bed.

The Yoriandir rose up from his own pillows—the bed had been stripped of its funereal accouterments and the coverings were of simple wool—and reached for her hands.

But Ariadne threw her arms about him in a great hug. She babbled something no one caught or bothered to sort out, since it was obvious that the queen was, for the moment, overcome. Tristan stood behind her, arms crossed, enjoying the spectacle, while Alphonse nodded to him and winked. Kursh was on the other side of the bed openly smiling as he stroked his short beard.

She held the Yoriandir at arm's length. "It worked!" she whispered with awe. "I still can't believe it!"

The tree-tender regarded her with reverence. "I owe you my life, my queen. From this day forward, you have only to command me."

Red sprang beneath her cheekbones. "Well, now—it

seems a trifle early to talk o' that, Imris. I believe I'd rather just have a friend, if ye don't mind."

Smilingly, he shook his head, the silver torque glinting about his neck, but he answered, "As you wish, lady."

She saw the glow still in his eyes, however, and lightly countered, "Besides, what talk could there be from you to me of service? I may be Greenbriar, but you are now Eldest of Yoriand."

Pain lined a furrow between the green eyes, and she could have bitten off her tongue as soon as the words were out of her mouth, but he replied steadily enough, "Yes, that is true." To ease her humiliation, he made an attempt to sound as natural as if they had been discussing a treaty. "Very well, then; we shall leave off talk of debts owed, and take this day for its full worth—a honey summer day of bright sun between two times of darkness." Then he added to her alone a sent thought: 'Be comforted. You meant no harm, and I took none. Words of truth cut, but they do not kill. I *am* the Eldest.'

She dropped her eyes and sat back in the chair wearily. Can ye hire someone to speak for ye when you're a queen? she wondered.

At that moment a clattering arose from the portico and Peewit, balancing an enormous silver tray, came in followed by three adepts similarly burdened. "Breakfast! Someone told me there were hungry people hereabouts!"

As the jovial Littleman bowed to her and set the tray on the bed, a bannock slid onto the coverlet. Instinctively both the queen and the Yoriandir grabbed for it lest it should fall to the floor, and Imris caught it. Ariadne had to suppress a gasp, for through the flesh of his hand, she could see the outline of the flat oat cake! Her shocked eyes lifted to his and he saw that she had observed it. He sent, 'Hush, my queen! The wizards know, but I would not spoil this moment for my old comrades; let them think me fully healed, if you will.'

Her lips parted but she only looked to the hand and

back at him quizzically. Even Peewit, pouring milk for her, did not notice.

Imris sent, 'Yoriand is gone, and like the rest of my people, I cannot survive long without Nilarion.'

His gentle eyes held infinite sadness and within her mind, her thoughts shrieked, Have I brought him back to life only to lose him again? Powers, I will not have it so! There must be something, some way!

In her agitation her hand shook and milk splashed onto the quilt. "Blast! I'm sorry, my lady." The Littleman made haste to mop it up.

She answered him absently, and said little more throughout the happy meal, though for appearance's sake, she tried not to let them see anything more than weary faintness in her manner. When Tristan bent to ask if she would like to go back to her own room, she nodded and let him carry her next door. When she had drawn the covers up to her chin, she made him go back, and then she lay for a long time thinking.

The neat stitches the wizard-healer had used in her cut hand throbbed.

As if she had summoned him, Chiswic met her in the garden. Nels bowed and withdrew at the old enchanter's motion and Chiswic walked to where she sat on a smooth wooden bench. "You wanted to see me," he said without waiting for her to speak.

She opened her mouth with a quick shake of her head, but then appeared to reconsider. "Yes. Yes, I did." She regarded a bee buzzing noisily in the trumpet of a flower near her hand. "I need to know what is goin' to happen to Imris."

It must be the Greenbriar Blood in her that saw it, Chiswic thought. "Would you believe me if I told you I don't know? But it is true. I have had no vision concerning this. If you want my guess"—he hesitated, and then finished quietly—"I think that only the leafkins your friends brought with them from Yoriand keep him on this side of the Zones. But as you have seen, lady, the power of the young trees is not enough to hold him fast to Earth. After a time, he will pass from this life again."

By her lack of reaction, he knew she had already come to the same conclusion. "Be there any Elixir left?"

This was unexpected. "A dram, or so. We have put it carefully by. But more will not help him, unless you mean to call him across the Zones again months or years from now."

She lifted her head. "I was not thinkin' of feedin' it to Imris. Can ye get me a boat to go across to Yoriand?"

"Nilarion?"

She nodded.

He said it as gently as possible: "Ariadne, a mere dram will not be enough."

A blaze kindled in the gray eyes. "Well, I can't just let him die again, can I? I've got to try something!"

In her mood, the wizard was almost afraid to tell her. "The Crystal is whole again." She was on her feet so quickly that the flowers nodded in the small wind her robe made. "It apparently mends itself." He held up a hand. "Wait! I do not say that you can use it again, not so soon. Why, you are not yet healed from last night. Besides, it would take an incredible quantity of Elixir to effect any good upon Nilarion. More than we could make without killing you by the bleeding."

"The Heir is supposed to be able to use the Crystal to heal the land. That's what you said." She faced him stubbornly.

"Only at last extremity, lady!"

"This *is* the last extremity! The Yoriandirkin were right, whatever Tristan may say! Nilarion *did* hold the earth together! I know it: I feel it! Can ye tell me that ye don't?"

Leaning on his staff, he regarded the frightened woman. "No," he answered. "I will not say that the lore about Nilarion is wrong. I too have felt the earth tremble, and overhead I fear a very great storm is gathering."

"Then help me do what I can." She grasped his arm and looked into his black eyes. "Can ye calmly watch the end coming closer unless we have done everything we can to stop it?"

He closed his eyes briefly, as if her intense gaze

were too much for him to face. "You are not yet ready for this trial, child. You have not yet grown into the power that will be yours."

"If I don't use me power now, I may not get the chance later." She smiled a little and patted his arm. "Let's get the Crystal. Oh, and Chiswic, don't tell the others, please. He'd only worry." The enchanter thought she probably hadn't even noticed the shift in words.

The old wizard nodded. "The Crystal is on the table in the bedchamber of your Aparting."

"I'll go there, then. Can ye mix up the Elixir there?"

"I shall not be doing the mixing. Alphonse must learn the formula. No, do not forbid this, lady; he will be the one who will be going out into the world with you when your company leaves Covencroft."

"Oh, very well. But he's sure to tell the others."

Chiswic shook his head. "It is a chance we shall have to take. Go now, and I will join you as soon as may be with the other things we will need."

Not long after, Ariadne took the Crystal from the table beneath the silver mirror and stood regarding it with mingled dread and hope. There was a discreet tap at the door and she went out to the other room to let the wizard in.

Alphonse was at his shoulder bearing several packets of twisted parchment, a mortar and pestle, and a bottle.

Chiswic said, "My lady, you will be more comfortable upon the bed, I think. Alphonse, get the rugs up. Let's see if we can avoid a mess."

Later, while Alphonse carefully mixed the Elixir under Chiswic's watchful eye, she regarded the new linen bandage on her wrist.

The trance had struck her with dizziness again as soon as she had dropped the Crystal onto the floor and it had broken, but lying down made it easier when Chiswic nicked open the vein. She had no headache this time, though she felt as if she was floating.

She mentioned this to the old enchanter who sat by her bedside. "I told you you were not ready for the Crystal trance again, lady. You must expect to feel the aftereffect for a little while. Try to drink some brandywine."

"It's ready," Alphonse announced.

She rose on one elbow. "Let's go, then."

Chiswic put out a hand to restrain her. "Rest! Another few hours will hurt nothing. You must eat too, and—" He broke off as the floor beneath his feet lifted. "Hold the flask!" he shouted at the younger wizard.

The earth rumbled and bucked again more strongly. They could hear pottery shattering in the outside room. They waited tensely for the next movement, but there was none.

The old enchanter drew a breath. "Maybe we'd better go now." He closed his eyes for a moment and sent a thought to one of the Meld-Mariners to have a small boat waiting for them. Alphonse handed the Elixir flask to Chiswic and bent to lift Ariadne.

As they went out the front door, Tristan came striding across the garden. "Oh, dear," the queen murmured.

He surveyed the group of three. "I looked for you when the shaking struck, my lady. I was concerned." His sharp eyes had noted the flask and the new bandage. When he spoke it was to Chiswic: "What are you about, Master Wizard? Why is my lady here rather than in the house of healing?"

The enchanter stiffened at his tone, but it was Ariadne who left Alphonse's arm and stepped forward. She looked up at the tall man. "We go to Yoriand, Captain," she stated. "To Nilarion, or what is left of her. There is Elixir and we hope that it will bring back the tree, as it brought back Imris. Master Chiswic doubts, but I am determined to try."

"There was not so much of the potion left after they fed it to Imris."

"That's right. We made more, just now."

He looked furiously at both wizards. "How could you put her through that again! Can't you see she can barely stand!"

The old man gripped his staff but said nothing and Alphonse, though he reddened, gave no ground.

"Captain! The idea was mine and the decision was

mine. I'll not hear sharp words spoken to the wizard on my account. Leave off at once, and if ye would help, come with us to the boat." Even as she spoke, she was aware that she had given her first order as queen. She was appalled.

He inclined his head. "As you will, my queen," he answered stonily and stood aside.

It was too late to call back the words and she did not want to shame him before the wizards, so she sighed and walked ahead.

They took it slowly down the winding path to the cove and by the time they arrived, the Meld ship was moored to a bollard off the pier's end with Peewit, Kursh, Fidelis, and a shaky Imris standing ready in a small knot near the gangway. Hrontin and several of the other wizards waited with them. Other ships were coming in from their anchorages off-shore, and Ariadne realized with a sinking feeling that the whole lot intended to go over to the mainland with her.

"Hail, lady of Ilyria!" Hrontin called as he caught sight of her and hurried forward. "We have heard of your errand to Yoriand. It is a brave thing you do."

She should have known she couldn't keep a secret on the Wizards' Isle. "I don't know about brave, Master Hrontin. I think 'tis more desperate than anything else."

She was uncomfortable with everyone staring at her, and the noonday sun dancing off the wavelets to either side of the boulder-built wharf made her head begin to ache as they walked toward the boat. Tristan seemed to sense this, for when she glanced up at him, she caught the look of exasperation he gave her. He held out his arm and she took it gratefully. She murmured for his ears alone, "Oh, don't be so grouchy. Ye know I have to do this."

"Mm."

"I'm sorry I spoke to ye that way."

"Mm."

It was her turn to look exasperated.

The other Watchmen bowed as she approached. She nodded to them, but said to Imris, "Are ye sure—I mean, it might be easier for you to stay here, y'know."

His fir eyes went to the farther shore and then came back to her. "Could you bear to ride past Wolf's Glen, my queen, and not turn aside to know?"

She reached to press his hand, and then Tristan helped her up the gangway and one of the mariner crew courteously led her to a cushion in the stern where she might sit for the short journey. The others followed, but the Yoriandir headed forward and stationed himself in the bow. Fidelis looked after him for a moment and then down at the queen. "I'll keep him company," he told her quietly, and went up. Kursh stood leaning over the rail, staring into the water and idly flexing his hands, as if thinking of the blisters the last trip had cost him. Thanks to the healing of the wizards, these were nearly gone the next day. When Chiswic, Alphonse, and Hrontin had boarded, the mooring line was cast off and the boat rocked away from the pier.

There were no rowers, and the wind stood against them, blowing still the acrid scent of woodsmoke from across the water, but the great sail lofted and billowed and they sped along as if a spanking breeze stood full at their stern. Ariadne frowned up at the multicolored sail which billowed in the wrong direction and was about to question old Chiswic, who was now sharing half the cushion, until she saw on the raised deck behind them one of the Meld-Mariners standing arms akimbo, looking steadily at the sail.

Alphonse stood at Chiswic's side. He was staring forward. "The Eldest begged me not to return," he remembered aloud.

The old man twisted to look up at him. "He did not reckon on your coming back with succor for Earth Pillar. Set your nerve, my boy."

The redhead cast him a quick look. Tristan, who had heard both the comment and the reply, thought the boy was trembling. The captain's attention went to Ariadne. Her head was bent so that her hair swung forward and hid her face, but she was fingering the bandages with her good hand. She did not look up for the length of the journey.

Finally the sail slacked and the mariners called or-

ders the length of the boat. Tristan reached to help
her to her feet, and now she saw that they stood just
off the Yoriand shore. On her first look inland, she
lost her breath.

She was still staring when the Meld-Mariner came to
her elbow. "The skiff is ready for you, lady."

"What? Oh. Yes." With the captain's steadying hand
under her arm, she walked down the gangway to the
flat-bottomed skiff and they were poled ashore. Imris
had not waited; he had jumped over the side of the
boat and splashed to the rocky beach with Fidelis at
his side, with Kursh close behind. As the Yoriandir set
foot on the soil of his home, a moan passed his lips,
but he made no other outcry and walked forward
steadily enough. The healer hovered at his side, fearing he would collapse, and the dwarf hurried to catch
up with them.

Ariadne drew breath to call to him from the shore
as he crossed what had been the verge of the wood,
but Chiswic counseled, "No, child. Let him go. It is his
own death he sees now, and you cannot temper that
for him, whatever may be the effect of Elixir upon
Nilarion. Soon or late, Imris must face this."

"Can you manage, my lady?" Tristan asked. "Shall
I carry you?"

"No, thank ye, Captain. Only stay near, please."

Uphill through charred stumps and half trees they
made their way, hardly knowing where they were; all
the landmarks were gone, of course. "I think Aspenglade lies more this way," the young wizard said and
led them left. They could see the Yoriandir's azure
cloak ahead, a bright spot of unnatural color in the
wilderness of ash and charcoal.

Alphonse was right. Suddenly above the near skeletons rose the broken spire. Ariadne fixed her eyes
upon it as they came through the double belt of stumps
that marked the aspens surrounding the glade. Imris
had fallen to his knees at the roots of Nilarion and
even across the clearing she could see that his face was
as gray as last year's leaves. Fidelis and Kursh stood
above him helplessly, too stunned to offer comfort.

Alphonse came forward, but Chiswic stopped within

the aspens and watched the young wizard. Hrontin came to the old enchanter's shoulder and said in a low voice, "There is deep illness in the earth, my friend. Deep."

Chiswic did not look at him, instead gazing at the others in the clearing. "Do any of the roots live?"

Hrontin's brows came together. "I don't know. I can't be certain. There seems . . . to be a Warding upon the place," he said in a puzzled voice.

The old wizard threw him a sharp look then. "What kind of Warding?"

Hrontin searched in his mind. "I've never felt it before. It is no song I know."

"But is it a Warding of Earth?"

"Yes. But no. It has other notes as well, I think." Hrontin withdrew into the Warding trance to see whether he could hear it better.

Meanwhile Ariadne, with Tristan at her side, had come to stand in the shadow of the huge trunk. Nilarion still trailed thin plumes of smoke a day and half after the inferno. The queen was aware of the uncanny silence: not a leaf to rustle, not a bird to trill, not a person to laugh.

A quick ripple of water entered her thought and she looked for the source. Nearby, Alphonse had stooped to the well of Nose-Tickler and dabbled his fingers in the pool that lapped at the rim. Imris raised his head at the sound, and rose heavily to his feet. The silver necklace gleamed as he looked down into the reflecting water. Alphonse made way for him, and the Yoriandir slowly bent to touch the surface as one might a fragile flower, or a child's cheek. His voice when he spoke was composed. "My lady, my lords, you are welcome all. Drink of Nose-Tickler, if you will. Taste Sileaught and be merry for a little time at least."

To honor the Eldest, Ariadne led them forward and was the first to bend beside him. She dipped her good hand and got barely a sip, but it was enough for the hospitality pledge. She rose gracefully and moved back into the crowd. When all of them had drunk, Ariadne said to Alphonse, "What now? Where shall we use the Elixir to do the most good?"

"I don't know." He frowned and looked around for Chiswic, but the old enchanter had gone again with Hrontin back to the belt of stumps, and only held up a forbidding hand when the boy was about to call. Alphonse regarded him nervously. "I think he means for me to find a way. But what if I ruin this?"

The queen said. " 'Tis likely ruined already, Alphonse. We might as well do our best and leave it at that. Come now, Master Wizard: how shall we apply the Elixir?"

"Sprinkle some on the trunk, I supposed," he answered doubtfully.

She looked up to Tristan, but he only shrugged. "Go ahead, then. Try it."

So the wizard unstoppered the flask and circled the tree, gently sprinkling drops onto the charred wood. Half the flask was left when he had made the complete round. He stood back.

The drops ran down into the blisters of sap and were gone.

Nothing.

Ariadne's hands had gone cold. "Try sprinkling some on the ground where the roots can get at it."

He did. Again, nothing. The queen began to tremble. "Empty it!" she whispered hoarsely. "Use all of it!"

But now the young wizard paused, taking a thoughtful slow look around. "Eldest," he said quietly to Imris. "Does Nose-Tickler feed Nilarion's roots?"

The Yoriandir nodded. "Everything in Yoriand drinks from—drank from Nose-Tickler."

The youth's amethyst surcoat shimmered as he quickly knelt and tipped the rest of the flask into the pool. He looked up at the spire hopefully.

Nothing.

Long moments later, the Eldest was the first to move. He went to Ariadne and raised her bandaged hand to his lips. Then he walked quickly from Aspenglade and never looked back all the way down to the Meld ship.

*   *   *

The lamp beside the bed flickered, sending wavering shadows about the small chamber. The trip back to
the island had been a silent one, and ignoring Chiswic
and even Tristan, she had come up the path from the
cove alone and locked the door behind her. It was
long past lamp lighting now.

She clung to the edge of the small table and fought
the weakness that came over her in waves. The faintness she had felt this morning after the first trance had
been minor compared to this. No good falling on your
face, she told herself. Get back to bed. Rest.

She knew that she probably just needed to eat; a
bannock, some berries, and milk didn't go very far,
though she had known times when there hadn't even
been that much, and she had still toiled with the rest
of the family to get in hay or to seed the fields.

With an abrupt, angry gesture she pulled the woolen
robe about her and staggered back to the bed. The fire
in the hearth kindled as she went by it, but in this
place of magics, it no longer startled her. When, a
moment later, the latch lifted on her window shutter,
however, she turned quickly.

The round green shutter swung inward and a small
hand grasped the sill from outside. Curly hair followed, and then Peewit's strained face. "Could you
just give me a hand, my lady?" he puffed.

She moved too quickly and shook her head to clear
it as she went to haul him up until he sat astride the
sill. A large sack was tied to his belt and this had made
his maneuvers more difficult. He went to work on the
knot, explaining, "Supper. Tristan's on the front door
and I'd sooner try to get past a riled dragon."

Her face went stiff. "I have not said I would eat
supper, and I have not invited ye in, Master Littleman."

He looked up, surprised, and then he gave her a
slow measuring look. In her own dialect, he said,
'Ye've had a bad day, sure, but there be no need to
take me ould head off, is there then?"

She thought he was mocking her with her peasant
fostering and flushed angrily.

He saw it and struck his forehead. "Now I've done

it!" he said in his normal voice. "I was forgetting that you wouldn't know that we Hearthfolk occasionally live among other folk. In fact, I was born not far from Wolf's Glen." He made himself at ease up on the wide sill and went back to working on the knot.

"Really?"

He nodded. "That would have been long before your time of course, but my father once worked at Coombe's Echo."

"I've been there to fair!" Despite herself, she sniffed the toothsome aroma of new bread.

"Shh! I beg you! If the captain finds out I'm in here, he'll—well, I don't know what, but something. In olden days, he'd have had me polishing armor till my arms dropped off."

He said this engagingly, but she had the feeling he had drawn the punishment more than once. A smile played about the corners of her mouth, and she waved him in. He dropped down to the floor and she swung the shutters closed again. When she turned, he had the sack open and was pulling out a small wooden platter, a cup, gilt knife, and fine embroidered napkin. She sat down on the bed and watched him set service for her as carefully as if this had been a great hall. He had brought dark bread, cheese, pears, and a leather flask. He uncorked this and poured her some drink.

"What's this?"

"Mostly water," he answered evasively.

She sniffed. "It smells like licorice."

"It does rather, doesn't it?" he busied himself slicing cheese.

"Where did ye get it?"

"Kursh. I'm trying to stay out of his way, actually. He bet me I couldn't get in here, and now he's lost."

She smiled and sipped. A pleasantly warm glow spread through her. "Mmm."

He lifted an eyebrow. "You like it?"

She nodded, and feeling slightly dumbfounded, he passed her the plate. She attacked it like a starving cat and he watched in amusement as the food rapidly disappeared. All at once she stopped. "Oh, Peewit, I'm so sorry. Have ye eaten?"

"Hours ago," he assured her. "And a good thing too."

She giggled and took another sip of the watered flotjin. Oddly enough, the spirits seemed to ease her swimming head, or perhaps it was only the food, but she was beginning to feel better than she had all day. "I suppose I should have come out for dinner," she confessed, "but I just couldn't face everyone."

He sat cross-legged upon the rugs. "We were worried about you. Tristan was like a bear with colic."

She cast her eyes down. "Was he?" she murmured.

The Littleman shrewdly guessed what the pink in her face might mean. Brickleburr quietly punctured her dream. "The captain takes his duties very seriously, my queen." The emphasis he put upon both their titles was not lost upon her.

She looked up. "I'm not your queen anymore, Peewit. The heir can use the Crystal, remember? Nothing happened in Yoriand today. Whatever power there was is gone. Maybe 'twas only a chance happening the first time."

"Tell that to Imris."

Pain twisted her face and she blurted, "He is not healed, either. Already he's dyin' again! I've brought him back to suffer it all over again!"

"No. You brought him back to live, and you tried to heal Nilarion to make the world back the way it was. But you cannot expect always to have things come out right when it is Rasullis's black art that has put them wrong. Even the wizards here admit that the Fallen knows much more than he should ever have been allowed to learn." He was staring now over his shoulder at the fire, which hissed as sap ran from the firewood. "They say that they can't oppose him directly because of their Rule, but I'm not sure they could beat him if they tried."

She did not understand what he was talking about, except that he did not blame her. Her heart was lightened as if some burden had been lifted off her. "Peewit, I think ye be not the jester everyone makes ye out to be." He looked startled and then uncomfortable, and before he could say anything, she rushed into it.

"I have a question I long to ask someone, and there is no one else who will tell me, I think." He was waiting tensely for what she might say, and she avoided his eyes. "If I am to be queen . . . that is, if we can somehow—get through whatever is ahead, well . . ." She foundered to a halt, and then her chin came up. "Has the captain a wife?"

Peewit kept his face carefully expressionless, but he let out his breath suddenly. He was silent for so long that she thought he would not answer, but finally he said, "No. There was a girl once, a long time ago . . . but when he came back from the war, she loved him no longer." He thought to himself, in for a penny, in for a pound, and told her the rest of it. "Because of his scars, you see."

"What scars?"

He sighed. "He was burned by Rasullis's fire out there on the Sweep. His hands and arms. It was long before he could use his right hand again, and then he trained himself to hold a sword and fight once more. Now, you would not guess."

"And that is why he always wears the gloves."

He nodded and his merry face was unaccustomedly solemn. "He has never said, but I think she must have rejected him because of what she saw. I know that he left in haste and went away—to King Ka-Nishon's court, I guess—and when next he came back to Ilyria she had died. Or been killed. I've never been able to find out which."

She said her thought aloud: "She cannot have loved him much."

One shoulder lifted in an unwilling shrug. "I don't know." His eyes met hers. "But *he* loved *her*." He added softly, "More than anything else, I think Tristan would pay Rasullis back for that, if he could. 'Tis bad enough to kill a man, but 'tis fouler by far to kill his dreams. Don't you think?"

She nodded silently, staring into the fire. He jumped to his feet. "Well, I'd better be going." He carried a stool over to the window. "Get some rest, my lady. The wizards are planning a ceremony for Alphonse tomorrow, and you'll be the honored guest. No outsid-

ers have seen it before, they tell me." He climbed
upon the stool and cocked an eye at her. "Will you be
all right, or would you want one of the healers?"

"I'm feeling much better, thanks to you. And don't
worry: I'll not tell the captain—anything."

"You might say a nice word to him before you
retire."

She nodded, and he swung himself up to the sill,
balanced for a moment, and then with a wink, he was
gone. She went to peer out, and saw him just disap-
pearing into the clump of dwarf pine diagonally out
from the back corner of the Aparting. Pulling the
shutters closed, she turned from the window and absently picked up a pear, and went thoughtfully to sit by
the fire.

Higher on the terraces, Hrontin and Chiswic sat in
the old man's Aparting, and the two of them seemed
to be staring into the dancing flames of the hearth.
But there was sweat on Hrontin's brow and Chiswic's
hands trembled with palsy. They were trying desperately to hear the notes of the new Warding.

Somewhere out in the night, probably high on the
cone of Covencroft, the boy was entranced. For these
past hours Alphonse would have lain staring into the
winking sky, deep in the drug that brought the Meld-
ing and his own Warding. The other wizards on the
island, though they were all aware of his trial, could
not help him. If he were not strong enough to master
the night visions, he was not strong enough to have
the Serpent imprinted in his flesh as the Meld was
imprinted in his mind.

Finally Hrontin wiped a hand over his forehead. "I
cannot hear any new phrases."

Chiswic's eyes were narrowed. "I think I can—very
faintly. But it is a long time coming to him."

"You are worried for him."

The old wizard reached for his tea. "I am more
worried about the strange notes of Warding you heard
from the earth in Yoriand today. The boy has already
manifested himself in Fire, and yet you say there was
music also of Earth, so I do not think the strange

Warding you heard can be his. The notes never come commingled that way."

"They never *have*." When Chiswic gave him a sharp look, Hrontin said in a low voice, "But there was a foretelling once—"

"I knew that lore before you were born," the old man interrupted sharply. "Alphonse is not the Abomination. He will be the Unmaker, but he will be true, Hrontin. You will see."

"None of us saw Rasullis for what he was, either, until it was too late, master."

"Llodin did. I should have listened to him, but I took it as a fault in him and bade him heal himself before he disrupted the Meld." He shook his head. "And all the while, the Fallen was turning the Warding against us."

There was a silence until Hrontin said, "He found out about the girl." Chiswic knew that the other did not mean Llodin.

"There's another place we've failed," the old man said bitterly. "When the Greenbriar King brought the Crystal here for safekeeping, he charged us to prevent Rasullis from giving a Warding to the Bastard and his army. And—to live by our Rule—we would not. Llodin spoke against that decision too." Chiswic set his tea down untouched and stared into the fire. "All his counsel was good."

Quietly Hrontin said, "He broke the Rule, Chiswic, you know it as well as I: the girl and the others have his Warding upon them."

"And a good thing too!" the old wizard flared. "She'd have been dead in some soldier's bed by now."

"And instead she is the heir to the power of the Crystal, the first woman ever. How did that happen, master?" This was difficult ground and Hrontin knew Chiswic was already angry. "King Dhonald had a son— her brother. The power should have passed to the Lordling, to die with him it may be above Willowsrill Falls, but still, his. The girl, like all the other Greenbriar women, should only be the bearer of the Blood, to pass it on to her offspring if she had no brother. It has been that way since Beod's time." He paused, but

Chiswic said nothing. "This is the truth, Chiswic—you know it. What does it mean?"

The coal-black eyes regarded him. "It may only mean that none of the Greenbriar women were tested. We have always read the runes to say that the power of the Crystal was bound with the kingship. How do we know that the Crystal's power has never resided in a woman before? None of them has ever even tried to use it. You see, my friend? Even we, who are reckoned wise by the rest of the world, have our blind spots. It is bound with that portion of us that is still mortal, I think. Be that as it may, we need not worry overlong about how Ariadne got the power; she has it; that is all we know. But we must decide before this company leaves Covencroft whether or not we will support them in their attempt to wrest the kingdom of Ilyria back from Dendron and Rasullis. We debated this once in Meld-Meet, and then we decided badly. Now the choice is before us again." He shuddered suddenly and Hrontin made haste to hand him his tea. Then he used his Warding to bring up the heat under the floor of the old wizard's Aparting. "Thank you," Chiswic murmured absently. "Llodin's vision about the Lordling troubles me, Hrontin. Something awaits discovery at the Guardian, but what it may be, I cannot imagine. The boy obviously died years ago; otherwise, Ariadne would not now be able to use the Crystal. What then could be so urgent that such a vision would come to Llodin, who of all of us was the least receptive to Sight?"

Hrontin shifted in his chair. "Maybe the boy did not die. Maybe even now he is alive somewhere and this group will find him." He saw the look on the old man's face and turned one hand palm-up on his knee. "The Crystal worked for her once and not again, don't forget. And that may have been because Imris will be needed later."

"The healing of the Yoriandir may have been fortuitous, you think?"

"Yes."

The old man finally nodded. "Stranger things have

happened, I suppose, though I can't remember when. But I tell you, if the Lordling lives, he will have to be great in Blood, because Ariadne has the greatest untutored power I have ever seen—and I have seen Greenbriar Kings come and go back to the oldest chronicles. Royalty ripples from her and she does not even know it!"

Whatever Hrontin might have answered was cut off by the swelling rumble and sudden fierce jolt that seemed to erupt under their feet. Chiswic looked toward the window and had the weird sensation that it was at least two feet higher in the paneled wall than it should have been, and then he was catapulted from his armchair as though a giant hand had sent him sprawling. He braced himself on the cone-shaped chimney to avoid the fire and Hrontin fell to his knees and crawled over to him to pull the old man back. A board was sprung in the doorframe and the door popped open. The round opening skewed and went oval. The old man's teacup fell and broke, and his staff fell full length from the corner where it had been propped.

As abruptly as it had begun, the shaking stopped. Cautiously the wizards looked at each other. When nothing further happened, Hrontin rose and pulled Chiswic to his feet.

No sooner had Hrontin hastily kicked embers back into the hearth and helped the old wizard back to his seat than he froze. "It comes again!" he shouted, and immediately the surging earth moved. The shaking was more violent than ever and bits of plaster pattered from the ceiling while tiles in the floor heaved out of their mortar and broke. A split opened along the diagonal seam where two of the wall planks joined. Then, suddenly, sweet through all that sensory madness, a full sure song rose—and not just a fragment: this was a Song in its own right, weaving notes of Earth, Wind, and Fire.

Both wizards turned their heads to it at the same time, just as the tortured earth relaxed its spasms and the rumble died away, lulled back to its accustomed slumber by the strains of the extraordinary Warding.

"Freckles!" old Chiswic breathed hoarsely. He pushed off Hrontin's arm and struggled to rise.

Full in the moonlight of the warped door appeared a mantled dark shape, outlined with garnet. Power was in his voice and he said, "The end of the world is at hand, my brothers. Come out and look at the stars."

Chiswic rose heavily from his chair. Hrontin stooped to collect the old man's staff while clear on the night air the three of them could hear fearful voices calling across the garden and up and down the hillside. Chiswic walked to the wizard of the Three. "How do you, Alphonse?" He could not see the boy's eyes in the deep shadow.

"I am the Unmaker." The voice was hollow and Chiswic was touched by fear. "I have no other name." In the pause that followed, Chiswic felt his breath come short and Hrontin straightened with the staff clutched in his hands as though he faced an enemy. The dark figure nodded and his hood fell away, showing the ginger hair that caught the moonlight. "Yes. I may be the Abomination. I am the power that destroys, and you have wrought me. Come, behold your creation." He waved them outside and both of them saw the ring he bore flash garnet.

When Chiswic glanced over his shoulder he saw the horror staring in Hrontin's eyes and knew it was reflected in his own, but they followed the Unmaker outside.

On the dark hillside, high above the lanterns plying to and fro as adepts checked the buildings, a fountain of fire spewed from a vent that had opened in the highest terrace. Already the lava wended its way toward them. "Alphonse!" the old man gasped. "In the name of the Three, *why have you done this*?"

The Unmaker turned to him. "Because we of the Meld do not suffer when great evil is done; we never feel it here. So I have taken the power of the Meld-Meet and set it loose in the world as should have been done when Rasullis first escaped from here. Your own fear has undone you, my brothers, and whether Covencroft survives will depend upon how bravely you meet doom when it happens not in Ilyria, not in

Yoriand, but here. This is the sacrifice you required of others by withholding your help. Measure yourselves against it." He turned on is heel and strode off across the ruined garden, but his thought pierced their minds and stuck there: "And if you decide to break your Rule, try to begin knitting together the fabric of earth again, for it is sore rent and Tydranth, the Wild Fire, lurks just beyond the Zones!"

There would be a barque waiting for them at the pier, Alphonse had come to tell them. His voice had been unnaturally deep and Imris had looked thoughtful. Kursh had asked over the dice, "Why? What's wrong? Besides the shaking, I mean."

The wizard in his dark wine-colored cloak had stood in the doorway of Imris's room. "We are leaving, Master Dwarf. The island is no longer safe. Look. See for yourself." He went out and the lamps flickered.

The dwarf had bounded off the bed, run to the door, taken one look, and told Peewit, "Pack! I'll be right back!" He had run off across the garden toward the queen's Aparting. When Peewit and Imris had gone to the doorway to see why, both of them jumped for the packs.

Now, nervously waiting for the queen and the captain to come down the path from the small cottage, Peewit aimlessly picked a flower and stuck it in his cloak pin. Imris and Kursh had already gone ahead with the baggage to give the Yoriandir a little more time; he was still weak. The Littleman sighed impatiently and raised his eyes to the river of burning rock that slid straight for the garden. It posed no immediate threat, but he was glad he wouldn't be here in another day or two.

When he lowered his gaze, the young leafkin he had watered while Imris lay dying just the night before showed silver in the moonlight. The other saplings were in no danger, for they had been planted high on the hillside, on a level with the vent but nearly around the semicircular cone from it. But this one of Nilarion's children stood directly in the path of the lava.

On a sudden impulse, Peewit bent to it and grasped

the young trunk carefully. He gave the gentlest of pulls and the tree came out of the soil easily. "Not again, little fellow," he muttered, straightening with the leafkin in his fist and staring up at the fire. "No more burning for Nilarion's seedlings."

The Littleman turned and ran for the shore with the leafkin bundled close in his cloak.

Later that night, after Alphonse had driven the barque across the strait with his power and they had unloaded their gear, the companions climbed up through the charred valley. They looked neither left nor right, going quickly, thinking only to come as fast as might be to Rimwall and begin their descent into Ilyria. Peewit brought up the rear and his footsteps were so light that when he stopped and let them walk on, none of them was aware of it.

Slipping away through the black skeletons, the Littleman made for Aspenglade. Dark in the moonlight, the spike of Nilarion loomed above him finally and he walked around to the well of Nose-Tickler with the uncanny sense that something in the night was holding its breath. As quickly as he could, he dug a shallow hole just at the side of the spring, and before he could place the leafkin in it, the bottom filled with seeping water. He planted the sapling, drawing a mound of earth up around its young trunk and tamping it gently with his hands.

In the dim light, the silver leaves rustled, though there was no wind. One eyebrow went up toward his curly hair and he murmured, "You're welcome, I'm sure." He rinsed his hands in the well and cupped a handful of the cool Sileaught to his lips. When he sat back on his heels and looked about, he seemed to see a sleeping landscape of silver and black, dreaming in a velvet midnight. A serene peace flooded through him and he rose to go.

The little tree rustled again.

He drew a finger along a silver-veined leaf. "Grow!" he told it in a fierce whisper. Then he left the clearing at a trot, reckoning that by now the others must be well ahead.

It was not until he was climbing through burned and twisted apple trees that he realized he had drunk of the well that had been laced with Elixir, and it was not until Kursh suddenly stepped out from behind a thick charred stump and cursed him roundly that he realized he could hear out of his damaged ear.

The dwarf did not understand why the Littleman laughed as they gained the Rimwall.

⭐ 10 ⭐

The restless clanking stopped the moment the key grated in the lock. The bolt was corroded by the dampness and shrieked in protest as it slid back. The scarred door swung open. Not an eye in the dungeon was looking anywhere else. It was past feeding time and not yet early enough to be roused for work parties. When the dungeon door opened in the middle of the night, it meant the wolves would run.

Torchlight flared against stonework stained with mold and water. Through the archway came two of the guards, the sable and crimson of their uniforms incongruously bright in the gray subterranean cavern. The taller of the two Barreners, his flat-planed face catching the light as he looked slowly about the room, was slapping a ring of keys against his thigh.

His fellow held the smoking torch higher. "Pitiful-lookin' lot, ain't they?" He said it loudly.

"Naught but a mouthful," the taller guard agreed in the same tone. "Seems hardly worth the trouble. But Beldis will have hisself some exercise, I don't doubt." The two laughed.

The prisoners who lined the walls, each strung in his own set of leg irons, stared back, but if the guards hoped for one of them to betray himself by a cry, they were disappointed: the dungeon was silent. The shorter guard swung the torch at a rat that scurried out of the way as they went toward the far end. The first soldier stopped a few feet from a figure crouched in the dark. "You. Up."

"Up yer own," a rasping voice answered.

There was no laughter in the cell, but a feeling as though there might be.

The guard drew his truncheon and casually brought the club down twice. There were thuds and one soft grunt, but that was all. The guard backed a pace, splay-footed and ready. "Up," he repeated.

The tall, large-framed prisoner got stiffly to his feet. He was broad of shoulder still, but the near-starvation of the past weeks had stripped pounds from him and his tunic hung like a sack. He was bleeding from a gash near the crown of his head and the blood ran down through his stringy hair. The irons had cut his flesh where he had struggled to get free and the swelling had begun to fester. But his eyes still burned.

Surveying him, the guard willed him to make a wrong move, but the prisoner stood absolutely still, and finally the Barrener's red lips stretched in a feral grin. "You're the one. Be proud, slave: Beldis has chosen you."

"Old doggie himself tell you, did he?" The blasphemous words were barely out of his mouth before the guard slammed him again with the club.

Bending over him, the guard hissed, "You will have more respect for our Wolf before this night is through!" He signaled roughly to the other and the pair of them hauled the prisoner to his feet.

"Courage, Quint," a pockmarked man murmured from the other wall.

"Don't ye worry none about me, Ian Rigby. 'Twill be a treat to be out in the open air. The reek in here is gettin' worse all the time," he ground between his teeth as they stretched his elbows up behind his back.

"Shut up!" the shorter guard roared.

But Quint managed a final, "For the Greenbriar!" as they dragged him out and slammed the door.

The key turned, the bolt fell into place, and darkness flooded back. With it came the rats. A moment later in the pitch, Rigby's voice murmured, "For the Greenbriar. Aye."

And there was silence.

The moon was in her dark phase and there was nothing to guide his foundering footsteps, but the taut rope about his neck hauled him forward and he fought to remain upright. If he fell, the rope would choke him and the guards would let him writhe into unconsciousness, but then the line would be loosened. They did not want him dead; the meat had to be alive for the god.

Quint could not tell exactly how long he had been in the king's dungeon, but he did not think it could have been more than a month. That was what reason told him. The evidence of his eyes, however, seemed to contradict this. He knew that it had been high summer when he had met the strange group near the old posting station, and only a few days after that he and most of his men had been captured. It should still have been summer, but already the leaves had mostly fallen from the trees and there was a frosty edge to the wind that came down off the ridge. He shook his head to clear it, but however he added it up, he could not make the days stretch into autumn.

The ground underfoot was too wet to take frost. From his repeated falls he was begrimed with mud up to his eyes, and he could feel the channels under his feet where floodwaters must have gushed down from the heights behind the castle. In the dungeon they had caught some snatches of conversation as the guards' watch was changed, and from this he knew that the skies above Ilyria had been leaden almost from the time that they themselves had been captured. The country had been hit with the worst rains in its history, if he had understood the Barreners correctly. No wonder they wanted sacrifice to their Wolf god.

Quint had heard tales of the sacrifices: a man was set free in the crags above Ravenholt near the place where the wolf pack had its lair. After so many easy meals, the beasts had acquired a taste for man flesh, and would eat little else. He had never heard of any "sacrifice" escaping; if the man turned back down the mountain, the soldiers simply caught him and repeated the procedure.

He was not nearly as afraid for himself as he was for his wife and the children, who waited in the cave which was their home back near the Yoriand border. Well, some of the lads had gotten free and she and the bairns would be taken care of. For a moment, grief so smote him that he stumbled and fell. When they finally loosened the knot, he was nearly beyond caring, but then the soldiers cursed him for an Ilyrian whore's back passage, and he pulled himself to his feet and went on.

At last they climbed the final stretch through the darkly silent pines and untied him. One of the guards swung from his skittish horse and unlocked his wrist manacles while another held the point of a spear at his chest. There was a snuffling in the underbrush and from further up the hill a sudden shuddering howl. The men curbed their horses sharply and cast anxious looks around them.

Through his painfully swollen throat, he croaked, " 'Fraid of the dark, gents?"

The officer smiled and was still smiling when they broke Quint's right leg and left him gasping in the middle of the trail.

Near dawn, Dendron was awakened from a restless sleep by the howling from the crags above the castle. Even in his fuzzy first thoughts, he remembered that the sacrifice had been made during the night. Beldis had feasted his peers, and today in the second half of the ancient ritual, the Barrener king would feast his.

The girl stirred and murmured something in her sleep. She was burrowed under the wolfskin rug that covered the royal bed, and nothing but a tangle of long dark hair showed. The king was disconcerted momentarily when he realized that he could not remember what she looked like.

He had drunk too much again last night. It was the damned rain; you couldn't hunt, you couldn't hawk, you couldn't even practice at arms. It was enough to drive a man mad. And then Rasullis with his eyes that looked right through you and his forever spells and magics, and his wanting more blood. Since they'd come back from the mess at the tree-tenders' valley, the wizard had been worse than ever, locking himself for days in his north tower or his underground rooms. Not that he'd minded having the chilly whoreson out of the way, the king reflected; it was just that the blue fire of enchantment had flickered night and day in the tower, and there had been an awful lot of Ilyrian peasants taken to the the dungeons. Even his own men were starting to talk.

If the men had known what the Fallen was trying to do, they'd have laughed. Bloody fool was trying to make a Crystal. By the Wolf, it was funny to see him so serious about it too. Nearly worth the bleedings. Oh, you had to humor him—what choice?—but the whole thing was absurd. If he'd been inventing another enchanted sword, now, that would have made sense. But you talked to him about that and what did the whoreson say? "You lost your toy, my king. You can't be trusted with another." *Lost it*, by Beldis! Like a youngling! Never mind that bloody thieves and villains had come in under the damn wizard's very nose and stolen both the sword and the girl! Lost it, he says. Ass.

You'd think with all his bloody magic he could do something useful like stopping this rain. It was going to be a long, tough winter. The captains all reported the crops ruined, some riverside villages flooded. That didn't affect Ravenholt itself, of course; the royal granaries were already full from the taxes, but it would mean unrest among the Ilyrian dogs. Maybe some show of strength now would remind them who was who and what was what. Yes. Cut off this whispering about the Greenbriar King returning too. Fools—they saw him dead under the rubble at the gate twenty years ago. What more did they need?

Ariadne, Rasullis said she was. *Did* look like Dhonald, curse him. But looks aren't everything. Who should know better, eh? Besides, wouldn't put it past

my oh-so-good brother to have a couple of by-blows
scattered about among some of these peasant women.
There are outdoor sports besides hunting and hawk-
ing, by Beldis. Lots of kiddies looking like *me* out
there. A few of them here in the slaves' quarters too.
You just can't beat a good Ilyrian whore.

Wonder why none of mine and Eowyn's lived? Probably took one look at the bitch's face and it curdled
their little lives right then and there. Still, it's odd—all
those bastards, and never one true-born.

Ariadne. Not bad looking, for an Ilyrian; face too
round, odd color eyes and all that, but even so. Can't
believe that whoreson wizard actually thought I'd ever
. . . especially so's he could have the kid she'd throw.
By the Wolf, it's enough to turn your stomach. He
must be out of his mind. Not that he's ever been
altogether normal.

Last night, for instance. Sends that queer dwarf of
his. The whoreson flaps his hand at me and I'm supposed to know that his master bids me come to the
tower. So I leave my dinner and all, and follow him.
Get there and Rasullis says "A slight inconvenience,
my king. I need some of your blood." "Again?" I
says. "If I'm right, you'll never have to do this again
after tonight," he says. I saw eyes like that on an
adder once. Well, what could I say? He bleeds me.
After, he bids me break this glass thing. I do, and he
picks out the seeds that were inside of it and drops
them into the cup of blood. Then he stands staring
down into it like it was the well of life. So after a
while, I says, "Looks like we'll be doing this again"
—trying to be nice, because I could see he's about to
boil and I wanted to get out of there. And he gives me
a look like to freeze the marrow of my bones. The
dwarf hustles me out as if I were a peasant come to
collect a mercy. Crazy, he is. Crazy and dangerous.

And scared. I can see that. Started back at that old
burned tree. Do believe the wizard is slipping. Visions
of the end of the world, by the Wolf. Scared by a little
rain and some shakings. Not like we've never had
them before. What of it? They're just a little stronger
and a little commoner than they used to be. We'll

make the sacrifice, and after today everyone will feel much better. Maybe the shaking will stop too, and the rain, if Beldis wills it.

Not like the end of the world.

The king stretched and turned to the girl with desire, but after a short, unsuccessful time, he shouted for the chamberlain and pushed her from the bed. "Get a bloody fire going!" he roared at the surprised and sleep-fuddled man. "It's cold as Frost-Month in here! No, no breakfast, you fool! I must fast—there's the sacrifice today! Just bring me some ale and have a groom saddle my horse. I *know* it's raining again, damn you! Just do as I say!"

The river had risen so high that it was actually lapping at the underside of the planking as they crossed. Even here, three miles above the First Falls, they could hear the thundering cascade. The captain opined that the bridge would go before noon if the rain continued.

They were all soaked to the skin and had been so for days. Soon after crossing the Rimwall out of Yoriand, they had been caught in a downpour, and the rain had not slackened ever since. The last time they'd been able to have a fire and hot food was two weeks ago in the shelter of a cave that reeked of bear. Luckily, it had been the wrong season for the animals to be hibernating.

They had seen no patrols, and the Watchmen agreed that the unnatural storm was probably a blessing in that respect, but otherwise the journey had been a nightmare. They had passed through a land that lay under the shadow of doom: oats and wheat lay matted and beaten into the mud, and hayfields were blackened with mildew; bloated carcasses of cattle lay in pastures where they had fallen as their hooves rotted; more than a few thatched roofs had caved in, and very little smoke wreathed about the chimney holes of the others.

Tristan led them quickly away from the banks of the river, fearing a flash crest might sweep through at any moment. They climbed through scrubby pine where the water sluiced off the hillside down to the river. When the earth began to shake, Ariadne thought at first it was another attack of the dizziness that had plagued her since leaving Covencroft, but when Fidelis threw an arm about her shoulders, and Kursh—ahead of her—was tossed off his feet, she dropped quickly to her hands and knees. They had found that it was safest.

Gravel loosened by the rain skittered down the slope and pattered against them. A few larger rocks tumbled also, but thankfully nothing larger. As the shakings went, this was not a bad one. When it was over, Fidelis helped her to her feet, and the captain came down the hillside planting his feet sideways not to lose his balance. "Is everyone all right?" No one answered. They were too weary and the momentary quake had been only a minor nuisance. "Let's go on, then. Kursh, go you before and keep a sharp eye for patrols; this close to Ravenholt, there will be sentries."

"Aye. Wet as dogs and looking for their relief, I don't doubt," the dwarf rumbled. Shouldering his ax, which he had not sheathed since they left the Rimwall, he turned and scrambled up the hillside.

The tall man cast an anxious glance at Imris, who stood slope-shouldered and exhausted under the dripping branches. The Yoriandir was far weaker than the Watchmen had suspected when they had left the Wizards' Isle. Imris had said nothing of his condition, but where his light step had led them on many a trail, the Yoriandir now lagged behind. Once he had begun to apologize, but Tristan had cut him off with a friendly clap on the shoulder and shake of the head. But he was worried. If they ran afoul of the Bastard's men, they would need Imris's bow, and the captain didn't think he could use it.

While Peewit and the queen began the ascent, the captain turned his attention to the wizard. Alphonse stood staring up into the sky. The garnet cloak and shimmering surcoat seemed dry and the rain beating into his wide eyes seemed not to bother the red-headed youth at all. Since they had left the island of the Meld, Alphonse had seemed remote, and he bore himself with the air of one whose thoughts were deep and cold. Almost, Tristan could have thought the boy was entranced, save that he walked open-eyed and—when necessary—communicated with them. But there was a kind of simmering threat about him and none of the young innocent bondsman they had known scarce two months ago. He had aged from boy to man, and the captain was not much sure he liked the man.

Irritably Tristan told him now, "Come along. Let us catch up with the others."

The cool blue eyes came down to meet his. "Let them go on a bit. I want to talk to you."

The presumption in his tone stiffened Tristan's spine. "Boy, I do not know what passed with you on the island, but do not think you can put on airs in this group. I have suffered your insolence thus far only because the queen bade me leave you be. While we are on the trail, *I* give the orders!"

A slow grin broke across the young man's face, but it was rather a calculating smile and devoid of humor. "Oh, you need not fear me as a rival, Captain." He sobered. "You have your job, and I have mine. We will work together whether we want to or not. But there is a rage growing in me like a canker, and you will do well not to anger me. I say this as fair warning, and because I recognize that in all matters concerning the Greenbriar Queen's protection, you lead."

There was such suppressed emotion in his voice that the soldier rested his hand upon his sword haft and stared at him. "What did they do to you at Covencroft?"

The new lines in the wizard's face settled. "*They* did what they have long done—nothing. But much was done that lay outside their power."

"You riddle."

"It is difficult to explain the inexplicable." He looked down, regarding the gleaming new ring encircling the garnet that shone on his finger. "It is enough perhaps for you to know that I am not the person you knew. He is gone. I am now rather a force than a man, or even a wizard." The captain made an impatient movement and some gravel bounced down the path. "I am

sent to be the Fallen's doom. So you see, our paths
are parallel, but we do not walk the same way."

"Leave Rasullis to you, you mean, and everything
else is our problem."

"In essence, yes."

"No. You forget, our vengeance has waited nearly
twenty years. Add to that Kursh's right to repay his
nephew's murder, our right to repay Llodin's, and
Imris's to—"

"Hold! You speak as if this were simply a matter of
bringing a murderer to justice! And yet you are not an
untutored man, Tristan Faring. You know the evil the
Fallen has loosed. You saw Nilarion, and Llodin told you
what it meant. You hear the rain and feel the shaking."

The captain's gauntleted hands had knotted. "I do.
But myth is a matter for wizards. I must deal in blood
and bone. For me, the world has long been dead, and
now I see a chance to make it live again. I will not be
gainsaid. I claim this death: do whatsoever else you
will, Alphonse, but Rasullis is mine."

The Unmaker smiled. "Or you are his. Who can
say? And at the last, sword wielder, you may feel dif-
ferently. Even the rock recognizes the ice that splits it,
so it is said."

Cold dread struck at the captain's heart and the
scars that drew his flesh from fingertip to shoulder
burned anew. He wondered for a startled instant
whether the young wizard had thrown a spell on him.

Alphonse shook his head. "No. I put no spell on
you. Nor would I ever. My Warding is only to undo
the Fallen's. Do you understand?"

Coldly the soldier regarded him. "I understand only
that you are a wizard unlike your master, who was
both powerful and good."

At this reference to Llodin, Alphonse first flushed,
then gew pale and nodded slowly. "You perceive me
well, Captain. I am *not* like him." Should I tell him
how different? Shall I tell him that where Llodin—and
all the others—hear only a portion of the Song, I hear
it *all*? Would he realize what power that gives me?
Can he guess that I must become even as Rasullis is to
Unmake him, and then—at the last—having all power,

both Rasullis's and my own and all the others' of the Meld, I must abnegate the Song and become Alphonse again? Or keep it, and become the Abomination—the one who wrests the Great Song to his own will.

The captain was looking at him with something very like disgust. "No, you are not like him. Would that we could have *him* back."

The youth did not reply, only turning his head suddenly and holding up a hand for silence.

Tristan could hear nothing above the sound of the rushing water, but he was aware that the others had long disappeared over the crest.

The Unmaker said, "You are needed!"

Cursing, the captain attacked the slope, trying vainly to put on speed on the sliding surface. He drew his sword clumsily and spat over his shoulder, "If harm's come to her, I'll kill you!"

The wizard made no answer.

As the tall man stumbled up over the last ledge, the rain-soaked wind brought to his ears what the torrent below had masked: the howling of wolves. He put on a burst of speed and crashed through the pines toward the sound. He got a glimpse of something slinking through the trees ahead and then snapping jaws passed so close to his face that he could feel the hot panting on his neck as the large gray wolf missed its hold and sprang past him. He flailed with his sword as it landed and bunched for another try, and got a slice of one ear. Maddened with pain, the beast sprang again even as he threw himself off to the side and whipped the sword up to impale it. The animal coughed a bark and lay gushing blood and bowel.

Another set of slavering teeth caught in his calf. He could not get the blade reversed to stab at the wolf and thrashed at its head with his sword hilt. The animal snarled away for an instant and flattened for a fatal lunge. The man rose to his knee, sword poised. At that moment a gout of garnet fire singed the wolf's muzzle.

The beast shrieked, tucked its tail, and bounded away. The man leaped to put his back against a tree trunk and looked wildly about for more of them.

The wizard ran past him. "This way!"

The captain raced after him, for the moment not even feeling the torn flesh of his leg. They burst through into a patch of boulder-strewn ground and saw at once that the pack had their companions surrounded. With natural cunning, the wolves were attacking a few at a time, while the rest paced just outside the perimeter of the Watchmen's slashing weapons. Peewit had just thrown himself at one huge beast. The Littleman's short sword looked ridiculously small, naught but a child's toy dagger with which to slay a sinewy bolt of lightning.

Kursh recovered from a two-handed swipe that dropped a decapitated carcass at his feet and glanced down to check his footing. In the instant a dirty brown fury struck him from his blind side and he went down with the handle of his ax fending off the fangs. Fidelis took a swift stride away from the queen, reached in and clamped his hands about the animal's neck. The next moment, the raking claws scored his chest and he gasped, but squeezed desperately and the dwarf rolled free. Kursh flicked the dagger into his hand and plunged it in under the healer's grip. Blood sprayed and Fidelis pushed the thing from him in disgust, then brought a hand down to discover the claw marks through his robe.

Imris strung arrows and fired them as quickly as might be, but many of the shots went wide of the mark and he was running out of shafts. Peewit snatched back his ripped hands and furiously swung his sword.

In all that swirling action, the captain could not see Ariadne.

His breath stopped and he leaped to the top of a high boulder to cast himself down into the melee. From that vantage he got a glimpse of her crouched behind the Littleman and the Yoriandir. There was a mess on the ground at her feet.

Tristan attacked. He fought as if he were two men, or three. Wolves dropped to his sword as if they had been practice dummies on a training field. And when the remaining beasts silently slunk away and he turned to the queen, he was not even breathing heavily. "My lady, are you hurt?" He grasped her arm and pulled her up, then realized that if she was injured, he'd just worsened the wound. Silently he cursed himself for an idiot and stepped in close to support her.

She pulled away angrily and stooped again. "Let me go, can't you! Look!" She reached to hold up the man's head and Tristan was shocked beyond measure when he recognized William Quint in the fear-stretched rictus that stared back at him.

Hugging his own wounds, Fidelis knelt and ran quick professional eyes over the shuddering body. One of Quint's hands was mangled, evidently from a wolf's jaws, and his right leg was folded beneath him at an impossible angle. He was scratched and bleeding from too many lacerations to count and there were swollen bruises over his eye and on his head. But he was alive and conscious. The healer leaned over him. "Hold on, Quint! We'll get you someplace safe!"

Through thin blue lips, the outlaw leader gasped, "Save yourselves!"

"It's all right—they're gone," Ariadne assured him. His eyes wandered up to her face, but she was not sure he understood.

Peewit eased himself down and dispassionately studied the gashes on his hands. "Wouldn't happen to have a drop of flotjin, would you, Kursh?"

The dwarf shook droplets of blood from his fingers and wordlessly dug in his pack, which was strewn with the others on the ground around them.

The captain looked down with surprise at the warmth trickling down into his boot and only then discovered that he too was injured. He looked around like a man coming out of a daydream and met the Yoriandir's fir eyes. "Nasty bit of work," he admitted, wincing.

"We must get to the Guardian, Tristan. At least the rock itself may afford some protection against the weather, and if the wolves come at us again, we'll have stone at our backs."

"Right." He tallied the hurts of the group and only then realized the wizard was not among them. He whirled quickly and had taken a stride to go back up the path for Alphonse, fearing him gravely hurt or worse, when he chanced to look up and see the boy standing atop the very boulder from which he himself had charged. Fear turned in an instant to anger. "What ails you, that you could not help us!"

Rain shimmered on the wizard's robes. "You did not need me. Besides, I wanted to watch a master at work. Worthily are you captain of the Watch, Tristan, nor has time diminished your skills. It was a lesson." He bowed.

Nonplussed, the tall man stared back. Behind him he heard Kursh mutter, ". . . comes down here, I'll teach him another, the little snot."

Something went sideways in the captain's mind and he could not hold back the laugh that swelled in his throat. Up on the rock, the young wizard laughed too, as though he knew the joke. The rest of the group looked from one mirthful figure to the other, and then at each other. The captain finally grinned. "Is it beneath your station, then, Master Wizard, to offer your strong back to carry this wounded officer to safety?"

"Indeed not." The freckled youth grinned back. "And the sergeant major can help me." He lifted his head to the rain, and the smile left his face as if a rolling cloud had covered the sun. Again he seemed to be listening. "There are hooves," the Unmaker said gravely, "and a small boy, crying. Make haste."

When they shifted Quint's leg to splint it, he gave one hoarse cry and lapsed into unconsciousness. Peewit saw the swollen bruises at throat, wrists, and ankles. "Captain, he's been in chains."

Tristan looked down the trail that led, as they all knew, to Ravenholt. "And the broken leg, the wolves . . . He's a sacrifice!"

"Aye," Kursh grunted as they lifted the large-framed man, "and now there are hooves, wizard says."

Ariadne gave the captain one stricken look and he saw terror in her eyes. He drew his sword, grasped her hand, and they led the way, running, while Imris covered their retreat.

Up the ridge they struggled, slowed by the mud and the necessity of carrying Quint's inert form. Above the pines the upthrust spire of rock loomed against slanting sheets of rain. The Guardian stood like a forbidding boundary marker of some long-forgotten kingdom.

Spurred by Alphonse's cryptic warning, they moved as quickly as possible, though Imris—even with his keen sight—spotted no pursuit. To each of the Watchmen except Fidelis, the place was familiar from patrols, though they had not passed that way for more than two decades. Then, when they had searched for the Greenbriar King's wife and children, the trail had led only as high as First Falls, and that lay behind them nearly four miles now. Tristan had known where Melchior and the queen were headed, but there had been no reason until Llodin's strange vision to believe that the chamberlain, the king's lady, or the young Lordling might have reached the solitary crag.

The captain peered up through the rain to the tall sentry rock. As chief of the king's bodyguard, he knew what he was looking for; time out of mind, the legend of the red tree and the chamber it guarded had been linked to the Ilyrian throne. Folk said it was an enchanted cave or tower, or perhaps the entrance to a vast underground realm, but whatever the form, it was a magical place to which the king could retire when the world failed him.

But when the world had failed him, the doomed Greenbriar King had chosen not to flee to the Guardian.

These thoughts were in the tall man's mind as he tugged the girl forward with him—these thoughts and more besides; when the old captain, Eodward, had trained young Faring to succeed him, he had brought the new officer up this trail. "You will not find the red tree unless there's real need. I've looked for it many a time as I've passed this way and never caught a glimpse. But that's as it should be. Just remember: if our king ever needs to use the retreat, the tree will be there, at the very top of the trail. Use the notch at First Falls as your guide—through it, the exact site of the entrance can be seen. Please the Powers, you'll be able to pass this lore on to your successor without ever having seen the tree."

The captain remembered the words well, but all his old commander's careful preparation had come to

naught—now, when the Watchman needed to find the
Guardian's entrance, he could not go back down the
trail to take a sighting on the notch. With this realization was paired another: if a patrol of the Bastard
King's army was even now on their trail and the companions could not find the marker tree, they would be
caught in open ground like crabs at ebb tide.

He pulled Ariadne to a walk and then to a stand-
still. "Alphonse," he said quickly, "do you know where
the entrance to the Guardian lies?"

The wizard, laboring to support Quint's feet, puffed,
"You do not?"

The captain turned on him. *"Do you know?"*.

The youth carefully shifted the wounded man's legs.
"I can feel the Warding around it already." He looked
ahead, and a look of wonder came into his face. "Look!
Nilarion!"

They all looked where he was staring, but not one
of them saw anything but twisted pine. "Where?"
Peewit demanded.

The captain was frowning, but suddenly the queen
gasped and flung out a pointing finger. "There! By the
rock at the base! By the Powers, it *is* Nilarion!"

Still the tall man could see nothing, and he looked
down at her now as though he suspected that she was
seeing visions, but Imris walked slowly up beside him
and when the soldier glanced sideways at him, he
beheld tears in the Yoriandir's eyes. "No," the green
figure said softly, "it is not Nilarion. But it is one of
Nilarion's children. I had not known till now that any
of them were abroad in the world. Oh, can you smell
it?" He drew a lungful of air and straightened, and
years seemed to drop from him. The silver torque
about his neck shone as if new-polished.

Tristan shook his head and looked again. And suddenly it sparkled into his vision, glowing ruby and pearl
in some sun that did not shine where they were. "By
the Powers! I see it now! Come—quickly!" On his last
word came a keening howl from the trail behind them.
He dropped Ariadne's hand. "Lead on, my lady! Imris,
go before with the queen." He himself ran to the rear
to cover their retreat if the wolves should attack again.

They needed no urging. In a short time they broke from the cover of the pines and raced across slippery scrub undergrowth. Beyond the base of the great cloven boulder out of which the tree grew, the land fell off in a precipice, and low-lying clouds hung there. They could hear animals crashing through the forest behind them, and just as Imris reached the split rock, the first of the pack raced out of the trees and halted, stiff-legged, with hackles raised and fangs bared.

The Yoriandir peered into the dark cave that opened before them. He motioned Ariadne back and thrust his bow before him, tapping cautiously to see that there was a floor and then to either side to determine how much space they would have.

"Get in!" the captain shouted.

Imris obeyed and the queen followed, reaching out to touch his cloak in the darkness. Jostling each other, the group shuffled forward until Tristan was safely inside. Suddenly there was a piercing brilliance and they all gasped and squeezed their eyes shut for an instant. Past one gauntleted hand Tristan looked upward and beheld a torch flare against the wall above their heads. As his eyes adjusted it became an ordinary cresset, burning clean and smokeless. But the flame was silver.

There was a frustrated howl and snuffling behind the captain and he turned quickly, sword at the ready. Outside, just a few feet from the huddled group, the leader of the wolf pack sank back on its haunches, tongue lolling, and in the lupine face, the captain was certain he could read puzzlement. Experimentally, he waved the blade of his sword back and forth, but the beast made no sign that it could see him.

"There is strong Warding about the place, Captain. They will not follow us in, be assured of it," the wizard said.

"Did you light the torch?"

The boy shook his head.

"All right." The tall man looked over the heads of his group. "Peewit, go on slowly before us." The Littleman turned with a raised eyebrow. It was usually the dwarf or the Yoriandir who led. Tristan explained impatiently, "If there are springs in the floor, you are the lightest and may not trip them. And if there is some sort of trap, it will probably be set at man height."

The small figure grumbled to himself, " 'May not,' he says. 'Probably,' he says," but he stepped cautiously past the Yoriandir. Holding his breath, he gingerly put one foot in front of the other and constantly darted his eyes all about. He disappeared into the darkness ahead.

The rest of the group waited silently, straining to hear his light footfalls. Imris very nearly let fly the arrow he had prepared when suddenly there was a flash of light further down the passage. But he perceived quickly that it was another of the silver torches. From just below the farther light, Peewit called back, "Well, I'm still here. I think it's safe for all of you tallfolk to come along now."

Despite his assurances, they went carefully. The passage would permit two of them to walk abreast with a good margin of room in which to maneuver. The stone out of which the tunnel had been burrowed was smooth to the touch and dry, and underfoot there was firm sand. The arch rose some two feet over Tristan's head. At intervals along the wall jutted more torches, and as the group slowed a little to let Peewit make his way on ahead, these lit, one after the other as the Littleman walked past them.

The captain of the Watch did not like the torches, and he didn't like the slight coolness he could feel blowing against his chin from further up the passage. The place seemed sound enough, and there was one of Nilarion's children outside the entrance, but still . . . you could never be entirely sure about wizardry.

The tunnel now began to descend at a degree sufficient to be noticed immediately, but not steep enough to cause them any problem. Peewit looked back once, inquiringly, and Tristan waved him on. At last the Littleman came to a turn in the corridor, and there he waited for the others. "I can't hear anything further ahead," he told them. "Shall I go on?" There was an eager light in his eyes: for all his jesting, Brickleburr had a lively sense of adventure. Now, as the captain nodded, the Littleman took a tighter grip on his short sword, lay down on his belly, and wriggled around the corner. "Well!" they heard him say. "There's an entrance ahead, Captain—or so it seems to be. At any rate a large door, wooden, with sculpted stone lintel and columns. The motif is a Greenbriar. I do believe we've come to the right place."

"Is it guarded?" Tristan demanded. "Is there any sign of a trap?"

"No guards—would I be talking if there were? As for traps, I can't tell. I don't think so."

Tristan made no answer, merely stepping around the corner himself, while motioning the others to stay where they were. Bright light from two silver torches flanking the doorway invited them on. At his feet Peewit stood and brushed sand off his clothing.

The captain made a swift decision. "It must be safe. If it is the Guardian, then it cannot harm us." He raised his voice, "Come ahead. My lady, please stay behind everyone else. Alphonse, do you sense any wrongness in this place?"

"Not wrongness. It is strange to me, though. This isn't like wizard-warding at all. It feels very ancient, as though it stood here even when the Great Song was plain for all to hear."

Ariadne made her way forward, careful not to jostle Kursh or Alphonse as they set Quint down for a moment. "This place was made as a refuge for the Greenbriar Kings, right? Then wouldn't it be safer if I went first through the door?"

"No!" the captain said instantly. "No, my lady, I think not. We have no idea what is on the other side."

"Well, of course not, and we won't until we open the door. Quint is wet and hurt. At the very least, there ought to be a place to camp and dry out. Let's go."

She tried to step past Tristan, but he gently took her arm and held her back. Motioning her to stand clear, he grasped the huge iron ring and pulled. As the door swung silently outward, they got a glimpse of firelit chamber beyond.

The captain gripped his sword and stepped through

with the queen at his elbow. The room was spacious, royally appointed. Ariadne's quick glance around showed tapestries softening stone walls, thick rugs, a bit of fire in the hearth, a canopied, gilded bed. The velvet counterpane on it heaved suddenly and a small tousled head popped up.

Knuckling the sleep from his eyes, Gerrit, the young Lordling of Ilyria who had not been seen outside these walls for twenty years, said quite calmly, "Oh. You've come."

Smoke of aromatic wood in censers. Torchlight. The wolf muzzle and ears of the Bastard King's headdress casting deep beast shadow. A vaulted chamber echoing guttural chanting. The snarling of the drugged animal.

Beldis's priest nodded to the Wolf king and there was, suddenly, silence. Solemn in this ritual, almost regal, Dendron lifted a hand to the keepers and the wolf was set free. Even dulled as the beast was, the fangs and claws were still real. The Barrener licked his lips, raised the long ceremonial knife, and walked forward.

The wolf, eyes glittering in the torchlight, backed away, staggering. Dendron tried to prolong the climax. 'Spring, Lord Beldis,' he willed.

But even when he closed with it, the wolf only trembled and ducked its head, snarling. And at the last, when the king plunged the blade, Beldis's spirit departed without protest.

There was uneasy shuffling.

As the closing words of the ritual droned on, Dendron saw the sidelong glances at him. The portent was bad, but not the worst; Beldis had shown no strength, but at least the animal that carried the god's spirit had stayed on its feet long enough to establish the Wolf's presence. That was really all that mattered, he tried to tell himself, listening through the rise and fall of the chant to the rain sluicing off the roof tiles outside.

Finally it was done. He led the way from the shrine. The vaulted building stood to one side of the broad lawn before the hall, and now he allowed himself to be escorted through a central archway into the castle interior. There would be an interval while the wolf meat was being roasted wherein the king and other worshipers could retire to their chambers to doff the heavy ceremonial robes, robes that ordinarily were spattered with blood from the ritual slaying. There wasn't a spot on anyone's save the king's today, and his only because he had been so close when the blade went home.

His chamberlain flung wide the doors to the royal apartment, anxiously trying to gauge the king's mood. Dendron snapped his fingers and pointed to the ale pitcher. A page hastily poured some into a golden horn. The Bastard took a swallow and swung to the commander of the Home Guard. "Make ready an expeditionary force. It's come to my ears that the peasants are talking sedition. Let's put an end to it before it has a chance to spread. Pick out a village or two for object lessons. Have you had any report on that damned island from your watchers?"

"No, sire."

Dendron grunted, and shook off the chamberlain's hands as the man reached for his wolfskin-trimmed mantle. Undoing the clasps for himself, the king let the thing slide to the floor and stepped to the fire. "Double the guards on our granaries. When this rain stops—*if* it ever does," he said irritably, "there will be hunger, and probably some will be desperate enough to try to steal. See that they can't." He dismissed the man with a flick of his fingers.

The commander bowed and withdrew. "Will you wear the red robe, my lord, or the blue?" the chamberlain was asking.

"The red," Dendron muttered absently. He stared into the flames. The shaking came so suddenly that the king staggered toward the hearth and, instantly reacting to his danger, thrust himself backward. The heaving floor made it impossible to recover his balance and he went down heavily, bruising his hunched shoulder. He lay for a moment half stunned, listening to the metallic clatter as his sword fell off its hangers near the bed and to the creaking of overburdened stone. By the time he had groped to a sitting position, clutching his arm, the tremor was over. He got gingerly to his feet, cursing the chamberlain back, and his eyes found the page. "You!" he roared. "Go bid the wizard come here immediately!"

The boy scuttled off, and the king allowed himself to be helped to a chair.

Dendron had bathed and changed by the time there was a response from the wizard. There came a tap at the door, and he prepared to blast Rasullis, but it was the dwarf Nolin the chamberlain admitted. The enchanter's slave bowed and held it.

"Where's your master?"

Nolin pointed out the window and upward. Still in the tower, Dendron thought.

"When I give an order, I expect it will be obeyed. Even by him." The dwarf remained impassive. "Why does he not attend me, dwarf?"

Nolin bowed again and indicated the door with a courteous gesture.

"I am not his creature, to go or come at his will." But that wasn't exactly true. "Ah, well, by the Wolf's death, I suppose he won't even come down for the feast unless I drag him to the hall, will he?"

The dwarf shrugged slightly but shook his head no.

The king dropped his voice. "Does he want to bleed me again?"

Nolin indicated a negative reply, but something Dendron could not identify flickered in the deep eyes.

For a moment, the king forgot the distance between them, and asked, "What is he *doing* up there?"

Nolin hesitated. He glanced up at the chamberlain and the mask dropped down over his face again. Once more, he waved the king to the door.

The Bastard sighed. "Yes. All right."

The dwarf swung open the door at the top of the stairs to the wizard's tower apartment. Dendron, who was puffing as much from nervous anticipation as from the unaccustomed exercise, stepped through, motioning his guard to remain outside. The man saluted, but frowned as the door closed.

Nolin quietly went to put more wood on the fire and

this left the king to approach the enchanter, who was seated on a high stool at a curved work table that fit into the arc of the tower wall. Resullis looked decidedly seedy, the king thought with relish. The wizard's robe was rumpled, as if he'd slept in it, and in the face that turned to him there were deep lines and blue-tinged shadows. The Fallen looked like a very sick man.

But a smile lightened his demeanor as he swung around on the stool. "It's good of you to climb all the way up here, my king."

Dendron was taken aback. "Yes. Well, it seemed to be the only way I'd ever get a chance to talk to you." His anger reasserted itself. "Why didn't you come when I sent for you?"

The wizard laughed, but it seemed to be with genuine amusement rather than with his customary derision. "Because I had to get you up here without every fool guard in the castle following."

The hairs rose on the back of Dendron's neck. "Why?" He wondered if the man out on the stairs could hear him if he yelled.

"I have something to show you, my king. Something wonderful."

The Bastard's eyes slid to the right and left, and he listened for the dwarf to come up behind him. "Really? So wonderful that you could not be present at the sacrifice?"

The enchanter waved that aside. He did not seem aware of the king's rising discomfort. He jumped up— Dendron flinched—and went through the door to the inner chamber, to return almost immediately with a flask of some amber liquid. He carried it carefully, and when he placed it on the table the Bastard had the uncanny sense that the wizard was presenting his first-born. Dendron did not move to pick it up. "What is it?"

"Please sit, my king." Reluctantly, the Bastard did. Rasullis crossed his arms on his chest and regarded him. "You are great in the Blood, my king. Much greater than I had any reason to guess. It is quite extraordinary, really." He had trailed off into a murmur.

"What's extraordinary about it? You knew I drew

half my pedigree from that damned old man. But it's my mother's people who are mine now. I'm no dog of an Ilyrian, wizard, and even you had better not try to say that I am!"

Rasullis was unperturbed. "Nevertheless, it seems you are Greenbriar enough, my king." He paused like a bard, to gain attention. "I've made a Crystal, Dendron, and it worked with your Blood to make the Elixir."

The Bastard sat stiffly. "Rot."

The black eyebrows went up. "Oh, yes. Last night after you left to your . . . well-earned rest"—that sounded like the old Rasullis, Dendron thought—"I chanced to pass by the table here and can you guess what I saw?"

Dendron shook his head once.

"A briar, my king. A weak and spindly little vine was edging over the rim of the cup. It was nothing like the old manuscript described, but I knew at once that it was beyond doubt a Briar. All night I watched it." His eyes were lit. "Toward dawn this morning, it set its first blossom. And then there was another, and finally a third. Just as the old lore had said, these dropped off, and in their place, fruits began to swell. They were tiny when I picked them, but they were enough; I made up the Elixir."

The Bastard King, who had not the faintest idea what Rasullis was talking about, carefully dropped a hand to his dagger.

"You wonder how I knew that the Elixir would work?" The Fallen smiled. "I tried it, my king. This morning I put a man to death—oh, don't worry, just a slave—and then I sprinkled the corpse with this." He caressed the flask. "He lives now." He smiled beatifically. "I opened the gates to the Zones."

Dendron was aware of his heart pounding, and he thought perhaps if he dove for the door he could make it out before the wizard could recover and incinerate him.

A frown drew the black brows into a straight bar. "You do not believe me, my king? You would like proof, perhaps? Very well." Before Dendron could protest, Rasullis stepped to the door of the inner chamber, calling, "Nolin? Come out here for a moment." Dendron rose quickly, but the enchanter's hand was already upon the haft of the dagger at his waist, and as the dwarf came through the doorway, he struck. On Nolin's face was a look of ultimate surprise and then the beginning of horror. His legs went, and he was dead before he hit the stone floor.

The Bastard King stood staring at the twitching legs and then his eyes leaped to the wizard. His own knife was suddenly in his hand, but Rasullis seemed not to notice. The blue-robed figure was saying, "Now, watch," as he reached for the flask, poured a scant sip into a cup, and bent over the slave's body.

Dendron backed away and was halfway to the door when the wizard forced the liquid into the clenched jaw. The king was never afterward sure what happened next, but he thought he saw the dwarf swallow and then Nolin's mouth stretched wide in a contortion that would have been a scream if he had had a tongue. As it was, air was forced from his throat in a hoarse gasp when Rasullis casually wrested the dagger out of his chest and turned to the king. "You see?"

Dendron was shaking, but he dared not let the enchanter see this. "Y-yes."

"Oh, come, my king! You need not fear. Think! The world is ours, yours and mine! Your Blood and my Crystal! Who could oppose us?"

The Bastard knew he was dealing with a madman, but a clever and powerful one; in his own sight, the wizard's words had been proven. Nolin was now pulling himself to his feet. Rasullis did not even look down at him, but Dendron could not look away; he saw the murder in the mute slave's eyes. The king answered with a calm he did not feel: "So all along you were right. I thought the Crystal of Healing was just a myth, like that of the old tree you burned back in Yoriand."

"Ah, no, Dendron Half-Greenbriar!" The Fallen saw the flush that washed through the Bastard's pale face. "No, the Crystal is quite real—I saw it once at Covencroft. This one is not the original Crystal, of course. I had to guess at its structure and figure out how to put the Warding upon it. Nor did I know what the mysterious seeds spoken of in the ancient manuscript might be, and that has long kept me from success. But in Yoriand I found the final answer." He motioned the king to the stool and dismissed the dwarf to the other room. Nolin glared, his hand still rubbing at his chest, and Dendron hoped that the slave would turn on the enchanter. But after a moment, he went.

The wizard excitedly perched on a corner of the table. His dark eyes gleamed and there were spots of color in his cheeks. "Nilarion, my king, Nilarion was the answer." A shadow of remembrance crossed his face, and he said as if to himself, "Chiswic always thought that the seeds in the original Crystal were berries of First Nilarion, and now I see that this was true. But apparently the berries of Now-Nilarion work nearly as well—especially if they are toasted a little first, eh?" He leaned to clap the Bastard on the arm, and Dendron felt his flesh crawl beneath the heavy wool.

Now that the shock of the cold-blooded "demonstration" was wearing off and the wizard seemed to intend no immediate threat to him, the Bastard King was beginning to focus more on what he was saying. Dendron found his voice again. "My blood and the tree's berries make what's in there?" He gestured to the flask.

The Fallen nodded. "That, and a few more things besides," he said owlishly. "Altogether, my king, our Blood, the berries, and other things make immortality. Ah, you begin to be touched by the grandeur that is rightfully ours, I see. Yes. Immortality is ours to give or not, as we will." He caught the flicker in the king's eyes. "And now, more than ever, I cannot do without you, and you cannot do without me. We shall be joint emperors of all the earth, and even of the Zones themselves. Does your head not swim with it?"

The Bastard regarded the mad wizard and thought, I wonder how I can get rid of him? Aloud he said, "I have long wanted the sea plain. We can take it from that whoreson, Ka-Nishon, now."

Rasullis smiled. "Why not? It will make a rich colony. But first, we will humble a much prouder foe." At the king's frown, his smile broadened. "First, we will bring the Meld of Wizards to its knees. We will get back the rebels, the girl, and your sword, my king. And the real Crystal too, so that they can harbor no hope of ever overturning us. Once we have done that, we may do as we will and none will be strong enough to oppose us."

"Won't they try to use their Crystal against us?"

"How? Only the heir can use it. And not all the Wizards of the Meld can gainsay that; not one of them can make it work. Only you, my king. Only you. And me, the one they despised."

Dendron began to see a future open out before him: lord of broad lands and rich treasure; his own Barreners a great people; perhaps a more loving queen, a line of sturdy sons. And somewhere in the background, there was no wizard. "Very well. The Meld first."

The old accustomed mockery crept back into the Fallen's voice. "A wise decision."

Dendron met his eyes. "But I want Ariadne." He rushed on, though the enchanter had made no denial. "The Wolf breeds within his own pack. Why shouldn't I, the Wolf king, do the same?"

The red lips drew back. "Why not, indeed?"

In the open doorway of the slave kitchen, the overseer squinted up at the pouring sky and spat into a puddle. "Damn rain," he muttered.

From behind him came the slap of bare feet running and a voice roughened by fear. "Orsa, come quickly! It's Bors!"

The steward turned to see a tall, rawboned youth whose agitation showed clearly in his worried expression. He was holding a piece of sacking over his head, having just come through the slave block from the court on the other side. Orsa asked sternly, "Jed, is this any way to be shouting with all of *them* just looking for an excuse to deal out some punishment?" The tall young man waved away his words, and the overseer squinted. "Now, what in the name of the Powers is so important?"

"*Bors,* I tell you! Come see. There's no time to explain!"

The steward levered himself off the doorframe. "What, did they hurt him bad when they took him up to the tower this morning? I thought he looked well enough when he came back."

Impatiently Jed grasped his sleeve and literally pulled him through the kitchen toward the connecting passage to the rest of the block. "He's sick, Orsa. I think it's some kind of fever."

Orsa jerked to a halt. "A fever!"

"Aye. And it came on him suddenly. Already he's so bad—" He broke off.

"Dying?"

A quick nod. "I fear so."

They broke into a run.

The word had spread quickly. There was a crowd about the doorway to the male slaves' shed. Orsa thrust through roughly, Jed at his heels. "Stay out!" the overseer roared into the frightened faces. "Get torches!"

He went in. There was only the dim overcast light from the one door to show the piles of bracken bedding, the few strips of sacking that served as covers, the oddments of ragged clothing or foot bindings, and lying stretched with a crying girl at his head, the dead man.

Orsa flung his sleeve over his nose and mouth and stooped to take a hurried look. Sweat still stood on the mottled brow, there were purpled swellings like goose eggs under both ears, and one hand was fixed by rigor into a claw. The steward did not need more confirmation. He thrust the youth beside him back out the door and from that safe distance told the girl, "You should never have touched him, Xena." Beneath the fear, there was compassion in his voice.

Listlessly, she wiped at her eyes. "I know," she agreed in a whisper. She looked out at them. "But he was alone."

Orsa heard the torches they had brought hissing in

the rain. He asked the tall youth without taking his eyes off the girl, "Did you touch him, Jed?"

"No." When the steward looked up at him, he said quietly, "I swear it, Orsa. I did not touch him."

"It is true. He did not," the maid Xena confirmed.

The steward licked his lips. To her he said, "You know that if we tell *them* . . ."

She was composed now, stroking the lank hair off the dead man's brow. "I know." She found a friend's eyes in the crowd. "Make the prayer to the Powers for me," she requested. The stout woman answered with a nod and turned away.

After a moment, Orsa reached a hand to take the torch from a man at his elbow. "Fare ye well, Xena. May the Powers bless you."

When she made no reply except to avert her head, he tossed the flaring torch through the door into the crisp bracken.

The shouts of revelry from the hall reached even the dwarf in the tower, and his face twisted with rage and pain. The spasms were strengthening moment by moment. When the first onslaught had hit, he had known at once that he had been poisoned. Now he struggled to rise from the floor.

By grimmest effort, he managed to lurch to his feet. Staggering to the table, he clenched the flask of the damned stuff the Fallen had made last night close to his chest and careened to the window. Nolin hurled the flask as far as he could, but could not hear it crash on the paved court below. He turned to the door, braced for a moment against the casement, and pulled it open. Sweat ran from every pore and he could feel his throat constricting.

By the time he had made it all the long way down the stairs and through the corridors approaching the Wolf's Hall, he could hear nothing, see little more, and feel nothing but consuming pain. The Home Guards on duty at the entrance were drunk and saw no reason why he should not be so too. One of them clapped him on the shoulder and waved him through.

Nolin marshaled every bit of his remaining strength

and achieved enough clarity of mind to be able to make his way up the long room unnoticed, but when he was almost up to the high dais, his tortured body betrayed him and he bent double, retching blood.

The sound brought the nearest guard whirling around. "Here, you, get away!" the Barrener shouted angrily, thinking for a moment that the dwarf was only one of the many overcome by feasting, drink, and the heat of the hall. But when the guard got a good look, he snatched back his hand and leaped out of the dwarf's way as Nolin swung toward him. "Plague!" the fellow roared.

Merrymakers looked around from their horns of ale, attracted by the sound of the shout, but unaware of what the guard had said. Grins turned to horrified stares, and suddenly there was a scramble as the nearest benches emptied.

Left in the midst of an open place, the dwarf staggered forward. Those at the head table seemed still unaware of his presence. With agonizing slowness, he found the long dagger at his thigh and drew it.

Now there came a warning yell from the Home Guard stationed on the platform itself, and the Bastard King frowned down at the twisted figure while the wizard glanced first at the guard behind his own chair. Recognition was breaking across Dendron's face as the dwarf suddenly jerked back his arm and threw the dagger.

But one of the soldiers leaped into the blade, taking it high in the chest. The Home Guard behind the sick dwarf brought his sword in a slashing arc into the short figure even as Rasullis, fully aware now, flung sapphire flame and burned both the contaminated slave and the soldier who had killed him.

In that instant the shaking struck, jerking men from their feet while stressed roof trees cracked and the great columns running the length of the hall twisted. Crawling, shouting, the Barreners made their ways to one of the entrances and clambered through, desperately seeking safety from crashing roof tiles and falling beams.

Rasullis followed the king as he staggered and lurched

out into the antechamber and past the fresco mural. Bits of bright paint lay strewn about and even in that moment of confusion, the Fallen had time to notice that most of the picture had crumbled off the wall. He and Dendron flung themselves down the stairs, falling and sliding as the steps heaved like a stormy ocean. Finally they leaped through the doorway and went sprawling onto the lawn.

The shaking went on for minutes more, a rending and grinding that moved columns from their pediments, skewed walls, opened vast rents in floors, emptied rainwater cisterns, and started fires. Then, mumbling and growling to itself like a hungry beast, the tremor subsided.

Home Guards came running to lift the king to his feet and the wizard stood also. Dendron shouted, "Fire teams! Damage and casualty reports by commanders of twenty immediately." Some of the soldiers ran off to act upon the king's orders. "Lachish, send some of the engineers through the place. I want to know when it's safe to go back inside." The second-in-command saluted and raced away.

The Bastard hid the trembling of his hands by thrusting them into his broad belt. He said to the wizard, "It was fever."

"Yes. I saw." If Rasullis was upset either by the threat of plague or the shaking, he did not show it. He was dusting a bit of dirt off his robe. "He must have picked it up in the village. I sent him down there a couple of days ago."

Now there was fear in the Bastard's tight voice. "Plague, by Beldis!"

The enchanter looked at him sharply and then smiled. "You are not afraid, my king, surely? You forget, there is more Eli—"

He drained of color visibly, and then mastered himself. He began to walk away and Dendron followed. Each of them had a sudden vision of the Elixir flask knocked from the work table in the tower room. Quickly they made their way across the lawn and into the stone court beyond, with several Home Guards escorting them.

Crossing the cracked and tilted paving blocks, they were met by an officer and some of his men who took the king aside to show him an odd sight. Amidst fragments of glass, a scrawny vine looped for the nearest wall. Already it had sunk roots into the earth between the paving stones and gripping tendrils into crevices in the tower wall. It quested upward, trembling in some wind they could not feel. But the stem and foliage were black as if bitten by a killing frost.

The Fallen came to stand behind the small group and Dendron's glance showed him the wizard's eyes gleaming. Rasullis said, "Behold the Greenbriar of myth, gentlemen. Even in your cold hills, you must have heard of it."

They looked at him doubtfully and then with anger. The Ilyrian symbol? Here? One of the troopers swept out his sword and hewed at the stem, but even the stern iron could not penetrate it. Rasullis laughed and the man flushed.

The first blooms opened above them and the foul putrescence of rotting flesh pervaded the air. The men coughed and clamped their cloaks against their noses, staring up. Petals black as the bowels of the earth itself began to float down. Rasullis seemed to shrink into himself. "No! It cannot be!" he cried.

Alarmed at his tone, Dendron demanded, "What is it? What's wrong?"

The wizard was backing away, eyes bulging. "The Bane of Ritnym wakes!"

Caught by his fear, the guards drew away from the twisting vine. Dendron grasped him roughly. "What does it mean?"

"The . . . the Elixir—gone wrong somehow—not supposed to be this way!"

The Bastard shook him, fighting his own rising fear. "Burn it!" he commanded. When the enchanter licked his lips and only stared, the king struck him full in the face. "Burn it, damn you!"

Blue flame kindled at the Fallen's fingertips and he wildly let fly an arc toward the foul plant. The flames fed greedily and soon the entire thing was alight. As the sapphire consumed the leaves and branches, the black flowers shook off their last few petals.

Watching the vine turned to so much char, the wizard felt his breath begin to steady. "Good," he muttered. "I got it in time."

A few moments later there was nothing left of the Black Briar but scorched tendrils against the tower's stones. Rasullis sighed and Dendron moved for the first time in many minutes. The king looked around at his officers. "Say nothing of this to anyone. It was not important. Understand?" They all nodded, though more than one glance went the wizard's way. "All right. Off with you, now. There's work aplenty to be done. Get the slaves out and get my castle cleaned up." Except for his personal guard, they went to do his bidding.

"It isn't a great loss, my king," Rasullis said. "We can go to Yoriand, collect more of the berries—there must be some that were not totally consumed in the fire—and then we can make more Elixir."

"What went wrong with that batch?" the king questioned as they stood alone in the courtyard. "Isn't it the same stuff you gave Nolin?"

"Well, yes, but—"

"And then the dwarf died of fever."

Rasullis's lips tightened. "Unrelated!" he snapped.

"I don't think so. In fact, wizard, I think you've got the wrong recipe for the potion. So until you get the bloody thing figured out, stay away from me!" He turned on his heel and strode out of the courtyard, flanked by his bodyguard.

His back was unprotected and the enchanter ached to release a bolt that would kill the ingrate before his next breath, but he restrained himself. When the king was gone, Rasullis turned back to the scorched and shriveled vine. It had certainly looked like Ritnym's Bane, he thought, and the smell had been described in lore. But Ritnym's Bane should have been impervious to his flame, since it was of the ancient Warding itself.

He decided that this vine had been only a sport of the true Greenbriar. Dangerous, but effectively exterminated. The dwarf had only contracted a fever; his death had nothing to do with the Elixir.

He felt better as he stepped through the sagging doorway and made his way up the intact stairway to his own rooms.

Some time later, as the scorched seed pods of the Black Briar cooled, each tough receptacle popped open. Thousands of spores were released onto the slight breeze. They eddied about the stonework, out over the broad lawn, past the great gates, down the Sweep, and finally wafted with the night mist that rose from Willowsrill to cover the broad river valley of Ilyria.

As soon as Alphonse stepped inside the door, he stopped and lifted his head, but he was not looking at the child in the bed. He was listening, and he knew even as the first notes rolled over his mind that he was hearing the Song sung by one who knew it best. He was hardly aware of easing the unconscious Quint to the floor.

"Lordling!" Peewit cried joyfully, and Kursh blurted, "By the Powers!" The rest of the Watchmen stared.

Gerrit threw back the covers and bounded from the high bed. His nightshirt was rumpled and he ran up to Tristan and took the tall man's hand. "I am to be your guide," the boy said. "Come along, everyone." He looked up at Ariadne. "You're my sister, aren't you?"

His eyes were the same gray as her own and the tilt to the chin was the same. Impulsively she stroked his mussed hair. "Yes. I am Ariadne."

"The lady said you would look like Papa." He regarded her with bird-bright eyes. "You do." He took her hand.

Before any of the stunned group could gather their wits, the walls of the chamber dissolved, or maybe their eyes began to see more clearly, and suddenly they were not in a chamber at all, but standing on the bank of a broad river that flowed through an underground cavern. A warm wind blew and they saw that the walls of the cavern were sparkling, but whether this was water sliding over rock, or firelight in gems, they could not be sure.

They heard a splash out on the water. "There is a barge," Gerrit said, "but sometimes you have to wait for it."

Kursh was the first to find his voice. "Where are we, Lordling?"

The boy said matter-of-factly, "You know."

A draft of fear blew over the Watchmen. "I do not wish to cross the water," the dwarf said for all of them.

Gerrit assured him, "It's all right, Master Kursh. You are guests, only, the Lady says."

"What Lady?" the captain demanded.

The boy regarded him. "The Lady of Earth, of course." He pointed across the echoing water. "Over there is Ritnym's Realm." It was the folk name for the kingdom of the dead.

Wild panic ignited in the dwarf and he turned back, thinking to wrench open the door through which they had entered the Guardian, but he found only rock behind him. "We can't get out!" he shouted.

From out on the water came a hail: "Will you kindly stuff your mustache in your mouth, Master Longbeard! There is no need for a lot of foolish carrying on."

A barge, high-prowed and dark, glided out of the shadows and nudged the landing. In it stood an old man, the Serpent of the Meld tattooed about his throat, his surcoat gleaming amethyst.

"*Llodin!*" the captain cried.

The old wizard allowed a broad grin to spread over his face. "Well met, my friends. I am glad to see you well, even in these darkest of times. Come aboard, now; we've not a moment to lose."

No one moved except Gerrit, who dropped Ariadne and Tristan's hands and hopped nimbly into the boat.

Llodin shook his head and told them, "You have nothing to fear. It is as Gerrit has told you: you are the lady's guests. I assure you that when the time comes, you may return to the world above." Still they hesitated, and the wizard saw the glances that passed among them. "I never deceived you in my life. I would not do it here."

Alphonse listened a moment more to the music from over the water, and then went to his old master. "May the Unmaker cross? Is this for me?"

Llodin placed a hand upon his shoulder. "While you are here, you are not the Unmaker, my lad. Listen to your heart's delight." Alphonse nodded and took a seat.

Tristan glanced to Imris, and the Eldest smiled. "I smell Nilarion. I will go across the water, and trust the Lady to send us back."

Fidelis looked down at Quint. "May we bring our friend?"

The old wizard waved impatiently. "Yes! *All* of you! And be quick about it!" Somewhere there was a subdued rumble, like distant thunder, and the enchanter looked up tensely. "Get aboard! Above us the earth is breaking up and you stand there like children amazed in an enchanted wood!" He extended a hand to Ariadne. "Haste, Queen of Ilyria!"

She did not know why she trusted this stranger, but she did. Grasping Tristan by the arm, she tugged him forward. Peewit followed, and Fidelis stooped to Quint's shoulders. Only Kursh still hesitated.

Llodin's eyebrows bristled. "Fool of a dwarf!" he roared. "She knew you would be the difficult one! Here." He withdrew a small object from the pocket of his robe. "The lady sends you a token." He tossed it, and the dwarf's broad hand caught the shining thing out of the air. When Kursh looked, he held in his palm a brooch pin of ancient dwarfish design, out of which a ruby gleamed. Llodin told him, "You may speak with him."

With a fierce light in his eye, Korimson thrust it into the pouch at his belt and bent to take Quint's feet.

They were quickly aboard and the dark boat glided out onto the river. The twinkling lights of the cavern walls and vault were reflected in the water and as they went further from the bank, it grew more difficult for Ariadne to tell where the walls left off and the water began. Like the boats at Covencroft, this one had no oars and no helmsman. The barge just went.

Whether it was awe of the place or fear of what lay on the farther bank, none of the company spoke. When the queen looked around at them, each seemed lost in his own thoughts, gazing about him at the vast cavern and its mirror. Then, before Ariadne was ready, the Lordling lifted a hand to point and she perceived a dark strip of shore. There was a dock, and among its boulders huge leaves and bright flowers bent to their twins in the water. The air was pleasantly warm and threaded with a strong scent of some spice she could not quite identify. Though she saw no torches or lamps, the place was lit with a greenish radiance—an effect like that of the sun through a canopy of leaves—and she found that deep moss cushioned her steps as she ventured a little past the landing. Before her was luxuriant foliage and twists of ropy vines, but she could not tell whether these were roots hanging down or plants growing up. That was an odd thought, but it came and went too quickly for her to grasp.

She was, all at once, very tired.

"It is the mist from the river," said a musical voice, a woman's voice, with an undertone like a trilled flute. Ariadne swung her head. The Lady of this place had come among them so quietly they had not been aware of her, and now she stood near Gerrit and Llodin. Long white hair, white as a swan's wing, was bound back from her brow by a circlet of leaves, and under this her face was a shock, for it seemed as young as Ariadne's own. The Lady's eyes were the deep rich brown of freshly turned earth in the spring, and her complexion was golden, with peach blooming over the high cheekbones and rose at the lips. Her robe was the color of new grass, and it was drawn in with a girdle of woven straw. She was smiling. "If you will come a little away, children, you will find your heads clearer." Without waiting, she turned and walked away and now Ariadne saw a path where she had not seen one before.

Gerrit came to take her hand. "Come along, and mind you don't step on the flowers." His voice dropped to a confidential whisper. "The Lady's a bit fussy about that."

Ariadne smiled. In the next instant—without knowing whether she had actually moved a step—she found herself stepping from stone to stone across a small pond. Water lilies bloomed about her feet and when a moment later she gained the tiny island in the midst of the water garden, she looked up and gasped.

As Yoriand had been all autumn, Ritnym's Realm was all springtime.

Plum and cherry trees flowered magenta and light pink by the banks of the pond. Deep blue of iris spiked through the lush grass, topping nodding yellow trumpets of daffodils and there were drifts of pale white windflowers all about. Further off, through the branches of the nearest trees, Ariadne glimpsed the rose and white of apple blossoms and the bright green of new beech. Everywhere there was the smell of moist, fertile earth. A gentle rain was falling, but this did not seem disagreeable in the least.

Ariadne laughed with delight and turned to the Lady. Ritnym nodded and smiled and waved them all to the simple benches of stone grouped about a sundial. As they sat, she herself served them all, bearing around to each a tray on which earthenware goblets of clear liquid sparkled. "It is quite all right for you to drink this. It is water from Earth-Above, from a certain spring I know." Her soft brown eyes went to Imris as she said this and seemed to twinkle.

The Yoriandir sipped. "Sileaught!"

The Lady laughed lightly and offered a glass to Fidelis, but he only stared at her, held fast by awe. Her look softened. "Will you not drink with us, Retreat Master?"

He started then and swallowed, holding out a trembling hand to receive the goblet.

She gave it to him and patted his arm before moving on. Ritnym stooped to Gerrit last, saying, "You may go now, child. I have things to say to them."

Her eyes were on a level with his. The boy dropped his voice to a whisper. "Why are they all so sad? Is it because of—"

"Yes. They have already been part of the fight, and they do not even know it. But I would prefer to tell them when their hearts are strengthened."

Gerrit clasped his hands behind him. "Would it be all right if I gave my sister something?"

"You know our rules: she may take nothing with her."

A child-sly smile touched his mouth. "She could if *you* gave it to her."

The Lady's eyes widened, and suddenly she laughed, straightening. "The ages have been long since I have been surprised, little one, but you have managed it! Give your present then, and we will call it Ritnym's second gift to the House of Beod Earth-Friend!"

Flushed with his success, Gerrit went to Ariadne and stood shyly looking down at his feet. The group waited.

Behind him the Lady prompted, "Hurry, Gerrit. Time races in Earth-Above!"

"What is it?" Ariadne leaned a little toward him.

"It isn't much," he mumbled. "I didn't know you were coming." He suddenly lifted his chin. "But you see, it's my job to take care of these." When he brought his hand from behind his back, a smooth, egg-shaped stone lay in his palm.

Ariadne smiled as a fond woman does when a little child gives her a rock. "It is very beautiful. Why, I can see the prettiest shades of blue and green, and this dark part here looks like a tiny forest!"

Gerrit looked back over his shoulder at Ritnym. She smiled and nodded. The boy handed the stone to Ariadne. "I must go now. I'm glad I got to meet you before—"

The Lady broke in. "That's enough, now."

He folded Ariadne's fingers about the rock, reached to give her a peck on the cheek, and circled around the sundial. As he passed by Peewit, he suddenly looked the Littleman full in the face and said quietly, "You had better take care of her." Before the surprised Brickleburr could find anything to answer, the boy skipped away over the stones and ran up past the cherry blossoms.

Watching him go, Imris said, "He did not ever make it to the Guardian all those years ago, did he?"

The Lady shook her head silently.

The captain frowned and shifted in his chair, and when he spoke it was to Llodin. "Then why did you bid me seek the Guardian? What was your vision of the prince?"

The enchanter looked to the Lady. "I was given the vision precisely to bring you here. You, and the queen. It was not my power, Tristan; I was only the tool. But I did not understand it myself until I . . . came here."

"I should be the one to explain, Master Wizard," the Lady of Earth said. "Captain, you and your group have played a valiant part in something you had not the slightest inkling about. You have brought together at this fateful time my gift and the one who has the power in herself to wield it. It is no accident that now, for the first time in all the long line of Greenbriar heirs back to Beod himself, a queen holds the Crystal. Indeed, my daughter"—she fixed her eyes upon Ariadne—"I made it for you."

Ariadne started to ask, "But how did you know that I would be—" and then she realized what a stupid question that would seem to a Power.

But Ritnym did not smile at her gaffe. "It was woven into the foundation of the world, my Robin." When the queen started at this use of her adoptive name, the Immortal's expression softened. "If Earth survives, it will not be healing that is needed, but rebirth."

Ariadne suddenly got a glimmering, possibly a fragment of the Lady's thought: "It is not just Lord Rasullis."

"No," the Lady confirmed, "it is not just he. In fact, the Fallen himself has very little understanding of what he has wrought."

"And I am to put it right?"

The Watchmen, together with old Llodin and the boy-wizard, stared at the queen. Ritnym regarded Ariadne confidently, but with compassion in the brown eyes. "I think you will choose to try." She held up one hand to stay the girl's next question, and turned to the captain. "When you return to Earth-Above, ye servants of the Greenbriar Queen, you will need certain aids for your task." She pointed away through the trees. "Follow the path a way and you will find a place where things have been made ready for you. It would be well to make haste—we have not much time left. Llodin, will you help them?" The enchanter nodded and rose, gesturing the group to follow him.

"What about Quint?" Fidelis asked. He hesitated. "Is he . . . to stay here?"

"Oh, no. That would not do at all," Ritnym said, and bent her gaze upon the recumbent figure. The burly man sighed and stirred. The Lady looked up at the healer. "He is well. Take him now and make you ready." Fidelis grasped Quint's arm and tugged him to his feet. The big man blinked and squinted as though suddenly roused from a deep sleep.

But Kursh stood fast. "Begging your pardon, Lady, but . . ." He swallowed and looked hastily down. Uncharacteristically for Kursh, now that it had come to it, he could not speak what was in his mind.

Ritnym smiled gently. "I have not forgot you, Master Dwarf. He waits yonder." She pointed past a willow that draped its catkins to the water. "Speak with him if you wish."

Without looking up, the dwarf followed the others across the stepping-stones. Ariadne was looking after him and suddenly realized they were gone. She wasn't sure whether or not she had seen them gain the other side of the pond, and she frowned.

"Come," Ritnym said, and suddenly she and Ariadne were standing on the crest of a hill. The landscape sloped away beneath their feet. A river twinkled through trees at the bottom of the hill. The queen turned slowly in a circle. To the east, mountains of dusty blackberry; to the north, the river flowed away into the distance and there a haze told of salt water; southward forested land lay below her vantage point and stretched far away in a pine-green plain until it rose to a series of hills; lastly to the west, an upland downs, thin with gorse and heather.

" 'Twas a bonny place, was it not? Do ye feel the wind

soft in your hair?" The voice was deep and clear, and Ariadne turned hastily to find the man it belonged to.

The sun was in her eyes, or else the bright light shone from him, and at first she could see nothing but a dark shape.

He spoke to Ritnym. "This is she? Nay, do not answer—I can tell that for myself. Well met, daughter."

Ariadne brought a hand up to shade her eyes and under her palm she looked at him. A tall man, broad of shoulder and thick of arm, with a streaming mane of blackest hair and eyes the color of woodsmoke. Ritnym answered the question in her mind: "No, this is not King Dhonald who was your father. Rather, this is your kinsman of old, Beod—he who is called Greenbriar and Earth-Friend."

The queen was struck mute; Ritnym, the Immortal herself, had not seemed half so remote to her. The gods are no part of our flesh, but the man before her stared back with eyes as gray as her own. She gathered her wits and made a deep reverence. "M'lord."

He raised her kindly, but his hand was cold as a winter stone. "Pretty as a wee nodding daisy," he murmured. Then his eyes sharpened and went to Ritnym. " 'Tis a heavy burden for such slender shoulders, Lady."

Ritnym clasped her hands before her. "Yes," she agreed. "But it is not the shoulders that will bear it, my friend; it is the heart, and this may not be measured by the outward form."

Still he seemed doubtful and shook his head slightly, with his eyes fixed the while on Ariadne. The queen straightened under that brooding gaze and she lifted her chin. "Will ye tell me what I am to do?" she asked quietly.

Ritnym pronounced, "The others are here," and suddenly they were—seated each in a high, gilded, jeweled throne. Five pairs of eyes beheld Ariadne. There were thrones for Ritnym and Beod too, and they sat. For Ariadne herself, there was a plain wooden chair. She glanced down at it, and elected to stand. "Now, let us take counsel again as once we did, my friends," said Ritnym.

"And let our choice be more illumined," Beod added.

The Lady of Earth continued, looking at Ariadne, "You have heard these names before, I think." She indicated the figure to her right, whose light gray hair billowed about his face as though stirred by a strong breeze. "My brother, Aashis, Lord of the Winds." The Immortal did not nod to her, but Ariadne sensed approval in the deep eyes. She bent her head and covered her eyes in token of reverence.

"Nay, fear me not, child," Aashis comforted in a voice as light as a summer draft around an open doorway. The queen took down her hand, but did not look at him again.

Ritnym continued, "And on my left, my brother Tychanor, Lord of the Warm Fire."

This Immortal was in the form of a young man of radiant good humor and leaping, ruddy complexion under hair redder by three shades than even Alphonse's. Sparks twinkled like gems down the front of his golden robe. "Welcome!" he said, and Ariadne felt immediately comfortable with him, as though someone had put a kettle on the hob, and there was a tabby purring on the hearth.

Next to Tychanor on Ritnym's left, a small figure grinned up at Ariadne. This was a Littleman of bright brown eyes and sandy curly hair. Unlike Peewit, this one wore a full beard, which swept about his round jawline and made him seem much younger than Brickleburr. "How do, dear?"

Even Ritnym was cajoled from her solemnity to smile. "Forefather of the little folk, Comfrey Lichen."

Ariadne dropped him a curtsy, and the Lady of Earth passed to the Yoriandir beside him. "And this is Dlietrian, First among Yoriandirkin." Though he wore no silver torque about his neck, he looked in every other respect so much like the Eldest that Ariadne experienced a pang of grief and had to look down quickly.

"I know," the soft voice said. "But you need not blame yourself." When she lifted stinging eyes to him, he added, "Your Eldest knew the price that would be exacted to keep you safe, and he made the choice freely." He smiled and lifted a hand, and there was a swishing of wings and bright flash of white. A pair of

Binoyr settled to her feet. As she gave an astonished
cry, he added, "Even as the Binoyr did. The spirit of
Yoriand is with you, lady."

Ritnym waved past Beod to the last throne. In this
sat a dwarf who had his long black beard looped over
his arm like the tail of a cloak. His brows met in a
bushy line across deep-set eyes and he neither nodded
nor smiled as Ritnym introduced him: "This is Ochram."

Ariadne regarded him and ventured, "Kursh has
been very stalwart." When still he did not react, she
said, "He favors you."

"Who?" Ochram barked.

"Kursh."

"Never heard of him."

Ritnym interjected quietly, "Tell no falsehood, my
friend. You have watched with as much interest as the
rest of us." The dwarf grunted and smoothed his beard,
and the Lady of Earth turned her gaze back to the
girl. "Will you sit?"

Absently, Ariadne did. "You have watched us?"

"Oh, yes," Ritnym assured her. "We could do no
otherwise; we have feared this for longer than memory
serves."

Beod said darkly and with sudden vehemence, "I
knew we should have destroyed him utterly when we
had the chance!"

"No!" Dlietrian objected as strongly. "We could
not, without unbalancing the forces!"

The dwarf swept his eyes about the group trucu-
lently. "And then *he* unbalanced them anyway."

Ariadne's eyes widened and fear raised sudden bumps
on her skin. "Ye speak of—"

"Name him not!" the Lady of Earth commanded.
"We will not give him the power of his own name!"
She gripped the carved armrests of her throne. "But,
yes—our other brother, Tychanor's twin."

The Lord of the Warm Fire murmured, "Tydranth."

When Ritnym turned to him, eyes widening, he
continued quietly, "His own name was good, sister,
just as he was himself. If we are to deal now with the
evil that he has become, let us remember that once we
called him brother and were fond."

Ritnym regarded him sternly. "You, being his twin, may do so. For myself, I have no memory of him thus. He is no part of me."

Ariadne sat with her eyes on the hands knotting themselves of their own accord in her lap. A voice said in her mind, 'You see? Even the Powers themselves pine when love turns to hate.' She knew before she looked up that the words belonged to Dlietrian. As if he knew where her thoughts went next, he sent, 'Your foster family is well. We have let them know by dreams that you are safe, though they will not let themselves do more than hope that their dreams are true ones. Still, it has been something for them to hold on to.'

The queen's eyes lit up and she thanked him with a grateful smile.

"It is well that you have such love for them, and they for you, my Robin," Ritnym said, and her voice was sad. There was a far-off rumbling, and Ariadne saw them all tense and listen. When it passed, the Lady of Earth drew herself straight. "We waste time. The Unnamed comes closer to breaking through each instant that we spend in talk. Ariadne, we have brought you here to ponder with you what shall be done. You have the Crystal, and you have seen how Rasullis the Fallen has burned the Earthgate and opened a way for Tychanor's brother to enter the world once more. Should that happen, we would have no choice—we would have to destroy all to destroy him. Everything— everything!—that we once created would be corrupted. And"—her voice fell—"even then, we might lose. With every evil, his power grows and ours weakens. *He* might very well destroy *us*."

The queen shivered and Aashis of the Winds puffed a breath of warmth to comfort her.

Ritnym continued, "We have debated long whether I should take back the Crystal of Healing, Robin." Ariadne bowed her head. "No, it is not that we do not trust you, child. Do not think so. But I put some of my own Power into your heirloom, and perhaps with it I could face the Unnamed and win. And therein lies our second danger: if we Immortals and these our friends exercise our Powers in the world, we should change the pattern of the earth as surely as if the Unnamed himself had done it, and perhaps to no less harm, though—unlike him—we would not intend it."

The queen raised her head. "But if a mortal uses the Crystal, it will be like sealing a door from the inside: it cannot be broken down from without, only unlocked from within."

The Lady of Earth nodded. "Even so."

"The . . . Unnamed will be shut out."

"Yes."

"Forever?"

Ritnym hesitated, and it was Tychanor who answered, "Even we Immortals cannot see down all the spirals of time. We did not foresee that this Rasullis would destroy Earthgate by burning Nilarion. But I think it will be forever—as mortals conceive it."

Ariadne said cautiously, "Forgive me. I do not understand why you brought me here. Had I a choice but to use the Crystal? And would I not have done this whether or not I knew all of this?"

Ritnym looked to Beod as if there were a weighty thing that needed saying and she herself was loath to do it. The gray-eyed man said, "There is a choice, daughter, and we felt you should know what you chose before you elected to try your fate with the Crystal." In measured tones he explained, "You see, if you manage to mend the rent in the Zones with the Crystal's power, the Earthgate will be closed. This will keep the Unnamed out, and that is the great good we hope for. But it will also prevent you from recalling anyone who has already passed into death. You will not be able to do for them as you did for your Imris."

"The Crystal was not supposed to heal Imris, then?"

Ritnym answered, "To heal, my Robin, but not to bring back. Never that. It is only because Rasullis had burned Earthgate that you were able to raise Imris. It was, if you will forgive me, a corruption."

Cold terror whipped through her. "Must he die again, then, when I use the Crystal?"

"No," Ritnym said softly. "No, not he."

The silence stretched until Comfrey Lichen slid from his high throne and came to take her hand. He looked

up into her fearful eyes. "We must tell you." He
swallowed. "It's Tristan." He squeezed her limp hand.
"By the time you use the Crystal, the man you love
will be dead. You won't be able to call him back
across the Zones."

All at once, she could not breathe. Past the knot in
her throat, she choked, "He will not die!"

They only regarded her with compassion as she struggled to her feet.

"He can't die! I—" She glared at them wildly. "I'll
order him to stay here, then! Or across the water in
the Guardian. If he doesn't go to Ravenholt with us,
he'll be all right!"

Ritnym caught her fluttering hands. "Robin. You
cannot keep him from his fate. Even if he were to
remain in the Guardian, death would find him. A
rockslide, a fall on the stone floor, his own sword.
Yes. Think of that—he would not suffer being twice
forsworn. He did not die with your father and it has
tormented him. Would he see you go into danger and
know that he could not follow?" As the queen began
to tremble, the Lady said softly, "You know him
better than to think so. Therefore, let his death at
least count for something. Allow him to accompany
you, and do not betray to him that you see his doom."

Almost soundlessly, the girl said, "I cannot. 'Tis too
heavy to be borne. Take the Crystal, Lady. You use it."

Far and near there was silence.

Then with a shudder beneath their feet and a crack
like that of the worst lightning, some far-off chunk of
the earth let go and they all heard plainly the crash of
falling stone and soil. Still, the council kept their eyes
fixed on the Greenbriar Queen, while Dlietrian said as
though quoting lore, " 'The ceiling of Earthcave falls
with an echoing crash.' The Fallen dreams true."

"Aye," Ochram rasped. "Truer than we do." His
smoldering eyes caught Ariadne's, and for an instant
she saw him with an eyepatch and a murdered nephew.

An icy calm clamped itself over the terror in her
heart. "I will take the Crystal. I do not think I can
defeat him, but I will try. We have come this far, and
too many have already died. There will be a stop to it,

one way or another." She was looking down at the Binoyr.

Tychanor sprang up. "I was sure you would!" Joyfully he caught her about the waist and lifted her off her feet, twirling in a circle. At his touch, the cold calm eased, and she wept in sorrow.

Ritnym smiled at her brothers. "I told you she would say yes."

"Well, Orin."

"Hello, Uncle."

They faced each other on a bank fragrant with rosemary. Seemingly, neither could find anything to say until they blurted at the same instant, "Why in blazes did you stay in the tavern?" and "How is Kathy?"

Both stopped and Orin drew back a pace. Kursh answered, "She's well. Sad, as you can imagine."

The young dwarf had flushed and drew his toe through the grass. "It was pretty stupid of me, I guess. Should have done what you told me." He sighed and looked up, studying his uncle. "You shaved your beard for me, didn't you?"

"It's custom," Kursh answered gruffly. The boy looked well. He tried to block from his memory the body by the hearth.

Orin nodded.

"I left your brooch for the girl," Kursh told him.

The boy nodded again.

"Well." The older dwarf cleared his throat. "That's all, I suppose. Just wanted to talk to you for a bit. You know."

"I know."

Kursh abruptly turned on his heel and strode down through the herbs. When he got to the bottom, he stopped suddenly, and said over his shoulder, "You were a good lad, Orin."

The dwarven boy stood at the top of the bank. "And you were a father to me."

When Kursh swung to look up at him, Orin ran down toward him. The sergeant major found himself moving too. They met in a tangle of rosemary leaves, and Kursh clasped the boy in a fierce bear hug.

* * *

Peewit drew the sword belt snugly to his waist and slipped the fine weapon into the damasked sheath. He had turned his curly head to remark to Quint that the garments were an exceedingly fine fit when Kursh came striding through the flowering shrubbery. The Littleman caught a fragment of a whistled song that sounded like "Marian the Fair," but the dwarf stopped when he realized they were all staring at him. "What's the matter with you, then?" Kursh growled.

The Littleman grinned and winked at the Yoriandir, who hid his own smile.

Kursh walked forward and looked down at the neatly folded uniform. "This is mine, I take it?" He shook it out. "Seems well made."

"As good as anything that ever came out of our own workrooms," Peewit assured him as the dwarf cast his cloak aside.

The earth suddenly lifted under their feet. Above their heads they heard a rending crack, and the Littleman ducked instinctively and squeezed his eyes shut. After a long moment he opened them to find the others staring nervously around and, like him, waiting for the next shock. Petals sifted off the apple tree above them.

"Imagine what's going on at the surface if it's like this down here," Imris murmured.

"A sorry old time of it they'll be having," Quint said. He was thinking what it would be like in a cave near the Yoriand border.

Peewit heard something lost and sad in his voice and to take his mind off whatever it was, observed, "You're looking much more like an officer of the Briar, Master Outlaw." The huge man made an imposing picture. Like the others, save for the two wizards and Fidelis, William was clad now in full battle uniform of the First Watch: a long-sleeved, knee-length tunic of bright green; over this, a sleeveless hip-length vest of burnished iron rings; pine-green leggings cross-gartered with silver strips; supple high boots and thick green gauntlets. At his waist was girt a long sword and he held his padded helm in the crook of one elbow.

Quint looked down at himself. "Never thought I'd see the day I'd wear the colors of the Rose into battle again."

"Nor did any of us, William." The captain stepped from behind the tree. The embroidered Greenbriar on his surcoat twined from his sword hilt up to his right shoulder, and his eyes glittered behind the noseguard of his helm. He half drew his sword and studied the etched Briar that, despite so many years, was still cleanly graven down the blade.

Llodin cautioned, "Weapons and uniforms will not defeat the Bastard's troops, and mail will not turn aside the Fallen's fire." When the captain's eyes snapped to his, he added, "This you already know. Therefore be not too confident. You *may* win, but the odds stand against you."

There was a silence.

Imris settled a quiver of arrows slung from his belt. "With Nilarion gone, it is only a matter of time. We could simply leave Rasullis and Dendron to their fate. Now that we know the Lordling is here, Under-Earth, there is no hope that he may prove greater in the ability to use the Crystal of Healing than Ariadne is. If she could not heal Earth-Pillar, it cannot be healed."

Alphonse, who until now had dreamed over the Song he was hearing, suddenly looked at the Yoriandir sharply. "No! You do not understand, Eldest. Nilarion lives!"

Even Llodin looked surprised, but it was Peewit who demanded, "How do you know?"

The redhead smiled and his blue eyes focused on something beyond them. "Because I hear it."

The captain shot a look at the older wizard. "Is this true?"

Llodin bowed his head. "I do not know, my friend. When a wizard comes here, his power is poured back into the Song itself. Thus he becomes—mortal, I suppose you would say. I cannot hear now what Alphonse can. But I do not doubt that what he says is so."

Cautious hope lit the Eldest's eyes. "But Nilarion must be very feeble, else why does the earth shake so, and the skies stay as open as a sore?"

Alphonse, lost in the music, did not answer, but

Peewit grinned to himself, remembering the leafkin he had planted by the side of Nose-Tickler.

"You're bloody cheerful for someone who's in the halls of the dead," Kursh told him as he buckled a broad belt.

Like a cold touch, the dwarf's comment drove the smile from the Littleman's face. "And you're enough to give a goblin collywobbles," Brickleburr snapped. "It hasn't been half bad so far, and I expect as soon as the Lady brings back the queen, we'll be getting out of here."

Under the strap of the eyepatch, one bushy eyebrow lifted. "Do you?" His voice dropped. "Ever hear of anybody who's come out of here alive, Peewit?"

The Littleman bristled and faced him squarely. "Ever hear of anybody who's *come* here alive? This is a rare privilege!"

The captain looked over their heads to Llodin. The wizard interjected mildly, "You might more profitably spend your time planning what you will do in Earth-Above when the Lady sends you back. Since she has given you these armaments, it seems likely there will be need of them."

"Just one chance at Rasullis, that's all I ask," the dwarf rasped, his hand going to the ax at his hip.

Alphonse's eyes sharpened and he said, "Do not ask boons in this place! You may get your wish!"

A shadow flitted across Kursh's face and his fist clenched round the ax haft, but then he smiled grimly and deliberately repeated, "Just one chance."

Too hastily, Fidelis jumped into the silence. "Maybe we won't have to deal with the Fallen. Maybe the Lady herself will do that."

As Llodin shook his head, Alphonse sighed. "No," he said. "Rasullis is my responsibility." The lines that ran across his brow as he frowned seemed to age him enormously, and a light seemed to go out of his countenance.

The old wizard comforted, "You will not fail."

"Think you not?" the boy muttered, and there was in his tone an echo of the despair Tristan had heard in their talk before the wolf attack.

"You dare not."

One corner of Alphonse's mouth dragged down. "No, I dare not."

Before the captain could contribute a bracing thought, the air seemed to shimmer and suddenly the Lady stood there with Ariadne. When Tristan saw the red in the queen's eyes, his instant thought was that, somehow, she had met the king her father and the queen her mother. Of all the people in the group under the apple tree, her gray eyes sought him out first and rested on him. Her lips parted and she seemed about to say something, but then Ritnym touched her arm lightly and Ariadne dropped her gaze. "We shall go now," the queen ordered, and not one of the group missed the catch in her voice. The Watchmen exchanged glances.

Thinking to offer her some reassurance, the captain suddenly brought his fist to his chest in a salute, and there was a stir as the others did the same.

Ariadne waved an acknowledgment, but she did it halfheartedly, and Tristan thought he saw irritation in the way she pulled her new green cloak about her shoulders. If the others had not been present, he would have asked what so troubled her, but inhibited from this, he could only surmise that the queen's parley with the Lady had brought some bitter news. "Tell us what we must do, my queen," he said staunchly.

Once more her eyes met his and after a moment she replied, "The barge awaits us. We go above, and thence to Ravenholt." She stopped.

"And then?" the tall man prodded, trying to be patient.

Alphonse went to the queen and, with a presumption that raised hackles down the captain's back, put a finger under Ariadne's chin and lifted her downcast head. "And then we shall need every scrap of courage we've got," the Unmaker answered for her.

She put her hand on his wrist and tried to smile. When he withdrew his hand, she straightened and advanced a step to stand before Llodin. "I did not know you, master, but I am told your wisdom has long protected me. For this I thank you."

Old Llodin, who never in life had bowed to any man, raised her hand to his bearded lips. "Go well, my lady. May you find the peace denied you now."

The queen swallowed and then turned to face her men. "Gentlemen, I am very glad to have such friends as you. Let us go." Her voice was sad and royal; even her diction was no longer that of the farm-fostered girl.

Thus far the Lady of Earth had said nothing, but now she looked around at all of them. "Be of good cheer. You have more allies than you know. Remember your Oath!"

Still rankling at Alphonse, Tristan stated with cold formality, "We have never forgotten it, Lady."

The soft brown eyes rested on his stern figure and the captain's heart thawed suddenly; behind the iron helm, his look went to Ariadne and he very much wished they could go someplace far from here where he was not a man of war and she was not his queen. Ritnym smiled gently. "Go now."

With a final sweet breath of Ritnym's Realm behind them, they were immediately back at the bank of the river, standing on the stones of the dock. The barge floated on the mirroring water. Neither the Lady nor Llodin was with them. Ariadne did not even look around for them, but led the way and stepped into the boat. The group followed her and as soon as they were seated, the craft left the shore. Silently they passed to the middle of the river and then the current caught them and sent them downstream. Kursh grabbed fearfully for the thwarts. "The door is on the other side, back up there. We're going the wrong way!"

"No," the queen corrected. "This is another way. You have only to hold on tight and trust. Nay, do not stand, any of you. The boat will bear us, no fear." As she spoke, the boat picked up speed until it was fairly arrowing through the water. On the surface of the river there appeared now eddies and visible currents.

The captain's instincts woke with horror. "There is whitewater ahead!" he had time to shout before the boat shot through a misty pall and sunlight struck them with blinding brilliance. They gasped and shielded their eyes.

Ritnym's barge was borne like a leaf on the foaming water and by the time their eyes had adjusted to the light, which dimmed suddenly as they drew away from the cavern, the scenery on either side of the river was streaking by at a dizzying rate. Alphonse let out a wild cry and grasped his head with both hands as though a sword had cloven his skull. "No-o-o," he moaned, and a weight too heavy for him seemed to crush him to the bottom of the boat, where he lay huddled.

The queen moved as surely as if the rocking vessel had been a smooth floor. She put a hand firmly on the back of the wizard's neck. "Alphonse, get up." As the banks on both sides of the river abruptly showed white with drifted snow, she said sharply, "Get up! I can't do this alone!"

The Unmaker appeared jolted by the urgency in her voice, for he fought himself upright and clamped his jaw against a further outcry.

"What is it?" the captain demanded of them.

When she turned on him, her eyes were blazing with fear and anger. "Can't you smell it?" She flung out an arm, encompassing the whole landscape. *"It's all dying!"*

As Tristan leaned to look past the Yoriandir, who was next to him, he saw that the Eldest had his eyes closed and his color was bad. "Imris, are you well?"

The Yoriandir gathered himself. He spoke with difficulty. "Yes. It is hard, that is all. I am so tired, Tristan." A tremor ran through him. "If Nilarion lives, as Alphonse says, it is no good to me; I cannot feel it at all."

Peewit turned to face him. "Hold on, Imris," he pleaded. "The leafkin—er, that is . . ." He broke off as the tree-tender raised his head.

The Eldest searched his face. A snowflake drifted lazily down and lit on his flaxen hair, and in a moment they were in the thick of the storm. The Yoriandir blinked away a cold touch upon his eyelid. "So you think there will be spring again, my friend?"

"I do," the Littleman told him stoutly, though he wondered behind his eyes whether any Yoriandirkin would be left to welcome it.

As they spoke, the landscape sped by and the snow

became thicker, but so swift was their passage that it did not settle upon them. With the rush of wind came a rotten stench that enveloped them as if they had broken through into a charnel house. The trees were stripped of needles and leaves and at any moment the Watchmen expected to see a huge herd of slaughtered animals or of Ilyrian slaves among the bare thickets, but there was nothing to account for the smell.

"By the Powers!" Kursh swore from behind a gauntlet.

"What can it be?" the Littleman asked, squeezing his nostrils shut.

The Unmaker stared ahead. The color had drained from his face, leaving his freckles marooned. "Ritnym's Bane," he said, and his voice was as lifeless as the landscape.

As the stinging pellets of ice found their way through the cheek guards of his helm, the captain's eyes suddenly narrowed. The last vestiges of the trance of the Zones were dispelled by the cold gusts. Even as the remnants of a fallen bridge flashed by, his hands flew out to grasp the thwarts. "The falls!" he shouted. "Turn! Turn, as you love your lives!"

But there was nothing to use for a rudder, and no oars. The First Falls of Willowsrill were less than three miles away.

While Kursh and Peewit, who had been wakened to action by the captain's hoarse yell, frantically strove to use their hands as paddles, Ariadne spoke up calmly. "Fear not! This craft will bear us even over the falls."

Tristan flung her a look as though she had told a joke at a deathbed vigil, and scrambled to the stern, where a neat coil of glistening rope had caught his desperate eye. "Kursh!" When the dwarf turned, the captain held up the line.

The stalwart sergeant major never hesitated. "Aye. Give it here."

"No. *I'll* go," the tall commander shouted and over-rode the dwarf's protest with, "I need your strength on this end! If I fail, you'll be able to pull me in—I couldn't do the same for you."

Kursh clamped his jaw and nodded once, reaching for the free end of the rope as Tristan threw it.

But it was the queen who caught it, and she leaped to her feet. "Wait! I tell you, we shall be safe!"

"*Ariadne!*" Tristan bellowed.

The Unmaker rose beside her. "It is true, Captain. The barge is Warded. It is *meant* to ride the falls. Sit now, lest you be thrown from your feet."

Ignoring what he took to be a sudden fit of insanity from the two of them, the captain jerked the rope out of Ariadne's hands and quickly gathered it once more. The dwarf grasped the boy-wizard's shoulders and firmly moved him a step aside in order to pass. "Pardon, lad."

A surge of garnet stung Kursh's hands and he released the Unmaker with an oath. "Sit down, Kursh," the wizard ordered coldly.

The dwarf saw his duty clearly, and he swung a ham-sized fist.

In the same instant, Ariadne cried out, and whether the plea reached him, or whether his own nature restrained him, the Wizard of the Three choked the hot fire that rose in him and only pushed Kursh's fist back at him. The dwarf went backward over the thwarts, and lay groggily waggling his head. Tristan was already going for Alphonse's back, while Peewit scrambled back from the bow to take the dwarf's place. The enchanter flung out both arms and held all three of them in a spell of command. Carefully he maneuvered them until they were safely seated and then glanced back to where Imris sat quietly in the stern. "Please don't move, Eldest."

The Yoriandir regarded him gravely, and the rushing river beyond him. "The Lady told you we would be safe?"

"Yes!" the queen answered with exasperation. She had to shriek to be heard; the river here narrowed into a chasm, and now even this enchanted craft was rocking.

Imris watched the blurred lands rush by. "Then you had better sit too, hadn't you?" he said.

12

The day was a glittering gray. Ice paved the ground, and the earth was frozen in a winding sheet of cold. The wind sheared like a knife across the hedgerows and fields, and cut the heart out of the Willowsrill valley. Not once in their passage down the river had they seen a flicker of life. The cots were silent, the occasional smithy smokeless and rime-encrusted. If folk were within the frozen walls, they apparently did not dare venture forth. Ariadne's heart ached.

Time and time again Alphonse was forced to kindle his fire just to keep them from freezing. It was fortunate that the Lady's barge traveled swiftly even after it leaped First Falls and descended through the minor cascades to the valley. The Willowsrill made a wide loop southwestward and then came about to flow down east to the sea. A journey that on a horse might have taken as much as two months—if any horse had been able to make its way in such weather—thus was accomplished in a little less than a week.

Through all this time—for the days were long indeed with flying snow and ice needling them, and the nights were even worse—Imris had not said more than a few words. He only huddled with the rest of them 'neath the tent of cloaks they tried to hold over their heads. The cold, or the force that sent it seemed to sap his spirit and his strength. The queen and the Unmaker exchanged knowing looks and to each came a picture of a smooth sapling, its green and silver leaves curled tight against the steely wind, standing deep in drifted snow. Beneath its roots, Nose-Tickler was locked in ice.

Peewit had told all of his merriest jests, some of

them twice, and since they all knew what he was doing and why he was doing it, they let him rattle on. Even Kursh showed more forbearance than the queen had thought him capable of. It was not until the third day that she realized he was holding his fingers in his ears and chewing the ends of the short mustache that had grown back in. A giggle rose in her tired heart and she looked away from the two of them to stifle it. Tristan's eyes met hers and he smiled for her alone. Beneath the folds of the thick cloak, she reached for his hand and held it for a long time.

Alphonse would often mutter under his breath and in each day's grayer light, they could see the flesh pared away from the planes of his face, revealing an emerging adult countenance. The mobility, the shy curiosity, the sudden embarrassed blush, these were gone. In their place were a chin firm to the point of brittleness and a focused gaze that looked at something the rest of them did not see and found it bitter as wormwood.

Quint spoke of his men, of how the countryfolk had sometimes hidden them or exchanged fresh vegetables for a haunch of venison, of the caves where they took refuge, and finally of his own family. There was an eight-year-old son, Thom; a five-year-old daughter, Elen; and the baby, little Wills. His wife, Meri, could make a right good loaf from acorn mast, he vowed. And then he fell silent and picked at a loose bit of rawhide at the cuff of one green gauntlet. Peewit deftly turned the talk to a journey he had once taken with a troupe of traveling minstrels.

Fidelis was another who did not talk much, but not from depression or sorrow, and Ariadne concluded eventually that it was not fear, either. The healer listened, laughed to encourage the Littleman, and kept a watchful eye on the Yoriandir. Once, the queen blew into her hands and looked over her blue fingernails to find him watching her. "What are you thinking?" she asked in a low voice.

Within his hood, Fidelis's face showed a rueful twist to the lips. "I am thinking that I shan't be left behind in the village this time," he answered. Then, seeing that she did not understand, he explained how it had happened that he had not been with the others on the day of the fateful battle. "For many years," he added, "I felt somehow as if fate had betrayed me. I even thought of riding up to Ravenholt and challenging them to kill me." He smiled at her and shrugged. "And now, when I soon shall do exactly what I dreamed of doing, I suddenly find that I would very much rather not."

"Then do not. I certainly shall not hold it against you."

For a moment he thought she doubted him, and then read her response for what it was. "Ah, no, my lady. A man does not often get a chance twice in his lifetime to do something that he knows is utterly right. No, I will not stay in the barque with the baggage!" The hood fell further forward and his eyes receded into it. "But I am afraid."

"So am I."

The Eldest sighed and stirred and from somewhere in the Yoriand of his heart, he summoned a shining smile. "Take courage, Chosen of the Binoyr! You shall not fail!"

This drew an answering smile from her, but she wondered if he knew how close Tydranth was to breaking through.

Imris's golden voice filled her mind: 'You shall not fail, my queen. This I believe with all my heart, though the Lord of the Wild Fire even now reaches his finger of death toward us.' When her eyes widened, she heard him add, 'After all, spring always defeats winter, does it not?' Again the brilliant smile flooded his face with light, and then a spasm seemed to freeze his marrow, and he sank again into a cold stupor.

She wiped tears on the rough woolen cloak, but her lashes froze anyway.

Near noon on the fifth day, the queen woke with a start. At first she could not imagine what had called her back to consciousness. She squinted and peered around at the other bundled shapes. A thick scum of icy snow lay crusted on their cloaks, but that was common now, and did not concern her. There had been no change in the wind; it lashed at her exposed face. The sky—what she could glimpse of it between the hands she threw up to protect her eyes—was the same leaden gray.

Then she realized that the boat was not moving.

She reached down near her feet and shook the captain awake. When he raised his head, scowling, she said, "The river is frozen. We're stuck."

Disentangling his long legs, he woke the others and everyone stared. The Willowsrill was a solid sheet, fissured and heaved in places. Earlier that morning they must have passed into an even colder sphere. Ariadne could feel the center of it like a canker in the back of her mind. "How far to Ravenholt, would you guess?"

Tristan peered from one dimly glimpsed embankment to the other. "If I am not mistaken, we are near the Lower Tollhouse. Wouldn't you say so, Peewit?"

The Littleman rubbed a powder of diamonds from his eyebrows and stared into the storm. "I think so. That knoll yonder could be the one above Coll's Corner, but I am not sure."

"It is," the dwarf confirmed. "Look, you can just see the jut of the tower round the bend." They looked where he pointed and could spy the toll station.

Peewit scanned the river ice. "Do you think it will bear us?" He sounded doubtful.

"Wait," the wizard cautioned. "Let me try something first." He raised his ringed hand and flung a garnet arc before the prow of their boat. A cloud of steam blew back in their faces and the barge rocked itself free. Steadily he cut a path for them and they proceeded slowly down the river.

"Careful," Ariadne said as the tower grew closer. "They'll see us."

"No matter," he replied, and then his teeth showed in a smile that she did not like. "The troops up there won't be near windows in this weather, and even if they were, they couldn't kindle a beacon. Besides, Rasullis knows we are coming." So saying, he brought them right under the looming window slits of the toll tower and, storm or no, Ariadne found that the Watchmen blocked her with their own bodies from a chance arrow.

The barge had barely cleared the next crook of the river when it jolted to a stop and Alphonse gasped. "His strength is far more than I thought!"

The queen looked up at him fearfully. "Whose?"

"The One we do not name," he ground between chattering teeth, and extinguished his fire.

"Is he here?" she cried.

With difficulty he shook his head. "Not yet. But already his power finds its way through the rent in the Zones." He pulled his garnet cloak about him, staring forward. "Ahead. At Ravenholt, I think. Yes, that is where he will break through. It is the weakest place. Almost I could think . . ."

Imris roused himself and a light shone in his fir eyes that made the queen think of the unnatural green of the sky before a destructive thunderstorm. "There *is*! There is another Crystal at work in the world—I can feel it! Now I perceive why my pith feels so frozen: Rasullis has made a Crystal and it wreaks this evil for Tydranth, its master! Oh, my friends, quickly, quickly we must begin to heal ere it is too late!" Feverishly he reached a slender hand to grasp the wizard's arm. "Forward, Alphonse, burn us free!"

The Unmaker did not shrug off his touch, but the effect of his next words was the same: "Master yourself, Eldest."

Stung, the Yoriandir stared up at him. "Earth dies," he said as if he spoke to the youth alone. "Will you not bring us where we can succor her with what small power we have?"

His garnet hood blew back and the redhead stood still in the storm's fury. "Indeed, it is one of my tasks," he acknowledged. If possible his blue eyes became colder. "But I must save what strength I can. I cannot squander it to melt ice." He raised his head and looked over to the right-hand bank. "There is a small village at the base of the hill. We will go there."

Tristan stood. "I have told you, wizard: we do not take our orders from you. We will go only if the queen wills it."

The Unmaker turned to Ariadne and there was a suggestion of a sneer as he waited for her order. Under that look, she rose slowly, taking a moment to gather the mantle about her and when she was ready, she fixed him with an equally cold gaze. "I don't like you this way, Alphonse. Only the burden you bear excuses your behavior. If and when we win through, I shall require greater civility to me and mine."

The iron-blue eyes widened and for a moment the bright color of forget-me-nots peeped through. He inclined his head slightly. "If and when we win through, Lady Queen, you shall have it."

Without acknowledging him, she turned to the captain and ordered quietly, "We'll go to the village. There may be some refuge for us there until we can see a way out of this mess."

"Yes, my queen." She could not miss the pride in his deep eyes, but she did not acknowledge this, either. Shortly, the band was ready with the packs and Tristan ordered them to run the end of the rope through their belts so that no one could become separated in the driving snow. Too, if someone broke through the ice, they would all immediately haul backward and hope to save him. He himself would go first, untethered, to try the passage.

When he had made these arrangements, they all turned to her expectantly. "The sooner we start, the sooner we get there. Onward, Captain." But when she saw him step over the side and advance onto the frozen surface, she had an almost overwhelming urge to call him back, to fling him an end of rope, to order William Quint to go first. None of these she did, but only watched as he fought for balance and led the way for the farther bank.

As bad as it was slipping across the river, it was far worse when they finally reached the bank. Out on the ice at least they could see somewhat where they were going and the surface did not betray them: it looked slick, and it was. But foundering through the deep snow as Tristan tugged them up the steep embankment was harder: the snow looked solid, but it was not. There were places, to be sure, where Peewit could slide along and not break through the crust, and once or twice even Ariadne found herself standing on a firm surface and the Eldest walked as easily as if the snow had been a cobbled road. Most of the time, however, the drifts were nearly to her waist and Quint had to keep a constant hand under her elbow to help her along. Tristan labored to break a path and Kursh followed him, widening it. Before they had reached the wooded road that led up to the village gates, they were all exhausted. They went grimly on.

No howling dog came to yap at their heels, no woodsman with a bundle of firewood swung into step beside them, no cooking smells beckoned them forward. If it had not been for the rough palisade they could glimpse through the trees at last, they would not have known there was a village.

Finally they stood beneath the timbered gate, yelling for someone, anyone, to open up. The sweat of their exertions turned cold while they listened for approaching footsteps and maybe the curses of the bailiff.

Save for the howling storm, all was quiet.

Peewit tilted his head to study the pointed logs that topped the wall. He did not have to ask; they made a ladder for him, Kursh the base and Tristan standing on his broad back. The Littleman clambered up, carefully negotiated the slippery palisade, and dropped down inside. A moment later, they heard the bar knocked from its holders. When Quint tried to push the gate inward, though, they heard Peewit call to wait a moment and he would try to clear away some of the drifted snow. While Kursh stamped and clapped his hands together to bring a tingle back to them, they could hear the Littleman working to free the bottom of the gate. Finally he had it and the timbered portal swung in a yard or so before it stuck fast.

The captain was the first through, his drawn sword ready. The others followed after. Quint and Kursh had a hard time of it. Within the wooden wall, the huts of the village crowded the smallish enclosure. It looked to be a poor enough place; they spied no smithy or mill, and the space for the common could not afford much grazing. The place seemed deserted. The captain noticed that there were no tracks in the snow.

"Halloo," Kursh suddenly shouted.

They all jumped and the Littleman rolled his eyes. "Well, we might as well find out the fast way," the dwarf rasped. "Makes more sense than standing about, freezing to death."

"Kursh, Peewit, take the houses on the right. Quint, you and I will go left. The rest of you stay here with my lady."

But before they could move, Imris lifted his head and told Tristan, "There is a tavern at the far end. Look you there first. Once I passed this way, and the landlord was better than the place warrants. His name is Dirk, I think."

The Littleman nodded and ran off, and the dwarf tromped along behind him. The captain and William Quint waited with the others. They watched the short figure and the broad one disappear into a long, low building at the end of the row.

The Littleman's shrill shout and the dwarf's booming "Captain!" came together. Tristan sprang forward and the rest followed. When they were nearly at the end of the row, the dwarf and the Littleman came tumbling through the doorway of the tavern and waved their companions back. Peewit's face was strained with fear. "It's plague! Stand off! Don't come any closer!"

As though he had put a spell of command on them, the queen's party halted in the snow.

"They've all got it—there must be twenty of them in here, I suppose it was the biggest building—and I think some may still be alive, but there's nothing we can do for them," Peewit rushed on. He ran out of things to say then because he and Kursh had both just been infected, and both of them knew what would happen next.

"Fire's surest," the dwarf said steadily, meeting the captain's eye.

Tristan nodded slowly.

The queen suddenly pushed past him, flinging them all a scathing glance. "Will you men kindly *think*! Alphonse!" she ordered.

"Here, lady," the wizard answered with no trace of sullenness. He followed her into the tavern before the others were loosed from their shock.

Imris was the first to move toward the door and, feeling foolish, the rest came after.

Inside, the queen was already bent over one of the nearer villagers, a middle-aged woman with badly decayed teeth gnawing at her lower lip as she strove to get a breath through her swollen throat. Ariadne straightened, pulling off her cloak. "Fidelis, you have a knife in your kit, I know. Alphonse will clean it with fire, first." She pointed to the hearth. "Can you do something about this?" she asked the Unmaker impatiently.

He looked about the room. "They have already burned even the furniture," he observed. "Well, no matter." The garnet flared at his fingertips and he directed it toward the thick damp ashes. These caught as if they had been pitch-soaked and within a moment welcome gusts of hot air radiated out into the room. One of the few people who was not ill was a pink-cheeked tot, perhaps two years old, who set up a howl as the fire crackled and popped. Peewit gathered him up and made faces until the child hushed, staring wide-eyed at the stranger.

As he had at Covencroft, the captain held the queen during the trance and if, after the Greenbriar had blossomed and fruited and Alphonse had collected the hips, Tristan held her for a few moments longer than was strictly necessary, no one seemed to notice. Ariadne herself was grateful for his strong arm around her. The dizziness this time was the worst yet. All at once the room was too warm.

Fidelis's face swam into her vision. "My lady? Will you be all right?"

"Of course," she muttered sturdily. She heard Tristan say something about water and eventually Kursh shoved a cup before her nose. She sipped, but it didn't help.

While the queen suffered the aftermath of the Crystal trance, the wizard concocted the Elixir. He directed Quint to fill a pail with snow and set it to melt near the hearth and by the time this was done, the healing potion was ready. Alphonse diluted the powerful Elixir with hot water and poured some into two bowls. Fidelis and Quint bore these around to the living and Alphonse followed with the full-strength liquid to feed it to the dead.

In less time than it had sometimes taken Fidelis to bandage a cut finger, the firelit tavern was full of people who yawned and stretched and only then stopped to stare at one another and at the strangers. A hush fell. When Tristan looked around, a man's voice from the back of the room asked, "Who be ye?"

The queen's men looked first to the captain and then to the queen. The first public proclamation should be a stately matter. Each of them felt instinctively that it would be better to wait. The Unmaker stood off to one side, alone, and it was he who answered, "Friends of the briar."

A plump young woman, her cap askew, stammered, "But . . . but— " Her trembling hands went to her throat as if searching for the swellings she dimly remembered.

The silence grew. "I seen that plant." This came in an elderly treble and a thin old man pushed himself up using the wall. " 'Twas a Greenbriar, wasn't it?" The Watchmen avoided his eyes, but Alphonse nodded once. A knobby old finger came up to point at Ariadne. "That's the lady what done it." Again the wizard confirmed this.

An underswell of murmuring began.

Slowly the queen rose, clutching Tristan's arm. She stood for a moment, looking around at the warm and living people she had reclaimed, and then she dropped his arm and her chin came up. "My name is Ariadne."

Thus it was that for the last part of the journey to Ravenholt the queen traveled in a broad-bottomed woodcutter's sledge, with two villagers leading the horses and nearly everyone else following in the ruts the sleigh cut in Willowsrill's ice. So strong was the surge of Elixir within the people that they swung along, heads up and as jaunty as if it had been midsummer and a market day. Men and women and children, they escorted their queen.

Along the two-mile run to the main landing below the Sweep, they were buoyed by a fair voice that sang both sweet and bold, but always with glad ease. Before they had left the poor tavern, amidst the excited bustle of cloaks and hats and leggings, Ariadne had taken the last of a cup and found Imris. "We need you hale," she had said without preamble, and pressed the wooden mug into his hands.

He had regarded the Elixir, tilting the cup so that the amber stuff had glowed in the firelight. Silently he raised the mug to her and drank the salute.

Now, as the Eldest stepped lightly beside her sledge and sang in the teeth of the storm, Ariadne found herself with a bittersweet sense that his was a treacherous January thaw. She hoped she was wrong, but knowing what they faced she could not feel as confident as she must try to look for them. "Captain," she called over the noisy throng, and when he leaned to hear, she told him, "Have Fidelis give the flask with the rest of the Elixir to Dirk. Tell the villagers to go with it to that village below Ravenholt. If plague is loose in the country, it will have hit there first. We must bring as many back as we can before—" She bit off what she had been going to say, remembering that he did not—could not—know.

Beneath the glittering pride, he was puzzled. "Surely that can wait, my lady," he suggested.

She lied. "I want these people out of the way, Tristan. They can do no good against swords." He bowed and withdrew, seeking out first the healer and then the village tavern keeper.

She tried to empty her mind, tried to steel herself, but her eyes followed his tall figure and suddenly her breath caught. She thrust a leather mitten against her teeth as though she were trying to protect her nose and chin from the cutting wind, and squeezed her eyes shut. A moment later, she felt a soft touch upon her arm and when she looked, Alphonse was there. He said nothing, only searched her eyes. Then he turned his head to watch the man with the embroidered Rose upon his uniform. After a moment he regarded the queen again, and mutely reached to brush a finger lightly across her cheek and then to bring a length of woolen stuff closer around her shoulders. Whether he knew, Ariadne could not tell, but she drew a fold of the material across her face and allowed the tears to come. Later, there would not be time.

If there were troops stationed at the small house at the landing, they were keeping very quiet. No smoke curled from the place. After watching it for several minutes, the captain told Quint and Kursh to check the shed. The villagers were silent, barely suppressing their excited chatter and craning to see. The queen's Watchmen approached the building on opposite sides and suddenly leaped through the doorway one after the other. A moment later, Kursh stuck his head out and waved them forward. A woman in the crowd clapped.

As Ariadne had been dreading the whole time they had been out on the river, a shaking struck the moment they set foot on the embankment. The terrified horses tried to bolt with the heavy sled and jammed it into the snowy bank. Ariadne managed to jump clear and landed in icy powder that stuffed itself up her sleeves. The river ice shrieked behind them and the villagers scrambled up the heaving slope, making for the track that led up to the castle. They cowered where they fell and fear replaced the exuberance with which they had left Coll's Corner. The queen shouted to the wizard, "This will not stop now! He knows we are come to Ravenholt!"

Alphonse nodded and fought himself to his feet, extending a hand to her. The captain and Kursh staggered to them, and Fidelis, Peewit, and Quint managed to lurch through the snow. She looked at each of them, measuring them—and herself—against the task. "Well," she said. "Now we are here." She wanted to say more, but between the quake and the fear, she could not find words.

The captain smiled, the hard smile of a warrior. "And now let us do what we came for."

She supposed it made him the brilliant soldier she had always heard tell he was. "Captain, you and your men are responsible for getting the Unmaker and me into the castle and for taking care of whatever of the Bastard's troops we shall meet. The king I leave also to you, but"—she put a hand on his sword arm—"please spare as many of the Barreners as you can." He stared as if she had told him to cut off his hand.

She turned to the dwarf. "Kursh, I must ask of you that you leave Rasullis to Alphonse."

The dwarf stared past her up at the looming walls. "As you order, my queen. But by the Powers, boy, if he gets away from you, he's mine." He tugged at the eyepatch, and hefted his ax.

The Unmaker made no answer. The shaking calmed to a tremor.

It was time.

The queen whispered, "I love all of you very much. You know that, don't ye?" Her eyes found all of them and came to rest on Tristan.

His hazel eyes warmed and he seemed about to reach for her. But he saluted instead.

"Let us go," the Unmaker urged.

So with many things left unsaid on the promise of a better time, they moved through the crowd of villagers and set their feet to the wain road. Before the queen and her party had gone far, a cheer came to their ears. Ariadne looked back and waved.

As the land trembled under them and the sky darkened to a false night above them, they climbed the Sweep until they stood at last under the very eaves of the castle. Boldly they stood before King's Gate and Kursh, acting as herald, boomed her name and lineage and claimed Ravenholt for the Queen of Ilyria.

Nothing happened.

"Try again," Peewit said. "Maybe they couldn't hear you over the storm."

"Maybe there is no one to hear," the captain said grimly.

Darkness was thick about them and the wind intensified, staggering them with its force. They felt more than heard the rumbling of the earth, and rode its swelling as though balancing on a barrel. Suddenly from the tower a hissing arc of sapphire lanced down over the battlements, even as the Unmaker flung up his ringed hand and answered with garnet.

Immediately, the group was caught in a hail of arrows from the rampart above King's Gate. Whether it was due to the wind or to their own quick action in flattening themselves against the iron-bound timbers, none of the Watchmen was hit and they shielded the queen as well as they could. The Unmaker alone stood in plain view before the gate and steadily held the Fallen's fire from reaching earth. Then, as easily as if it had been an adept's exercise, Alphonse pushed the sapphire back. When the blue flame flickered, he at once threw his power against the gate itself, but here he got a shock. "Woe!" he gasped. "This is not Rasullis's power!"

Ariadne knew immediately what he meant, so she went directly to the point: "Can you open it?"

Without answering, he stared steadily at the timbered portal. His eyes widened and a kind of corona appeared about the ring on his hand, a shimmering iridescence of garnet and amethyst, emerald and copper. The gate splintered like kindling and its iron strapping melted like lead. The shattered halves blew back against the inside tunnel walls.

Imris was the first through, and with deadly precision he dispatched half a dozen scarlet-and-sable-clad bowmen. The others fled their exposed position and retreated into the guardhouse at the right side of the gate. The Watchmen together with the queen and the Unmaker ran up the broad road and dodged into the first lane. Tristan led them, bearing for the hall. He was astonished that more of Dendron's troops were not in evidence.

By the time he had led them through the lane by the patched-up horse barns and taken a turn into the smithy, it was obvious why they had met so little resistance. They had had to leap over at least a dozen bodies, and all of them showed the purple swellings under jaws that jutted toward the darkened sky. "This may be easier than we thought," Kursh rasped as they halted for a moment in the lee of the armory.

"Don't be too sure," the captain snapped. "If there

were enough of them left to man the gate, then someone is still alive to give the orders. We know the
Fallen, at least, awaits us.''

The Unmaker looked where none of them could.
"Both Rasullis and the Bastard survived the unleash-
ing of the Bane. They think you already doomed by
it.'' At the look that passed among them, he added,
"Remember, they do not know that the Crystal of
Healing is in the hands of the heiress. Though the
Fallen knows that Ariadne is with us, he is confused
by what he can perceive of her power.'' He smiled at
the flicker of fear that reached him from Rasullis's
mind. "He rightly thinks me the chief threat to him.''

Peewit looked back the way they had come. "I hear
followers!''

The captain reacted immediately. "Through here!''
The group raced through the dark archway that con-
nected the smiths' row with the slaves' block. Bursting
through a door, they found themselves in a low shed
that apparently had burned out in some accident. Tristan
went along the half wall that was all that remained and
peered carefully around the rubble. In the unnatural
dark, he could see very little, but the courtyard beyond
seemed deserted. He waved his group on and they
followed as he ran across the packed snow and through
another doorway. This should be the slave kitchen, he
remembered.

A dim glow seemed bright by contrast to the outside
and he made the Watch hand code: danger ahead.
Peewit appeared at his side and he gestured the
Littleman forward while the rest of them waited.
Brickleburr stole down the short corridor and flattened himself against a wall. They saw him peek around
the corner where the light came from. Quickly he
jerked his head back and looked down to them. His
hands moved: eight men, three women, a child; slaves;
Ilyrians.

As the captain moved to answer with a sign, the
Unmaker blew an impatient breath and walked briskly
past the Littleman. "Come along," he told the Watchmen. Peewit grasped at his arm, but a crackle of
garnet warned him off.

Furiously Tristan ran after the wizard with the queen at his heels and the rest of their group behind.

When they rounded the corner into the large room, the Unmaker was already at the far door, poised as if listening. He glanced back at the captain. "They think to trap us on the stairs leading up to the hall. Dendron has packed the building with nearly all of the troops he has left to him, and he and the Fallen wait within."

As the tall man took a swift stride toward him, intending to say something of the danger into which the wizard may have put them all, a sizzle of lightning clove the stormy sky. For a moment, Ariadne could see snowflakes falling beyond the door. An overwhelming cold struck her and she cried aloud. Both men jumped to her side.

The enslaved Ilyrians were huddled into the hearth corner as far from the strangers as possible, and they stared fearfully as the queen gasped, "Ah, it is split in twain! The last Zone is rent! The Dark One is nearly through! Look where he comes!" The Watchmen whirled to look where her trembling finger pointed, but they could see nothing save the darkness outside the door.

But now the Unmaker quailed and backed, his hands feeling blindly behind him for a safe wall, and whatever the queen saw, he saw also. Until that moment, the captain had not been afraid.

Scarcely had the sharp crack of thunder echoed over the castle when they all became aware of some other sound, a low noise on the very edge of their senses. Breathlessly, forgetting all pursuit, they strained to listen. The noise assumed dimension; it was singing, and it was coming, it seemed, from beneath their feet. Such a song they had not heard before. The Eldest of the Yoriandirkin twisted as if in pain and his numbed hands dropped his bow and reached for the silver torque about his neck. Instantly the queen grasped his arm. "No!" she said. "He shall not have it if you are strong, Imris! Think what he did to Nilarion!" The tree-tender's breath steadied and he fought his hands back to his sides. Sweat popped out on his brow.

Ariadne raised her chin and reached into the purse

at her girdle, taking hold of the Crystal. She withdrew it and Ritnym's gift recognized the subterranean singer. In the blinking of an eye, the Crystal began to glow, and then to flare, and by the time the Watchmen dared look directly at it, the thing was shining like a star in the confined space. In its radiance, the queen was revealed standing straight and slim as a sword. For a moment as Tristan stared, her face blended with other features—those of an older, more regal woman whose hair was bound off her brow with a circlet of gold.

She closed her hand about the Crystal and her living flesh glowed red and so translucent that the Eldest could see the dark tracery of blood vessels like imperfections in alabaster. When she spoke her voice was the one they knew, but strangely richer, larger, as though the queen spoke from an oracle. "Go quickly!" she told them. "Use the stairway to the kitchen of the hall—they do not look for you to come that way. Unmaker, your time is come." Her gray eyes summed him. "If you cannot perform your task, I shall fail. You realize this, I know. Go." She opened her hand, and where the Crystal had lain in her palm, now there was nothing.

From the dark singer a laugh ripped through the earth.

As if this had unleashed it—and the Watchmen thought it probably had—shaking rocked them, and somehow each of them knew that this time the foundations would crumble. Lurching from the doorway, Tristan led them in a drunken race. He did not know why the queen had elected to send them on ahead, but he was more at ease with her safely left behind—if any place in this cursed time was safe. He set his mind on gaining King's Hall and sped on.

Even as she herself left the slaves' block, crossing again the courtyard and back through the burned shed, the queen followed them with her thought and saw how her green-uniformed men ran for the highest point in the fortress. The great hall loomed over Ravenholt with its dark, blind glass eyes reflecting the flashes of lightning that now forked over the Sweep. She was scarcely aware of the lightning or of the shaking earth, but she heard every note of the song, every clashing dissonance. And woven into the disharmonic she heard her own name.

Tydranth of the Wild Fire would enter Earth on the long slope outside the castle walls. She would meet him there.

A tall, rawboned youth cautiously ventured after her a pace or two. A young woman of about his own age hissed at him, "Jed, ye can't be thinkin' to go after her!"

Caught by his vision of the lady's face, Jed made no answer.

" 'Twas a Power, ye fool—maybe the Lady herself! Leave it! It isn't for the likes of you nor me!"

Thoughtfully, the young man replied, "Maybe. But, you know, she looked awfully like . . . what was her name? Robin? And those men; I've seen them before too. They were the ones who came to steal her away. And did you see their uniforms?" Jed slipped to the corridor where she had gone and stole after her, drawn by some force he did not understand. The girl merely stared after him and did not dare call out.

The queen walked straight down the main road in plain sight of the archer company if they still held the guardhouse. She saw the shattered gate; she knew enemies might be there; but she went on as if this were no longer important. Her mind was divided between the cold spot in the snow-swept field that fell away from the castle walls and the pictures that unfolded against the back of her eyes with the blurred edges of a dream. Eventually, when she stood alone on the icy Sweep, waiting, she watched elsewhere.

Tristan and the others were in the storerooms below the great kitchen. She was with them when they climbed the wooden stairs, clutching the walls, the steps, each other for balance when the stairway swayed. She followed when they flitted from shadow to shadow along the long corridor that led from the kitchen to the fresco hall. She saw them slip behind the guards posted at the top of the marble stairway, and she saw Kursh bring back his arm and whip the knife end over end as Tristan took the other with one thrust of his sword. The Watchmen crept to the great doors of the hall, but only the queen saw that the Greenbriar glowed turquoise in the painting.

She saw them look to the captain, and when he nodded grimly, they burst together through the carven entrance, and the Unmaker set a Warding upon it so that none might enter after them. From both sides lances flashed down in front of them and a cool voice said from the upper end of the hall, "Come in. We've been expecting you."

But the Watchmen never hesitated. Before the words were out of the Fallen's mouth, Kursh's ax swept two of the spear shafts out of the soldiers' hands, while Tristan's sword found a mark and another pikeman crumpled to the dirty rushes. Quint hurtled through the opening they had made, and met the first of the Bastard's swordsmen in a clang of metal on metal, while Peewit leaped upon a table and held that side against two Home Guards. Imris fired so rapidly that no one saw him notch his arrows and draw back his bowstring. Fidelis grasped a lance, reversed it, and brought it down in a solid whack across the sword arm of a Home Guard who lunged for the captain's unprotected back. Tristan whirled and dispatched the man easily. "Thanks!" he called, and only then noticed that Alphonse was not with them. Quickly he looked up the length of the hall, but the only person he saw was the Bastard King. His lips tightened and he threw himself back into the fight.

The queen watched while the captain steadily cut his way toward the upper end of the hall, where Dendron, seated in his high gilded chair, watched and finally sent his own two bodyguards into the fight. At last the captain swung a mighty blow at the last crimson and sable uniform that stood between him and the high table. Pushing the dying trooper away, he raised his eyes to the Bastard, but the latter did not move, only regarding him with an unreadable expression. "Damn you!" the leader of the Watchmen yelled. "Get on your feet!" He jumped the steps to the platform.

Still Dendron did not move, only surveyed the ruin of his troops on the floor of the hall below. "I can't get up," he rasped harshly. "Lucky for you, Ilyrian."

Furious, the captain reached to drag him out of the chair and then saw beneath the fur-trimmed collar of the royal scarlet robe a purpled swelling. He froze.

"Go ahead. Kill me. It'll be a blessing to die quick. Not that this isn't." Dendron grimaced. "An hour ago, I was as hale as you are now." A gurgling chuckle made it past the swelling. "Let that be a lesson to you."

The captain's fist clenched on the hilt of his sword and his face darkened with hot blood. "No! Not after all these years! Get up!" he bellowed insanely.

"Disappointed, are you? So am I. I've got you to thank for this shoulder. But you and your men had guts, I'll give you that. Pity you followed my brother." He tried to twist his head to look at the tall man. "By the Wolf, how did he think he could shut out me and my people forever?" One blunt forefinger jabbed at the table. "This land is *ours*!"

"Never," the captain told him coldly over the leveled sword.

Another bubbling chuckle. "Haven't done a bad job of holding it for these past twenty years, have I?"

Pity and revulsion and rage made Tristan's hands shake. He cast a quick look about the hall and saw that it was secured. The last few Barreners crouched on the floor under Quint's baleful eye. The others of the Watchmen had seen him and now began to come forward. The captain's eyes returned to the Bastard King and he saw how Dendron labored for breath and tried to lick his lips. Abruptly the commander of the Watch rammed his sword into its sheath and dumped some wine from a lidded flagon into a golden cup. He slid it within Dendron's grasp.

The Bastard's eyes widened. His thick hands raised the cup as a child does and he swallowed. When he tried to set the goblet down again, it slipped from his fingers and rolled in a semicircle on the embroidered cloth, the wine spreading in a quick gush. Something that sounded like a curse twisted from his lips. ". . . one more favor," he was saying gutturally. "Get that whoreson Rasullis."

Before Tristan could answer, the Bastard fell heavily forward across the table.

The queen saw the captain bend to check the pulse in his wrist and she saw a gleaming sword lift behind the scarlet drapery at the rear of the platform. A Home Guard leaped out and before Imris's shout could alert Tristan, his enemy brought the sword slicing down. She saw the captain's hands fly out and his bulging eyes seemed to look right through her. I couldn't tell you, she whispered in her mind. I couldn't, my love. And whether there was forgiveness in those filming eyes she did not know.

The dark singer's harsh laughter whipped out at her and turned her grief to white hot anger. "Come you," she breathed, "come you."

But he waited, as she did, for the Unmaker.

The Fallen was at the top of the stairs. The Unmaker knew this, just as he was aware of Ariadne's watching eyes, and of the singer who threatened them. The part of him that was still Alphonse knew fear, but also a boyishly extravagant courage: for the Eldest and for the people of Yoriand, he would give everything he had to defeat the evil wizard and dent the dark singer's evil power. But the part of him that had metamorphosed into the Wizard of Earth, Wind, and Fire climbed the steps deliberately and as heavily as a man who risks all in an instant and hopes only that he may take his enemy with him.

With his foot uplifted to take the last stair, he halted, all at once perceiving the Warding that barred his way. A sigh escaped him and he bent his mind to the task. When he touched the barrier with his power, the thing burst into visible light—a wall of sapphire as brilliant as a mountain lake and ten times ten colder. For a moment, the Unmaker strove with the Warding, seeking to dominate it. He found, though, that nothing Rasullis did now was done solely with the power that

had been his own, and the barrier was not a mere
wizard's trick. Now the Unmaker took a step into the
icy water of his own fate: he withdrew his own power
and sought to unmake Rasullis's Warding.

Whether there was actually a gasp from the blue
wizard in the tower room beyond the thick door, or
whether Alphonse only heard this in his mind made
little difference: the Fallen had perceived his intent
immediately and with it, the nature of the threat the
boy represented. The Unmaker sent a sardonic smile
through the door. Yes, he told the Fallen, there *is* a
new wizard in the Meld.

At once the sapphire Warding acquired a black tint
around the edges, and this was none of Rasullis's
doing. 'Beware,' the Queen said within the Unmaker's
mind. He sent an impatient snap back her way and
then bent himself in earnest to eliminating the Warding. It was a subtle song that wove the barrier, but he
sang a counterpoint, slowly, note by note, and there
was nowhere Rasullis's fragment led that Alphonse
could not follow. When it was done, he marveled that
one who knew so little of the Song itself could have
wrought such unspeakable harm.

The Warded barrier shattered like a mirror, and the
Unmaker stepped through its fragments. "Now, Fallen,"
he said aloud, and pushed open the door.

Rasullis stood by the window, dark even against the
dark sky beyond. "So," the Fallen wizard said. "They
must send a boy to do their work. Even now the fools
will not break the Rule."

The redhead smiled, though perhaps in that dark
the other could not see it. "Rasullis," he said gently,
"I *am* the Rule."

Silence fell between them, and Alphonse shut from
his mind the queen's lonely fear out there on the
storm-riven Sweep.

"You will fail," the Fallen stated. "He will not let
you destroy me." When the Unmaker made no answer, a touch of fear entered Rasullis's voice. "Join
us. You are already great in power. You could be
greater."

Still the boy made no answer, only standing so abso-

lutely still that he might have been a phantom of
Rasullis's imagination. When Alphonse abruptly began to speak, the Fallen started visibly. "I offer you
one last chance to save yourself, Fallen. Unmake the
crystal you formed."

"Do you really think I would, even if I could?"

The Unmaker gave him another moment to think
about it, even though he could hear the other singer
shift to a deeper melody. Then the Wizard of Earth,
Wind, and Fire sang strong and clear every note of
Rasullis's own personal Warding, overbearing the Fall-
en's shocked flurry of incantations. Alphonse held the
last note and flung his own Warding at the panicky
man.

Instantly the room was lit with a wine-red glow and
by this the Unmaker saw his spell take effect: the
Serpent tattoo imprinted in Rasullis's flesh on one
long-ago night seemed to swell. Coiled about the enchanter's neck, it slithered and looped, defeating
Rasullis's efforts to tug it away from him and throw it
to the floor. The head lifted, forked tongue darting,
tasting the fear in the air. Swaying, the snake wove
before the wizard's terrified eyes and then struck suddenly between them.

So venomous was the Serpent of the Meld that the
Fallen was reduced to mortal man—dying mortal man—
within seconds. He stared past the obsidian eyes at his
Unmaker. "You," he breathed.

"The crystal. Where it is?"

The broken wizard's knees gave and he sprawled.
The Serpent rippled away into the dark. The Unmaker
approached and knelt quickly. "Where is it?"

A fragment of thought whispered back at him. "You'll
never . . ."

The Unmaker tugged at the corpse's robe and discovered the crystal. He held it up and it glowed redly
in the light of his own fire. Awareness flooded through
him. Another presence was near. The dark singing
had stopped. There was silence. "Well, now," a voice
breathed in his ear. "Well, now. Who have we here?"

The Unmaker gritted his teeth and gripped the false
crystal.

"Ah. The Abomination. The one who kills his own brothers—they who bore the robe of amethyst, the silver torque of Yoriand, and the embroidered rose of Ilyria." The voice sounded amused. "Death follows you, my boy."

"I did not kill them. You did."

A harsh laugh floated out of the stone beneath his feet. "Believe as you wish." The singer knew when the boy drew breath to begin unlocking the crystal. "You do not want to destroy it, boy. Think what will happen to you when you do. Shall you go back to being the wretched little creature you were? Or do you think she will regret much that you died up here in a futile effort to aid her? Have any of them given you the respect due the Wizard of the Three? Can you honestly say that you matter a whit to any of them?" He had read the cold spot in the boy's heart aright. "And for these miserable folk, you would throw away the power that lies in your palm? Shall she have a Crystal and you none?"

The Unmaker was staggered by the force of the relentless words, and came perilously close to falling under the singer's dark spell. He seemed to see a vast land subject to his command, the wizards of Covencroft coming humbly to him for counsel, Ariadne on a throne, but a throne a step lower than his own.

Then, in place of the cold crystal he held, he felt again a pole of carven ash thrust into his hands and saw snapping old eyes that summed him and found him suited for the task. Amethyst light bathed his memory and he knew himself once more. Deliberately he began to sing and the staff faded like the vision it was, until only the dingy crystal was left in his hand.

The dark song rose against him, drowning him, but he fought grimly and slipped a few notes into the other singer's Warding. He began to work on the unmaking of the crystal. It took days, years, lifetimes, though only a few minutes were registered in the world outside his mind. At the last, he gasped under the crushing weight of the dark song, seized the crystal, and hurled it against the opposite wall. The sphere shattered, and he crawled through the fragments to collect the wrinkled, fire-blackened seeds. When he had them grasped safely in his fist, his strength left him and he collapsed full-length. Too scorched by the Wild Fire to move, he gathered all his Warding—the Earth, the Wind, and the Fire—and threw the power to the woman who waited on the Sweep. Tydranth had not expected this: Alphonse could hear the subterranean scream of rage even as his human consciousness left him.

The Serpent of the Meld slithered from the cold hearth and approached him. Its cool skin touched his as it gently explored his face with its flicking tongue, and then the snake coiled in the crook of his chin and kept watch.

Alphonse had shut her out. She had no way of knowing whether his strength of purpose had been equal to his doom. She had been out in the swirling icy snow for a long time, and she had stared up at the tower until her tearing eyes forced her to look away. There had been no reassuring flash of garnet light.

So now, she thought, I am alone.

The voice, when it came, seemed to echo as though coming from the bottom of a well. "You are alone, indeed. Did my sister not tell you it would end this way?"

Ariadne didn't think the Lady Ritnym had told her anything of the kind, but suddenly she wasn't sure. Her hands were frozen and her feet, and now her heart. She whispered, "Do not dare come forth!"

He laughed. "And what will you do to prevent me, mortal? Do you really think your puny Crystal can mend the tear in the world that my servant made when he burned the Earthgate?"

She saw Nilarion burning like a torch and the shapes of green-skinned people in the flames. But there was ice over the ashes now. She could not answer him.

"Ah, your own reason tells you otherwise. Listen to it!" The voice dropped to a more conversational level. "Did my sister in her talk with you ever happen to mention that you have a choice besides meaningless death? No? Well, that is not to be wondered at, I suppose. Ritnym has always been set against me, for purposes of her own. Make no mistake, mortal: you

are her pawn and she will sacrifice you without
thought."

As Ariadne drew breath to answer this, he continued, "Your choice is life. You doubt that I will grant
it? But I will—I would give much to defeat my sister. I
would even grant you your kingdom, and the man you
want for consort beside you. Think, mortal: the gates
are open; he need not remain dead; you have the
power to recall him as you recalled the Yoriandir."

She swallowed but the words nearly stuck in her
throat anyway. "But if I call him back across the
Zones now, you will come with him." Her voice hardened and she spoke across the beginnings of a reply,
"And I will not have his love for doing that, I can tell
you."

The voice remained calm, friendly even, but by
some other sense she knew that the singer was gathering his fury for one last attempt. "If immortality for
him affects you not, then think of it for yourself. If
you managed to close the gate, you yourself would be
locked in the Zones and prevented from returning
when your own time comes."

She cast one last despairing glance up to the tower,
but all of Ravenholt showed as dark and brooding as a
ruin. No way out but through, she told herself. She
raised her chin. "For my people," she said proudly,
and in the instant was thrown off her feet by the
slantwise tearing of the earth beneath her. The gaping
crack widened until she lay almost at the edge. When
she managed to raise her head and peer past the icy
fringe of her hood she saw the dark crevasse snake
away down the Sweep and run across the drifted grassland to the northeast, quick as molten rock or the
leading edge of a forest fire. And then her breath
stopped, for she perceived that the deep crack in the
earth's crust was headed straight for the heart of
Yoriand, where a leafkin stood above a locked spring.

Wild white-hot rage swelled and burst within her,
that he should kill again what was so lately reborn.
She leaped to her feet, flaring, and standing as easily
as if she were rooted in the earth itself. "You shall
not!" she shrieked and flung out her hands. Power

surged from her fingertips and she threw it at the leading point of the crevasse.

Born of the Crystal, of the woman who had herself become the Crystal, a quickening force caught the rift just as it climbed Rimwall and instantly sealed it off. There was a screech of rock sliding against rock and then deep silence.

She could feel evil boil from the pit at her feet; indeed, she could *see* it blow the snow away. When she looked down, all was darkness except that a pair of eyes looked back at her. They could have been a mile down, they could have been inches. "Go back," she told him, and now there was no trace of fear in her voice.

He answered not, as she had expected. The eyes winked out even as she hurled her power into the pit, down to the rent in the world. The dark singer countered, entrapping her power with his own, and suddenly she found herself gasping in a lightless, airless void. She persisted, summoning every bit of Healing she possessed and then reaching desperately beyond that for more. Amethyst winked now in the peal of her fire, and garnet, emerald, copper. Silver joined, metallic in the darkness, and she saw a flurry of red leaves with white berries blow down the way her power had opened. Finally, as his dark power swallowed all these and fear shot through her, a single emerald feather drifted in lazy spirals around and around, down into the depths.

The sight of that feather made her heart bound, and her Healing flooded through the Zones, washing even to the rift itself. Chased by the rising flood of her pity, the dark singer who had been brother to the good, fled and whisked back through the rent to avoid its touch. At once there was a snick deep in the earth and a puff of balmy air wafted to fan her cheek.

The sun split the lowering clouds.

She laughed aloud for joy, whirling in a circle, trailing Healing from her fingertips. It was not until she grew tired and slowed to a stop that she realized that the Healing was pouring from her like blood; she could not stop it, and soon it would drain her of her own life. Joy turned to dread and she knew with bitter certainty that the dark singer would have his revenge. She had closed the gate and now she would indeed be locked behind it.

Stricken, she looked out across the land. Bright sun bathed the Willowsrill valley and already she could hear melting snow trickling down the Sweep. The ugly scar of the crevasse was black against the slushy snow. There was not much time to do the last thing.

With fingers that had only begun to tingle with returning warmth, she opened the purse at her girdle and extracted the smooth, egg-shaped stone that had been her little brother Gerrit's present from Ritnym's Realm. Green and blue it shone in her palm, and the tiny dark lines like trees. As her dazed eyes studied it, a boy's young face showed in its smooth surface and he grinned at her. Slowly she grinned back and hefted the stone in her hand. Ariadne lifted her chin, drew back her arm, and as expertly as she had once skipped stones across the mill pond at Wolf's Glen, she skipped this stone down the crevasse. She must have thrown it harder than she had thought, for she watched until it was out of sight.

It did not seem long to her, but she was dizzy and could not be sure. Where Gerrit's stone touched, good rich earth filled in the void. Velvet-green turf sprouted and knit with the snow-watered grassland to either side, and all at once there were tiny saplings already leafing. The Greenbriar Queen smiled vacantly and then the good green grass was under her cheek and she sank into a dangerous sleep.

Near her head, a vine poked through the earth and climbed for the sun.

So they found her, with a tall, rawboned youth who stammered and tried to explain what he had seen, but finally left off as his words could not tell the half of it.

Kursh and Quint nearly came to blows over the privilege of carrying the unconscious queen up to the castle, but the Eldest silenced them with a reference to the captain, and the dwarf yielded to the huge man as having two good eyes to see where he was going on the muddy hillside.

Gently Quint lifted her, and as the villagers thronged out of the settlement beneath the Sweep, the First Watch brought her back inside her own gates. Here they met a grave youth clad in a garnet cloak coming down through the ruins. His eyes were bright, clear blue. He was very quiet when he looked at the queen's closed face. "There is a Greenbriar on the hillside, you say?"

Peewit nodded eagerly. "A big one too! I warrant it will make enough Elixir to heal everything and everybody!"

The redhead's voice was soft. "I hope not."

Kursh bristled at that, for his gruff heart was at that moment so full of worship for the slender woman that he would have chewed his way through granite to reach anyone who dared speak against her. "By the Powers, I've had enough of you and your bloody naysaying! Can you not feel the sun and smell the air? By the Briar, *it's spring, boy*!"

For a surprised moment Alphonse's eyes widened and then a grin spread over his face and shone in his eyes. "I know, Master Kursh, I know." He sobered. "But you see the price she has paid to bring it."

Now when they looked at her pale face there seemed an ominous shadow over it. Amid all that white and new-green landscape, the Watchmen looked at each other and fear struck at them again. Peewit spoke with a lightness he did not feel. "It is just the Crystal trance; she will wake soon."

Alphonse did not answer. A warm breeze fluttered their cloaks. "Well," he said at last, "let us make the Elixir anyway. She would not want less than a complete victory. We shall need to collect the Rose hips." He took Peewit with him to gather them, and the others carried the queen up through the rubble.

They were just wondering where to take her, when from a small crowd of people at the entrance to a lane, a plump woman stepped forward, grasping at Fidelis's sleeve. "Please, sirs, if I might say, there be no place up yonder fit for my lady." She lowered her voice.

"Them damn Barreners was real pigs, y'know." She gave a push to her cap. "Anyways, I reckon my kitchen be the cleanest place hereabouts. We've a stick or two of wood put by secretlike, and my lady'll be well cared for, I tell you." She nodded vigorously and others in the crowd echoed her sentiment.

Imris looked around at them and a smile touched his eyes. "We accept in the name of the queen, madam. If you would be good enough to show us where to go?"

Flustered and blushing crimson, she hiked her ample skirts, did a passable imitation of a polite curtsy, and led off with the air of a contented goose. Even Kursh grinned.

As soon as they had collected clean straw, made a pallet for the queen, and tucked warm woolen blankets about her, Alphonse and Peewit were shown in by Jed. Both of them had their cloaks full of rose fruits. Alphonse made up the Elixir. Kursh said immediately, "The captain first."

Alphonse avoided his eyes, and it was the Eldest who guessed what this meant. "The gates are shut, Kursh." When the dwarf still did not seem to understand and the Littleman stood by his side smiling brightly, Imris said it plainly: "He cannot come back. Ariadne has closed the way from the Zones."

The one eye narrowed. "You can't be serious."

The wizard swirled the liquid in the cooking pot, the biggest vessel they'd been able to find. "It is true."

The dwarf flung away from them out into the courtyard.

The Littleman looked down at the queen. "How are we going to tell her?" he asked softly.

"She knew before we left the Guardian," Alphonse said, "but she could say nothing of it to us. Or to him."

Peewit turned away, saying in a choked voice, "Think I'll take a walk down to the river," and he too left.

Fidelis looked at Imris, who looked at the wizard. William Quint stood near the fire and did not know what to say, nor to whom to say it. Alphonse said, "We should bury him with all honor."

"Yes," the Eldest agreed, "but we must look to the people too. Kursh and I will take the Elixir up the river to the folk who cannot come here. I saw at least a few horses left in the stables. Then, when I return, I will go to Yoriand, for my heart tells me to go home and tend Nilarion. The thaw has reached there too." He regarded the queen's still form. "She did win, you know." That sounded too much like an elegy, so he added hastily, "We will be back ere you have time to look for us."

Later, when the Yoriandir and the dwarf rode down the cart road to the river landing, they met the Littleman coming back. There was a swarm of glad people on the road, walking in the moist new grass, throwing off cloaks, and calling up and down the Sweep to friends and family. The small figure was standing with his thumbs jammed in the belt of his uniform, watching them. He looked up as the two horsemen drew close. "Does she wake?" he called.

"Nay, not yet," the dwarf answered as they drew rein. "We go upriver carrying Elixir." Kursh cleared his throat. "I've been thinking. You are captain now, ye know." He made an abrupt silencing gesture as the Littleman started to deny it. "First Watchman always gets the promotion, don't be such an ass, Peewit. That's not what I've been thinking about. Someone should light the signal beacon." He saw the slow realization come to the Littleman's eyes. "There may be some of our fellows left out there who will remember what it means, and they'll gather here. It's going to take a powerful lot of people to put this place to rights," he pointed out.

Peewit knew that he was right. "Good idea. I'll take care of it." The dwarf nodded and moved his heel to spur his horse on down the hill. "But I'm only acting captain till the queen wakes." He grinned. "Then I'll flip you for it."

Something that may have been an amused snort escaped the burly dwarf, but he brought his fist to his chest in a salute, and when Peewit returned it, set his horse to a trot. The Eldest waved and followed him.

"Oh, botheration," the new captain sighed and made his way through the villagers back to the castle.

But the queen did not wake, not that day or evening, and so Peewit took it on his own to light the beacon and call her people together. She did not wake when they buried Tristan. She did not wake when the village below the Sweep swelled by hundreds of Ilyrians, or when William Quint directed their labors in cleaning and restoring the castle. They made quick progress; the men were willing now that they worked for their queen.

She was still not awake when Imris and Kursh came riding back up the hill. In fact, if anything, she was worse, Alphonse told them when he met them at the rebuilt gate.

"What the bloody hell's wrong with Fidelis?" Kursh demanded bluntly.

"It is nothing he can heal!" the wizard said with exasperation.

"Well, you then?"

"Kursh, sometimes you are the thickest—"

The Eldest intervened. "Is it then some trance, something Tydranth put upon her?"

The wizard was thoughtful and he put up a hand to Kursh's horse's bit and led them toward the stable. "I don't know. I don't think so. It is like a trance, but it seems to be coming from within her. It is as if she sinks under the weight of the Healing she is still sending forth." He cast an eye up at the puffy white clouds that floated in the blue sky. "Is it as well in other parts of the land as it is here?" They passed into the dimness of the stable.

"Just as fine." Kursh beamed. "Just as fine. A better spring I've never seen. Already the fields are dry enough to plow. We saw several farmers out in their fields, didn't we, Imris, and by the Powers! You ought to see the apple blossoms in the West Riding!" He stopped abruptly, and the wizard was certain he saw him blush.

"May we see her?" Imris asked.

"Of course." They handed the horses off to an old ostler who smiled and waved the Watchmen off.

Fidelis was sitting in the sunlight in the kitchen, grinding herbs with a mortar and pestle, while the buxom cook bustled about his stool and chided him because he was not quick enough to suit her. "My land, we'll *never* be ready to feed all them hungry people!"

"They they'll wait," he answered reasonably, but she clucked and pounded at the bread dough.

When Alphonse stepped through from the courtyard, he led the other two to the far corner. The Eldest was shocked and went quickly to one knee beside the bed they had made for her. Kursh stared. "This is a pretty pass," he muttered.

"If you menfolk would just leave the poor thing be, she might wake sooner." The cook, her face flushed, advanced on them. She glared at Kursh. "How would *you* like to wake up and look at that face?" she asked.

The fierce eyebrows lowered.

At that moment Captain Peewit came in. "You're back!" he exclaimed. "Good. Now maybe we can get this place straightened out."

The Eldest rose, still gazing down at the queen. "Yes. Maybe," he murmured.

Late that night, Peewit walked out alone on the battlements, as had become his custom. He could not do enough star-gazing, for they had not seen them in so long. Besides this, he missed Tristan terribly and did not feel equal to succeeding him.

Leaning against the rough stonework, he looked out over the Sweep and the river and sniffed deep of the blooming air. His thoughts were full of fear for the queen, though, and even the peaceful night could not calm his spirit. He looked down along the hillside and studied the Briar, which had spread like a rambler all over the slope, so that the villagers came and collected the hips as if they were picking strawberries. It was a sweet smell, he thought grudgingly. Even if it *was* going to kill her.

Tiredly he wrested his mind away from the nagging thought. He wondered how the leafkin was doing. It must be stronger; Imris certainly seemed to be feeling hale. He remembered how the moonlight had shone on its green and silver leaves, and how he had made sure it could drink from Nose-Tickler. The Elixir-laced water would do it good, he had judged.

His head jerked as if he had been slapped and he cursed himself for a fool. "Alphonse!" he shouted as he leaped away down the battlement stairs. "Alphonse, we are such idiots!"

When he burst into the kitchen, he dragged the wizard from Kursh's instructive dice game, jabbering so that they could barely understand him. Finally he had it all out. Kursh slapped his back so hard it raised a welt, and then raced down to the Briar to collect hips.

They fed the queen Elixir by the light of a lamp the cook held high, and when Ariadne sighed and stirred and opened her gray eyes, they raised such a mighty shout that they woke the families who were encamped on the Sweep to be received by the queen.

⤛ Epilogue ⤜

Amidsummer breeze fluttered the pennants above the queen's head as the procession wound its slow way up the Sweep toward the castle. The day had dawned fair for her coronation, but that was no surprise—this had been the fairest summer in memory.

She reined her gray stallion to a sedate walk. The First Watchman rode at her right, and she studied the dwarf in his resplendent dress uniform. "Come now, you must tell me where Captain Peewit is."

He shook his head and smiled. "I may not, my queen. He swore he'd pull out every hair in my beard if I told you." The eyepatch wrinkled as he grinned at her.

She pretended irritation to whet their teasing fun. "Well, then, *you'll* tell me, Sergeant Major?"

Quint smilingly shook his head. "I have me orders, beggin' yer pardon, my queen."

She shook her head at the two of them and drew a finger lightly down the throat of the white and emerald bird perched on her fist. She knew that Imris was up ahead, waiting for her at Queen's Gate. As most senior in royalty, the Eldest would place the crown upon her head. Chiswic and Alphonse were there too, to witness for the Meld.

Her eyes strayed to the patch of hillside where her Watch had established a cordoned area. Kursh saw the direction of her gaze. "Wherever he is, he thinks of you today, my lady."

There was sorrow in the look she gave him, but she summoned a smile. "That was a good place you picked. I believe he is satisfied to lie by my father and the other brave ones."

"Well, it seemed right."

A young boy's voice rose over the noisy exclamations of the crowd. "Hallo, Dad!"

Quint laughed self-consciously. "My boy," he explained, and saluted the small figure at the fringe of people.

They went on and presently she caught sight of a richly attired retinue standing grouped about a dark-haired young man. He was handsome and bold enough, she thought, for he did not bow as she passed, only inclining his head briefly and smiling into her eyes. "Who is yon dandy?"

Kursh answered, "Why, my queen, that is young Prince Ka-Salin."

Ah, the southerner whose father's borders march with our own, she thought. See if I don't have something to say to *you*.

The crowd cheered, for she was come nigh unto the castle and the Briar standard above the gate was dipped in salute. Among the knot of people richly dressed were some who made her eyes sting. Happiness broke through the restraint of the occasion, and she waved as enthusiastically as a girl. Stiff in their new clothes, her family waved back and Iris blew her a kiss.

Jed, in the uniform of the Watch, stepped forward to take her horse's head, and Quint lifted the queen lightly to the fine tapestry they had unrolled for her to walk upon. She placed her hand on Kursh's arm and went forward to stand before the Eldest. Imris smiled and his green eyes danced. He raised his bard's voice and proclaimed, "Welcome to your own, Queen Ariadne." Turning to the pillow Alphonse held, he took from it a crown that sparkled with amethysts, emeralds, garnets, and inlaid copper roses. When he placed it upon her head, the whole Sweep erupted with cheering. Then, when he would have bent the knee before her, she pulled him up and kissed him.

On the battlements above, Peewit hung over the wall, listening. A streaming torch was in his hand, and the fire rockets waited in their cradles. He'd never seen them before, but old Chiswic had said the effect would be spectacular, and by the Powers, nothing else would do for the queen's coronation day.

When he heard the cheer go up, the Littleman chortled, ran back to the rockets, and lit the fuses.

About the Author

Sheila Gilluly was born in Rhode Island and attended high school and college in Arizona, graduating from the University of Arizona with a BA in English in 1973. Since then, she has earned an MA in Religious Studies from Maryknoll School of Theology, lived in Taiwan briefly, taught for a couple of years in Guam, and now teaches English and Creative Writing at a rural district high school in Maine. Ms. Gilluly is an avid gardener. Since midcoast Maine has only two seasons (winter and July Fourth), she has a lot of time left over from gardening to devote to her writing.